P9-ELV-919

The COURTSHIP of the
VICAR'S DAUGHTER

A Table by the Window

THE GRESHAM CHRONICLES

The Widow of Larkspur Inn
The Courtship of the Vicar's Daughter
The Dowry of Miss Lydia Clark

TALES OF LONDON

The Maiden of Mayfair
Catherine's Heart
Leading Lady

LAWANA BLACKWELL

The COURTSHIP of the VICAR'S DAUGHTER

THE GRESHAM CHRONICLES | BOOK TWO

BETHANYHOUSE
Minneapolis, Minnesota

The Courtship of the Vicar's Daughter
Copyright © 1998
Lawana Blackwell

Cover design by Jennifer Parker

All rights reserved. No part of this publication may be reproduced, stored in a retrieval system, or transmitted in any form or by any means—electronic, mechanical, photocopying, recording, or otherwise—without the prior written permission of the publisher. The only exception is brief quotations in printed reviews.

Published by Bethany House Publishers
11400 Hampshire Avenue South
Bloomington, Minnesota 55438

Bethany House Publishers is a division of
Baker Publishing Group, Grand Rapids, Michigan.

Printed in the United States of America

ISBN-13:   978-0-7642-0268-1
ISBN-10:   0-7642-0268-5

Library of Congress has cataloged the original edition as follows:

Blackwell, Lawana, 1952-
    The courtship of the vicar's daughter / by Lawana Blackwell.
        p.   cm. — (Gresham chronicles ; bk.2)
    ISBN 1-55661-948-0
    1. Children of clergy—Fiction. 2. England—Fiction. I. Title. II. Series: Blackwell, Lawana, 1952- Gresham chronicles ; bk 2.
    PS3552.L3429   1998
    813'.54—dc21

00502460

This book is lovingly dedicated

to my father,

Earl Chandler,

who taught me the value of integrity.

LAWANA BLACKWELL has eleven published novels to her credit including the bestselling GRESHAM CHRONICLES series. She and her husband have three grown sons and live in Baton Rouge, Louisiana.

July, 1870

*A*nd now with your kind indulgence, my lovely and talented daughter, Ernestine, will sing for us," Vicar Nippert announced after tea had been poured in the parlor of the vicarage behind Saint Stephen's. "She will be accompanied on the pianoforte by my equally lovely and talented wife, Aurea."

Andrew Phelps, balancing a plate of little watercress sandwiches on one knee and a cup and saucer on the other, winced inwardly. Not because Ernestine's talent had been exaggerated—on the contrary, as the girl began the first notes of "Ye Servants of God," it became quite obvious that she possessed a pleasant singing voice. But since his arrival in Prescott this morning for the quarterly regional meeting, he and a dozen other country vicars had been subjected to their host's incessant boasting.

Oh, he could understand the man's pride. The most beautiful stained-glass windows in Shropshire graced Prescott's three-hundred-year-old Gothic cathedral. The parishioners were such enthusiastic givers, according to Vicar Nippert, that they practically pounded upon the church doors at the first of each month, demanding to be allowed to tithe immediately. And, of course, as he had mentioned more than once, his wife and daughter were musical virtuosos, worthy of leading angel choirs.

It was just that Andrew had assumed that, as was the case with past diocese meetings hosted by other vicars, most of the time would be devoted to discussing *church* issues.

"Well, what do you think?" came a low voice from Andrew's right. He turned to find Vicar Nippert leaning over his chair, his proud grin exposing a row of teeth as white and prominent as the piano keys upon which Mrs. Nippert's nimble fingers glided effortlessly. "Sings like an angel, eh?"

"Very talented," Andrew agreed reluctantly, not because he had aught against the girl, but because he suspected the door was being opened for more boasting. His suspicion was confirmed right away, for Vicar Nippert immediately launched into a litany of his daughter's other talents. Andrew assumed an attentive expression and consoled himself with the thought that at least when this meeting was over, he wouldn't have to endure Vicar Nippert's company for another three months.

And then a certain name snapped him out of his reverie.

"Did you say Saint Julien's Academy at Shrewsbury?" Andrew asked as Ernestine began the fourth stanza.

"This will be her second year," Vicar Nippert replied after sending a nod of approval across to his daughter. "Outstanding institution, and of course she was at the head of her class last term." His expression suddenly brightened. "Say, you've a daughter about Ernestine's age, eh? Are you considering enrolling her? Because I feel compelled to warn you that a waiting list begins to accumulate this time every year."

Andrew swallowed. "I already have enrolled her."

"Well, capital!" The vicar clapped him on the back, the toothy smile even wider. "You'll be fetching her on weekends, yes? No doubt we'll be seeing a lot of each other come September, eh?"

"Y-yes," Andrew nodded.

"Capital!" Vicar Nippert clapped him on the back again and moved on to converse with other clergy across the room.

While Ernestine sang the first few words to a second hymn, "Come, Thou Long Expected Jesus," Andrew added under his breath, "And could you possibly come before September, Lord?" But then he thought about his upcoming marriage to Julia Hollis and amended his prayer. "With all due respect, Lord, could you please wait until after December?"

The four high-backed willow benches Julia had commissioned the Keegans, the Irish basket weavers, to make for the *Larkspur Inn*'s garden looked quite rustic among the flower beds and shrubbery. She was pleased with the effect. A two-hundred-year-old building of weathered red sandstone would look a little silly looming behind lawn furniture made of the dainty-looking wrought-iron lace that was so popular in London.

Or at least it was popular sixteen months ago, when her late husband's gambling debts caused Julia to lose her home and almost everything else she had in the world, save the *Larkspur*, an old abandoned coaching inn that the London bankers had deemed too worthless to claim. With a courage born out of desperation and a loan from her former butler, Julia had moved to Gresham with her three children and loyal chambermaid, Fiona O'Shea. By God's grace and plenty of hard work, they had transformed the *Larkspur* into a lodging house, successful beyond even their most optimistic dreams.

It was upon one of these willow benches that Julia and Andrew met every weekday morning before Andrew paid calls to his parishioners. Over cups of tea the two shared news from the *Shrewsbury Chronicle*, tidbits of the goings-on in their separate households, and plans for the life they would begin together in December. For propriety's sake, the tea tray occupied the space between them upon the bench—an arrangement the vicar understood and conceded was necessary, but disliked immensely.

"But you know what happened the last time you tried to speak to the Sanderses," Julia said on Monday morning as she handed her fiancé the cup of tea she had just poured. She was a little miffed that Andrew had charmed her into a jovial mood by relating the events of Saturday's diocese meeting in Prescott before mentioning in passing that he would be making a certain call today.

"Yes, but this time there will be four of us." He took an appreciative sip from his cup. "Please compliment Mrs. Herrick on her most excellent tea, as usual."

"Please don't change the subject, Andrew. You'll only be providing him with more targets. And who's to say the next cracked forehead won't be yours?"

This warning had the opposite effect from the one Julia had intended, for the corners of his hazel eyes crinkled. "So you're worried about me, are you, Julia Hollis?"

Julia refused to return his smile. "I'm in no mood to be teased." During the three weeks since she had accepted his proposal of marriage, she found that he was growing more and more dear to her. And the thought of Mr. Sanders crowning him with a rock, as he had poor Mr. Clay, frightened her immensely.

He reached across the tray, picked up her hand, and brought it to his bearded cheek. "It's rather nice, you know, having you fuss over me."

"Do you plan to indulge in rash behavior all during our marriage so you can be fussed over?"

"Now, there's a thought."

She could no longer resist the coaxing in his warm eyes and squeezed the hand that held hers. "Just be careful, Andrew."

"Of course," he promised, giving the back of her hand a quick kiss before releasing it. "I'll turn and start sprinting if Sanders so much as *looks* at a rock. And I'll warn the others to do the same."

"Why do they want you along anyway? The man has already proven he has no respect for the clergy."

"I suppose they're hoping Mr. Sanders will feel contrite enough about his last show of temper toward Mr. Clay and me to grant us audience. I couldn't refuse them."

The "they" and "them" of whom Andrew and Julia spoke consisted of Messrs. Sykes, Sway, and Casper, Gresham's newly elected school board. Because of Parliament's passage of the Elementary Education Act this year, local school boards were now responsible for seeing that English and Welsh schools met certain universal standards of education. Pressure was also brought upon these boards to increase school enrollment.

There was no easy way to accomplish this latter goal, however, because without a compulsory education law, the choice still lay in the hands of the parents. But the three men of Gresham's school board had made it their mission to enroll every child of school age in the village for the coming academic year.

Their enthusiasm was contagious, and the whole town had become infected with it. The ladies of the Women's Charity Society applied themselves to knitting caps, stockings, and gloves for the children of the less fortunate in anticipation of the winter months when they would be walking to and from school. Worshipers at Saint Jude's, as well as the Baptist and Wesleyan chapels, dropped pennies in vestibule boxes for the purchase of boots for these same children. Even Squire Bartley had made a surprise donation of three dozen slates and a carton of chalk to the school.

But the most exciting development was the offer made by Mr. Durwin, one of the *Larkspur*'s lodgers. His oldest son, an engineer building a bridge in India, had sent him the design for a merry-go-round he had constructed for some of the colonists' children. Mr. Durwin pledged to have one built in the school yard if one hundred percent enrollment was reached by the beginning of the school year. It was the talk of the town, especially among the children.

So far, seven of the nine unschooled children had been registered. Even the Keegan family from Ireland had been persuaded that their three school-aged children should receive an education. That only left the two youngest Sanders boys, and it was no accident that the school board had saved that particular family for last.

"Even if Mr. Sanders agrees to send them, how do we know they'll behave?" Julia asked Andrew. "What if the new teacher isn't as good a disciplinarian as Captain Powell?" Captain Powell had given his resignation in June and was now to assume a position as one of Her Majesty's Inspectors. His new responsibility would be to travel throughout the county of Shropshire, seeing that schools met at least the minimum standards of education.

"We have to give them a chance," Andrew reminded her. "And as to their, or any other child's, failure to behave, the board has decided that expulsion would be swift. It's been difficult enough trying to find a new teacher. We can't have him or her resigning out of frustration."

"Him or her? I take it that the board hasn't heard from Miss Clark yet?"

"Not yet. Perhaps tomorrow." He smiled and replaced his empty cup on the tray. "It will work out, Julia. Things usually do."

"When you say that, I believe it," Julia replied, returning his smile. "Would you care for more tea?"

"I could stay here with you all day, drinking Mrs. Herrick's fine tea and staring at the most beautiful woman in England. But duty calls." After setting his bowler hat atop his blond head, he sent a glance in all directions, then put an arm around her shoulders and leaned over the tray for a covert kiss. It lasted longer than it should have, and when their lips finally came apart, Julia darted a glance at the *Larkspur*'s windows to make sure their little indiscretion hadn't been witnessed.

" 'They do not love that do not show their love,' " said a voice with a faint Cornish accent and a liberal dose of humor.

Julia and Andrew turned their heads to gape at Ambrose and Fiona Clay, smiling as they walked hand in hand from the side of the house facing the carriage drive. Their fortnight's stay in the apartment above the stables was halfway over now, for in another week Mr. Clay would be returning to London's Prince of Wales Theatre to take the lead role in a comedy titled *The Barrister*.

While warmth stole through Julia's cheeks, Andrew got to his feet, obviously not the least bit embarrassed at being caught. "Shakespeare?" he ventured as he and the actor shook hands.

"But of course. *The Two Gentlemen of Verona*."

Rising to embrace Fiona, Julia said, "You're up early. Have you plans for today?" The Clays were late risers out of necessity, for life revolving around the London theatre required long evenings.

"We thought we would enjoy watching the excavation before the sun gets too overbearing," Fiona explained. Mr. Ellis and Mr. Pitney, new *Larkspur* residents, were conducting an excavation on the Roman ruins atop the Anwyl. It had become a pleasant outing for villagers to hike up the steep hill to the west of Gresham and watch from distances that did not interfere with the archeologists' work.

Mr. Clay smiled. "Marriage agrees with me. I never had the energy to take on the Anwyl when I lived here before. Even Mrs. Kingston couldn't bully me into it."

"It sounds like a grand adventure," Andrew told them, then motioned to the nearest bench. "Have you a minute or two for a visit?"

"That's why we came out here first," the actor replied, guiding his wife to the bench. "Mrs. Herrick is packing some fruit and biscuits for us to share with Mr. Ellis and Mr. Pitney. Why don't you two join us?"

As Julia resumed her seat, with Andrew again settling on the other side of the tea tray, she made the silent observation that marriage certainly did agree with the couple. Mr. Clay seemed not to be in one of his despondent moods, for his gray eyes were bright and his posture erect. Fiona's face still wore the glow of a wife who is adored by her husband and, judging by her wardrobe, pampered as well. This morning she wore a striped silk gown of rich strawberry and gunmetal gray that flattered her fair complexion with a straw hat trimmed in matching ribbons.

"I still find myself reaching back to untie imaginary apron strings when I change clothes," she'd confessed yesterday when Julia complimented her wardrobe. Which was all the more reason Julia was happy to see her with nice things. Having spent most of her twenty-seven years in servitude, Fiona deserved no less.

Andrew's voice broke into her reverie. "Speaking for myself, I've a full plate today," he was saying, then turned to her. "But why don't you go, Julia?"

"Yes, Julia, do come with us," Fiona urged. After an awkward first day or two, she finally seemed to be at ease addressing Julia by her given name. The men still used formal titles out of habit, even though they had great affection for each other.

"Thank you, but I'm afraid I've several things to do as well," Julia replied with a regretful smile, though truly, she could have put some off until tomorrow. No matter how sincere the invitation, she couldn't help but feel that the newlyweds would enjoy ambling up the Anwyl's footpaths without a third person along. Changing the subject before a second invitation could be issued, she said, "I was just trying to talk Andrew out of accompanying the school board to call on the Sanderses."

"Yes?" Mr. Clay raised an eyebrow. The scar upon his forehead was still noticeable, but it added a rugged quality to his aristocratic face that was not unattractive. "And will you be needing someone to escort you to Doctor Rhodes' afterward?"

"That won't be necessary, thank you," Andrew replied with a chuckle, then got to his feet again. "But I must run along now. Supper at the vicarage tomorrow night?"

"It sounds lovely," Mr. Clay replied after exchanging a meaningful glance with his wife. They were already becoming proficient in the silent language of married couples.

"Excellent!" To Julia, Andrew said, "Please bring the children along, too."

"Are you sure Mrs. Paget won't mind? She's not used to cooking for so many."

"My dear, I've already spoken to her about it and she's delighted. Besides, she'll need the practice for later."

After Andrew bade them farewell, Julia watched him walk up the garden path and through the gate. He wore the broad shoulders of a man who should be taller than his five-foot-eight frame, and his bearded face was plain, according to his own description. But Julia had come to realize months ago, even before she had begun to love him, that Vicar Phelps had the most beautiful soul of any man she had ever met. And that meant far more to her than any aesthetic features.

––––––––

Andrew took his horse and trap only when his calls were not within walking distance of the vicarage. On those occasions he left Rusty, his blue roan, hitched outside the *Larkspur*'s front gate during his morning visits with Julia. Propriety, the same taskmaster that dictated the tea tray should rest between them, was why he did not pull into the carriage drive around back and sit with her in the courtyard, out of the sight of most villagers. *Avoid even the appearance of evil*, the Scriptures said. It wasn't exactly fair that most people held ministers up to a higher code of conduct than they did themselves, but it was an unchangeable fact of life.

It wasn't that the inhabitants of Gresham were malicious. On the contrary, most were warmhearted and had embraced his family in the year they'd lived here. But because of the remoteness of their village and the long hours spent hard at work, they had little else but gossip to keep themselves entertained. Even something as mundane as Mrs. Shelton's purchase of a new lamp or the Moores' overnight visit to cousins in Lilleshall was chewed over, discussed, and often embellished on its way to the next set of eager ears.

Climbing up into the seat of the trap, Andrew unwound his reins from the whip socket and turned for a last look at Julia. She never wore hats during their morning visits, and he wondered if it was because she was aware that he loved the way the morning sunlight turned her auburn hair to burnished copper and lit sparks to the emeralds that were her eyes. *I'm truly a blessed man*, he thought, as he did most mornings.

––––––––

When Andrew's trap was finally out of sight up Market Lane, Julia realized the Clays were both staring at her with the sentimental expressions usually reserved for small children who have done something particularly winsome.

She gave them an embarrassed smile. "I feel I should recite something for you now."

"Oh, do forgive us, Julia," Fiona said. "It was just so . . . sweet, the

15

way you were watching the vicar just now."

Mr. Clay nodded, his smile positively simpering. "I could tell you were meant for each other the first time I saw you in the same room."

"Yes? Well then, you should have told me and saved us some trouble."

"Do you suppose you would have listened to me?"

"Actually . . ." Julia assumed a thoughtful pose. "I'm sure it would have frightened me away. I suppose things have to happen in their own good time."

"*Sometimes* they do," the actor said with a wink at his wife.

Julia smiled again. She had momentarily forgotten that Mr. Clay and Fiona had married on the same day he proposed.

"When will Mr. Jensen be moving here?" Fiona asked. Mr. Jensen was Julia's former butler, whose loan and advice had rescued her and the children, along with Fiona, from impending poverty.

Julia sent a sideways glance at the new sign above the door to her lodging house. *Larkspur Inn* was carved into oak above a spray of flowers. While she looked forward to living in the vicarage and forming one family from the two, it was a comfort to know that the *Larkspur* would always be nearby. "Not until the first of December, so I'll have only one week before the wedding to show him how to manage the place. But it shouldn't take him long to learn. And of course he'll only have to send word to the vicarage should he need assistance later."

His scarred brow furrowing, Mr. Clay said, "Surely you aren't planning to forgo a honeymoon."

Even though Mr. Clay was a dear friend, and Julia not the seventeen-year-old bride she had been at her first marriage, she felt another blush steal across her cheeks. Still, she managed to answer with a casual, "We plan to spend a week or so in Wales. We don't wish to leave the children for too long during the Christmas season."

Mercifully Fiona changed the subject, or rather veered it off in another direction. "Speaking of the children, Julia, have you met Elizabeth's beau?" Elizabeth was Andrew's nineteen-year-old daughter.

Julia sent her a grateful smile. "Why yes, two or three times. Paul Treves—he's a curate in Alveley."

"Do you think he'll propose?"

"Elizabeth says he plans to do so formally as soon as he's promoted to vicar in eight months or so." Her smile faded. "I'm a little concerned about that situation . . . and so is Andrew."

"You don't care for the young man?" Mr. Clay asked.

"Oh, it's not that," she hastened to reassure him. "He seems very decent. It's just that we wonder if she's completely over someone from her past."

Recognition came into Fiona's expression. "The young man from Cambridge."

"He broke her heart in the worst possible way, but I believe she still longs to see him again."

"Then it's fortunate that Andrew moved his family here," said Mr. Clay. "At least the possibility of that happening is remote."

"Yes," Julia nodded, but for some reason she couldn't feel completely reassured.

Gertie, the scullery maid, came outside then with a basket of treats from Mrs. Herrick's kitchen, putting an end to the discussion. "Are you quite sure you won't come with us?" Fiona asked as Julia walked the two to the gate. "You could bring the children along."

She smiled and waved them away. "Thank you, but Andrew has brought them up there at least a dozen times. And I've duties around here, so you'll just have to try to enjoy yourselves without me."

*J*ulia lingered at the gate as Fiona and Mr. Clay walked the length of the garden wall, exchanging waves on the way with the driver of one of the red-and-white wagons from Anwyl Mountain Savory Cheeses. The wagon turned west at the crossroads, and it seemed from the ring of hooves and the rattle of wheels against the cobbled stones that it was turning into the carriage drive behind the inn.

Mrs. Beemish must have ordered cheeses, Julia thought. Which was odd, because although Squire Bartley's factory, north of the River Bryce, sent its famous Cheshire cheeses all over Great Britain, the wagons did not make local deliveries. They were kept busy enough, it seemed, carting their wares down to the railway station at Shrewsbury. Gresham residents made their purchases directly from the factory.

Deciding that policy must have recently changed, she shrugged the matter off and went into the house. The choppy notes of "London Bridge" greeted her in the hall—Mrs. Dearing had asked Julia's twelve-year-old daughter, Aleda, to give her piano lessons, and the two sat at the bench.

"Very good!" Julia exclaimed, walking over to stand at the piano's side. Up until now, all she had heard Mrs. Dearing attempt were simple scales. The elderly lodger smiled up at her, looking like an Indian princess with her turquoise necklace and long gray braid draped over one shoulder.

"Aleda is so patient with me," she said. "I'm afraid I'm rather slow."

"No, ma'am, you're doing very well," Aleda assured her. Like Julia and fourteen-year-old Philip, she had thick auburn hair and a scattering of freckles across her cheeks. Patiently she repositioned her pupil's slightly gnarled fingers on the keys so that the wrists did not droop, then smiled up at Julia. "Did you recognize 'London Bridge,' Mother?"

"As soon as I heard it." To Mrs. Dearing, Julia said, "Will you play it again?"

That pleased both tutor and pupil, and Julia stood and listened appreciatively. When the song was finished, she complimented them again, then walked up the corridor toward the kitchen to remind Mrs. Herrick that tomorrow her family and the Clays would be having supper at the vicarage. She heard voices in the short corridor leading to the courtyard door and looked to her left. There stood the cook along with housekeeper Mrs. Beemish, kitchen maid Mildred, and lodger Mrs. Kingston. The latter was dressed for her morning walk, straw bonnet over her gray head and stout walking stick in hand. From the tone of her voice it was obvious that she was not pleased.

"I care not one whit about your orders!" she was declaring to a man in the open doorway. Julia could see from the space between Mrs. Kingston and Mildred that he held two huge round cheese boxes in his arms, his face red from the effort.

"What's wrong?" Julia whispered to Mrs. Beemish.

The housekeeper turned wide brown eyes at her and said, "The squire—he sent cheeses this time and Mrs. Kingston will have none of it."

"Oh dear," Julia whispered. Faintly she could hear the halting notes of "Baa, Baa, Black Sheep" drifting from the hall, while in front of her Mrs. Kingston assumed her most imperious voice.

"You will remove yourself and these cheeses from the premises immediately, young man! And please inform Squire Bartley that any further offerings will be delivered to the parish poor box!"

The driver was obliged to yield at this point and backed away from the door. Mrs. Kingston turned to the group of onlookers. Julia wasn't certain if the flush across her wrinkled cheeks was from anger or embarrassment, or a combination of both.

"The stubborn old goat," she muttered.

"But he *did* stop sendin' the flowers, ma'am," Mildred reminded her in a humble tone. For her efforts at consoling, the kitchen maid was rewarded with an icy stare from Mrs. Kingston's blue eyes.

"And so what will it be next?" Mrs. Kingston demanded. "A side of beef?"

"Oooh! If he does, ma'am, please don't send it back!" Mrs. Herrick exclaimed.

Julia had to look away for a second to keep her composure. For Audrey Herrick's small stature—she was a dwarf, as was her husband, Karl—the cook possessed more dry wit than most people of normal size.

Deciding it was time to restore some order, Julia gently nudged her way through to the door. "Why don't we chat outside for a little while?" she asked, linking arms with Mrs. Kingston. Behind her she heard the trio of servants return to their duties.

The elderly woman raised her chin. "I'm late for my walk, and that

19

man has me so vexed that I doubt very much if I shall be able to go the whole three miles."

"Of course you will." Julia opened the door again and peered out, then pulled her head back in to smile at Mrs. Kingston. "The wagon is gone."

"The Worthy sisters . . ."

"Can't see the courtyard bench. I shan't keep you too long. Please?"

Mrs. Kingston's shoulders rose and fell with a sigh. "Oh, very well, Mrs. Hollis."

When they had settled themselves under the wide-spreading oak, Julia put a hand upon the woman's shoulder. The first lodger to arrive at the *Larkspur*, Mrs. Kingston occupied a special place in her heart. It hadn't been so at first, for the woman had arrived last year seemingly intent upon running the establishment to her own liking.

"Mrs. Kingston," Julia began gently. "The squire has been a bachelor for some seventy years now. Shouldn't you be a little flattered that he's trying to court you?"

Mrs. Kingston propped her walking stick against one of her knees so that she could tighten the strings to her bonnet. "If it were for the right reasons, Mrs. Hollis, I would be very flattered."

Julia blinked at such frankness. "You would?"

"Of course. He's not the ogre everyone makes him out to be, and we certainly share the same passion for gardening." She gave Julia a quick sideways look. "And it doesn't hurt that he's wealthy as Croesus, I might add."

"Then why. . . ?"

"Why don't I encourage him?"

"Yes," Julia said, though she would have rephrased the question to *Why do I do everything in my power to discourage him?* At least twice lately the squire had attempted to pay calls on Mrs. Kingston while she was out working in the garden, and on both occasions she gave an excuse to go inside immediately after returning his greeting.

Folding her arms across her ample chest, Mrs. Kingston replied, "I may not be as educated as Miss Rawlins and Mrs. Dearing, but I am not a fool, Mrs. Hollis."

"Of course not," Julia readily agreed.

"I know exactly why the squire fancies himself fond of me."

"Yes?"

"I figured it out after that first time he asked me to the manor to tour his gardens. When I arrived back here my heart was fairly swooning over the pleasantness of the whole afternoon." She gave Julia another sideways look, this time wistful. "My late husband, Norwood, was the only man who had ever courted me. It felt nice to be treated as a lady again."

That made Julia think of Andrew, which caused her to smile. She reined in the corners of her lips before Mrs. Kingston could notice. "He sent flowers from his garden the very next day, didn't he?"

"Yes," Mrs. Kingston nodded. "Mrs. Herrick received them at the back door, then proceeded to warn me about him."

"About the squire?"

"She worked in his kitchen for some years, remember. Mrs. Herrick said she felt compelled to inform me that according to some of the older servants in the manor, the squire courted several different women in his younger days."

Julia could hardly believe her ears. It was difficult enough imagining Squire Bartley ever being young, but the notion of his having any interest in romance was almost impossible to conceive—regardless of the attention he now showered upon Mrs. Kingston. "Then why did he never marry?"

Mrs. Kingston blew out her cheeks. "Because once a young woman showed signs of returning his professed affection, he lost interest. Time and time again."

"But that doesn't make sense. Wouldn't he *want* his affection to be returned?"

"According to the information Mrs. Herrick received, the squire's parents doted upon him and his sister, never refusing them anything. The sister married and moved away, but Squire Bartley was so used to being catered to by his parents and servants alike that getting his way became boring to him. As long as a young woman seemed unattainable, that represented a challenge for him, you see?"

"But that's so shallow. Surely the years have matured him."

Giving her an indulgent smile, Mrs. Kingston said, "Age is no guarantee of maturity, Mrs. Hollis."

Julia supposed she was right and upon further reflection recalled that Squire Bartley had never shown himself to possess any great maturity. He obviously still held a grudge over the Herricks leaving the manor to work at the *Larkspur*—she could see it lurking behind the forced smile he would direct at her whenever their carriages passed in the lane. "So when you carried away that blue ribbon at the flower show last month . . ."

"It was one of the few times anyone has dared to refuse him anything. I believe his interest in me grew out of that incident. After all, I had lived here in Gresham over a year and passed his church pew many a time. Why did he never speak to me then?"

"Perhaps he—" Julia began but found herself lacking the words to fin-

21

ish. Now it was she who let out a sigh. Even though the squire was a vinegary old blister, she had entertained great hopes that he would bring some romance to Mrs. Kingston's life. She had learned many things from her mostly elderly lodgers, and one of these was that the yearning to love and be loved didn't diminish with age.

"So you're afraid if you accept his gifts and attentions, he'll lose interest?"

"Oh, I'm most sure of it." Mrs. Kingston's lips tightened for the fraction of a second. "And I'll not be made a fool of again, Mrs. Hollis."

Julia knew she was referring to the time when she had displayed affection for Mr. Durwin, who ultimately chose Mrs. Hyatt. She patted Mrs. Kingston's spotted hand. "No one thought you a fool, Mrs. Kingston. It's not a crime to have feelings for someone."

"Hmph!" she snorted but shot Julia a grateful look before pushing herself to her feet. "If you'll excuse me now, Mrs. Hollis, the miles are getting no shorter."

Julia watched her disappear around the short L wing of the house, then heard her exchange greetings with their nearest neighbors, the Worthy sisters—two lace spinners who sat in their garden with their lap pillows. *She's a good soul, Lord,* Julia prayed. *And in spite of the companionship she has here, I believe she's lonely. Please help her to find someone.*

————

Intent upon collecting his fishing gear from the gardening hut, Philip hurried through the courtyard door and almost collided with his mother. He automatically reached for her arms to steady her.

"Philip!" she exclaimed, a hand flying to her chest.

"Sorry, Mother! Are you all right?"

"Yes, fine. I'm afraid I was woolgathering."

She seemed to do that a lot lately, but Philip reckoned she had more to think about than usual, what with the wedding and all. He was glad she was marrying Vicar Phelps, now that he'd had time to get used to the idea. With his leaving for school in early September, he would seldom be home to look after her and his sisters. *All four sisters,* he thought, for with that marriage would come two more—Elizabeth and Laurel Phelps.

"That's dangerous to do around doors," he cautioned.

"Yes. I'll be more careful."

Then she smiled at him in that sentimental way she'd developed lately. He knew what was coming next.

"Why did you have to grow up so fast?" she asked, her green eyes staring into his and looking suspiciously close to watering.

Philip supposed she would still be asking him the same thing when

22

he was a thirty-year-old man. Nevertheless, he forced himself to forget that Ben and Jeremiah were waiting for him at the River Bryce. After all, she *was* his mother. Reassuringly he said, "I'll still be home for visits, Mother."

"I know," came out with a sigh. "But won't you be terribly homesick?"

Perhaps if he were being sent away to Africa or Siberia, Philip thought, but to *Worcester?* However, he had the good sense to reply, "Of course I'll miss you terribly, but I can't become a doctor without schooling."

"I just wish we had a school here in Gresham for you. And for Laurel. You're both so young." His soon-to-be stepsister would be attending school in Shrewsbury and allowed to spend every weekend at home. The Josiah Smith Preparatory Academy in Worcester, however, only allowed one visit home per month in addition to a fortnight at Christmas and Easter. But it would be worth that drawback because it was the only preparatory school in Great Britain designed specifically for boys with aspirations toward the medical field.

"Now just a minute ago you were scolding me for growing up too fast," he teased. To his relief, she laughed and the sentimental expression faded away.

"I did at that, didn't I? Be sure to leave some fish in the river for everyone else."

The calls of rooks sweeping the air above with their black wings grew louder as Philip approached the bridge. As he suspected they would, Ben and Jeremiah had already wet their hooks. "Caught one already," Jeremiah Toft beamed, a flush of pleasure all the way to the roots of his coarse brown hair. "He put up a good fight, too. Look at 'im."

Philip raised the string tied off at the bank to admire the fat perch with a flipping tail, then lowered it back into the water. "He's a fine one, all right."

"I was beginning to think you weren't coming," Ben Mayhew scolded. Like Philip he had red hair beneath his cap, but Ben's was more the shade of a carrot, and his face a mass of freckles.

"Mrs. Dearing and Aleda asked me to listen to a couple of songs on the piano," Philip explained sheepishly as he baited his hook with one of the fat grubs Mr. Herrick had helped him dig yesterday afternoon. "Then my mother wanted to talk about my going away."

"She's still fretting?"

In spite of Ben's casual tone, Philip could recognize the envy in his voice. He felt sorry for his friend, who wanted to become an architect more than anything in the world. Though Ben's father made an adequate income as the village wheelwright, it did not lend itself to luxuries such as boarding schools. Ben's lot in life was to become a wheelwright like his father and brother, and most likely the same profession would be handed down to his sons.

"About my being homesick," Philip replied. Then for Ben's benefit he sighed and added, "You know, she may be right. I've always said there's no better place on earth than Gresham."

"Then why don't you tell her you don't want to go?" asked Jeremiah, who like his perch had fallen for the bait.

Ben simply smiled knowingly and said, "You know you're dying to go off to school, Philip Hollis. You don't have to pretend otherwise for my benefit."

"I'm not pretending," Philip said weakly but then shrugged. "All right—I want to go." The fact that eighty percent of all Josiah Smith Preparatory Academy graduates were accepted into Oxford or Cambridge—as the headmaster had boasted when Philip toured the school with his mother—was not the only reason he looked forward to going. It seemed a great adventure upon which he was embarking, a rite of passage into manhood. He would be able to bring home all sorts of news about happenings in another part of the country. The way Philip figured it, he would have the best of both worlds.

"But we'll still see each other when I'm home," he told his friends. "I doubt there's fishing at the school, so we'll likely have to spend every spare minute here during my monthly visits."

"Every minute," Ben echoed with a smile.

Philip could still detect the longing in his voice. He touched his friend's arm. "I'm sorry, Ben. I wish you could come with me." The irony of it all was that Ben could likely find a way to finance his way through one of the universities, for most had work-study programs for students without means. But one couldn't leap from sixth standard at a village school to the university.

Ben shrugged. "Oh well, I probably wouldn't be able to keep up anyway."

"That's not true," Philip protested. "You're very clever."

"Perhaps." Another selfless smile. "But honestly, I'm glad you get to go."

A silence followed, broken only by the rustle of willow boughs in the breezes and the lifting and dropping of fishing lines into the water. From downriver drifted the happy sounds of the blond-headed Keegan children, gathering rushes for basket making. After a while Jeremiah obviously mistook the lack of conversation for sadness on Ben's part, for he said in a cheerful voice, "Wheelwrights are important, y'know. May be some of the

24

most important folk in England. Why, without wheels, how would we get our wagons to go?"

"Why, that's a thought," Ben said, clapping him on the back while sending an amused glance to Philip. "Thank you, Jeremiah."

Jeremiah ducked his head modestly at this affirmation. "Carriages, too, don't forget."

There's going to be trouble, Mercy Sanders thought as she watched her father talk with the four men at the gate. Though judging from his upraised and shaking fist, it was more likely he was shouting threats at them. She pressed her forehead against the window glass to get a better view. She recognized Mr. Sykes, Mr. Sway, and Mr. Casper, members of Gresham's newly formed school board. They were with Vicar Phelps. This obviously had to do with her youngest brothers, Jack and Edgar, ages ten and eleven.

Her suspicions were confirmed when her father turned on his heel and began stalking up the path toward the cottage. The thunder in his expression was enough to send her flying to where his shotgun sat propped in the narrow space between a cupboard and a wall. Grabbing the stock with both hands, she hurried over and lifted the tablecloth long enough to lay the gun across the seats of two kitchen chairs. She quickly went to the stove and picked up a wooden stirring spoon just as her father burst through the door.

"Where did you put it, girl!" he bellowed a second later, wheeling around from the empty corner. Rage stained his already ruddy complexion to the color of the bandana around his neck.

After casually stirring the pot of cabbage that simmered on a back burner, Mercy turned down the knob a notch. The Durwin oil stove was a luxury that had taken her three years to talk her father into buying. By his way of thinking, she should have been content to continue cooking meals for a father and six brothers over the fireplace for the rest of her life. What else did she have to do—besides wash and sew their clothes, tend the garden, and keep the cottage in some semblance of order? "I'm not telling you, Papa," she said calmly. "You can't go shooting people."

Her father disappeared into the pantry for a second, then returned to the kitchen to glare at her. "I'm just gonter shoot over their heads. A man has a right to protect his property!"

"And Constable Reed has the right to lock you up."

26

Her words seemed to give him pause for thought, for as Mercy had heard it, her father had developed more than a nodding acquaintance with the damp old sandstone lockup behind the village hall in his earlier years. How would he oversee the operations of his dairy farm and herd of forty-three Friesian cattle if he were incarcerated? He certainly couldn't depend upon his sons, who were so lazy that they had to be bullied into work and would run him into ruin if left in charge. Mercy looked across the room through the door he had left open and was relieved to see no sign of the four men.

But that wasn't the end of it, she knew. "You're just going to have to send them to school, Papa," Mercy told him. "The whole village looks down on us. It's not right that none of the boys can even write his own name."

"Well, what about *me*?" he practically whined. "I need help around this place."

"They would be home afternoons and weekends. Besides, it wouldn't hurt the older boys to have to take up the slack. Perhaps if they had a little less idle time, they wouldn't get into so much trouble."

He appeared not to have heard her reply, for his heavy-lidded eyes were still traveling the length of the large room that served as kitchen and parlor in the half-timbered cottage. It was the color of those eyes that one first noticed about him, the restful green of a forest at twilight. Set in a face more disposed to generosity and good will, they would have been considered handsome and thoughtful.

Sighing, Mercy told him, "Those men are gone, so you might as well give up looking for that gun."

Her father hurried to the door and peered outside. When he turned back to her, disappointment had deepened the lines in his perpetually dour face. "I should strap you for thet, Mercy," he muttered.

Ten years ago Mercy would have quailed and perhaps even surrendered the shotgun now that the callers appeared to be on their way. But the thirteen-year-old girl she was back then had not yet reconciled herself to the fact that her father was the most selfish man upon the face of the earth. As long as his sons did their share of work, he had no concern that each was almost completely devoid of good character.

Of late Mercy had begun to wonder if the pneumonia was not what had killed her mother five years ago, but rather the years of living a life with very little appreciation to soften the drudgery. As a believer, Mercy was aware of the obligation upon her to honor her father. But she would leave the house before surrendering to a strapping at the age of twenty-three. Calmly, she told him after peeking at the joint of beef in the oven,

"You do, and I'll go live with Mrs. Brent, and who would cook and clean up after you then?"

"It's thet sharp tongue thet keeps men from courting, girl."

"It's our family's reputation," she shot back, hiding the effect of his hurtful words behind a bustle of cooking activity. *There was one once*, she thought. Orville Trumble, the owner of Gresham's general shop, had been interested in her when she was nineteen. But having to brave a gauntlet of surly brothers and a hostile father every time he paid a call had finally gotten the best of him. Now she had heard that the shopkeeper was courting Miss Hillock, the beginners' schoolmistress. It was not that Mercy had lost her one true love those four years ago, for their courtship had not had the chance to blossom that far. It was the thought of what *might* have been that was difficult to swallow.

Don't think about that, she told herself. It became quite easy to keep her mind occupied some minutes later when her brothers bustled into the house for their lunch. Dale and Harold were the oldest, at twenty-six and twenty-nine years of age. Oram and Fernie, fourteen and fifteen, were next in ages, then Jack and Edgar. Except for Mercy and Edgar, who had inherited their mother's hazel eyes, the Sanders siblings were all cast from the same mold as their father, with green eyes, ruddy complexions, and strapping physiques.

"After we eat, I want you to scrub the water trough," her father was saying to Jack from the head of the table between bites of roast beef, boiled potatoes, and cabbage. Clicks of pewter cutlery against crockery plates provided background noises against the usual mixture of banter and complaint, sprinkled with occasional profanity.

"Aw, Papa—" the ten-year-old started but then clamped his mouth shut after receiving a look of warning. While Willet Sanders had taught his sons by example that authority in general was to be scorned, his own rule was supreme—and correction came swiftly in the form of a blow with the back of a hand or a strapping.

"I seen those school men out front," Oram said while managing to chew at the same time. "You ran 'em off, didn't you, Papa?"

Busy with the meal in front of him, Mercy's father grunted something in the affirmative.

"You should ha' called me," Fernie said. With one deft movement he transferred cabbage juice from his chin to his sleeve. "I would've took the shotgun after 'em."

"Tried to." He flung Mercy a wounded glance. "Now they'll only be comin' back to pester us."

"They were just trying to help Jack and Edgar," Mercy argued, grimacing inwardly as Dale plunged a food-grimed fork into the butter crock.

Long ago she'd given up trying to get her family to use a butter knife. And about the same time she'd stopped putting butter on her own bread.

"They don't care nothin' about Jack and Edgar," Harold, the oldest, declared. "They just want that spinnin' jenny for the school yard."

"It's a merry-go-round, not a spinning jenny," Mercy corrected. "And they do care about Jack and Edgar. Why would they risk coming out here for the sake of something they're too old to enjoy?"

"Well, what's the difference anyhow?"

After the meaning of his question became clear to her, Mercy replied, "A spinning jenny is for weaving, a merry-go-round is for playing. It twirls around in a circle as children ride upon it." At least that was what she had read in a book.

"It does?" asked Edgar, perking up considerably. "Can it go fast?"

"Now, don't you go getting ideas." His father waved a fork at him. "You've enough to do here without takin' fancy notions about school."

"Mebbe they should put a spinnin' jenny in the school yard instead," Harold snickered. "Give 'em somethin' useful to do instead of recitin' poems." This caused several more snickers, for Harold was considered the family wit.

"Give 'em something useful to do," Jack echoed.

"Shut up and eat," their father ordered.

Until she began attending the Wesleyan Chapel two years ago, Mercy had not known that there were families who actually prayed before meals and carried on pleasant conversation as they ate. Did those families know how blessed they were?

She cleaned up the kitchen, put a pot of soup on the stove for supper, then went upstairs into her room. At the mirror over her chest of drawers, she stood untying the blue ribbon so she could comb her hair. She knew she was too old, at twenty-three, to tie her light brown hair at the nape of her neck, but it was so thick and curly that it tended to shed pins all day when she attempted a chignon. *Nobody cares how I look anyway*, she thought. Mother had been the only person to tell her she was pretty, but then, Mercy supposed all mothers told their daughters that. At least she hoped they did, for it had been nice to hear.

After retying the ribbon, she stared at the mirror in a rare moment of self-scrutiny. The heavy-lidded eyes of her father and brothers had some-how bypassed her. While her own hazel eyes were not disproportionately small, they were fringed with short, wispy brown lashes that certainly did nothing to call attention to them. Two straight, fawn-colored slashes formed her eyebrows, and her nose turned slightly upward at the tip. Un-derneath curved a nondescript mouth with lips neither too heavy nor too thin. At least her complexion and teeth were good, for she was meticulous in her grooming, if only to prove to herself that being a Sanders did not mean a total lack of pride in one's appearance.

She went downstairs to the pantry next, where dozens of quart jars stood in neat rows on the shelves. Most were filled with the bounty of her well-tended vegetable garden, along with jams of sloeberry and crab apple, preserved pears and apples, and honey from the beehives behind the barn. Taking a basket from the bottom shelf, she set a jar of pickled beets at one end, some crab apple jam at the other, and wedged a loaf of raisin bread between them to keep the jars from knocking against each other.

"Where you goin', Mercy?" Edgar asked, coming into the kitchen for a dipper of water just as she turned the corner from the pantry.

Mercy smiled. She loved her brothers, all of them, but felt particularly responsible for Jack and Edgar. If only she had come to know the Lord when they were much younger and still very pliable! For now, try as she might, she could not persuade them to accompany her to chapel. A contempt for religion was another legacy passed on to them by their father. Any conversations she attempted with them about her newfound faith were met with blank stares and much fidgeting. Their need for spiritual training was another reason Mercy *had* to persuade her father to allow the two youngest to go to school. At least there, they would have no choice but to sit through Vicar Phelps's chapel services every Monday.

"I'm going to Mrs. Brent's," she replied. "Would you ask Papa to let you come inside and stir the soup every now and then?"

"All right," he shrugged. "Why do you spend so much time with that old woman?"

"Because she's my friend."

But her friend was dying. Mrs. Brent, who lived at the end of Nettle Lane, was instrumental in getting Mercy to attend the Wesleyan Chapel. Every Sunday for years the elderly woman had passed by in a wagon pulled by two black dray horses driven by her caretaker, Elliott. If Mercy or one of her family happened to be outside, Mrs. Brent would have Elliott stop. "We've lots of room back here," she would call, her wrinkled face bearing a sunny smile. Even Mercy's father couldn't bring himself to be rude, though he never accepted the invitation. But one day over two years ago, Mercy found herself sitting between the white-haired woman and her housemaid, Janet, in the bed of the wagon.

Mercy's friendship with Mrs. Brent opened up a whole new world to her. Besides introducing her to the Gospel, the former schoolmistress taught Mercy to speak correctly, to read and cipher numbers, to use proper table manners, to embroider, and other little niceties that her mother had never had the opportunity to learn.

Mercy's flock of a dozen guineas accompanied her across the yard, clucking their usual *pot-rack!* sounds. The size of small chickens, they were a dark gray color with light gray speckles. "Go back!" She shooed them away from the gate lest they follow her.

Alternating the heavy basket from the crook of one arm to the other, she walked the half mile. Mrs. Brent's stone cottage was in a sad state of disrepair, with weeds choking the garden, a shutter hanging askew beside an upstairs window, and broken shingles on the roof. Mercy hated to think that Elliott was as lazy as her brothers, but she didn't recall his allowing things to go to pieces when Mrs. Brent was up and about. If she could spend more time here, she would be willing to attempt some of the repairs. But her father already complained enough about her leaving her chores to make the daily visit down the lane.

Janet, who seemed to be more conscientious than her husband, answered the door. "You're so dear to visit her, Miss Sanders," she said, greeting Mercy with a smile. She was a softly rounded young woman with soot-colored hair and a jutting chin.

Mercy glanced at the staircase and lowered her voice. "How is she today?"

"The same—perhaps a little worse," Janet whispered. "Would you like to go on up?"

"Yes," she replied and scooped the jar of pickled beets from the basket before handing it to Janet. The first bedroom from the upstairs landing was Mrs. Brent's. A rock the size of a teapot kept the door propped open so that Janet could listen for her call.

"I *thought* I heard your voice, Mercy," Mrs. Brent said. She lay propped on pillows against an iron bedstead, so frail that it appeared a mild wind could sweep her away like a fallen leaf. Palsy, Doctor Rhodes had diagnosed, had robbed her of the ability to walk and now was moving its way up through her arms.

"I brought you some beets," Mercy said, leaning forward to kiss the wrinkled forehead.

"You did?"

She held the jar up so that the sunlight slanting through the window would touch the glass.

"Look how they sparkle like rubies," Mrs. Brent breathed, lifting a trembling hand to touch the jar.

"There, there—don't tire yourself." Mercy eased the hand back to her friend's chest and took a seat in the bedside chair. "I just hope your digestion can still bear them."

"Oh, I can bear them all right. Do you think there will be pickled beets in heaven, Mercy?"

"Mrs. Brent . . . don't talk that way."

"Oh, forgive me," the gentle soul replied. "I don't want to cause you sadness. But you must understand that I'm looking forward to that place, dear child. Remember, we weren't created for this world."

A lump came to Mercy's throat. "It's just that I'm going to miss you so much."

"But only for a little while." Mrs. Brent's faded blue eyes were shining now. "But here . . . hold my hand. We've plans to make."

Memories of sitting at her dying mother's bedside assailed Mercy as she wrapped her fingers carefully around the fragile hand. Yes, she knew that a better place awaited her friend, but such talk was so hard to hear. And deep inside she believed, though without rationale, that if plans were not made for the afterlife, then the death could not occur. If she did not love Mrs. Brent so much, she would have made some excuse and left the room.

"First, my little herd," the woman said, seeming not to notice her discomfort. "There are six now, counting the two calves born this spring. I want you to have them when I'm gone."

Mercy had to shake her head. Mrs. Brent's cattle, named after flowers, were like the children she never had. "Mrs. Brent . . ."

"They'll not be allowed to accompany me to heaven, Mercy," she said in a thin but firm voice. "And I know you'll take good care of them."

"But Elliott and Janet . . ."

"I'm leaving them the horses and wagon and whatever money is left. But they're planning to live with Elliott's family and hire on at the cheese factory, so there will be no place for my herd." Beseechingly the old woman looked at Mercy. "I'm too weak to argue over this, dear. Please say you'll take them."

Mercy gave her a careful squeeze of the hand. "If it will make you happy."

"Yes." Letting out a sigh, Mrs. Brent lay back on her pillows to collect her breath for a moment. "The land and house go back to the squire," she said presently. "Janet will be taking my clothes for her mother-in-law— except the nightgown I'll be buried in, of course. Please remind her it's the blue one."

"Yes, the blue one."

"As for the rest of my belongings—they've been in this house for so long that I feel as if I should leave them for whoever settles here. But I want you to take my Bible. And if there is anything else you would like to have—"

"Mrs. Brent, I can't talk about this anymore." Mercy blinked the sting from her eyes.

"Have I made you sad? I'll stop then." She looked up at Mercy with the most tender of expressions. "Sing to me, child?"

"Yes, of course. What would you like to hear?"

"Oh, you choose this time. Something about heaven?"

"Very well." Mercy thought for a minute, and managing to stay on key in spite of a lump in her throat, she sang one of the hymns she'd learned at chapel:

> There is a land of pure delight, where saints immortal reign,
> Infinite day excludes the night, and pleasures banish pain.
> Could we but climb where Moses stood, and view the landscape o'er,
> Not Jordan's stream, nor death's cold flood, should fright us
> from the shore.

Mrs. Brent's eyes were closed as she lay back on the pillow, but her creased lips moved along with the words. Mercy completed two more verses, and then sang "Jesus, Still Lead On," one of her friend's particular favorites. After she was finished, she thought Mrs. Brent was asleep and wondered if she should leave, but then the faded eyes opened.

"You've such a pure voice," the woman said with a little smile. "Your babies will be so sweet tempered from listening to your lullabies."

Mercy felt a dull sadness at the futility of those words, but it wasn't the appropriate time to contradict her just now. She returned the smile. "Thank you, Mrs. Brent. Now why don't you try to sleep?"

Mrs. Brent closed her eyes obediently, but her lips still moved. "God has told me that He's going to send you a husband, Mercy."

*S*eated at the head of the *Larkspur*'s long dining room table that evening, Julia Hollis took in the homey scene before her. Savory aromas rose from plates loaded with Mrs. Herrick's specialties and mingled with the pleasant conversation of people who had become almost family to one another.

"Actually, they were used for weaving cloth, not for grooming," Mr. Ellis was saying of the bone combs he and his assistant, Mr. Pitney, had uncovered in the Anwyl's ruins today. Mr. Ellis looked every bit the archeologist with his studious gray eyes, tall, slightly stooped frame, and graying beard. "And they are not Roman, by the way."

"Not Roman, Mr. Ellis?" Mrs. Dearing asked from his immediate right. "But the fort *is* Roman, isn't it?"

"Oh, absolutely. But Mr. Pitney and I have come to the conclusion that there was a fortified village there sometime during the Late Iron Age—around 50 B.C., if you will. The Romans apparently leveled this village some two hundred years later to construct their fort atop the ruins."

"And so the combs are Celtic?" Mr. Durwin, retired founder of *Durwin Stoves*, asked.

"Indeed they are. It was Mr. Pitney who established that. He has a deep abiding interest in Celtic artifacts."

Julia recognized that Mr. Ellis was generously attempting to draw his younger associate into the conversation. Perhaps it was his great size that contributed to Jacob Pitney's timidity, for the dark-haired man towered above everyone else in the *Larkspur*. Big-boned he was, with hands that looked as if they should be swinging a pickax at a quarry rather than handling delicate antiquities. But it was obvious that he loved his work, for his brown eyes lit up when Fiona asked him to describe how the combs were used in weaving.

"Aren't you hungry, Mother?" Aleda asked from Julia's adjacent right. Julia looked down at her plate and realized her fork had been idly plowing swirls in her creamed turnips for some time now.

34

"It must be the turnips," Grace, at Aleda's other elbow, suggested before Julia could reply. The seven-year-old had an acute dislike for the root vegetable and seemed to assume it was only a matter of time before the rest of the household came to their senses and formed the same opinion.

Julia didn't force her to eat them, for she could recall a similar enmity with peas when she was a young girl. "The turnips are fine," she told Grace. "I'm still not used to having everyone here again. It's nice."

"Everyone" consisted of, in order of seating beginning with her son on the left, Mrs. Hyatt and Mr. Durwin, who were to marry in September, Mrs. Dearing, who had spent some years in California gold country with her late husband, Mr. Ellis, and Miss Rawlins, author of such penny novelettes as *Dominique's Peril*.

From Grace's right were seated Mrs. Kingston, Mr. Pitney, Fiona, and Mr. Clay. Counting Julia and her children and parlormaids, Georgette and Sarah, who were flanking the sideboard in their black alpaca gowns and white aprons, fifteen people were gathered in the room.

Good people, Julia thought. Oh, some had their minor peculiarities, as she suspected she did herself, but she could not have imagined a more congenial group living under her roof. She became aware that Mrs. Dearing was attempting to establish eye contact and said, "Yes, Mrs. Dearing?"

"Have you heard whether the school board's call on the Sanderses was successful, Mrs. Hollis?"

All eyes turned to her now. Julia shook her head. "I'm afraid I haven't." But as the day wore on, she had ceased worrying about her fiancé being the target of a rock, for surely she would have heard by now if he had.

"I do pray they were able to persuade him." Mrs. Kingston glanced at the girls at her left. "A merry-go-round would be such a novelty—why, I doubt there's another village in Shropshire that can boast such a wonder!"

Mrs. Dearing nodded. "It looks as if the whole outcome depends upon Mr. Sanders, doesn't it? I avoid gossip like the plague, but from what bits and pieces I've heard concerning him, he cares for nothing above his cattle—not even his own children."

"I've heard that as well," Mrs. Hyatt sighed.

The mood of the assemblage turned somber, with the scroll clock on the chimneypiece ticking off several seconds of silence. Presently Mr. Clay, whose face betrayed an apparent struggle with some sort of emotion, said, "We can only hope Mr. Sanders was in an agreeable *moo-ood*." He winced afterward. "Forgive me—I just couldn't help myself."

Another silence followed, during which everyone appeared to be collecting his thoughts. Mr. Durwin was the first to speak, scrutinizing Mr.

Clay unsmilingly, but with eyes that held a suspicious glint. "I suppose you find that *a-moosing*, Mr. Clay?"

Now somber expressions turned to chuckles. Even Georgette and Sarah sent giggles from the sideboard. "May I give it a try?" asked Mr. Ellis.

"But of course," Mr. Durwin invited.

He assumed an eloquent pose. "It would be-*hoof* any child to be educated."

"Wait—I have one!" Miss Rawlins said above the laughter that followed Mr. Ellis's contribution. "I *cud* listen to you make puns for days."

"Thank you, Miss Rawlins." Mr. Clay inclined his head toward the head of the table. "But wouldn't you rather listen to Aleda play the piano?"

The mirth that erupted fizzled out in the same breath. Before anyone could ask Mr. Clay to explain his answer, he sent Aleda a wink. "*Mooo-sic.*"

It seemed a dam had been broken. An assortment of nonsense words were twittered and guffawed over—even those that weren't quite up to mark, such as Mrs. Kingston's "It was *beast-ly* of Mr. Sanders to crown poor Mr. Clay with a rock."

"Aren't you going to say one, Mother?" Aleda whispered.

"I've been trying to think," Julia whispered back. "*Moon* is the only word I can come up with, but it hasn't anything to do with the subject."

Philip turned to her, his face flushed from laughter. "May I?"

"If you like," she nodded, relieved that at least one person from the Hollis family would be represented. Her son turned to the others, raised a timid hand as if in school, and was soon noticed by Mrs. Hyatt.

"Have you a good one for us, Philip?"

"I think so."

"Well, let's hear it, young man," Mrs. Dearing urged.

"This is *udderly* the funniest supper I've ever had," he said, which caused Mr. Clay to roar and Mr. Ellis to remove his spectacles and wipe his eyes with his napkin. By the time dessert was served—raspberry torte with cream—everyone had settled down somewhat, though the mood was still light.

As the lodgers moved from the room later, Mr. Clay accepted Mr. Durwin's request for a game of draughts "for old time's sake." Julia suspected that he did so to give Fiona and her some time to spend together and appreciated him all the more for it. "Why don't you show me the rest of your new wardrobe?" she asked her friend.

"I would love to," Fiona said, linking her arm through Julia's. They ambled down the corridor toward the courtyard door, first stepping into the kitchen to compliment Mrs. Herrick and the kitchen maids on the meal. Inside, the women were laying the table for the servants' supper.

"Ah, so's Mr. Clay *does* allow you out of his sight now and then," Mrs. Herrick told Fiona, causing a shocked giggle from scullery maid Gertie and a smile from Mildred.

"Now and then" was Fiona's smiling reply. "I'm happy to know that the cooking here is still the best in England."

"Flattery will land you another dish of raspberry torte, Mrs. Clay."

Fiona raised a hand to her waist. "It sounds wonderful, but I'm afraid I've no room for it, Mrs. Herrick."

They stayed only a minute or two longer, for the rest of the servants had begun drifting into the kitchen for their meal. In the comfortably furnished apartment over the stables, Julia sat at Fiona's dressing table and tried on an assortment of hats. She angled her face to study herself wearing a particularly flattering one of midnight blue felt, the brim turned up at one side and adorned with feathers and ribbons. "Is this French?"

Standing behind her like in the old days when she used to brush Julia's hair, Fiona nodded. "It looks stunning on you."

"It does?" Julia allowed Fiona to tilt the brim a bit farther down on her forehead, then looked in the mirror again. She had begun to feel pretty again in spite of her thirty-two years, for Andrew told her so every day. Her waist-length auburn hair had no gray as of yet, and her slightly freckled cheeks were still smooth. "I do look like I'm about to have tea with the Queen, don't I?"

"Why don't you keep it?"

"Oh no, I couldn't."

"You could wear it to the vicarage tomorrow evening."

The idea was tempting. For just a few seconds, Julia relived the years when the latest Parisian fashions were something she took for granted. The richness of her clothing had been important to her then, for there was little else in her life over which she had any control. But before temptation could take too great a hold upon her, she removed the hat. "Thank you, Fiona, but I can't."

"If you're worried that Ambrose might object . . ."

"No, it's not that." Julia sighed and tried to explain. "Most women here in Gresham can't afford anything so fine. I don't want to set myself apart from them."

She had given much thought on how she should conduct herself now that she was betrothed to a minister. There was no sin in being fashionable, and she had no intention of dressing dowdy. But how could she help her husband minister to people like Mrs. Burrell if she were bedecked out in

Parisian finery, when the poor woman couldn't clothe herself or her children without parish assistance?

"I understand," Fiona said, which of course came as no surprise to Julia. Taking the hat and handing over another, this time a muslin morning cap, her friend said, "Then we'll just have our own Easter parade right here. Try this one on, please."

Julia did as she was told. After every hat had been modeled and every gown admired, they sat on a small settee in front of the empty fireplace and propped their feet on the fender. Mr. Trumble had sent the Clays a tin of Belgium chocolate bonbons last week, and the two managed to find room for two or three each in spite of Mrs. Herrick's torte. Fiona entertained Julia with tidbits she'd learned about the theatre, and Julia told Fiona about her wedding plans.

And then abruptly Fiona asked, "You don't think I'm prideful, do you?"

Stifling a smile, Julia replied, "Are you referring to your wardrobe?"

"It's not that I require all that finery to be happy. Ambrose insists upon buying them for me."

"Fiona, there's not a prideful bone in your body."

"I'm afraid I'm capable of any emotion," she sighed. "In London we're often approached by people who recognize my husband. I must admit it's rather flattering being at his side. During my quiet times with God, I often have to remind myself from whence I came."

Julia nodded, understanding. Fiona's origins had indeed been humble, beginning with servitude in Ireland as soon as she was old enough to labor, then marriage to a brutal man at fourteen. She ran away from her husband, now dead, four years later to emigrate to London and was hired into Julia's household as a chambermaid. Fiona rose in position to become housekeeper of the *Larkspur*, but when she was twenty-six years old, her servitude became a thing of the past with her marriage to Mr. Clay.

"You know, I have to remind myself of that as well," Julia told her. "Or rather, where the children and I could have ended up had God not taken care of us. He's brought us both a long way, hasn't He?"

"Aye, missus," Fiona replied.

"Missus?"

The former housekeeper smiled at her slip of the tongue. "Old habits die hard. But yes, He has brought us far. And just think . . . our journeys aren't over yet."

Presently they joined the others in the hall. Both archeologists were absent, but that was not unusual, since they spent some evenings after supper cataloging the day's findings. Julia imagined that Philip was with them—they were patient about allowing him to watch. Mrs. Dearing and

Mrs. Hyatt sat on one of the sofas with needlework on their laps. On the facing sofa, Miss Rawlins read passages from a recently finished manuscript to Mrs. Kingston. And on the carpet, Aleda helped Grace cut paper dolls from a book. While Fiona watched the remainder of the draughts match, Julia moved an ottoman over to her daughters to admire their work.

"Let's clean our teeth and wash our faces," she told the two when the grandfather clock chimed eight times. Grace looked up from her paper dolls with pleading eyes, but Julia shook her head. She had learned last year, upon assuming the responsibility of mothering her children instead of allowing a nanny to do so, that if bedtime were allowed to be negotiated *one* night, it would have to be negotiated *every* night. And since she didn't wish their last conversations of the day to consist of arguments and pleadings, she enforced the rule with the rigidity of a garrison sergeant except on special occasions.

While the girls headed with reluctant steps for the water closet to take care of their toilet, she went to the bedroom they shared and laid out their nightgowns. Philip's bedtime was pushed back thirty minutes when he graduated from Gresham School, so she had plenty of time to hear the girls' prayers and read a story before it would be time to bid him goodnight.

And the boy's bedtime ritual would end with that, for shortly after his graduation he had approached her with the request that he not be tucked into bed anymore. "I'm too old to be coddled now," he'd explained after some hesitation. "You don't mind, do you?" Julia had smiled and assured him she understood, then went to her room and wept for a little while. Her son no longer *needed* her. If Gresham were Alaska, she would be one step closer to being set adrift on an ice floe.

But she had forced herself to see reason. It only meant that he was trying as best he could to become a man—*not* that he had no use for a mother. She had come to accept that for her son, "tucking in" now meant a kiss on his cheek in his doorway and exchanging wishes for pleasant dreams.

The story Julia selected from Grace's big book of fairy tales was *The Ugly Duckling* by Hans Christian Andersen. Two well-scrubbed faces listened intently from their pillows as Julia read:

> "It was so lovely in the country—it was summer! The wheat was yellow, the oats were green, the hay was stacked in the meadows and the stork went tiptoeing about on his red legs, jabbering Egyptian, a language his mother had taught him. . . ."

She could tell that Aleda enjoyed the story as much as her younger sister did, though she would have been loathe to admit it—for she, like

Philip, was beginning to feel the constraints of her age. But in Aleda's case, having a younger sister afforded her the opportunity to listen in.

When both daughters had been properly tucked in for the night, Julia went two rooms down the family corridor and knocked upon Philip's door. There was no answer, so she returned to the hall. The Clays had retired to their apartment, and Mr. Ellis had come downstairs and was reading Mrs. Hyatt a portion of a letter from his wife back in Liverpool. Shortly after the archeologist had arrived at the *Larkspur*, he and Mrs. Hyatt had been pleased to discover they were second cousins twice-removed. Mr. Durwin did not seem to mind the shared tidbits of family gossip between his fiancée and Mr. Ellis, for he listened with eyes half-closed and a pleasant smile.

"You must hear this part, Mrs. Hollis," Miss Rawlins said from the opposite sofa, where she and Mrs. Kingston still sat. "I based the heroine on you."

"You did?"

"Well, her appearance anyway."

Mrs. Kingston nodded up at Julia. "As soon as she read it to me, I said, 'Why, she sounds just like Mrs. Hollis!' "

Philip will likely come along soon, Julia thought. The two women moved apart to give her room, and she settled in between them. With a sideways smile that seemed to say, *Just wait until you hear this!* Miss Rawlins cleared her throat and began to read.

> "Penelope St. Martin was a beautiful woman, slender and well-proportioned, who carried herself with a quiet grace that belied her tempestuous spirit. Oh, the eyes were calm enough—green like the sparkling sea under the noon sun—but in contradiction with hair that flamed crimson about her shoulders."

"Why, that's very good," Julia said as the author lowered the page. "I'm flattered, but I must confess I don't think of myself in quite so exotic terms."

"I realize your hair is longer." Miss Rawlins gave Julia's chignon a glance. "But 'flamed crimson to her waist' just didn't sound as poetic as the shoulders bit. And of course Penelope is much younger."

Julia's smile stiffened just a little. "Yes?"

"I pray you don't take offense, Mrs. Hollis. But I'm sure you realize no one wants to read about older people. I seldom write about any woman past the age of eighteen."

Being termed "older people" from someone one year older than her own thirty-two years was a bit of a sting, but Julia managed to reply, "Yes, of course."

Mrs. Kingston, however, took issue with that notion. "And why is that,

Miss Rawlins? Why should I, as a woman in her sixties, wish to read about a child barely out of pinafores?"

Favoring her with a patient smile, Miss Rawlins said, "That's just the way it is, Mrs. Kingston. Surely you'll concede that youthful courtship is the most romantic."

"I quite disagree."

"Then you would be in the minority among readers. You have to understand that there is the market to consider."

While the issue was cordially but adamantly debated upon on either side of her, Julia sank back into the sofa and allowed her mind to carry her back to the kiss Andrew and she had shared in the garden this morning. She imagined she could still feel the gentle pressure of his lips upon hers, the fresh smell of lavender soap in his beard, and the security of his strong arm around her shoulders. *And what do you think of that, Penelope St. Martin?*

Silence on either side of her jolted her back to the present.

Why are you smiling so? both sets of eyes seemed to question. Julia made a self-conscious little shrug and decided this was the perfect time to absent herself. "Excuse me," she said, getting to her feet. She turned to the two, aware that the debate would continue, but appreciating the fact that neither would bear a grudge as a result. "Thank you for sharing the passage with me. I really must find Philip now."

"He was in the library last time I looked," offered Sarah, who had just walked into the room with a tray of hot chocolate. "Shall I fetch him, ma'am?"

"No, thank you. I'll go myself." Indeed, Philip sat in an armchair in a circle of lamplight, a book open in his lap, his chin tilted upward, and his gaping mouth emitting snoring sounds. She shook his shoulder gently. "Philip."

He blinked at her. "Huh?"

"It's time for bed."

"Huh?"

"Just come with me." As she guided her half-conscious son by the arm to his room, she thought it was nice to have a reminder once in a while that a boy-almost-a-man still needed his mother. *Perhaps I'm not ready for the ice floe yet after all.*

She returned to the hall afterward to bid the six remaining lodgers good-night. Miss Rawlins, however, asked her to sit for a moment. Fearing she would be subjected to another reading, Julia was about to politely decline when she noticed the gravity in the writer's expression.

"I didn't want to mention this with the children around," Miss Rawlins began when Julia had settled into a chair. "But I was at *Trumbles* purchasing some writing paper for my latest manuscript, *Lord Sullivan's Daughters,* and overheard Mr. Sway tell Mr. Trumble that Mr. Sanders was not at all receptive today."

"Oh dear," Mrs. Hyatt said to Mr. Durwin. "Then the school won't have full enrollment, will it?"

"I'm afraid not, unless Mr. Sanders changes his mind," he replied. "He has two eligible children."

"Oh, surely you can go ahead and get the thing," Mrs. Kingston said. "It's not the other children's fault that Mr. Sanders is muleheaded."

"Yes, can't you?" Mrs. Hyatt asked hopefully.

"Nothing would please me more, but I wonder if that would be wise." Mr. Durwin sent an apologetic look to Julia. "Every child in Gresham is aware of the condition for the offer. What kind of example would it set for them if I were to alter the goal now to fit the circumstance?"

"You don't believe they'll become larcenists as a result, do you?" Mr. Ellis scoffed mildly, causing Mrs. Kingston and Miss Rawlins to nod their heads in agreement.

Mrs. Dearing, however, held her head at a thoughtful angle. After a second's hesitation she replied, "I would like the children to have the merry-go-round just as much as all of you do. But I believe Mr. Durwin has a valid consideration. Our word is supposed to be our bond. If exceptions were to be given, they should have been announced back when the offer was made."

"But they're only *children,*" Mrs. Kingston pleaded.

Mr. Durwin nodded gravely. "All the more reason to keep our word. The example we set, you know. If we capitulate on this issue, what happens later on when we hold up another goal before them?" He gave a heavy sigh. "There is always next year. I'll make the offer stand indefinitely."

Julia didn't know which side was more reasonable, but having two daughters who would be affected caused her to hope Mr. Durwin would reconsider. *Yet I can't tell him how to spend his money.*

She happened to glance at Mrs. Kingston. The set of the woman's chin—with her lips pressed together under her hawkish nose—caused Julia to wonder if she considered the matter settled.

Jesus shall reign where'er the sun
Does his successive journeys run:
His kingdom spread from shore to shore
Till moons shall wax and wane no more. . . .

Mercy did not miss a note as she picked another marrow from its vine and tossed it gently into the pail at her feet. There was a technique to knowing exactly when the vegetable should be harvested—picked too soon and the taste was sometimes bitter, too late and the pulp was too dry. Today's offering from her garden would soon be simmering in a pot with slices of onion and bits of ham for the dinner table.

She had finished the second stanza and was about to launch into the third when she heard a woman's voice from behind her. "Excuse me, dear?"

Mrs. Brent? Hopefully she turned to look at the figure standing at the beginning of her row, but alas, a stranger stood there. Or rather, someone she had not met, for during the course of attending errands in the village, she had seen the elderly woman walking the lanes.

"Yes, ma'am?" Mercy said, still holding one of the vegetables. So seldom did a caller happen by that she found herself a little dumb struck. Surely the woman had lost her way.

The woman mopped her face with a handkerchief. She was quite becoming in spite of a hawkish nose. A blue calico gown draped from her squared shoulders as regally as a queen's robe—the walking stick in her hands could have easily been a scepter. "Would this be the Sanders place?"

"Why, yes it is, ma'am." Mercy's quick glance past the gate revealed no carriage in the lane. "Did you *walk* all the way from town?"

"I'm afraid I did, child." The handkerchief made another swipe across the wrinkled forehead. "Silly, yes? I had another call to make on the way here, so I assumed both would be equal to my usual morning walk. I didn't realize how far away you lived. I could have easily asked Karl to drive me here. He's caretaker at the *Larkspur*, Karl Herrick."

"Is that where you live?" Mercy had passed the old coaching inn many times and admired the stately look of it.

"How thoughtless of me!" Switching the handkerchief to her left hand, the woman took a couple of careful steps in the valley between the beans and the carrots and extended her right hand. "Octavia Kingston is my name, dear. And yes, I do live at the *Larkspur*. And you would be. . . ?"

"Mercy Sanders." Now that names had been exchanged and hands shaken, Mercy relaxed a little. "Would you like to come inside and have some tea?"

"Oh, water would be most lovely, dear."

Minutes later, after Mrs. Kingston had drained a tumbler of water and was resting herself in the rocking chair that had been Mercy's mother's, she smiled while removing her bonnet. "You have a beautiful singing voice, Miss Sanders. Have you ever performed for an audience?"

"Thank you." Mercy perched herself upon a cane-bottomed chair. "I sing at the Wesleyan Chapel on Sundays."

"And what better audience than God, eh? Well, the Wesleyans are blessed to have you. One of my parlormaids back in Sheffield was a Wesleyan. Fine person."

Mercy didn't know if she was expected to express thanks for the compliment, since it was mixed with one for the woman's former servant. She settled for a grateful smile. It was rather nice to have a visitor and be able to sit like two lady friends. Suddenly it occurred to her to wonder exactly *why* Mrs. Kingston would walk some five miles to her family's cottage. But since it would be rude to ask, she asked instead if Mrs. Kingston would care for more water or perhaps some bread and jam.

"Oh, no thank you, dear. I'm quite fine now."

"I'll ask one of my brothers to drive you home in the wagon when you're ready to leave," Mercy offered.

"How very kind of you." Mrs. Kingston's blue eyes swept across the room, missing nothing. Then she smiled again. "Would it be possible for me to speak with Mr. Sanders?"

"You want to speak with my father?" Mercy echoed, though she had heard her perfectly the first time.

"If it isn't too much of a bother. I shan't stay but a minute."

"Well . . ." Mercy stalled for time to consider the request. Her father had not been in the best of moods when he walked away from the breakfast table a couple of hours ago. Of course, that wasn't anything unusual, but what if he were to curse at Mrs. Kingston? Her family's reputation could hardly stand any more tarnishing.

Mrs. Kingston seemed to read her thoughts, for she said, "I informed no one that I was embarking upon anything other than my daily walk. Whatever we happen to discuss, I will keep to myself."

"Thank you," Mercy said, letting out a relieved breath. "I believe he's still in the hay barn patching a hole in the loft."

After Mrs. Kingston replaced her bonnet, they walked out toward the barnyard together. Faint hammering sounds drifted from that direction. The cows were all out to pasture, having been milked earlier in the morning. Mercy found herself wishing her brothers had been sent out to pasture as well, for as each caught sight of Mrs. Kingston, he stopped his chores to stare. Oram, who was supposed to be scrubbing milking pails, gaped with his jaw hung so low that Mercy worried it might lock. Harold was rude enough to look up from the post hole he was digging and say, "Papa's too busy for comp'ny, Mercy."

Mercy ignored him, and miraculously, he did not press the issue. At the barnyard gate she turned to Mrs. Kingston and said apologetically, "You'd best wait here. I'll see if Papa will come down."

Mrs. Kingston sent a doubtful glance back at Harold, who now stood glowering at both of them with hands upon hips. Fixing Mercy with her frank blue eyes, she said, "I don't wish to inconvenience your father, Miss Sanders. It will defeat my purpose in coming here if he becomes angry."

That's likely to happen anyway, Mercy thought.

"Why don't you lead me to him?"

Mercy would have argued had she not the feeling that Mrs. Kingston was not one to be discouraged so easily. Instead, she nodded down at the woman's shoes.

"You'll need to watch your step in there, ma'am." As if to illustrate her point, a shovelful of muck flew from the open door of the milking barn only ten feet away. "Dale is sluicing out the stalls," Mercy explained, highly embarrassed.

Mrs. Kingston was already gathering the folds of her skirt with both hands and smiled reassuringly. "I didn't expect your cows to be wearing nappies, Miss Sanders. Just lead the way, and we'll be fine."

The hammering sounds increased as the two gingerly made their way across the barnyard. Six feet away from the barn, Mercy stopped and cupped her hands to her mouth. "Papa?"

There was no answer, so she tried again a little louder. This time the hammering ceased, and a grunt floated down from the open hayloft door. It likely was his way of saying *what?* but could just as well translate into *go away!* or *this board is too heavy!* She gave Mrs. Kingston a helpless look, then raised her hands to her mouth again.

"Would you please come to the door, Papa?"

This time he actually articulated words from the recesses of the loft. "What for?"

Mercy sighed. Why did everything in her family have to be so difficult? "There's a Mrs. Kingston here to see you."

"Who?"

Before Mercy could reply, she felt a touch on her shoulder. "Allow me, dear. We can't have you damaging that lovely singing voice." Then raising her chin, the woman called out shrilly, "Octavia Kingston, Mr. Sanders! Would you be so kind as to allow me a word with you?"

There was a brief silence, in which Mercy could picture her father trying to place the name. And then, "Is this about thet school?"

"It is indeed, Mr. Sanders. How very perceptive of you!"

This time the grunt that issued from above had a distinctive familiar ring. Mercy felt her cheeks grow hot, and she prayed that the woman beside her hadn't figured out what he had actually said. But Mrs. Kingston seemed to be concentrating on something else, for after listening to the resumed hammering with pursed lips, she turned to Mercy and said, "Tell me, how does one get up there?"

"You want to climb up in the loft?"

"Frankly, dear, I am not looking forward to it. But there seems to be no other way."

With great misgivings Mercy led the older woman through the wide open barn door. Just inside, Mrs. Kingston paused. "Will you close and bolt that door?" She glanced down at her skirt. "Modesty, you know."

Mercy complied at once, plunging the barn into darkness save for the daylight seeping through the cracks between the door boards. After allowing a second or two for Mrs. Kingston's eyes to adjust to the dimness, Mercy pointed to a ladder. She felt compelled to give another warning at the bottom. "He may swear at you."

Mrs. Kingston again gathered her skirts about her knees, then lifted her foot to the first rung. "I'll box his ears if he does."

After the initial shock had passed, Mercy smiled to herself, gathered her skirts, and followed. Perhaps this woman would be a match for her father after all. This was much more interesting than picking vegetables.

"Would one of you gentlemen mind lending me a hand?" she heard Mrs. Kingston say, whose head and shoulders had disappeared into the floor of the loft. Mercy listened to the hammering cease and cringed at the expected explosion of words, but to her surprise, none came. Perhaps Mrs. Kingston's tenacity had rendered her papa speechless.

"Help her, Fernie," she even heard her father mutter, and Mrs. Kingston's feet presently disappeared. Her father and brother did not extend the same courtesy to Mercy when she reached the top of the ladder, but she had played up here hundreds of times as a girl and easily swung herself to the floor. Papa was on his knees staring, openmouthed, as Mrs. Kingston brushed stray bits of straw from her sleeves and surveyed the stacked bales of new hay as if they were fine furnishings.

"Your cattle will be nourished all winter, I can see. How wise of you to provide for them, Mr. Sanders."

Her father sent Mercy a look that would have set her to trembling had she been younger. Fernie resembled a kitten watching a pendulum as he shifted his attention from his papa to this visitor, and then back again.

"Just like the biblical ant, storing for the lean times," Mrs. Kingston was saying. "Some things never change, do they? I find that very reassuring."

"I ain't gonter send the boys to thet school," Mercy's papa finally glowered.

"No?"

"No!" He jabbed in the direction of the ladder with his hammer. "So's you may as well go away."

Mrs. Kingston merely shrugged her regal shoulders. "Very well then, Mr. Sanders. I can see it's useless to attempt to change your mind." Turning back to Mercy, she said, "Would you mind helping me with those top rungs, dear?"

As her father expressed his contempt with a resumed barrage of hammering on the patched floor, Mercy lowered herself by four rungs and then held out both hands toward Mrs. Kingston. The elderly woman leaned down as if she would take them but then straightened again.

"Oh, by the way, Mr. Sanders."

Mercy's father held the hammer poised above his repair work. He directed a grunt toward Mrs. Kingston, but mercifully it did not sound like any recognizable profanity.

"Would you happen to know of anyone in the market for a cow?"

"What?" he growled.

"Silly woman that I am, I happened to come into possession of a fine heifer from Mr. Fletcher of Arnold Lane this morning, and I don't quite know what to do with her. You see, I reside at the *Larkspur* and—"

Sitting back on his heels, he said in a disbelieving voice, "Mr. Fletcher sold *you* one of his cows?"

"Actually, we made a trade. You see, my morning rambles take me down almost every lane in Gresham. On Thursdays I pass their farm and have had the privilege of making the acquaintance of Mr. Fletcher and his lovely wife. I'm not surprised you've heard of them. Their herd—"

"The finest milk producers in Shropshire!" Mercy's father interrupted again. "But Fletcher won't sell to nobody, the stingy—"

"As I made mention, it was a trade." Mrs. Kingston picked another bit of straw from her sleeve.

Mercy could read her father's thoughts as he studied the woman standing at his hayloft ladder. To have such an animal among his herd would result in some outstanding calves one day, thereby increasing milk production considerably in just a few years.

"I don't suppose you'd be willin' to sell her to me, would you?" It was a statement, not a question, for clearly he was beginning to understand that she had some other motive in mind.

"I'm afraid not, Mr. Sanders."

His green eyes formed slits. "What do you want, Mrs. . . . . "

"Kingston," she supplied. "I believe you already know the answer to that."

"Thet school," he said resignedly.

She smiled. "A little education never hurt anyone, Mr. Sanders."

It was with a sense of great awe that Mercy accompanied the woman back through the barnyard. Finally when the gate was behind them, she sent out a long breath. "You knew you could make him change his mind, didn't you?"

"Why, of course not, Miss Sanders," Mrs. Kingston replied. "I'm not a prophet. I'm just as surprised as you are." But the look in her blue eyes said otherwise.

Mercy smiled. She had seen something remarkable this morning—an elderly woman had accomplished what four men couldn't.

She beckoned to Oram, who came trotting over right away and gladly accepted the responsibility of driving the visitor back to town. Handling the team and wagon was more enjoyable than scrubbing milk pails any day. "My papa doesn't believe women should drive," Mercy explained after Oram had hitched up Dan and Bob, the two speckled drays, to the wagon. "Or I would take you back myself."

"That's quite all right, dear." Mrs. Kingston allowed Oram to help her up into the seat beside him, then she patted his shoulder. "I do appreciate this young man saving me from that long walk."

"Yes'm," Oram mumbled. But before he could pick up the reins, Mercy stepped toward the wagon again.

"May I ask what you traded Mr. Fletcher for the cow?"

Mrs. Kingston smiled down at her. "Certainly you may, Miss Sanders. It was a bicycle."

"You have a bicycle?"

"You've heard of them, haven't you?"

Mercy nodded. She had seen an advertisement for one in an issue of *The Sunday Visitor* at the lending library. But she had never seen one on the lanes of Gresham.

"I haven't actually taken possession of it yet," Mrs. Kingston went on to explain. "Mr. Fletcher is well aware of that and knows I'm good for it. You see, my son, Norwood, has written that he's sending one for my birthday next week."

"Happy birthday," Mercy said, and Mrs. Kingston smiled.

"Thank you, dear." She shook her head. "Now, no doubt you're wondering why someone would send a sixty-four-year-old woman a bicycle. Norwood is obviously under the impression that, as much as I enjoy my morning walks, I would enjoy peddling along at breakneck speed even more so. I dare not send back his gift for fear of injuring his feelings, but I shan't go gadding about on a contraption that looks like something out of a medieval torture chamber. And if I were to keep it at the *Larkspur*, the Hollis children would no doubt ask to ride it, thereby risking their lives and limbs."

Mercy smiled. "Then it was good that Mr. Fletcher wanted a bicycle."

"Isn't it, dear?" Mrs. Kingston smiled again. "And I find people much more agreeable when there is something they want."

As easy as stealing a drunk man's purse, thought Mrs. Kingston, who would of course never actually *do* such a thing. And her conscience was quite clear about it all, for she had made no promises regarding Mr. Fletcher's heifer producing more milk than any other cow in Mr. Sanders' herd.

She smiled to herself and waved away a curious bee with a slow motion of her hand. It was odd that she, who had no experience with dairying, would have figured out what the rest of Gresham considered a big mystery. She had simply put two and two together one Sunday morning in church, or rather added one incident with another to form a theory.

The first incident had been Mr. Fletcher's rendition of "Come, Thou Almighty King" in the choir gallery. There was nothing unusual about that, as the self-educated Mr. Fletcher often played his violin before the church. Clearly he loved the instrument, for his eyes closed and rapture filled his expression as the bow swept across the strings. Even the children ceased to fidget when the sweet strains of his music floated out among the congregation.

It was the following message Vicar Phelps delivered about young David in the palace of his nemesis King Saul that set Mrs. Kingston to thinking.

Just as the chords of David's harp had refreshed Saul's troubled spirit, couldn't music also lull animals into a relaxed state? Even *she* knew that agitated cows produced less milk—didn't it stand to reason that relaxed cows would produce more?

She had the opportunity to voice her theory to Mr. Fletcher during her walk the following Thursday. His reaction had stunned her. Redness stole up from his collar over his clean-shaven face before he practically tore his gate off the hinges in his lunge through it and seized her hand.

"I don't know how you came up with such a notion, Mrs. Kingston," he protested.

"Are you saying it's not true?" She had him there, for a man who stood up in church and played hymns on the violin could not in good conscience stand on the side of Arnold Lane and perjure himself.

"If I tell you, will you promise to keep it a secret?"

"But I should think if you have a technique that will boost milk production, you would be happy to share it with everyone," she told him in the same tone she'd used when lecturing her son when he was a boy. "It seems rather selfish to keep it to yourself."

"It's not so simple, Mrs. Kingston. Please?"

In the end she had yielded to the pleading in his eyes. "Very well then, Mr. Fletcher. I'll tell no one, but only if you can give me a good reason."

"Thank you." He dropped her hand and let out a heavy sigh. "You're correct. I do play for my cows."

"Indeed?" It had been an exhilarating feeling, knowing she'd guessed correctly. "Now would you care to tell me why it's not so simple to share such a method?"

Mr. Fletcher nodded. "I am not a selfish man, Mrs. Kingston. How many times have you heard Vicar Phelps announce that I would be giving free violin lessons in the Village Hall on Saturday afternoons?"

"Well, several," she admitted. "But what does that have to do with—"

"Everything! Because though that announcement has been made many times, do you know how many people have come to take advantage of them?"

"No, I don't."

"Two! The Casper boy and Mrs. Moore. They are progressing well, but neither is in the business of dairying. I realize that there are few wealthy people in Gresham, but most make good livings. And a decent German violin can be ordered through Mr. Trumble for little more than a half-sovereign."

Mrs. Kingston felt sorry for him then, for there was nothing so disheartening as being enthused about something in which others had no

50

interest. "But surely if you told everyone your secret, you could fill your class."

"That's exactly why I cannot do so . . . don't you see? If a person wishes to learn the violin for any reason other than a love of music, he will never master the instrument. Yet I would be obliged to give lessons to those who are simply eager for more profit, for how could I refuse a fellow villager?" A shudder seized him. "I can think of no greater agony than attempting to teach music to a room filled with people with wooden ears. And the poor cows, Mrs. Kingston—they're such helpless creatures and a captive audience in their milking barns. The violin in the hands of a novice can produce sounds that are simply torturous."

Again Mrs. Kingston could see his point but had to ask, "But what will you do if a dairy farmer asks you for lessons? Simply because he loves the music, I mean."

For the first time during their exchange Mr. Fletcher produced a smile. "Should that wonderful event ever happen, Mrs. Kingston, I would feel privileged to include such person in on our secret."

"Our" secret, Mrs. Kingston thought as the Sanders wagon continued up Nettle Lane. A clever way of reminding her that she had given her word. "People are interesting, aren't they?" she said to the boy beside her.

"Yes'm," he mumbled, with his eyes still straight ahead, and no apparent curiosity as to why she would make such an observation out of the blue.

Probably *any* observation she could make, such as *hares have long ears*, would have gotten the same response. She didn't know what was taxing the boy's brain so, for it wasn't driving. Clearly in no hurry to return to his chores, he was allowing the two horses to meander along at a snail's pace.

"Interesting, indeed," she said.

————

"You should have seen the way she talked to Papa," Mercy said to Mrs. Brent after easing another spoonful of potato soup into the ailing woman's mouth.

Propped up on her pillows, Mrs. Brent swallowed, then smiled weakly. "So your father changed his mind about the schooling?"

"He did, indeed." Mercy chuckled at the memory.

"What did she give Mr. Fletcher for the cow? Did she tell you?"

Mercy wiped her friend's lips with an edge of the napkin she had tucked under her chin. "A bicycle."

"A what, dear?"

"It looks something like a dogcart, but with the two wheels front-to-

51

back instead of on each side. It has handles to hold on to in front, and you must pedal it with your feet."

"Do tell? But how does a body keep from toppling over?"

"I'm not quite sure about that part," Mercy admitted. "Let's have another bite, shall we?"

Mrs. Brent obeyed, taking a spoonful of soup into her mouth and then another. Presently the effort of eating something even as easy as soup took its toll on her, and she held up a trembling hand just as Mercy was lifting the spoon from the bowl again. "No more, Mercy."

"You really should try to finish the bowl," Mercy admonished gently. "You're wasting away to nothing."

"Ah, but my soul is fat, child, from feasting on the Word. Take it away—I'll have Janet give me some more later."

It was useless to argue once Mrs. Brent made up her mind. In her own softer way she was perhaps as stubborn as Mrs. Kingston. Setting the bowl and spoon on the bedside table, Mercy leaned over to take her friend's bony shoulders, move two of the pillows from behind her, and ease her back onto one. Mrs. Brent lovingly smiled up at her, and after Mercy had taken her chair again, she said in a voice growing hoarse, "When you take my little herd, dear, remind your father that they're yours."

The subject of Mrs. Brent's cows was not a pleasant one for Mercy because they would be in her possession only because of her friend's death. But to comfort her, Mercy mumbled something in agreement. However, that didn't satisfy the elderly woman.

"Of course they will be pastured with his herd, and he will profit from the milk. But only until your husband comes along," Mrs. Brent said.

"Yes, Mrs. Brent," Mercy replied obediently. She could not match Mrs. Brent's adamant faith regarding a husband but would not have argued with her dying friend had she declared that a prince would ride into Gresham upon a white horse and claim her for his bride.

"Thank you, child." Even the frailty of Mrs. Brent's voice could not prevent her affection for Mercy from coming through. "Now run along and tend to your chores at home. You've enough to do without listening to an old woman ramble."

Mrs. Brent's six cows had their heads loped over the drystone wall separating the pasture from the yard. Mercy could feel their gentle brown eyes following her as she walked out to the lane, as if the small herd had assembled themselves to inquire about their mistress's condition and were now mutely calling her back to them. Finally Mercy could stand it no longer, and she turned and went over to the wall. She pulled some long stalks of hawkweed from the ground. "There, there now," she cooed as they nudged one another gently for a better position to receive the treat. Her vision blurred. "Everything will be all right."

She had doubts about that herself, but she didn't think God would fault her for saying it to reassure a few pitiful cows.

*A*ndrew left Luther Sloane's small dairy farm north of the river later than he had intended and now wondered if he would reach the vicarage before his guests arrived for supper.

The Sloanes' four-month marriage had reached a crisis state when Mrs. Sloane demanded that her husband make a choice between her and his collie, Shep, that had enjoyed the run of the cottage and slept at his master's feet long before she was carried across the threshold. In reply to her demand, Mr. Sloane had requested a day or two to consider his answer, causing his wife to pack her belongings and threaten to leave.

As Rusty pulled the trap up Church Lane, Andrew flicked the reins lightly to coax a little more speed. Thankfully he'd been able to negotiate a compromise between the husband and wife. Mr. Sloane was brought to the understanding that wives were more important than pets and offered to clear a space in the hay barn for the dog's bed, keeping him outside from now on. Warmed by that concession, Mrs. Sloane had decided that a blanket in a corner of the gardening hut would provide more comfort for sleeping, and that the animal could continue taking meals at the cottage hearth.

Please grant my daughters good marriages, Lord, Andrew prayed as Rusty automatically turned north up Vicarage Lane. During his twenty-plus years in the ministry, he had witnessed the misery a bad one could cause. He believed strongly that a loving family was the core of a person's well-being. If there was strife and contention in the home, very little else in life could compensate for it.

The carriage from the *Larkspur* had not yet arrived at the vicarage, but he could see Mr. Treves' gray Welsh cob tethered to a low limb of the chestnut tree outside the garden.

"There you are, Papa!" He scarcely had climbed down from the trap and Laurel was at his side. "What took you so long? We were beginning to worry."

Andrew didn't answer but touched a spot on his cheek above his blond beard. Feigning a martyred sigh, his daughter dutifully planted a kiss on the spot before repeating her question.

"I was unavoidably detained during a call," he told her.

The girl's eyes lit up. "What happened? Something exciting?"

"You know I can't tell you. Are the children still here?"

The fourteen-year-old nodded. Like her father and sister, she had straight, wheat-colored hair and dimples in both cheeks. But that was where the resemblance to Andrew stopped, for both daughters had been blessed with their late mother's brown eyes, slender build, and fair complexion.

"Luke was wondering whether he should borrow Mr. Sykes's wagon."

"Well, he can use the trap now. I doubt their mother is home yet."

The Burrell situation was a sad one. Mr. Burrell, the village drunk and slacker, had left his long-suffering wife and seven children back in October of last year. It was then that Elizabeth had offered to tend the two youngest, Molly and David, while their mother worked at the cheese factory so the older children could attend school. She grew so attached to the children that the offer was extended to the summer months as well. The five older children were hardy, as were many from tragic circumstances—the girls kept house and tended a small garden while the boys kept odd jobs such as stripping bark from downed trees for the local tanner. They could manage their chores much easier without tending to the two youngest, and the arrangement gave Elizabeth something worthwhile to do with her days.

Just as Andrew and Laurel stepped up on the porch, Elizabeth came out of the door with David in her arms. Mr. Treves followed, holding Molly's hand. Andrew's daughter frowned and opened her mouth, but Andrew silenced her with a look.

"Your sister has already taken it upon herself to reprimand me, Beth." He shook Mr. Treves' free hand and patted Molly on the head, then held out both hands to David, who lunged his little body forward into his arms. "So, you're going to leave us again, are you?" he said to the child, who wove his little fingers through Andrew's beard and with the other hand pointed to the waiting trap.

"Tor?" he said.

Andrew took the boy to mean *horse* and replied, "Yes. And he's waiting to take you home."

"Luke is on his way around the back," Elizabeth told him. A little ridge appeared between her eyebrows, and she leaned forward to study the sleeve of his black coat. "You're shedding, Papa."

"Shedding, Papa," Molly echoed, her light brown curls a halo about her round face. "Papa read book now?"

55

"Tomorrow, Molly," he smiled. As touched as he was to be addressed so endearingly by both tots, it always caused a slight lurch in his heart. What kind of man would walk away and leave such beguiling children to the mercies of happenstance? "I'll read to you when I come home for lunch."

"Two books?"

"Very well." Andrew lifted a helpless smile to his daughter's beau. "I'm surprised she hasn't conscripted you into service, Mr. Treves."

The young man smiled back. He was three years older than Elizabeth and much taller than Andrew. His sandy hair was so light that even his eyelashes were blond, making his blue eyes seem all the more blue. "Actually, sir, I've just finished reading one."

"Papa, I can hear a carriage," Laurel said. She made a face and brushed at his sleeve. "And you *are* shedding dreadfully."

Andrew handed the boy back to Elizabeth. Julia's family and the Clays would be here within minutes. No time to change clothes, but surely the vigorous application of a clothes brush would remedy the situation. "It's not me. It was a dog."

"It was a dog," he could hear Molly echo as he went through the front door.

The supper Mrs. Paget had prepared, with Dora's assistance, was delicious from the broiled trout to the apple cobbler. Or at least the others had raved about the cobbler. Upon noticing what appeared to be a hair in the dish Andrew had passed her, Julia had used her fork to scatter it around a bit so no one would notice she had not actually taken a bite.

Afterward the adults assembled themselves upon wicker chairs in the garden for aftersupper tea. The children declined the gathering, choosing instead to play tag on the darkening green within sight of the vicarage. Several stars in the clear sky had begun to show themselves, and a breeze redolent with lilac and sage made for a pleasant evening.

Most of the dining room discussion had centered around Mrs. Kingston. Not only had she appeared in the *Larkspur*'s carriage drive this morning perched upon a wagon seat next to one of the Sanders boys, but she had also persuaded the child to come into the kitchen for lemonade and shortbread. It was only after he was gone, his pockets stuffed with peppermints, that Mrs. Kingston casually mentioned to Mrs. Beemish that Mr. Sanders had had a change of heart concerning the schooling of his two youngest. Of course word spread about the house like fire in broom sedge, and Aleda and Grace were overjoyed to the point of giddiness.

"As happy as I am for my soon-to-be daughters," Andrew said from his wicker chair beside Julia's, continuing the discussion about the school, "the biggest benefit will be the way the villagers regard education. Hopefully in the years to come it'll be unthinkable for children of school age not to attend."

Mr. Treves nodded, both elbows propped onto the arms of his chair, his long hands cradling a saucer and teacup. "You would think it would have become unthinkable years and years ago. But I've noticed the same situation in Alveley." He shook his head with disgust. "Why would any parent *not* desire to educate his children? I'm appalled at the legacies of ignorance handed down in so many British families."

There was a fractional silence, then Andrew replied tactfully, "It's often a sacrifice for the poorer families to send their children. Sometimes all hands are required just to keep the wolf from the door." He gave the young curate an understanding smile. "Even small hands."

To Mr. Treves' credit, he did not attempt to defend his position. *"He's still green,"* Andrew had once commented to Julia. *"Life has gone along according to plan for him, so he hasn't been humbled yet. He'll be a much better minister when his heart has been broken."*

Two years ago Julia would have thought such an observation unfeeling and callous. How could anyone wish sorrow upon another person? But it was through the pain of discovering her late husband had gambled away their fortune that she had experienced the most growth spiritually.

She glanced at Elizabeth, who kept her gaze on the tea table in the center of the group. Whether she was embarrassed that her beau had been gently rebuked by her father or was in deep thought was hard to tell, for Elizabeth had her father's habit of retreating within himself.

" . . . found a replacement for Captain Powell?" Julia realized then that Fiona had been speaking.

"Why yes," Andrew replied.

"Miss Clark sent a reply?" Julia asked.

"Mr. Sykes received the wire just today."

Julia breathed a sigh of relief. Six of the nine previously unschooled students would be in the class formerly taught by Captain Powell. Added to that were three, like Grace, who would be promoted from Miss Hillock's classroom. A class totaling thirty-one students would require the firm hand of someone with Lydia Clark's fourteen years' experience.

Julia had never actually met the woman, who still lived in Glasgow where she was schoolmistress in a girls' boarding school, but shared a friendly acquaintance with her parents. Mr. Clark owned the iron foundry on Walnut Tree Lane, and Mrs. Clark was a dear little woman who grew sunflowers along her garden hedges. They had asked the school board to consider their daughter for the position. How nice, Julia thought, that two needs had been met. Gresham would have a capable schoolmistress, and two lovely people would enjoy having their daughter with them during their golden years.

"How many days until you return to London?" Elizabeth asked Fiona and Mr. Clay, finally steering the subject away from school.

"Only six," Mr. Clay replied. "We leave August first."

"The first week passed so quickly," Fiona said.

Mr. Clay smiled apologetically. "And you've had very little time to spend with Mrs. Hollis. I'm still so enchanted with being married that I'm afraid I've dominated my wife's company."

"Why, that's not true, Ambrose," Fiona insisted.

"But you were so looking forward to this visit." He looked over at Andrew. "As was I. I've no male friends in London as close as our dear vicar. It could be a year or two before we can return—depending on how successful the play turns out to be."

"Just forget your lines every now and then," Andrew suggested good-naturedly but was obviously moved by Mr. Clay's declaration of friendship.

"Or deliver them in a falsetto voice," Elizabeth offered.

Julia caught the uncertain glance the girl immediately sent to Mr. Treves, as if she needed his reassurance that he found her little joke amusing. Whether he did or not was impossible to tell, for he simply stared down at his teacup.

Mr. Clay shuddered. "I'll keep those suggestions in mind, thank you. But while we're still here, why don't you ladies do something special together?"

"Something special?" Fiona asked.

"Why not a shopping trip to Shrewsbury? You could spend the day, have lunch at a restaurant, even tour the castle."

Julia exchanged smiles with Fiona. For over a year now, the twelfth-century castle had occupied a space on Julia's mental list of things to do "one day." And she was certain that Fiona had never toured it. "It sounds lovely."

"Lovely," Elizabeth agreed, then bit her lip. "I mean, for the two of you."

"Oh, but we insist that you come with us," Fiona assured her with typical graciousness.

"Thank you, but I've the children to watch."

"We wouldn't dream of going without you," Julia insisted. "Surely Dora wouldn't mind tending Molly and David, do you think?"

Elizabeth looked at her father.

"She has offered to before, you know," he answered. "The outing would be good for you."

"Are you aware that the castle is only open for tours on Saturdays?" Mr. Treves asked, speaking for the first time since his gentle admonishment from Andrew.

Fiona shook her head. "How good of you to warn us, Mr. Treves. It looks as though we should wait until Saturday, doesn't it?"

"That will give us more time to prepare," Julia said. Smiling at her fiancé, she asked, "What will you men do while we're gone? I don't believe either of you would care for a shopping trip."

"Heaven forbid!" he said, feigning horror, then turned to Mr. Clay. "Have you ever fished?"

"Not since I was a whelp. My grandfather would occasionally take us out in his boat in Cornwall. I daresay that I've forgotten everything he taught me."

"You may have retained more than you realize. And riverbank fishing is easier."

"Then let's have a try at it Saturday."

"We'll invite Philip along," Andrew nodded. "I doubt that he'll care to shop, and he knows all the best fishing spots anyway. How about you, Mr. Treves?"

The young man straightened, clearly surprised to be included. "Thank you, sir, but the Ladies' Floral Society is holding their annual tea, and Vicar McDonald and I are expected to attend."

Julia wondered if she only imagined the relief that crossed Andrew's expression.

―――――――

"Will you be able to see the road?" Elizabeth asked as she accompanied Paul to where his horse was tethered after the other guests had left. "I'm sure you could stay over the stables with Luke."

Her beau glanced up at the star-crusted sky and shook his head. "It's not too dark. Caesar has made the trip so many times, I believe he could make it blindfolded."

"Just be careful."

"I will," he said, smiling.

He had a nice smile, Elizabeth thought, that caused little lines at the corners of his mouth. Last month when she accompanied Paul to a choir cantata in Alveley, Mrs. McDonald, his vicar's wife, had jokingly informed her that female attendance at St. Matthew's had increased dramatically when Paul was assigned to the parish. Elizabeth had no trouble believing that. *And how fortunate you are that he's only interested in you*, she told herself. There were likely half a dozen women in Alveley, and not a few in Gresham, who would give their best bonnets to be in his company.

Papa only allowed ten minutes for them to say good-bye, and at least three had already passed. She wondered if Paul would kiss her tonight. He had never attempted it before, which she attributed to his being a gentleman. Perhaps if he were to kiss her, she would have deeper feelings for him. She *had* to have deeper feelings, for he was determined to ask Papa for her hand as soon as his promotion to vicar became a reality. She was as determined to accept his proposal, for Paul Treves would be a fine husband and father to the children they would have one day. And she knew the demands of being a minister's wife from helping her father and felt she could live up to them.

Another face flashed into her mind's eye, and she shook it away immediately.

"Elizabeth?"

She realized that Paul was staring at her curiously. "Yes?"

"Are you all right?" he asked.

"All right?"

"You jerked your head just now."

"I did?"

"Perhaps I just imagined it." Paul looked past her at the glowing windows of the vicarage. He was obviously making sure no paternal eyes were set in their direction. Elizabeth knew that her papa wouldn't spy—as long as she was inside within the time allowed. He took a step closer.

"I'd like to ask you something."

Should I close my eyes? Elizabeth decided against it. A lady shouldn't look as if she were *expecting* to be kissed until the faces were a little closer. "Yes, Paul?"

"Your father wasn't really angry at me earlier, was he?"

"What?"

"When I said that about the poor people educating their children." He threw a glance at the vicarage again and sighed. "I don't think he likes me at all. He can make me feel quite the child sometimes."

Elizabeth lowered her chin a little, not sure if it was relief or disappointment she was feeling. "He's very fond of you, Paul," she assured him, though earlier tonight some doubt had nudged at her mind. "He just has a softness for the less fortunate."

"Well, so have I." He frowned. "I just wasn't thinking when I spoke. In fact, my brain almost ceases to function whenever I'm in his company. I assume that he's expecting me to say something idiotic, and so I end up obliging him."

"He understands what it's like to be a young curate, you know."

"Are you sure?"

"I should know my own father, Paul." She sighed and caught sight of

60

the lamp now burning from the front window nearest to the door. "But our ten minutes are up. Be careful on your way home."

When they had said their good-night and she stepped back inside, her father gave her a wary look. "I suppose I'm about to be scolded."

"For what, Papa?" She knew what he meant but wanted to hear him say it.

"For correcting Mr. Treves." His hazel eyes narrowed a little. "You already knew what I was talking about, didn't you?"

"Yes, Papa. He's convinced you think he's an idiot."

Her father sighed. "Laurel should be ready to be tucked in now. Then let's sit for a while, shall we?"

Later, when he had settled himself into his favorite parlor armchair and Elizabeth occupied a place at the near end of the sofa, he explained, "It wasn't my intention to embarrass the young man, Elizabeth. But certain things had to be said in light of that comment he made. I thought I was as tactful as possible. Mr. Clay and I disagree at times, and he never takes offense."

"But don't you see, Papa? When you correct Paul, it's not the same as your verbal sparring with Mr. Clay. You're not on equal footing. He not only looks up to you as an older man, but as his senior in the church hierarchy."

" . . . who will very likely become his father-in-law," her father added, studying her face.

"Yes. Does that distress you?"

"Not if he makes you happy, Elizabeth. I don't fault Mr. Treves for his youth. He'll make a fine minister one day and a good husband and father."

She knew her father wouldn't say that if he didn't mean it, so she should have been pleased. Instead, she felt an odd sense of disappointment. *You're just in a blue mood*, she told herself.

"Beth?" he said softly.

Forcing lightness into her voice, she answered, "Yes, Papa?"

"How do you feel about him?"

About whom? was her immediate thought. "Paul is a wonderful person. Kind and considerate."

"But you didn't answer my question, did you?"

"I love him, Papa," she replied with a little more conviction than necessary.

————

Thank God she confides in Julia, Andrew thought later from his bed as he marked his place between the pages of Trollope's *Phineas Finn*. Reading any more of the novel tonight was futile, he realized upon discovering

61

that his eyes had traveled through the same paragraph three times. The subject could have been the latest horticultural methods for growing tea in the Orient for all he could remember of it.

He blew out his candle, allowing the darkness that had pressed against the window glass for the past half hour to flood the room. Why was it so difficult to say what was in his heart to his daughter? On the heels of that question came an unsettling answer. *Because I'm afraid if she follows my advice, another disaster will happen.* For he could no longer put off admitting it . . . *he* was the one who had encouraged Elizabeth's friendship with Jonathan Raleigh. He had been too blinded by the young man's courtly manners, his academic triumphs, and his well-connected family to see him for the scoundrel he was. What if he hadn't received the anonymous letter that caused him to discover Mr. Raleigh's secret life? What if they would have married? He would have had to blame himself for the rest of his life for the misery he had inflicted upon his daughter and even future grandchildren.

The sad episode with Jonathan Raleigh had caused him to question his own ability to advise Elizabeth in the matter of her future. If he encouraged her to marry Paul Treves, who was a decent man and probably loved her very much, and the marriage proved to be an unhappy one, how could he live with himself?

But on the other hand, if he continued to express doubts about Elizabeth's feelings toward the young man and caused her to reconsider the marriage—what if it turned out that he would have been the perfect husband for her?

I should be more like my own father was, he thought wryly. All his father had asked, when told of his betrothal to Kathleen, was, "Has she money or title?" But Andrew wouldn't even consider taking as little interest as that.

I know you want what's best for her, too, Lord, he prayed. *Please give her a wisdom beyond her years.* And as an afterthought he added . . . *and help me not to influence her in a direction not of your choosing.*

*W*ednesday morning, as Mercy closed Mrs. Brent's wooden gate behind her, the sound of weeping drifted from the upstairs window, mingling with pelts of rain against her umbrella. Inside Mrs. Brent's cottage, Mercy propped her umbrella and climbed the stairs with what felt like a stone centered in her chest. She paused at the first doorway—Janet was on her knees at the side of the bed, her back to the door and shoulders heaving. Elliott stood at the foot, reddened eyes set in a somber face. He nodded at Mercy as she stepped into the room.

Mrs. Brent lay with hands folded together upon her frail chest, her eyes closed. For the peacefulness on her face, she could have been merely having a pleasant dream. Surely she would open those eyes and smile at them if they just waited long enough!

It's Jesus she's smiling at now, Mercy thought, reaching out to touch her friend's cold hand. *Or perhaps her husband and all those babies she lost.* She was surprised at her own composure, but then Mrs. Brent had warned her that this time would come. And now there were things that had to be done.

She touched Janet's shoulder. The maid looked up at her with sodden cheeks. "We should bathe and dress her," Mercy said. "She asked for the blue nightgown."

"The blue one's nice," Janet sniffed, seemingly relieved to have something useful with which to occupy herself. "It's folded in the chest of drawers. I'll press it now."

To Elliott Mercy said, "Would you fetch Mr. Croft?" Generations of Crofts, the village joiners, had crafted coffins for Gresham's departed for as far back as anyone could remember. "And please stop at Reverend Seaton's on your way back."

"Laurel is beside herself with excitement over the Shrewsbury plans," Andrew told Julia over their morning cups of tea in the *Larkspur*'s garden.

"It was kind of you and Mrs. Clay to include the girls."

"Oh, but kindness had nothing to do with it," Julia assured him. "Outings are so much more fun when we can savor them through the children's eyes." As soon as her own girls heard about the trip they had begged to come along, so now the number had increased to six. "I invited Philip, too, so he wouldn't feel left out, but of course he said he would rather go fishing with you and Mr. Clay."

"Of course."

Julia took another sip of tea and sighed. "You know, boys turn into entirely different creatures when they reach fourteen. He seems to have a mood for every day of the week. I'm glad girls aren't that way. I don't believe I could live through this two more times."

"Mmhm," Andrew mumbled before taking a prolonged sip of tea.

Julia could see the corner of a smile lurking over the rim of his cup. "What are you smiling at?" she asked suspiciously.

"I don't think you want to know."

His hazel eyes were sparkling, and it suddenly dawned upon her that she knew exactly what he was thinking, which came as a rather pleasant shock. When her parents were still living, there had been occasions when they seemed to possess an uncanny ability to read each other's minds. It had never happened during her own marriage to Dr. Hollis, but she knew now that her late husband had had to shield his thoughts, lest she have suspicions about his secret life in the gaming houses. It pleased her to know she and Andrew already had such a bond between them.

"You're amused by my naïveté, aren't you?

"Why, no . . ."

Julia frowned. "It's a sin to lie, Vicar Phelps. You were just thinking that girls change into different creatures, too, weren't you?"

He let out a guilty sigh, but a hint of that maddening smile still remained. "I'm afraid they do, dearest. Don't you remember how it was when you were that age?"

"Actually, I was already at boarding school with three hundred other girls. If there was any moodiness, it must have seemed the natural order of things to me."

"Hundreds of moody young ladies under the same roof." He exaggerated a shudder. "But now tell me. Do you regret ever having any children?"

"Of course not." No longer able to resist the warmth in his hazel eyes, she smiled back at him. "Not for one minute, Andrew."

They sipped from their cups, wrapped in a comfortable silence, until Julia voiced the thought that had been nagging at the back of her mind for some days now. "Andrew, are we doing right by them—Philip and Laurel?"

He set his cup on the tray between them. "You mean by sending them to school? I believe so, Julia. They both want desperately to further their education, so what choice have we?"

"I wonder now if we should have looked for a tutor. It's not too late." She expected that he would gently chide her for her overprotectiveness, but his expression became serious.

"It's a thought that has crossed my mind more than once. I've even considered tutoring them myself, but my duties require so much time." He gave her a sad smile. "I don't know if I'm relieved or a little hurt that Laurel is so eager to leave. She thinks of it as a great adventure. It would crush her if I forbade her to go."

"It's the same with Philip. He can hardly wait. But at least you'll have Laurel at home every weekend."

Doctor Rhodes had recommended the academy to Philip, with its heavy emphasis on science and Latin. The lodging house account ledger showed a healthy balance every month, so Julia could afford to send him without too much of a financial strain. It just didn't seem natural to send a child so young away, even though her own boarding school experience had begun at age twelve.

"He'll be fine, Julia." Andrew gave her shoulder a reassuring pat. "We have to allow them to grow up sometime."

"I suppose so." Reaching up to cover his hand with her own, she said, "I wouldn't be able to go through this without you, Andrew. You're such a comfort."

"As you are to me, my dear. I cannot tell you how relieved I am to know Elizabeth seeks your counsel."

"She hasn't lately, Andrew."

He kissed her hand and then rose to make his calls. "But she will soon, I have no doubt. She's much confused, no matter how she tries to pretend otherwise."

Next year I should plant some sunflowers, Octavia Kingston thought. In order to keep her morning walks from becoming monotonous, she had six different routes through Gresham and the surrounding countryside. Wednesdays brought her past the iron foundry and the Clark cottage on Walnut Tree Lane, where an abundance of sunflowers raised their heads above a white picket fence to follow the path of the sun. They were such friendly looking flowers—if plants could be assigned personalities. *I know just the spot to put them too.*

65

She thought about how bitter she had been upon her arrival in Gresham last year. The person she was then seemed almost alien to her now. Norwood, her son, had made the arrangements for her to live at the *Larkspur*. She was a threat to his marriage, he had declared, and must leave his home while he still had one. Being forced from the place where she had lived for over forty years seemed like a death sentence. A horrid picture had loomed in her mind back then, of herself vegetating away in a hired room, with no one to care if she lived or died except for the rent that could be collected. Like old clothes assigned to a trunk in an attic, she felt she had outlived her usefulness.

But the compassion of Julia Hollis had changed all of that. And after being on the receiving end of such compassion, Mrs. Kingston had learned to give it. With the knowledge that her life did indeed matter came a commitment to fill her days with useful activity—which she fulfilled by turning the *Larkspur*'s practically nonexistent flower garden into a showplace.

Yes, I shall definitely plant sunflowers, she thought, turning her head for one last look over her shoulder. When she did, she caught a glimpse of motion.

Mrs. Kingston frowned. The same thing had happened Monday while she was walking back up Market Lane at the end of her southwestern route. *But why would someone be following you?* she asked herself. *Ridiculous!* Still, the uncanny feeling of being watched would not leave her, and she turned around to stare at the lane she had just walked. A wide elm spread its branches in front of the Clarks' cottage, more than wide enough to provide a hiding place. Mrs. Kingston looked in all directions to make sure there were no witnesses to the absurd display she was about to make.

"You there!" she called forcefully, pretending an assurance she didn't quite possess, for she wasn't totally sure that her imagination wasn't playing tricks upon her. There was no answer, nor did she see anything amiss.

"I say, you there!" she bluffed again. She shook the head of her walking stick. "I saw you duck behind that tree! You may as well show yourself!"

There was nothing except a curious raise of the head from a nutmeg-colored cat napping upon the Clarks' porch.

"Surely you're not afraid of an old woman!" she called, though not so loudly this time, for the foolishness of her actions was becoming clearer every second. When no lurker gave himself up and came forward for a scolding, Mrs. Kingston slowly turned back around and resumed her walk. She was almost positive she'd seen someone. But she couldn't very well go searching behind trees without appearing even more foolish, if only to the Clarks' cat. She reached the end of Walnut Tree Lane and turned east onto Church Lane to make her way back to the *Larkspur*. The Worthy sisters were, as usual, sitting under a patch of sunlight in their garden.

"Mrs. Kingston!" Iris called in a voice as soothing as a warm cup of tea. Her gnarled fingers never stopped winding threads around the pins sticking from the lace-making pillow in her lap. "I was just telling Jewel that you should be by soon."

Jewel nodded her white head as Mrs. Kingston advanced. Her fingers also seemed to move independently of their owner's thoughts. It occurred to Mrs. Kingston that the sisters could probably spin laces in their sleep if they could find a way to sleep sitting up in their chairs.

"And I told Iris that a body could set his clock by Mrs. Kingston's walks," Jewel said in a tone as raspy as Iris's was soothing. She turned to her sister-in-law for confirmation. "Didn't I, Iris?"

"You certainly did," Iris agreed.

Mrs. Kingston smiled. "What are you making now?"

"A tablecloth," Jewel replied and tilted her pillow so that Mrs. Kingston could admire the pattern. "We'll block the strips together when all the lace is finished. Someone in Whitchurch ordered it for a wedding gift."

"Lovely," Mrs. Kingston declared, eliciting smiles from both wrinkled faces.

"We thought we heard ye callin' out to someone just a little while ago," Jewel said in a questioning tone.

Mrs. Kingston sighed. So there had been witnesses to her lunacy after all. She should have known better, for there was little that escaped the notice of the Worthy sisters, situated as they were at the crossroads of the village. With great reluctance, she admitted, "I thought someone was following me."

The sisters exchanged understanding looks. "Have you considered spectacles?" asked Iris. " 'Tis no shame to wear them, you know."

"I don't need spectacles," Mrs. Kingston declared crisply and was immediately sorry, for she could see the injury across both faces. "Forgive me. It's just unsettling to feel like you're being watched every time you set foot outside."

"We understand, dear," Iris told her.

"We felt that same way when Jake Pitt used to watch us from the *Larkspur*'s window," Jewel added.

Mrs. Kingston was opening her mouth to say that surely the sisters didn't still believe in that ghost story when a new idea shoved all thought of the old knife sharpener from her mind. Without glancing back down the lane, she leaned closer to the cushion on Iris's lap and pretended to examine the lace. "I wonder if you ladies might do me a favor," she whispered while trying to keep her lips immobile.

"What is it, dear?"

"MY GOODNESS! YOU SHOULD BE SPINNING LACE FOR THE QUEEN!" Mrs. Kingston exclaimed, then whispered, "Don't look to your left, but I'm *convinced* someone has been following me."

The sisters exchanged glances, and for once both sets of fingers slowed their spinning. "What does he look like?" Jewel whispered.

"I don't even know who he is. Or if it's even a 'he,' " she said in a low voice. "I FEEL SO FOOLISH NOW, THINKING THAT SOMEONE WAS FOLLOWING ME. ONE WOULD THINK I WAS LOSING MY MIND. WELL, IT'S BEEN GOOD CHATTING WITH YOU, BUT I MUST RESUME MY WALK."

"But aren't you finished walking, dear?" asked Iris.

"He'll stop following me if he thinks I'm finished," Mrs. Kingston hissed through a gap in her lips. "Would you mind paying notice if anyone of a suspicious nature comes down the lane shortly?"

Jewel's eyes grew alive with excitement. "Spy on him, you mean?"

"Yes. Only act natural, so he doesn't suspect anything. I'll come back later." With a farewell wave she turned right at the crossroads instead of her usual left and made her way down Market Lane. She resumed her usual brisk pace, pausing occasionally to exchange greetings with customers leaving the greengrocer's and to admire the geraniums in the window boxes of the *Bow and Fiddle*.

Finally she decided she should go back home, lest her follower find it suspicious that today's walk was longer than usual. When she came upon Mr. Trumble sweeping the stoop of his general shop, post office, and bank, she stopped and announced in a voice clear and loud, "I suppose I should buy some peppermints, Mr. Trumble, since I'm finished with my walk and am now on my way back to the *Larkspur*."

She waited an hour before slipping out to visit the Worthy sisters. Both faces lit up as she drew closer.

"Remy Starks," Iris said in a conspiratorial whisper, as if Mrs. Kingston's follower still lurked nearby.

"He come strollin' past soon after ye left, pretty as ye please with his hands in his pockets," Jewel added.

"Remy Starks?" Mrs. Kingston shook her head. "But who is he?"

"The squire's boot boy," Iris replied. "Odd little man, I hate to say."

*T*hough the use of torture had long been outlawed in Great Britain, to the convicts of London's Newgate Prison the treadmill was almost as debilitating as the rack had been to their predecessors. It only took longer for the treadmill to wear a man down, both physically and mentally. The nasty device consisted of a wide iron cylinder made to revolve by marching around the steps fixed to it. Wooden panels separated each man from sight of his neighbor, and to his front was only another panel to stare at for six hours at a time. Fill the convict's day with the most useless activity imaginable, and he will be too weary and disheartened to cause trouble was the philosophy behind the treadmill's invention.

For ten years now, thirty-one-year-old Seth Langford had marched those steps daily. To keep himself sane, he mentally recited the Scriptures the Wesleyans taught in Sunday chapel. And toward the end of every six-hour session, he would tally anew the "miles." One step of the treadmill represented one linear foot, and taken at one step per second meant sixty feet per minute, thirty-six hundred feet per hour. Which added up to over four miles daily. During his ten-year confinement, Seth figured he had walked to China and back. *And uphill all the way*, he thought, lifting his foot again.

He became aware that the steps were becoming more and more difficult to take, which meant that one of the guards was tightening the screws to bring the device to a halt. Yet it seemed much too early for the lunch break. Turning to look over his shoulder was against the rules and could result in a jab in the small of the back with a club, so when the treadmill came to a dead stop, Seth stayed in place and stared at the panel in front of him.

"You! Langford!" came a voice behind him. Seth recognized it as belonging to Mr. Baker, one of the more decent guards. He turned his head to give him a sidelong look and waited for further instructions.

"Major Spencer wants to see you right away," the guard said, motioning for him to step down. Seth had no choice but to obey, yet he did so with a terrible sense of foreboding. A summons from the warden could only mean bad news. Yet he couldn't recall having done anything to deserve punishment. Oh, he had raised a row upon his arrival ten years ago, but when several guards explained to him, using their clubs for emphasis, that such behavior would lengthen his sentence, he settled down. They neither believed his protestations of innocence, nor cared, he realized. The best a man could do here was to serve his time quietly.

"Do you know why?" Seth asked Baker while holding out his hands for manacles. The guard shrugged but gave him a wry smile.

"Allst I know is there's a woman in there wi' him."

Immediately Seth's pulse jumped. *Elaine!* But it couldn't be so. He had lied to her when she tried to visit after his sentencing, claiming that he no longer loved her. Still, his heart clung to enough feeble hope that it gave a lurch when he was ushered into the warden's office and she wasn't there.

He did recognize the woman in spite of her black veil and clothes of mourning. It was Lady Esther Hamilton, wife of his former employer, Lord Arthur Hamilton. Seth had been head groomsman on their Kensington estate until accused of stealing a gold and ruby brooch from Lady Esther's boudoir. *Lord Hamilton must have died*, he thought with no emotion.

"You may release his chains," Major Spencer said from behind his desk to the guard. "And wait outside the door."

Baker complied immediately, though with a disappointed droop of the shoulders at being excluded from the meeting. As he held out his wrists again, Seth darted another glance in Lady Hamilton's direction. Two men sat on either side of her. The young one at her right looked vaguely familiar. *Benjamin?* he thought with wonder.

His last memory of young master Benjamin had been of a small face pressed against the glass of an upstairs window. Seth had happened to look up in that direction from the courtyard through the bars of the police wagon. He had locked eyes with the lad, and then the face disappeared. *He's grown so.*

The warden nodded toward a chair beside his desk, six feet away from the visitors. "Please have a seat, Mr. Langford."

Mr. Langford? As he obeyed, Seth felt his eyes sting at this small measure of respect directed toward him after so long. He stared at the floor, resisting the urge to wipe his eyes with the sleeve of his gray-and-white-striped prison shirt.

"I suppose you recognize Lady Hamilton and her son?" Major Spencer asked, staring through his steepled fingers. The prison warden was a man of an indeterminable age, with dark hair graying only at the temples and hooded brown eyes. A severe man he was reported to be, one almost as heavy-handed with the guards as with the prisoners, but a just one.

"Yes, sir," Seth mumbled, his eyes still directed toward the carpet in front of him. He heard a sniff and glanced again at Lady Hamilton. The veil hid any hint of expression upon her face, but young Benjamin's pale green eyes were rimmed with red. Seth had no time to wonder at this, for the portly gentleman seated at Lady Hamilton's left rose from his chair, took a few steps forward, and offered his hand.

"My name is Lyle Kelmscott, Mr. Langford. I was Lord Hamilton's solicitor."

Speechless at still another display of respect in so short a time span, Seth took the gentleman's soft hand in his large work-hardened one. When the solicitor had resumed his seat, he cleared his throat.

"The reason we are here, Mr. Langford—"

"Benjamin should be the one to tell him," Lady Hamilton's soft voice cut in.

Mr. Kelmscott gaped at her and at the young man. "I don't believe that is necessary, Lady Hamilton."

"I disagree." She nodded at her son. "Go ahead, Benjamin."

Now Seth looked at them squarely. Benjamin blew his nose again, then with trembling lips said, "Do you remember when you forbade me to ride Quicksilver?"

Seth nodded, clearly recalling the day. Lord Hamilton had been away at a session of Parliament, and Benjamin had wanted to impress some visiting older cousins by ordering his father's recently acquired Arabian race-horse to be saddled. The animal was high-strung and would have likely killed the boy, so Seth had stoutly refused.

Now it was Benjamin who stared down at the carpet. "My cousins mocked me, and I was furious at you for it."

The fog that had shrouded the events of those days lifted, allowing Seth to see with astonishing clarity. "*You* put the brooch in my trunk?"

"Yes." Benjamin's hands shot up to cover his face. "I'm so sorry!" he sobbed.

Stunned, Seth watched him weep. *Why ten years?* he wanted to ask but could not. But then Lady Hamilton provided a reply as if she had read his thoughts.

"He assumed you would simply be dismissed," she said somberly, placing a black-gloved hand on her son's wracking shoulders. "And then he feared his father's anger too much to admit to his prank. But now that Lord Hamilton has passed away . . ."

Seth blinked at her. "Prank?"

71

"He was but eleven years old at the time, Mr. Langford," the solicitor reminded.

A silence settled into the room, save the sound of Benjamin Hamilton's soft weeping. As the implications of his confession made their way into Seth's mind, he met the warden's eyes. "Does this mean I'll be allowed a new trial?"

Major Spencer shook his head. "No, Mr. Langford. It means you're to be released. Today, in fact."

"Today?" The word, so commonplace, had never sounded so beautiful and so strange. It was odd to think that he'd risen from his cot this morning with no inkling of the events to come. *Haven't you prayed for release?* he reminded himself. Apparently, with little faith. Still, God had looked down through walls of stone and heard him.

"Lady Hamilton wishes to offer some compensation for the years of your confinement," Mr. Kelmscott said magnanimously, as if about to bestow knighthood upon him.

Seth let out a sharp bark of laughter at the absurdity of it. "Will that restore ten years of my life, Mr. Kelmscott?"

The solicitor's well-fed cheeks reddened. "Of course not. But five hundred pounds can soften the rest of it. I daresay you would have earned less than half that amount in wages."

"Yes, and married the woman I loved and had children."

"No one is denying you've suffered, Mr. Langford."

Finally moving his hands away from his face, Benjamin Hamilton stared at Seth through swollen eyes and rasped, "If I could give you ten years of my life, I would."

"Actually, it could come to that," Major Spencer said, causing the solicitor and Lady Hamilton to exchange worried glances. "Mr. Langford has the right to register charges with the Crown Prosecutor for being falsely accused and imprisoned. No doubt you're aware of that, Mr. Kelmscott."

"I'll gladly—" the young man began with fervent voice but was silenced by his mother's hand upon his shoulder again.

Seth realized then the significance of the five hundred pounds. "You're offering to *pay* me not to register charges?"

"That is a condition, yes," Mr. Kelmscott admitted. "Surely you understand that there can be no profit in revenge." Again he cleared his throat. "*And* Lady Hamilton requests that you use the money to settle elsewhere. While you have been vindicated today, there is young Benjamin's reputation—"

"I'll accept the offer," Seth cut in, suddenly weary of the whole conversation. And as for leaving London, he was more than willing, for the city was a repository of too many painful memories.

"Then I take that to mean the matter is settled between you and young Lord Hamilton?" the warden asked.

"Not quite." Seth looked over at the young face, now as pale as whey save the reddened eyes. *The same age I was when I was arrested*, he thought. It would be so easy, even comforting, to give over to hatred. But by doing so, could he regain the third of his life lost to him? And it *had* taken courage to admit the wrongdoing, even after so many years. *The Wesleyans have gotten to you . . . made you soft*, Seth thought with self-disgust.

To the new Lord Hamilton he said, "I'm accepting the money as back wages for ten years of walking the treadmill. Spend one day on it, sir, and you'll see that you're paying out a fair price. And as for what you did . . ." In the thick silence that swelled about them, Seth imagined he could hear the young lord gulp. "I forgive you." He turned his head from the trio and looked at the warden again. "May I leave now?"

Major Spencer nodded. "Young Lord Hamilton has already signed his portion of the paper work. Your signature is required on two documents." He went to the door and said to the guard, "Fetch Mr. Langford's belongings."

Seth penned his signature to the two papers without reading them. For all he knew, they could have been confessions to murder. But obviously they were not, because the warden actually smiled as he handed one back to him.

"Proof of your exoneration, should it ever be questioned," the warden said.

Minutes later Seth found himself being led down the corridor to an empty office. Mr. Baker, disbelief thick upon his face, thrust a bundle at him—the clothing he had worn to prison ten years ago. Over the years maturity and the treadmill had built up muscles so slowly that Seth had not been aware of them, and now found them to be a hindrance because the corded trousers and muslin shirt were too tight for comfort. The guard was of the same opinion, for he grinned when Seth stepped back out into the main corridor.

"You'll be wantin' to buy some new clothes, won't yer? But I reckon yer got the money for it." This last part was said with a bit of envy in his voice, proof that the guard had listened at the door.

Seth merely nodded—he wasn't used to conversing with any of the guards on an equal level. Until he actually left the premises, he would not be fully convinced that Mr. Baker wasn't going to lead him back to his cell and declare the whole set of events a cruel joke.

He was led to the same thick oak door that had slammed behind him so ominously ten years ago. A gray, driving rain greeted him on the other side, with claps of thunder rolling across the distant sky.

"You can wait it out inside," the guard offered.

Seth politely declined and stepped out into the walkway of Newgate Street. He wouldn't have turned back if a blizzard had raged. His daily exercise breaks had consisted of a half hour in the prison yard, canceled in the event of rain. The deluge was the most wonderful thing he had experienced in years. Within seconds his shirt was plastered to his skin, his brown hair soaked, and water ran into his eyes so freely that he had to blink rapidly in order to see.

He wandered out to the roadside and watched the traffic pass as if he'd never seen it. Wagons and carriages and omnibuses, hansoms and delivery carts—their horses' hooves sent up great sprays of water, and wheels hissed upon the wet cobblestones. Drivers either wore mackintoshes or attempted to keep umbrellas aloft while holding reins at the same time. A hackney cab pulled to the walkway in front of him.

"A ride, sir?" the driver called out to him above another roll of thunder.

Seth looked over his shoulder to see whom the man was addressing and realized it was he. How strange to be addressed as "sir"! He nodded and felt the lump of money in his shirt pocket.

"Hey!" the driver of a butcher's cart in the rear bellowed. "Got a delivery to make here. Get moving!"

The hackney driver flung back a curse at him, then turned to Seth again. "Best be gettin' in, sir. Where to?"

"Are there still clothing shops on Regent Circus?"

As the question left his lips, Seth realized he was giving himself away as a former convict. Sure enough, the change in the driver's expression was evident in spite of the rain. "Plenty of 'em," he replied. No "sir" this time.

"People has work to do!" the voice from the rear called.

Seth stepped himself up into the carriage, and it began to move along with the flow of traffic. Rain sprayed in on him from the edge of the hood, and he was beginning to feel a chill in his bones despite the late July heat.

He was deposited at Slater & Sons on the north side of the circle of shops and intersections. After handing the hackney driver his threepence fare, Seth waited under the awning so that he would not go dripping into the shop. A ferret-looking little man approached when he finally entered, with shoulders hunched forward and protruding teeth. He swept a doubtful glance over Seth's wet, ill-fitting clothes.

"Yes?"

"I would like to buy some clothes," he said, feeling like some creature who had just crawled out from under a rock. "I have money."

At the word *money*, the man assumed a more respectful posture. "Certainly, sir. Do come in."

Seth looked self-consciously down at his sodden boots. "I'm sorry about the rug."

"That's to be expected," the shop assistant said, waving a dismissive hand. "Weather like this." He motioned Seth to a curtained compartment and instructed him to strip down to his linens. They were almost as soaked as his trousers and shirt, but Seth could do nothing about that, and he stood mute while the assistant took his measurements and penciled them in a small notebook. When he was finished, the little man said, "I can have a suit ready in nine days. We have some fine black wool, which is of course the most practical, but pinstripes are becoming rather popular—"

"Nine days?"

"Isn't that a wonder?" The assistant clicked his tongue against his protruding teeth. "Marvelous inventions, sewing machines. You would have had to wait three weeks just a few years ago."

Realizing that his reaction had been misunderstood, Seth shook his head. "I won't be here in nine days."

"You won't?" The man scratched his forehead with the blunt end of his pencil, then gave him a cagey look. "We've some orders ahead of yours, but if you pay an extra ten-bob, I'm sure we could have it ready in half that time."

Even five days in London was too much to consider. In fact, Seth could see no reason not to leave today. But he had to have something to wear. "Haven't you any ready-made?" He motioned to the heap of wet clothes on the floor. "Like these?"

With a disappointed heave of the narrow shoulders, the assistant left the compartment. He returned with a pair of navy trousers and a shirt of thick gray cotton. "Fustian—very sturdy," he said of the shirt, albeit with less enthusiasm than he had had for the black wool suit.

Seth bought three sets. When he left the curtained area, he peered at himself in the wall mirror. It was strange, seeing his own face again after ten years, for prisoners were not allowed mirrors or anything else that could be broken and turned into weapons.

A decade of scant acquaintance with the sun left his skin ghastly pale, save the dark shadows under his brown eyes. He had the droll thought that perhaps he might even glow in the dark. Elaine had been kind enough to tell him he was handsome, way back when, but he was aware that he had inherited his father's brutal looks—deep-set narrow eyes, high cheekbones, and a strong jaw. *I could hire out as a gargoyle*, he thought. But what did appearance matter when he was free?

Fortunately the rain had ceased when he walked out of the shop. He purchased boots from a cobbler three doors down and then crossed the circus to *Candler Brothers' General Mercantile*, where he purchased a canvas satchel, shaving kit, toothbrush, comb, handkerchiefs, underclothing, wool socks, a cap, and, after debating with himself, a watch and umbrella. By the time he walked outdoors again, his stomach was sending up signals that the noon hour had long passed.

He saw people entering and leaving a doorway with the words *Margate's* etched into a wooden signpost overhead. A policeman leaned against one of the posts, idly tapping his billy club against the side of his shoe as he watched passersby on the walkway. Seth felt his knees go weak. Would the shop assistants recall his face if he had to prove he'd purchased the items in his canvas bag? His anxiety deepened when the policeman looked in his direction and then past him, as if he were one of the gaslight poles lining the walkway. *You've every right to go in there*, Seth reminded himself, his shoulders relaxing a little with relief. The policeman gave him a nod as he approached the door, and Seth actually nodded back.

Halfway through his meal, he noticed that the smattering of other patrons still in the small café were sending curious glances his way. He realized he had been hunched over his bowl of soup and loaf of bread, wolfing it down as if a guard would blow the whistle, signaling the end of mealtime at any minute.

Not one whit did he give for their opinions, these people who lived their lives so blithely, unaware that at this very moment there were hundreds of convicts walking treadmills in not so pleasant surroundings. But as a concession to the manners that once used to matter to him, he forced himself to slow down. In doing so he rediscovered something he'd once taken for granted—that food could taste good as well as fill the belly.

A ripple of feminine laughter came from the window table. Seth started at the sound, but he could see at a glance that the young woman seated there, flush faced and smiling at the young man accompanying her, was not Elaine.

He had effectively blocked out all thoughts of her during the latter years of his term. Why torture oneself with pipe dreams that could never materialize? He was surprised that he could still picture her face so clearly. Could he really leave London without at least trying to see her? What if she hadn't believed his denial of love and had been waiting for him all of this time? Miracles did happen, or he wouldn't be sitting here this moment having a meal like any other Englishman.

I have to know, he thought as he left the café. Even if she had married someone else, at least the finality of the situation would help him to keep her out of his mind for his remaining years. The clock above a draper's shop showed half-past four. He would have to hurry if he still expected to board a train leaving the city.

He knew he would not be welcome on the Hamilton estate, where Elaine had worked as a chambermaid at the time of their covert courtship. Lord Hamilton hadn't allowed romances among his domestic staff, but there were only so many half-days off that one could assign the servants without repeating some. And Seth's and Elaine's had fallen on Tuesdays. Weather permitting they would walk the mile and a half to Chelsea, where Elaine's mother and aunt shared a small cottage. They sat at a well-scrubbed table with the two women and drank hot chocolate and played dominos until it was time to hurry back to the estate before the great wrought-iron gates were locked.

The memory was a pleasant one, and he became aware while hailing an approaching hansom cab that he was smiling inanely. He pulled a sober face so as not to frighten away the driver, perched precariously high in the rear of the passenger seat.

"Take yer somewhere, guv'nor?" he called down in a Cockney voice.

"Church Street, Chelsea," Seth told him.

Some thirty minutes later he was stepping around a clump of weeds in front of a faded whitewashed cottage. His knock went unanswered, and he was about to turn when he heard a noise from inside the cottage. Presently the door opened to reveal a stooped, white-haired woman. Seth remembered her right away as Elaine's Aunt Phoebe, and he had to restrain himself from leaping across the threshold and catching her up in his arms.

"Yes, sir?" she said in the manner of one who is not used to having callers.

Switching his satchel to his left hand, he removed his cap. "Mrs. Woodruff?"

"Yes." She tilted her head to study his face. "Who are you?"

"Seth Langford, Mrs. Woodruff. Do you remember me?"

"Who's there, Mother?" came a voice from another part of the cottage just as recognition flooded the woman's faded hazel eyes.

"Seth? Is that you?"

He almost laughed for the joy of it. He had not been totally forgotten by the people who mattered to him. "I was let out of prison today."

"Yes?"

Swallowing, for his mouth had gone suddenly dry, he said, "I'm here to ask about Elaine, Mrs. Woodruff."

Her expression clouded. "She's gone." Before she could say anything else, another face appeared in the doorway over her shoulder. This woman was much younger, perhaps forty years old, with blunt features and a suspicious expression.

"Who's this, Mother?" she asked, as if Seth were incapable of speech. Nevertheless, he took it upon himself to answer.

"I'm inquiring about Elaine. My name is Seth Langford, and I just want to hear how she is before leaving town."

The woman's expression softened just a little. Gently pulling her mother away from the door, she said, "I'm Lucille, Elaine's cousin. You'd best come inside."

Seconds later he was seated in the small parlor in a worn armchair. He listened as Lucille recounted somberly how her cousin Elaine had married Jack Norton, who owned a little greengrocery in the east side on Stepney Way. ". . . eight years ago," she continued after a thoughtful pause. "He was considerable older than her but treated her good. They both had to work hard to keep the business goin', so when Elaine had the baby, her mother—my aunt May—moved into their flat with them over the shop."

What did you expect? Seth asked himself, while a hard knot centered itself in his chest. *Her to spend twenty years scrubbing chamber pots in the hopes that you'd come back for her one day?*

It was time to catch a train, any train, and the sooner the better. But before he could apologize for his intrusion and get to his feet, Elaine's elderly aunt mumbled while staring at something visible only in her distant memory. "The shop burned like dry leaves, they told us."

"Excuse me?"

"I'll tell him, Mother." Lucille's chest rose and fell. "Seven years ago last June. It was the wee hours of the mornin', and the shop burned with the flat above it. The driver of a milk wagon saw Jack at a window. 'Catch the baby!' Elaine's husband called out, and the driver ran under the window and caught him. When he called for Jack to jump, too, he said he had to get his wife and mother-in-law. He never came back."

The two women became blurs in Seth's eyes. "Elaine is dead?"

"All dead, except the boy," the old woman said, rocking her body back and forth.

There was nothing left to say. The agony he'd felt over losing her to an unjust prison sentence was nothing compared to the mental picture evoked upon hearing how she died. As he got to his feet he pushed a fist into his chest, as if he could somehow make the knot go away. *My poor Elaine.*

It was only when Elaine's cousin had opened the door for him that Seth thought to ask about the child. The woman didn't answer but looked away for a second.

"You said the driver caught him," Seth said. "That means he lived, didn't he?"

"Aye, sir."

"Who has him now?"

Now she looked straight into his eyes, daring him to judge her. "I had eight of my own to raise at the time, sir, and a husband breakin' his back at the cotton mill to keep 'em from starvin'. And Mother hadn't the means nor the strength. We handed him over to the Whitechapel home."

"An orphanage, you mean?"

Her lips tightened. "Better than leavin' a basket on the church steps. And now if you please, I've Mother's things to pack. I'm takin' her with me to Enfield." The door closed with a final snap, ending Seth's last tenuous link with Elaine.

He's not my child, Seth reminded himself in the seat of the hansom carrying him to Paddington Station. *This has nothing to do with me.* At Queensway and Bishop's Bridge Roads, a crossing sweeper who couldn't have been more than ten years old grinned up at him with gaping teeth. Seth tossed him a shilling. *At least Elaine's son isn't having to fend for himself on the streets. He's fed and sheltered.*

"Just like you were at Newgate," he muttered. An image came to his mind, a face so beloved that it brought tears to his eyes. How Elaine would have grieved if she could have known what would happen to her child!

"Sir?"

It was the driver, waiting now at the side of his carriage as the remaining daylight was ebbing away. *I could just go have a look at him, reassure myself that he's well tended.* He owed Elaine that much. And since he would never return to London, this would be his only opportunity. But spend another night in the city he loathed?

"Sir?" Again the driver, this time looking impatient.

Seth gave a sigh. If only he hadn't stopped at Mrs. Woodruff's cottage! "Do you know of a reasonable place where I could lodge tonight?"

"Place on Chilworth has cheap lodging. Lumpy mattresses but clean sheets, bland food but plenty of it."

The driver could have described Buckingham Palace, and Seth could not have been less enthused. It was still London. He was deposited two blocks away at a narrow two-story building set between a butcher's shop and the apothecary. The mutton stew he was served for supper was the tastiest meal he'd had in ten years, and the bed was like a cloud—a lumpy cloud, perhaps, but infinitely more comfortable than a prison cot.

Thursday morning when habit woke him at six o'clock, the temptation to lie abed for a little while lasted only a couple of seconds. In just a matter of hours, London would be at his back—and the sooner he started, the more distance he would reach before nightfall. Just as soon as he took care of the one little errand that had compelled him to spend the night.

"Whitechapel," he told the driver of the first hackney he flagged down. "There's a children's home there. Do you know of it?"

The man touched the handle of his whip to his forehead. "Aye. On Cable Street."

Soon Seth was seated in the moving hackney cab. He watched the towering monument fade away into gray mist, for the morning was as overcast as the day before. To his right the Tower of London's gray stones rose above the press of wagons and carriages, and the masts of the shipping in London Dock cut sharp edges against the sky. As he alighted in front of a three-story building of sooty red brick, The Whitechapel Foundling Home, the first thing he noticed was a sharp unpleasant odor. It was far more irritating to the nostrils than the heavy stench of the Thames, which was but a short walk south. "What do I smell?" he asked as he paid the driver.

The man jerked a thumb toward the north. "Ammonia factory."

A woman in a gray uniform gown and apron answered his ring and left him in the vestibule. Minutes later an older woman appeared. "I'm Mrs. Briggs, the headmistress," she told him when he'd introduced himself. "Please follow me."

Her shoes thumped a dull staccato on the quarried tiles as she led Seth up a long corridor. From all appearances Mrs. Briggs seemed to be a woman who hurried through life. Her graying hair was pinned into a careless knot, her olive-colored linen dress serviceable and free of ornament. Even in her tiny office she sat perched on the edge of her chair as if begrudging having to surrender her body to it.

As she stared expectantly at him, Seth realized he had no idea of the boy's first name. He mentioned the circumstances that had orphaned him, that he should be seven years of age, and the father's last name. Mrs. Briggs nodded.

"Thomas Norton," she said. "Why do you ask about him?"

"I was once acquainted with his mother."

"Are you his father, Mr. Langford?" she asked, her gray eyes appraising.

Seth bristled at the innuendo but answered with a civil, "I am not."

"Then I must ask why you're inquiring about him."

He would have liked to have known that himself. After a fractional hesitation he replied, "Out of respect for his late mother. I'm leaving the city this morning and just wanted to reassure myself that he's being well cared for."

"Does that mean you wish to see him?"

The idea hadn't entered his mind, but now that she had mentioned it, he supposed he should. Better to take care of everything, since he was already here, than to have regrets later. "May I see him from a distance? He doesn't know me, so there is no point to our meeting."

"As you wish." Again her rapid footsteps proceeded him farther up the corridor. "The children are at breakfast," she said, reaching for a door-knob at the end. She ushered him through to the other side. A familiar institutional silence was what struck him first. Boys filled chairs surround-ing at least two dozen tables, yet the only sounds were the muffled clicks of spoons against tin porridge bowls and an occasional cough. Some waifish eyes strayed curiously in his direction, but for the most part the children ate mechanically. *They would feel right at home in Newgate*, he thought.

"There he is," Mrs. Briggs whispered beside him. He looked in the direction in which she was pointing. All the young boys looked alike to Seth, especially with their identical brown shirts. But then his eyes locked with those of a lad of about seven. Something in the tilt of his oval face, the way he held his lips together when not spooning porridge through them, made him certain that this was Elaine's child. Seth could tell even from that distance that he was small for his seven years. There was a sur-prising air of loneliness about him. It was memories of life on the outside that preyed upon those in prison and even drove some to madness. He would have imagined that a child with no memories beyond institution walls would feel at home.

"Is that him?" Seth whispered. As certain as he was, he thought he should ask anyway.

"It is," the headmistress replied. "Would you care to speak with him?"

He looked at her. "Why, no."

"Then I have duties." She turned to reach for the doorknob. "If you please."

They walked in silence back down the corridor, her shoes making the only sounds. When they reached the vestibule, he asked, "Is he happy here?"

"Happy?" Mrs. Briggs folded her arms across her bosom. "I find it curious that you should ask that question, Mr. Langford. Are *you* happy?"

"I only wondered about the boy—"

"Most never had happiness to begin with, so they make do with what they have. There are three hundred children here to my fourteen workers, counting kitchen and scullery. We're doing all we can to keep them fed and clothed and schooled. It's not uncommon to hear weeping at night."

"But they *are* treated kindly." It was a question, though he did not phrase it as such.

"They are. If our rules seem severe, it is because without order, we cannot hope to tend to their needs." Her gray eyes took on a melancholy expression. "It's family they weep for, Mr. Langford, even those who've never known such a thing. My years here have convinced me that God puts a longing for family in our hearts."

The longing in *Seth's* heart was to be rid of this place. "Thank you for your time," he told her and made for the door. Out in the feeble sunlight again, he felt suddenly drained of strength. So many emotions had raged through him in the past twenty-four hours! He almost longed for the bland sameness of the treadmill again. He leaned his back against the soot-begrimed bricks of the building and closed his eyes.

I was foolish to come here, he thought, dropping his satchel to the ground beside him. *God, why did you allow this to happen? He'll never know how wonderful his mother was. Even his father—he saved his life. Why did his family have to be snatched away like that?*

He half expected a bolt of lightning to put an end to his ungratefulness. Here he was, released from prison just yesterday, and already questioning the ways of the Almighty. But instead of censure, he felt a question rise from somewhere within him. *Why don't you be his family?*

Seth opened his eyes, reached down, and snatched up his canvas bag. This was ridiculous! The child didn't know him from Prince Edward and had lived without the pleasure of his company for seven years now. *I don't even know where I'm going.*

A sudden idea brought relief. *Money.* Surely the boy had material needs. That had to be why God had led him here. He turned to the door again.

Mrs. Briggs looked at him curiously from her office doorway. "Mr. Langford?"

"What happens to the boys when they leave here?" he blurted. The question had not even occurred to him until that very minute.

"We attempt to find apprenticeships for them at age twelve. It teaches them a trade."

I started working when I was younger than that. It didn't hurt me. "I see." Then he recalled how small the child had looked for his age. "What happens if you can't find apprenticeships for all of them?"

She looked away for a second, just as Elaine's cousin had done. "Some are able to find positions at factories and such."

"By 'such' do you mean workhouses?"

Her face hardened, clearly from resignation and not cruelty. "These are hard times, Mr. Langford. Our beds are never empty. If we keep a child a day longer than his twelfth birthday, we sentence a younger one to stay a day longer in the streets."

"I see." An image came to his mind of the destitute children who scavenged for salable bits of coal and iron in the mud of the Thames at low tide. Mudlarks, they were contemptuously called by Londoners.

Clearly growing impatient with Seth's silence, Mrs. Briggs said, "And now, Mr. Langford, I must return to my—"

"Would it be possible for him to come with me?"

Her eyebrows raised. "You wish to adopt him?"

"Well . . . yes."

"You didn't mention a wife."

"His mother was to be my wife. But something happened to prevent it. It's for her that I would like to take care of the boy."

She nodded thoughtfully. "Are you a Christian man, Mr. Langford?"

"I am."

"Can you produce someone to testify as to your character?"

"Reverend Mercer. He's a Wesleyan minister. I've known him for years."

"Yes? And where is his congregation located?"

Seth's shoulders sagged. "Newgate, among others."

"The prison, you mean?"

"Yes."

Mrs. Briggs' hand went back to the doorknob. "You had best step inside my office, Mr. Langford."

When they had seated themselves again, he told his story, leaving out the Hamiltons' name. It sounded incredible to his own ears, so he did not take offense when she said, "Can Reverend Mercer verify this?"

"I believe so." If the minister approached Major Spencer, surely the warden would at least confirm that he had been found innocent without giving the details. A chill snaked down his spine, raising cold sweat on the back of his neck. "He visits Newgate in the afternoons. I'll have to go back there and wait for him."

Seth didn't allow himself to think about what he had committed to as he bought Scotch eggs and an orange from street vendors for his lunch and then hailed another hackney cab to take him back to Newgate. Too much thinking was dangerous, for he knew he was but a hairsbreadth away from abandoning the whole idea.

He had been standing on the walkway of busy Newgate Street—as far as possible from the prison but close enough to watch the entrance door—when he felt a hand upon his back. Already unnerved by being so close to the dreadful place, he jumped.

"Seth Langford?" It was Reverend Mercer standing there, grinning like a boy who'd just found a shilling. Before Seth could collect himself, he was caught up in a bear hug by the young minister. "Praise God! It is true!"

When he was released and could draw a breath again, Seth smiled back. "How did you know?"

The minister slanted him a knowing look. "Apparently Mr. Baker eavesdropped on your meeting yesterday. No doubt half the prison knows why you were set loose."

That was disturbing to hear. "But I agreed to keep it to myself."

"It wasn't your doing, Mr. Langford."

But it was all the more reason he needed to put London behind him. What if the Hamilton family decided he had broken his word? He realized then that Reverend Mercer had been speaking. ". . . anything you need?"

"Yes, please," Seth replied. "There is."

Five minutes later they were seated in a hansom headed toward East London. "Mr. Langford is of sound moral character," the minister expressed at the orphanage to Mrs. Briggs and a Mr. Healy, who had been summoned in his capacity as head of the board of trustees. "He taught himself to read while in Newgate, so it's clear he suffers from no lack of industry. He has a document signed by the warden and a legal representative of the family involved, withdrawing all charges. I can testify to the validity of the facts he gave you, although you must understand that we haven't the liberty to give the name of his former employer."

Three identical documents were produced, one for the files of The Whitechapel Foundling Home, one for the magistrate's office, and one for Seth to keep, testifying that Thomas Norton shall henceforth be recognized as Thomas Langford. On each Mr. Healy penned his official signature, Mrs. Briggs and Reverend Mercer signed as witnesses, and lastly, Seth, with trembling hand, altered the fate of a young boy he had yet to meet.

But that would soon happen, for after Mr. Healy left and Reverend Mercer wrapped Seth in another bear hug before making his departure, Seth was alone again with Mrs. Briggs. "So soon," he said in a voice as unsteady as his hand.

"Having regrets already, Mr. Langford?"

I don't know, he thought but said evasively, "I'll take good care of him."

And so it was that Seth's hansom seat was shared by a small wide-eyed boy who looked about him in mute wonder on their way to Paddington Station. That was fine with Seth, for he really didn't know what he was expected to say. Mrs. Briggs had done all the talking when the boy was brought into her office. Thomas was then ushered away to collect his belongings—a change of clothing bundled with string that fit easily into Seth's canvas bag, and a small tin horse that had no doubt been a Christmas gift last year. Seth could easily imagine the overworked headmistress already making plans to find a replacement for the boy's bed and porridge bowl by nightfall.

Seth knew next to nothing about children. He had been the youngest in a family that scattered after his mother's death because his father lost interest in everything but gin. The little contact he had had with children on the Hamilton estate had resulted in disastrous consequences. From the corner of his eye he studied the boy. His close-cropped hair must have come from his father's side, for Elaine's had been reddish blond. The boy's hair looked almost gray in the sunlight, like ashes—an unusual color for a child. It was a bit disconcerting to see Elaine's blue eyes set in such a waifish face.

Does she know he's with me now? Seth wondered. Were those same blue eyes looking down on them from heaven right now? He hoped so. He had surely hurt her with his lie about ceasing to love her. True, she had married just two years later, but women married for more than one reason, and he suspected that security had been Elaine's. He couldn't fault her for that.

The platform at Paddington Station was an anthill of activity. Seth carried his bag with one hand and, after some hesitation, took Thomas's small hand in his. It wouldn't do to have the child get separated from him in the crowd and end up falling on the tracks. A black locomotive with *London-Birmingham Railway* on the door belched steam and sent out a shrill whistle.

"It's loading now," he said to the boy, leading him toward a ticket window. "We have to hurry." They were the first words Seth had spoken to him. Blue eyes wide, the boy nodded back and hurried along. At the window Seth waited anxiously as the three people ahead of him made their purchases. "Two tickets, please," he said when his turn came.

"Where to?"

"The end of the line." *As far from London as possible.*

The clerk gave him a brief appraising glance. "Second-class?"

Ten years of being treated like the dregs of society caught up with Seth. He clenched his teeth and entertained the notion of reaching through the window and taking the man by the collar. But it wasn't worth going back to Newgate over, so he relaxed his fist and stifled the urge. He considered the money in his pocket. Wouldn't it be satisfying to raise his chin haughtily and demand first-class tickets?

And so you'd allow one uncivil boor to influence how you spend your money? he chided himself. That money was to provide for his future, and now the boy's as well. "Yes," Seth replied as he handed over a pound note and then pocketed his change. Thankfully their second-class compartment wasn't crowded—the only other passengers being an older married couple and a young man who looked like a bank clerk. Seth allowed the boy the

86

place by the window so that they could both look out—he over Thomas's head. They traveled on in silence until the train pulled into Coventry Station at half-past seven, and Seth thought to ask if he would like anything to eat.

The boy turned to him with his large eyes. "Yes, sir, if you please, sir," he answered apologetically. Seth took his hand again outside the train, for though the platform was less crowded than in London, it seemed so large and the boy so small. He bought roast beef sandwiches in the depot, but the boarding whistle blew soon afterward and they had to eat them on the train. They arrived in Birmingham at half-past eight and found an inn within walking distance, The Christopher Columbus. An innkeeper led them upstairs, telling Seth they were fortunate because there was a trading fair going on and he had but one room left.

"Do you know how to ready yourself for bed?" Seth asked Thomas when the innkeeper left them. Surely boys of seven knew how to clean their teeth and bathe themselves, but he thought he should ask just to be sure.

"Yes, sir," Thomas replied and took his belongings out of Seth's canvas bag. It astonished Seth to see the boy's nightshirt, worn thin and patched in several places. As he pointed out the water closet at the end of the corridor and, as an afterthought, waited outside the door lest the boy forget his way back and become frightened, Seth reckoned he would need to purchase some clothing for him. *Some shoes as well*, he thought, for they were almost as thin as the nightshirt.

He waited until the boy had settled himself on the pillow to snuff out the candle. "Good night," Seth said.

"Good night, sir." The small voice seemed to have grown even smaller in the surrounding darkness. It was Seth's second night since his release to sleep in a real bed, and his limbs sank greedily into the soft mattress. Sleep had already begun to muddle his thoughts when he heard a noise and opened his eyes.

It was Thomas weeping behind him. Guilt struck Seth like a mallet. No one asked whether he wanted to leave the orphanage. And now here he is in a strange bed, likely wondering what's to become of him. Seth didn't know what to say but knew he had to say *something*. Turning on his pillow, he could see the boy's faint outline in the darkness. "Thomas?"

A sniff, and then, "Yes, sir?"

"Why are you crying?"

There was another sniff before the boy answered, "I don't know."

How was he to offer reassurance to that? Feeling more than a little awkward, he said lamely, "You've had a long day. You'll feel better in the morning."

After a second or two of silence, the small voice said, "Yes, sir. Thank you, sir."

The boy did seem in brighter spirits in the morning, as much as Seth was able to tell. But Seth's spirits took a downward turn upon walking out into the light of day. Congested and busy, the odors of factories and mills affronted his nostrils. "It looks just like London," he mumbled to himself.

"Sir?" asked the boy beside him.

Seth looked at him and sighed. "Let's go get our things."

Again there was a train preparing to leave at the station. *Severn Valley Railway* was stenciled in silver on the door of the locomotive. "Shrewsbury is the end of the line," the ticket agent informed them.

*M*ercy accepted a ride home with Janet and Elliott Friday afternoon after the funeral and burial in the little churchyard behind the Wesleyan Chapel. Before letting herself down from the wagon, which Mrs. Brent had left to the couple along with the horses, she embraced Janet.

"You was so good to her," Janet sniffed against Mercy's ear.

"And so were you." On the ground, Mercy nodded up at Elliott, sitting there with reins in hand. "Both of you."

"And now it's time to go on with our lives." The maid blew her nose into her handkerchief. "Like she wanted us to."

"Yes, time to go on," Mercy agreed, but as she turned and approached her family's cottage, she had the thought, *Go on to what?* There were no signs of activity outside, and when she walked through the doorway, the reason became obvious. Four disgruntled faces looked up at her from the table, and three more from chairs in the corner that served as a parlor of sorts.

"You been gone for hours," her father said with an injured tone.

Harold, who had apparently nodded off in his chair until hearing his father's voice, blinked and rubbed his eyes. "What took you so long?"

She stood just inside the doorway, eyes traveling from one sullen face to another. "If any of you would have cared to come with me, you wouldn't have to ask."

Fernie grumbled something about being famished, but his father, who had apparently decided to be magnanimous because his herd had become richer by six cows—seven counting the one Mrs. Kingston had traded to him—threw him a glare.

"You heard her, boy! Have some consideration. Takes time to bury a body." He gave Mercy a long-suffering frown as if to say, *You just can't teach manners to some people!* "We didn't mind waitin' at all, did we, fellows?"

"But *you* said you've a mind to use the strap—" Oram began but withered at his father's silencing look.

The full meaning of her father's last sentence dawned upon Mercy. She passed the table to the stove, where an iron pot still sat on a back burner. "You didn't heat up the stew?"

"What?" Dale said, exchanging puzzled looks with the others. "We have stew?"

"Surely *one* of you thought to raise the lid and look?"

They stared back at her as if she'd suggested they should have done the ironing in her absence. "But you didn't tell us. . . ." Harold declared defensively.

"That's because you were all in the milking barn when I left." She'd also left bread from yesterday's baking in the cupboard with a large wedge of cheese. Just *those* would have provided something to stave off the starvation pangs that were apparently tormenting them now. But she knew without even checking that no one had bothered to open the cupboard door.

Sighing to herself, Mercy crossed the room and reached for the tin of matches she'd left in plain sight. Yes, it was time to go on with her life, as Janet had said. *I want to have faith in your promise, Mrs. Brent,* she thought. But a dismal picture would not budge from her mind—herself twenty years from now, still cooking pots of stew for a group of men who became helpless once they crossed the cottage threshold and had yet to express anything resembling gratitude.

––––––––––

Some twelve miles south of Gresham, Shrewsbury sat within a horse-shoe loop of the River Severn. The steep-hilled town had thrived from its very beginnings as a defensive stronghold against the Welsh threat and had become a well-situated center of trade. There was a diversity of dwellings and shops—Queen Anne, Georgian, and Victorian structures were mingled with medieval and sixth-century half-timbered buildings, and winding cobbled lanes were overhung in places by Elizabethan storeys. It was bustling and busy and as different from the sedate atmosphere of Gresham as night from day. Not a place Julia would care to live, even after having spent most of her life in the far more metropolitan London, but certainly an exciting place to spend a Saturday.

Julia and Fiona, along with Elizabeth and the younger girls, had left Gresham before the sun rose in order to squeeze as much activity out of the day as possible. Since Karl Herrick would need to stay in the town to drive them back in the landau, Julia had insisted that Audrey come along so she could spend the day with her husband. It took some doing to coax the cook to surrender her kitchen to the care of Mildred, Gertie, and Mrs. Beemish. But as the couple waved farewell after depositing Julia and her group in the market square, Julia could see a flush of pleasure on the small woman's face.

Shopping was the first order of the day, and they spent more time looking than purchasing. Elizabeth found a shawl of fine India cashmere, and Fiona purchased the novel *Lorna Doone*. Laurel and Aleda bought identical watercolor cases, and Grace chose a small framed picture of a cocker spaniel suffering through a bath administered by a curly-haired child who looked strikingly similar to herself. Not aware of anything that she needed at the moment, Julia was content to admire the purchases of the others until Fiona insisted that they just "look" at the items in a jeweler's display.

The rows of stones and settings and pearls brought a tiny ache to her heart that she thought had long been extinguished. She'd been forced to surrender her jewelry when the Bank of England foreclosed on her house—even her wedding ring and some treasured heirlooms from her mother. In the busy uncertain days of establishing the *Larkspur* as a lodging house and learning to operate a business, her loss had seldom crossed her mind. She felt blessed just to keep the children clothed and fed. But being a woman she did enjoy pretty things, and some of the displayed pieces of jewelry were lovely indeed.

"I know you don't want to appear high and mighty for the vicar's sake," Fiona was saying from beside her. "But I can't imagine anyone begrudging you those amethyst earrings, can you?"

From her other side, Aleda coaxed, "Mother, you can wear them with your lavender dress."

"Or even gray." This came from Elizabeth, who had looked up from admiring a string of pearls.

"Yes," Julia said simply. This drew surprised looks from the others, who had obviously expected a battle. She smiled at the little group. "But I'll save them for my wedding day."

Upon Laurel's request they walked through the gardens of Saint Julien's Academy for Young Ladies next. She had toured the school with her father and Elizabeth three months ago, but she now expressed a desire to show at least the outside to everyone else. It was an impressive Georgian building of red brick, situated across the English bridge and within sight of the spire of Saint Alkmund's Church.

Soon after that they decided upon lunch—as much for the sake of their feet as their stomachs. The castle would be their last visit, where the Herricks had agreed to meet them at three o'clock for the return trip to Gresham. A hansom driver informed them that the Lion Hotel on Wyle Cop was famous city wide for its fidget pie—a combination of bacon, onions, and apples, rounded off by pastry.

The dining room of the Tudor-style building was packed with patrons, adding weight to the driver's recommendation. Perhaps the efficiency of the innkeeper had something to do with its popularity as well, Julia thought, for he greeted them almost immediately and led them to a table in the center of the room.

"Whew," Elizabeth breathed after an apron-clad server took their orders. "I'd forgotten how exhausting large towns could be."

"I'm not tired at all," Laurel declared, sitting up erect as if to prove it. "I could do this every day."

Her older sister smirked slightly. "Well, so could I when I was your age."

This caused an exchange of smiles across the table between Julia and Fiona. "You're hardly ready for the rocking chair," Julia told Elizabeth.

"Mrs. Rhodes has a green rocking chair in her sitting room," Grace put in so sweetly that no one cared to point out the irrelevance of her statement.

Fiona smiled. "But you're right about cities being exhausting, Elizabeth. I daresay it'll take me weeks to adjust to London's pace again."

Julia had detected no trace of sadness in her friend's voice, but just in case, she asked, "You don't mind living there, do you, Fiona?"

"Mind? Why, no, Julia. It's so good for my husband to be performing again. But if I could scoop up the Prince of Wales Theatre and bring it to Gresham, I would do so."

"And after the first performance the theatre would close," said Elizabeth with a wry little smile. "There would be no one left to buy tickets for any other nights—unless cows were allowed."

"Aye, there's the truth." Fiona smiled back. "But that's the charm of the place, isn't it? No crowds pushing this way and that. Everything so green and peaceful."

Julia smiled in agreement, then noticed the dark-haired man seated at the table behind Fiona. His manly and rugged face was pale—as if he had been ill. Yet judging from the shoulders his stature seemed hardy enough. A small boy sat with him—his son, no doubt, but the two could have been strangers for all the eye contact they made. In fact, the man's attention was centered upon Fiona, or rather her words, for his posture was set in a listening pose. There seemed a wistful expression about him until he moved his head a little and, in doing so, made eye contact with Julia. He immediately shifted his attention to the meal in front of him. Chagrined at being caught staring, Julia was careful not to look at him again.

"I wonder why sandwiches taste so much better out of doors?" Ambrose Clay said, stretched out on the grass and resting his head upon one crooked arm. With the other hand, he wiped his mouth with one of the linen napkins Mrs. Paget had packed in an oversized picnic hamper.

"I would imagine almost anything tastes better out of doors," the vicar replied dreamily. He still had half of a ham sandwich in one hand and a glass of lemonade from the crock in another. "It's just that sandwiches are the only foods we ever pack in picnic baskets. Right, Philip?"

Philip looked around from the hook he was baiting at water's edge. "Yes, sir." He had led the two men to a shady spot on the riverbank in Gipsy Woods so they could see if the fish were biting any better here than they had been below the bridge. Ben and Jeremiah had joined them for a while, but then had to leave to do their Saturday chores.

So far only two perch were on the string dangling into the water from the trunk of a willow. Some days were like that, but Philip had higher hopes for today after the two men had praised him, tagging him a fishing expert. Vicar Phelps had even boasted to Mr. Clay before they set out this morning, "Philip can smell the fish in the water."

He didn't feel as badly for the vicar as he did for Mr. Clay. He had fished with the vicar and Laurel a couple of times already, and both times had resulted in good catches. But Mr. Clay hadn't fished since he was a boy. It would be nice to watch the actor pull in at least one big one.

Still, neither man seemed disappointed. They lingered over their lunch as if there were no fish in the water waiting to surrender themselves to just the right cast of the line. That wouldn't be so if the morning had been successful, for a good spell of fishing left one craving for more.

"Have another sandwich, Philip?" the vicar asked from behind him.

Philip looked back over his shoulder. "No, thank you."

The vicar scratched his beard. "Then I suppose I should return to the task at hand."

"I believe we'll catch some here," Philip told him.

"Of course we will."

"I'll join you in a moment," Mr. Clay said. He was sitting up now, with a slice of chocolate cake on a saucer in one hand, a fork in the other. "I can't recall when I've had such a good appetite."

Philip exchanged smiles with Vicar Phelps, who was now on the bank baiting his hook with a grub worm. The vicar had had to bully Mr. Clay into coming along, for yesterday afternoon the actor had plunged into one of his dark moods. This morning he had insisted that Fiona go ahead with her plans for Shrewsbury, but apparently he planned then to spend his day in bed. Perhaps it wasn't a total loss, Philip thought, that Mr. Clay had yet

93

to catch a fish. If the outing had merely lightened his despondency, it was worth it.

"You may have my other sandwich if you like," Philip told him.

"Thank you, but the cake was the perfect *coup de grace*." The actor closed the lid to the hamper and picked up his fishing rod from the ground. He lowered himself to the bank on Philip's left. The three fished in silence, seasoned with occasional small talk for the better part of an hour. During that time Philip hooked a grayling and attached him to the string.

"Not again!" Mr. Clay exclaimed mildly, pulling his line up to discover his hook empty. "Greedy little creatures, aren't they?"

Vicar Phelps passed him the jar of dirt and grubs. "You don't begrudge them a good lunch, do you?"

"Actually, I feel a little sorry for them. Here we feasted just a few feet away on sandwiches and cake, and they have to make do with grubs." He paused then, his fingers poised above the jar. "I wonder . . ."

"Yes, sir?" Philip asked.

The actor looked back at the picnic basket. "Are you sure you don't want that sandwich, Philip?"

"Surely you're not thinking of feeding it to the fish, Mr. Clay." The vicar frowned uncertainly, as if wondering if his friend should have spent the day in bed after all.

"Just the ham." Mr. Clay was already on his feet at the picnic basket. He came back with the extra sandwich and unwrapped the brown paper covering.

Philip could only watch, bemused, as he tore off a sliver of ham and threaded it upon his hook. Some five minutes passed, with not even a bite for any of them. Philip smiled to himself at the mental picture of a school of perch under the water's surface, scratching their heads with their fins at this oddity. But then a curious thing happened.

"Say . . . my cork has disappeared," Mr. Clay said.

"Pull it up, man!" the vicar exclaimed.

The fish put up a fight, and Philip finally had to net it when the actor was able to get his line close enough to the bank. It was a trout, probably close to three pounds. Not to be outdone, Philip and Vicar Phelps both baited their hooks with pieces of the ham, but with no success. Another mental picture occurred to Philip, this time of the fish warning each other not to go near the mysterious pink food. This image seemed to be confirmed when he went back to grubs and snared a good-sized perch. The two men switched back to grubs as well, and by about three o'clock they actually had a full string—a good thing, since Mildred was expecting to fry their catch for supper.

Back at the *Larkspur* Vicar Phelps insisted that Mr. Clay go on upstairs to his apartment and get some rest. The actor had begun looking peaked again on their way back from the river. Philip filled a pail with water from the pump next to the stables, and Gertie brought out knives and spoons, a dishpan and towels. Last fall Mr. Herrick had crafted a narrow oak table behind the potting shed, and it was there that Philip and the vicar rolled up their shirtsleeves and began cleaning their catch.

The vicar held up Mr. Clay's trout. "I believe this made his day."

"It made mine too." Philip smiled back and picked up his knife. He enjoyed Vicar Phelps's company, the easygoing, pleasant way about him. He especially appreciated the fact that even though the vicar would become his stepfather in less than five months, he respected Philip's present position as man of the Hollis family. It would be terrible if Mother had chosen a man who made him feel like a little child, or worse, flattered him and his sisters unduly to win affection.

The thought occurred to him that his mother and sisters would likely not be back for supper, which meant Elizabeth and Laurel would be away as well. He looked up from the grayling he was scaling. "I'm sure Mildred won't mind setting another place at the supper table. Especially since you caught some of these. And *most* especially since you're helping clean them."

Busy scraping the scales from a bream with the edge of a spoon, the vicar thanked him but had to decline. "There's not time enough to give Mrs. Paget notice. I learned a long time ago it behooves me to stay on her good side." He looked up at Philip, and the hazel eyes had become serious. "I wonder if we might discuss something."

"About Mrs. Paget?"

He smiled at that but then shook his head. "I've debated with myself over whether to approach you about this. You're a bright lad, and I don't want you to think I haven't the confidence that you can cope with the world."

Now Philip was beginning to worry. "What is it, sir?"

The vicar sighed, as if whatever was on his mind had caused him great turmoil. "It's about school. You're still eager to go away, aren't you?"

"Yes, sir. But not because I don't like it here."

"I know that, Philip. And I understand your wanting to experience something new."

"Was it that way with you?"

"Well, not exactly. But you see, by the time I reached your age, I'd been in boarding schools for six years."

There was just a bit of sadness in those last words. Philip realized then that he knew very little about his future father's childhood. "I'm sorry, sir."

"All in the past, son," the vicar said with a wave of a scale-crusted hand. The "son" had seemed to come out automatically, as if he were unaware that he had said it. But Philip did not mind—in fact, he found that he rather liked it. It had been a long time since anyone besides Mother had called him that.

Vicar Phelps went on. "I just thought I should warn you about a nasty little element of boarding school of which your mother would likely be unaware."

"Yes, sir?"

"I've never heard of a boarding school for males that wasn't infested with bullies, Philip. And of the worst kind."

Philip let out a relieved breath. He had learned from last year's episodes with the Sanders brothers how to deal with bullies. But so as not to appear that he didn't appreciate the warning, he said, "Thank you, sir. I'll be careful."

"I hope you will, Philip. Because incoming younger students are the most likely targets. I'd like to think that things have changed since I was a young man, but unfortunately, I've seen little proof of that."

"You won't tell Mother, will you?" Philip asked. She already had misgivings about his living away from her. A thing like this, however inconsequential he thought it to be, would surely cause her to reconsider. Or add to her worries.

The vicar gave him a little smile that said *I understand how mothers are too.* "No, of course not. I'm sure you'll come through it all just fine, just as thousands of other young men have done. I just wanted you to be aware."

They worked on in silence and were just finishing the chore when Philip cocked his head at a familiar sound. Horses' hooves and carriage wheels were turning onto Church Lane and into the carriage drive. He had assumed his mother and sisters would return much later, but then he hadn't exactly inquired about what time to expect them. Vicar Phelps raised his head, too, indicating that he'd heard. Feminine voices began drifting around the walls of the potting shed.

"Mr. Herrick likely will be taking Elizabeth and Laurel back next," Philip said. "Would you like me to run around and stop him so you can ride too?"

Panic flooded the man's face. "Your mother can't see me like this!" he whispered. Indeed he looked a sight, with blood smeared upon his shirt and fish scales clinging even to his beard. He stank of grubs and fish innards, as did Philip and everything surrounding them. "I'll dash around the other side of the house and catch Mr. Herrick after she goes inside."

Philip couldn't resist a bit of a wicked smile. "She won't mind, sir.

She's seen me like this a hundred times."

"Yes? Well, it's a bit different in my case, now isn't it?" the vicar whispered hotly but then winked. They both listened while the landau pulled back out of the carriage drive. He could faintly make out his mother's voice, and then Mrs. Herrick's. Grace said something too. There was the click of the courtyard door, followed by silence.

"You can go now, Vicar," Philip whispered.

"Yes, thank you." With that, the vicar walked to the corner of the shed and peered around to the other side. He turned to give Philip a sheepish smile, lifted a hand in farewell, and was gone.

*M*r. Drummond has no need for a groomsman," a butler informed Seth at the back door of a High Street mansion. It was the sixth residence he'd called upon since lunch, totaling fourteen so far that day. He could have covered more ground had Thomas not been along, but it didn't seem right to leave him alone in their room at the inn. The boy didn't seem as robust as the children Seth noticed playing in the parks and alleys, yet his appetite was hearty enough. No doubt food had been stretched to the limit at The Whitechapel Home for Foundling Children.

He was beginning to despair of ever finding a position. Fortunately he was by no means desperate for cash. But he couldn't just idle away his time. He may as well go back to the treadmill in that case. If only he had a character reference! He'd been too stunned by his sudden release to ask Lady Hamilton for one. It was likely that he wouldn't have had the boldness to do so anyway; not after taking her money. How could he explain the last ten years of his life to any potential employer?

"Are you tired?" he asked the boy when they came upon a small park. After a hesitation, he replied apologetically, "Yes, sir."

"Then let's have a rest." They settled on a bench, and Seth wove both hands behind his head, leaned back, and closed his eyes. "*Everything green and peaceful*," the woman in the dining room had said. He felt a touch upon his arm and looked down at the boy beside him. "Yes?"

"There's a big house over there, sir," Thomas said, lifting a skinny arm to point at a rooftop rising above the others to the south of them.

"Yes, I see it. We'll have to see if they're in need of a groomsman, won't we?"

The child nodded back shyly, and Seth's thoughts returned to the conversation he had overheard at lunch. He'd never heard of a village called Gresham. *But it can't be far away if those women lived there.* Having been raised in the tenements of London, he knew almost nil about small villages. Were there stores where one could buy food? What did people do for a living? He looked at Thomas's thin wrists. What if a doctor was needed in the middle of the night?

"What can it hurt to find out?"

"Sir?"

Seth realized that he'd spoken his last thought. "Nothing," he replied to the boy. *I should really give him a day to rest.* He had dragged him from door to door for the past two days—not to mention uprooting him from the only life he'd ever known.

We should go to chapel in the morning, he thought but discarded the idea immediately. It was not that he had little affection for God. Without God's sustaining hand upon his shoulder, he would have gone mad in prison. It was the idea of having to congregate with others that terrified him. Chapel at Newgate had been the highlight of his weeks, but then he'd shared the pews with fellow convicts in the same situation. Outside prison walls people tended to want to know about each other. He would have to keep up his guard constantly for fear that any small talk or pleasantries— no matter how friendly—would stray into uncomfortable territory.

Not that he was ashamed of his past. He had done nothing wrong and was finally vindicated. But people tended to believe that where there was smoke, there was fire. What was he to do? Hang his acquittal paper about his neck on a string? And what if they asked questions about the boy? Even Mrs. Briggs had assumed he was the father, which would have made Thomas illegitimate. His young shoulders weren't strong enough to bear that burden.

"Sir?"

He looked again at the boy beside him. "Yes?"

"I'm not so tired anymore, if you want to move on."

"Then let's try the house you pointed out," Seth told him. *And if there's no position to be had there, we'll push on for Gresham early Monday.* He recalled again what the woman at the inn had said: "*No crowds pushing this way and that.*"

On Monday morning, the first of August, every resident of the *Larkspur* from lodger to servant, along with Andrew and his daughters, assembled in the courtyard to bid the Clays farewell. Julia and Andrew hung back and allowed the others to say their good-byes, for the two would be accompanying them in the landau to see them off at the railway station in Shrewsbury.

"Some lunch for you," a watery-eyed Mrs. Herrick said, handing over a basket to be put into the boot of the landau. "Those station meals would make a body ill."

Miss Rawlins pressed a copy of her latest novella, *Lord Elton's Niece*, into Fiona's hands. "I miss our discussions about my books. Insight such as yours is so rare."

"Sugared dried figs from Florence," Mrs. Kingston declared after clutching both husband and then wife to her ample bosom. "I was saving them for such an occasion."

Julia's children even presented gifts—Philip, three Roman marbles from the collection he'd gathered atop the Anwyl last year; Aleda, a fairly accurate watercoloring she'd painted yesterday of the *Larkspur*; and Grace, one of her paper dolls. The Worthy sisters even crossed the lane to give Fiona a card of fine ecru lace.

While Mr. Herrick sat at the reins behind Donny and Pete, the two Welsh cobs, Julia and Fiona occupied the front seat and Andrew and Mr. Clay the rear. Julia was painfully aware that every mile that drew them closer to Shrewsbury represented less time she'd have with her friends. It was likely that *The Barrister* could run at the Prince of Wales Theatre for years. Of course she hoped the production would be successful for Mr. Clay's sake, but a selfish side of her was reluctant to agree.

The landau was halfway to Shrewsbury when red-and-white *Anwyl Mountain Savory Cheeses'* wagons began passing on their way back from delivering their barrels to the railway station. Mr. Herrick returned the waves of one driver after another, many whose faces were known to Julia. The last wagon was passing when she turned her face to the right and met a familiar set of eyes.

"Fiona," she said, gently elbowing her friend. "Did you see that man?"

"What man?"

"In the bed of that wagon."

Fiona craned her neck to see, for the wagon was lumbering on past them. Julia now noticed that there were three riders in the bed of the wagon—two men and a young boy. "What's wrong, Julia?" Andrew asked from behind.

"It's nothing, really—just that I believe I saw that man when we were in Shrewsbury last Saturday." Andrew and Mr. Clay turned around to peer over their shoulders while Julia said to Fiona, "You remember. He sat near us at lunch."

"I don't recall seeing anyone there I would recognize now," Fiona responded doubtfully.

"That's right. Your back was to him."

"Was that Mr. Burrell?" Andrew asked. Julia looked back at her fiancé. He was twisted around in his seat, peering at the road behind them, but the wagon was too far away now to discern the faces.

"Mr. Burrell?" She had never met the man who had left his wife and seven children. Was he the one who had sat behind them at the Lion Hotel? But why would he have a boy with him? *Must have been the other man*, she thought, remembering there had been two in the wagon.

"Who is Mr. Burrell?" Mr. Clay asked.

"Molly and David's father," Andrew replied as they both returned to their original sitting positions. "A slacker with a soul as black as his fingernails."

Julia couldn't recall ever having heard such anger in her fiancé's voice, but she knew he had a soft spot for the Burrell children. "Why would he come back to Gresham?" she asked.

"To cause trouble, I'm afraid. And that poor family has suffered enough."

———

" . . . and of course he owns most o' the land," the man sharing the wagon bed with Seth and Thomas was saying.

"I beg your pardon?" Seth said. He had allowed his attention to stray to a passing carriage just a minute ago. The two women inside had looked vaguely familiar.

"Squire Bartley," the man went on. "Most dairymen lease from him."

He was a strange traveling companion. While this Mr. Burrell had bad teeth and a face that hinted at a past partnership with the bottle, he was clean and well-groomed. Even his suit of clothing was pressed and clean. It was by accident that they happened to share a wagon. Upon learning from the innkeeper of the Lion Hotel that no railway went up to Gresham, Seth had been directed to the livery stables near the railway station where they could rent a coach and driver. He took scant notice of several red-and-white wagons passing on their way to the station, stacked with barrels.

"What's a grissem?" Thomas had asked timidly.

"A what?" was Seth's reply.

The boy had pointed to the side of one of the wagons. *Anwyl Mountain Savory Cheeses* was stenciled in bold letters on the side—under which was written *T. Bartley esq., owner, Gresham, Shropshire.*

This brought a smile to Seth's face, for wagons leaving *from* Gresham obviously had to *return* to Gresham. Surely they wouldn't mind taking on paying passengers, at a fare much cheaper than what a coach would be.

"Might I ask the nature of your visit ter Gresham?" their traveling companion said, bringing Seth back to the present.

"We'd just like to see it," Seth replied guardedly. "Is there an inn?"

Mr. Burrell nodded. "Th' *Bow and Fiddle*. There used to be two afore the railway took coachin' business away. But there's still a good living in dairy farmin', if yer lookin' to settle."

Dairy farming? Seth restrained himself from smiling. He had seen cows only occasionally during his lifetime, and always from a distance. How a person went about extracting milk from such a creature was a mystery. "Is that what you do?"

"Me? Oh no, sir. I'm a carpenter. Been workin' steady for a Mister Green for near four months now." He stared at Seth, his eyes clouding over. "Wanted to see if I could stay off the bottle afore seeing if my family would move down there with me. Got a nice little cottage on Bridgeway and decent wages."

Seth nodded for lack of any other response. All too well he could recall his father's bouts with gin. He did not underestimate the holding power of strong drink, which was why he never touched it.

"It were Mister Green that taught me how to stay sober," Mr. Burrell went on. "Do you know Mister Hunter Green?"

"No."

"Good Christian man, he is. Prays with his workers every mornin'. Most are just like me, but Mister Green used to crave the bottle, too, so he knows how it is." He smiled apologetically at Seth. "Vicar Wilson and Vicar Phelps . . . well, they was good men. But they never knowed how it is to want a drink so bad you'd kill yer own mother fer it."

In spite of his determination not to get involved in anyone else's affairs, Seth found himself interested. "What did he do to help you stop?"

Mr. Burrell nodded. "First, he tells me that some people hated Jesus because he sat down at the table wi' drunkards. That made me get ter thinking that maybe Jesus don't despise the likes of me after all." He wiped an eye with the cuff of his sleeve. "And Mister Green, he says to me, 'Now Randy, every day that you show up fer work clean and sober, I adds a shilling to your wages for that day. A man can get hisself into a neat little cottage fer his family if he stays sober long enough.' "

Stopping his narrative, Mr. Burrell peered searchingly at Seth. "I sees you wi' yer boy, how you helped him in the wagon. I never treated my children that good, not one day. Are you a believer, Mr. Langford?"

"Yes."

"Would you pray that my family will take me back? Come live wi' me in Shrewsbury? I know I can stay sober wi' Mr. Green and the rest of the workers. We helps each other along, see?"

"Yes . . . all right." He found himself hoping the family would mend, even though he would likely never meet the wife and children.

"Thank you kindly, sir," Mr. Burrell said, forcing air through his teeth. "I'm gettin' nervous the closer we get."

"You'll do fine," Seth felt compelled to say. "Does that mean we're almost there?" The man smiled and turned to point to something behind them.

"You see that hill yonder?"

"Yes," Seth replied. Thomas shifted around to look as well. It was almost a small mountain, about five hundred feet high, that had sneaked up upon them while their backs were turned.

"Is that Gresham?" Seth asked.

The man chuckled. "No, but if you was to stand at the top, you could count the spots on the cows in Gresham."

———————

There was not much time for farewells on the platform at the Shrewsbury station. Outside the Clays' first-class compartment, Julia and Andrew attempted to keep the mood lighthearted. All that could be said about their forthcoming prolonged separation had been said, and it was not forever. Julia knew instinctively that they would return again and again to Gresham, as they both considered it their home.

"I'll send you a playbill and tell you all about the opening," Fiona promised as she and Julia pressed cheeks.

Mr. Clay had been a little quieter all morning. His eyes were shining as he faced Andrew and Julia and said simply, "Thank you for being our friends."

The last boarding whistle sounded, and five minutes later the train was moving east toward London. Not until the train was out of sight did Julia realize she was still waving. She turned to Andrew and shrugged. "Well, that's it then."

"You're crying," he said tenderly, touching her cheek with a finger.

"Am I?" A salty taste came to the back of her mouth. "Silly, aren't I?"

"In the nicest possible way," he teased, then made an abrupt change of subject. "Are you that keen on visiting Wales on our honeymoon?"

"Wales is supposed to be beautiful. Why?"

Andrew glanced in the direction of the tracks, as if he could still see the moving train. "I hear there are good hotels in London. Fine theatre too. We could do some Christmas shopping. And I've always wanted to see all those rooks fluttering around King Charles' statue in Trafalgar Square."

"Pigeons," Julia corrected, smiling. "As if you didn't know."

He raised an eyebrow. "Indeed? Well, what do you think?"

"What do I think?" Taking his arm, she replied, "I think I'm going to love being your wife."

*A*s Seth walked the shaded lanes with Thomas in hand, he was pleased to discover that while Gresham was certainly rural, all the ingredients necessary for civilized living were here. They had passed a school, churches, the smithy, a doctor's surgery, bakery and general store, greengrocery—even a lending library. If he couldn't find a position as a groomsman, perhaps he could hire on at the wheelwright's or joiner's or even the cheese factory. He had a strong back and was willing to learn.

"Don't know of anybody hiring, unless you've a mind to work at th' cheese factory," Mr. Pool, the innkeeper at the *Bow and Fiddle*, informed him as his wife served Seth and Thomas shepherd's pies. A heavyset man he was, with a fringe of gray whiskers extending from ear to ear below the jaw, while she was thin as a rail and anxious-looking. There was little activity in the dining room, and as a serving girl tended the other occupied tables, both husband and wife seemed eager to linger.

"But the squire won't allow the boy to come to the factory, even when he ain't in school," Mrs. Pool said. "He says children get in the way."

Seth masked his disappointment with a casual shrug. He would not consider leaving Thomas alone while he worked long hours anywhere. The boy had suffered enough loneliness in his life. But in the three hours since their arrival in Gresham, he had found the tranquillity of the village much to his liking. He had not known so many trees could grow in one place. Their aromas mingled with those of flowers from cottage gardens, lulling strollers with a sense of well-being. He had never known that river water could smell so clean, unlike that of the Thames. Even the odors that wafted in occasionally from the north pasturelands were not unpleasant. How fortunate were the people who lived here!

"You know," the innkeeper went on thoughtfully, "a young fellow like you could make a go of dairying. Th' squire's got a farm available now—he don't like them to sit empty. Got more than enough pasture for a decent-sized herd."

"Thank you, but I've no experience with cows."

"Just as well. It's practically at th' end of the world."

"The end of the world?"

"Well, th' end of Nettle Lane. Same thing. Nearest neighbor is a half mile away, and they ain't too sociable, if you know what I mean."

"A *wife* wouldn't be too happy about being stuck out there away from everybody," Mrs. Pool added with an arched eyebrow that invited him to explain why there was no one accompanying him and the boy.

Seth refused to take the bait, but the description touched something inside him. He found himself wanting to see the farm, if only to assure himself that there were places where one could live without the company of others. "Is it close enough to walk?"

"Maybe for you, but not the boy," the innkeeper said. He was silent for several seconds as his wife leaned close to whisper something in his ear, then nodded and added, "But if you'll agree to stay another night, I can lend you my horse and wagon."

Having to stay two nights in this village wasn't the worse deal he'd ever been offered. Besides, there was still the possibility of a job becoming available if he looked hard enough. "I'd appreciate that," he replied. Less than an hour later he and Thomas stood in front of a two-story stone cottage at the end of a winding dirt road. It was in need of some repairs, as were about half a dozen outbuildings clustered some distance from a drystone wall. Had the landlord not volunteered that the former resident had passed away recently, Seth would have guessed the place to have been uninhabited for a year or so.

The cottage door was unlocked, which struck Seth as odd, for when he and Thomas walked into the front parlor, they discovered it to be furnished, as if the owner were just on holiday. Obviously thieves were not as prolific here as in London. Old but serviceable furniture sat on faded rugs, and a needlework basket still filled with yarn rested beside a rocking chair near the fireplace. In the kitchen, pockmarked copper pans glinted from sunlight slanting through a gap between the curtains.

He had never lived in a cottage or house. Assorted tenements during his childhood became rooms over stables, and then of course there was the cell at Newgate. What must it be like to wake in the morning and draw one's own fire? To sit in the rocking chair at night and read, or perhaps just prop one's feet on the fender and daydream?

"Does it look cozy enough to you?" he asked the boy, catching him staring into one of the three bedrooms upstairs. Thomas turned to him with round eyes.

"Only one bed in a room, sir?"

Seth had to chuckle. *The poor mite's only known rows of beds.* "One person, one bed," he said to the boy. "And your own washstand." He spoke as if he already had signed a lease, and in his heart he had. The place was as welcoming as it was remote. A man could live at peace here.

But how would a man support himself? While Seth had enough money to last for years if he were frugal enough, he had to assume that it would run out, if not in his lifetime, certainly in Thomas's. It hadn't occurred to him until last night that he was responsible for more than just the boy's immediate needs. He had the boy's future to plan for now while he was still alive to do so.

With Thomas again silent at his side, he went around to the back of the cottage and peered over the wall at acres of browning grass spread out like an apron before him. *I could grow crops.* Of course he would have to acquire the skill somehow, but he had watched the gardeners at Lord Hamilton's estate, and their chores hadn't seemed overwhelmingly impossible. And certainly easier to learn than tending cows! Impulsively he picked up the boy and set him on top of the wall. "Well, what do you think?"

"It's so big, sir," he replied with awe in his young voice.

He realized Thomas was referring to the land. "Bigger than any place either of us has ever lived, that's for sure." Something such as farming was the wise thing to do, he thought, whether here in Gresham or anywhere else. Instead of looking for a position, he should invest some of the money and allow it to provide them with an income and a trade. The idea of being his own taskmaster was strange and yet compelling. *Not having to bow to any man* . . .

Seth looked at the boy. "Are you ready to go back to the inn?"

"Yes, sir." After some hesitation, as if he thought he had overstepped his bounds, Thomas added, "If you are, sir."

It pained Seth to see the boy still unable to relax totally in his presence. Shyness he could understand, for he himself sometimes suffered from the same affliction. But he was beginning to worry that it was homesickness for the orphanage that was the cause. If only he had some idea of how Thomas felt about being adopted by him! He wished he had the words to ask, but he couldn't bring himself to broach the subject for fear of what the answer might be.

"Farm that land?" Mr. Pool slapped his thigh that evening at supper. "And what would you grow, Mister Langford?"

Seth could feel his cheeks reddening. The joke that was lost to him had apparently been caught by the three elderly gentlemen at a nearby table, for their faces were creased in smiles. And just in case they hadn't caught on, the innkeeper turned to them and repeated Seth's question.

"What about farming that pastureland at the end of Nettle Lane, gents? Do you reckon there are enough folk in Gresham to eat sixty acres of cabbages?"

"If they does, I'm moving away!" one man with a long gray beard snorted, causing his friends to chortle until they wiped tears from their eyes.

Only the presence of the child prevented Seth from growling his opinion of innkeepers who encouraged people to mock their patrons. But then something unusual struck him. While the four men were enjoying a hearty laugh at his expense, there was no malice involved. With his own tongue he had shown himself to be completely naïve about farming ways. Why shouldn't they laugh?

"I confess I don't understand," he finally admitted in an affable manner. "What did I say that amused you?"

The trio at the table smiled indulgently at him while Mr. Pool leaned his hip against a chair and explained. "Most of Shropshire is what you call rural, see? And rural folk grow their own vegetables. The greengrocer here—Mr. Sway is his name—does a fair amount of trade for those without the land or time. He imports things we can't grow, like Spanish oranges. So if you grew vegetables, you'd likely find yourself without a market."

"What about wheat?" Seth asked, fully aware that he was risking more mockery. *In for a penny, in for a pound*, he thought wryly.

"Too much rain," one of the old men replied around the stem of a clay pipe, causing the others to bob heads in agreement. "Needs drier weather, wheat does."

Seth nodded as well. "Then you're saying that the only thing that land is practical for is raising cows?"

"Raising *cattle*," the landlord answered. His eyes glinted with humor, so Seth realized he had asked another foolish question. But for the life of him, he couldn't fathom what it was. Weren't cows the same thing as cattle?

The bearded elder gent took pity on him. "Only the females is cows, son. Males is bulls."

"I see," Seth gratefully responded.

"He would ha' found out sooner or later," added the man with the pipe.

"Thet's what I were afraid of."

This set off another round of chortles, and this time Seth caught on and smiled sheepishly. As the laughter trailed off, a sudden inspiration hit him. True, this was a dairying village, but he had yet to see a cow pull a wagon or carriage. "What about horses?" he asked.

The third elderly man, who had so far contributed only guffaws to the discussion, rubbed his bristled chin. "Horses come from Wolverhampton."

"Why?"

"Because that's where they're bred and raised, that's why," he shrugged. "No one wants to take up pastureland to raise 'em here, when we've a sure market for milk."

"Besides, the place already has a milking barn," Mr. Pool advised.

"Couldn't it be converted into horse stalls?"

"Well . . . yes," the innkeeper conceded. " 'Course there's the hay barn too. Likely needs a nail or two—the place went to seed when Mrs. Brent got to feeling poorly and had to sell off most of her cattle."

"Mrs. Brent?"

Now all four faces assumed expressions of somber respect. "Woman who lived there was buried Friday past," said the man with the pipe. "Died upstairs in the cottage, she did."

Seth glanced at Thomas, who was listening intently to the conversation. He could remember how his own childhood imagination could torment him in the dark of night. Would the fact that a woman had recently died in that cottage give the boy nightmares?

You're seriously considering this? he asked himself as the four other men moved on to speculating about the likelihood of an early autumn. *What do you know about operating your own business?* But hadn't everyone who operated his own business had to learn as well? *It's not as if you left your brains behind at Newgate.*

He was tempted right then and there to ask directions to the manor house. But then reason prevailed. A man couldn't go through the rest of his life making decisions as impulsively as he had when he adopted Thomas. He didn't regret it, for he was coming to realize he would be terribly lonesome without the boy's quiet company. But what if Thomas had turned out to be a whiny child or a sneaky one, like young Lord Hamilton had once been? There had been that possibility.

The cottage wasn't going anywhere. He would spend some time in thought and prayer over the matter. *And besides . . . we're committed to two nights here anyway.*

Thomas was looking a bit peaked from all the activities of the day, so Seth took him upstairs after their supper was finished. While the boy slept, Seth sat in a chair by the window, where evening light still seeped into the room, and read from a two-year-old issue of *The Cornhill Magazine* he had found in the hall. It was all new to him, so the date didn't matter. Across the room he could hear faint snoring sounds. He finished the magazine, then leaned back his head and listened for a while.

The next morning he and Thomas walked up the main road of the village, Market Lane. At the stone bridge they noticed a group of fair-haired children moving in the shallow water near the riverbank. Seth watched, fascinated, as the older children harvested the tall grasses and passed them on to younger hands on land. The Irish brogue in their young voices was unmistakable, and he supposed they were the children of basket weavers. One girl, who couldn't have been much younger than Thomas, graced them with a smile. The boy lifted his hand for a timid wave. His cheeks were getting flushed from the sun, and Seth realized he should have a cap.

They ambled on back toward the south. When *Trumbles General Merchandise* came into view, Seth asked the boy if he would like some candy.

"Sir?"

"Candy," Seth told him. "You know what it is, don't you?"

"Yes, sir. Mrs. Briggs gives it to us at Christmas."

"Well, it's Christmas now."

Thomas's blue eyes grew wider. "It is?"

"No, of course not. I was just . . ." Seth didn't quite know *what* he was doing, so he gave up and ushered the boy forward. The man behind the counter turned from dusting merchandise-laden shelves with a white cloth. Thinning blond hair framed the top of his round face, and a smile stretched under a drooping walrus mustache.

"Good mornin' to you!" he said, reaching a hand over the counter. "Orville Trumble is my name—welcome to Gresham."

Almost at a loss as to how to respond to such friendliness, Seth stepped up to shake his hand. "Thank you. Seth Langford."

"What can I do for you today?"

"He would like some candy, and he needs a cap as well." Seth couldn't quite form the words *my son*, though that was legally the case.

The shopkeeper seemed not to notice the awkward moment. "The children like sour balls and these new cinnamon candies the best," he told them, nodding to two jars on the counter filled with yellow and white hard candies. "And sweetmeats for them who don't want incarcerated taste buds."

He must mean "incinerated," Seth thought, but the morbid humor did not escape him. *Incarcerated* was what his taste buds had been for ten years.

"Of course we've peppermint sticks as well," Mr. Trumble was saying.

Seth looked at the boy, who seemed to be having trouble making up his mind. "Would you like to try a couple of each?"

"Oh . . . may I, sir?"

"If you don't eat them all at once."

"As to the cap," the shopkeeper said regretfully, "I'm all out of boy's

109

sizes. Should have some by next week, though."

"I don't mind a man's cap, sir," Thomas said with hopeful timidity.

Seth had to smile. "Have you ever owned a cap?"

"No, sir."

Some minutes later, Thomas held the candies wrapped tidy in a square of brown paper, save a sour ball tucked away in his bulging jaw. Only his ears prevented a short-brimmed cap of corded brown cloth from swallowing his face. "Good enough," Seth said and paid Mr. Trumble.

The shopkeeper, like Mr. Pool, seemed inclined to chat, for he leaned upon his counter and said, "You've a polite boy there, Mister Langford."

Seth was aware that he should express his gratitude for the compliment, but how could he take credit for Thomas's manners when he'd had nothing to do with them? "It's good of you to notice," he finally said instead, then touched the boy's shoulder and motioned toward the door. But Mr. Trumble wasn't deterred that easily.

"Thinking about Mrs. Brent's place, are you?"

"How did you—?"

The shopkeeper smiled and tugged on an earlobe. "I can tell you're from the city. You know that telegraph cable they got stretched under the Atlantic now?"

Seth actually didn't know.

"That's nothing over Gresham," Mr. Trumble went on. "Or any other village, I'll warrant. Gossip is just as much a reformation as cricket and horseshoes."

Does he mean "recreation"? Seth wondered.

"She was a sweet old soul, Mrs. Brent. Had Elliott drive her here every Tuesday back when she was able to sit in the wagon. Want to warn you, Mr. Langford. A wife would be powerful lonely out there, if she's used to the city."

"Well, thank you," Seth said, aware that within the shopkeeper's friendly warning was a hope that he would feel prompted to volunteer more information about himself. He supposed that strangers were a novelty here, and so if he were to stay, he would have to guard his privacy zealously. But surely that couldn't be too difficult when one lived at the end of the world.

*O*n Wednesday mornings Octavia Kingston's walks took her to the southern outskirts of Gresham, far past where the cobbled Market Lane had turned into macadamized roadway. Pink knapweed had all but taken over a field that had become her halfway marker. After pausing to admire the hundreds of butterflies drawn to the flowers, she would then turn and retrace her steps to the *Larkspur*.

"Good morning, Mrs. Sykes!" On her way south, she called to a young woman supervising a tot's frolic through a cottage garden. "And how are little Jimmy's ears?"

The young woman, the churchwarden's daughter-in-law, smiled and returned the wave. "Doctor Rhodes recommended drops of warmed cod liver oil. As you can see, they worked quite well."

"Excellent!" Mrs. Kingston called, pushing on. Yesterday she had not seen any sign of her shadower, presumably the squire's boot boy. This caused her great relief, for she had been mightily tempted to approach the old blister after church Sunday and show him the rough side of her tongue about having her followed. One thing alone had prevented her—that it wouldn't be honoring to the Lord's Day to have a row right outside Saint Jude's.

Now she wondered again if she had imagined the whole thing, or if perhaps the Worthy sisters had been mistaken. It wasn't against the law to wander the lanes of one's village, she thought, or *she* certainly would have been arrested by now.

———

Seth rolled over in bed, gathered his pillow up under his neck, and yawned as he became aware that the room was no longer dark. He opened the eye not pressed into his pillow. The curtains were still drawn, but not enough to disguise that the morning had started without him. *Daylight already?*

The night had seemed endless, until the wee hours of the morning when God had given him some peace about the matter. Still Seth had asked for a sign, like Gideon's fleece. *If I'm supposed to stay here, please let the squire agree to sell me the land.* Having lived in places belonging to other people all of his life, he had a longing to own the little piece of paradise on Nettle Lane. To walk across his own threshold, sit at his own table, and not be beholden to any landlord. It seemed the only way he could think of to ensure that Thomas would always have a place to live.

When the cobwebs had sufficiently cleared from his mind, Seth raised his head. Thomas's side of the bed was empty, save the toy horse propped at a restful angle upon his pillow. For a second or two he wondered where the boy had gone, and then sensing a presence, he turned his head to look over at the side of the bed behind him. Thomas stood there watching him. Seth blinked. "How long have you been standing there?"

Anxiety crossed the boy's face, as if he feared he would be scolded. "I don't know, sir."

Assuming a more moderate voice, Seth asked, "What are you doing?"

"I didn't know if you wanted to be awoked."

"Awakened," Seth corrected. One of the few good things that had occurred in Newgate was that he shared a cell for three years with a Professor Thorndike, who had killed a rival in a duel for the hand of a young woman. He was eventually hanged outside the walls of the prison, but not before giving Seth an appreciation for proper grammar. "But yes, I suppose I can't stay in bed all day. Are you hungry?"

"Yes, sir."

"You haven't been at the candy, have you?"

"No, sir."

"Well, the next time I oversleep, I give you permission to clout me on the head."

Horror filled the boy's expression, causing Seth to modify his statement to "give me a good shake." The waifish face still did not lose its stricken look. Seth sighed and realized he had never seen the child smile, even when offered candy yesterday. *Am I that fearsome-looking?*

He dressed hurriedly so that the boy would not faint from hunger. About one third of the tables in the dining room were filled when they sat down to bacon and eggs. Mr. Pool's wife served them, but fortunately she was kept too busy to attempt to needle personal information out of him. Seth was sopping the remainder of his egg yolk with his bread when Mr. Pool paid their table a visit.

"Would you mind directing me to the squire's house?" Seth asked him after politely enduring some idle chat about the likelihood of rain this afternoon.

"So you've decided to stay," the landlord said, using the tail of his

112

apron to wipe a bit of what appeared to be gravy from his chin.

In a polite tone that did not invite questions, Seth replied, "That depends."

Mr. Pool shrugged. "Just watch yourself, I would advise. Th' squire's a sharp one when it comes to negotiating. That's free advice, young man."

"I appreciate it," Seth replied sincerely.

"You just go up Market Lane, see—"

"The squire's just outside." The interruption had come from Mrs. Pool, newly returned to the room. "I seen him walking by."

Raising eyebrows, the innkeeper said, "You saw the squire *walking*?"

"Couldn't ha' been the squire." The bearded older man who had been at supper two days ago occupied a table by himself now. He grinned wickedly when all eyes turned to him. "He don't even walk to his own privy."

"Now, that ain't true and you know it," Mrs. Pool said sharply. "Besides, the manor has lavatories. Everybody knows that."

Seth, who had been attempting to get a word in edgewise since Mrs. Pool first made the announcement, seized upon the fraction of silence to ask, "Do you recall in which direction he was walking?"

"South."

He looked uneasily at the boy, who still had half a plate of food remaining. The idea of negotiating with the squire out in the open was infinitely more appealing than turning up at a manor house with hat in hand. But if he waited for Thomas, there was no hope of catching up with him. "I'm going to leave you for just a little while. Will you play in the courtyard if I'm not back when you've finished?"

The blue eyes became anxious, even as he answered, "Yes, sir."

Seth swallowed his guilty feelings, for he was in a hurry, and turned away. He almost reconsidered and turned back at the front door, but then he thought of the cottage again and hastened his steps.

———

How thoughtful of you to have fashioned such lovely creatures for us to admire, Octavia Kingston prayed silently as she watched butterflies flitting this way and that. Why, it was like a tonic to her soul to see such beauty— and there was something lovely to see on each of her routes, from sunflowers to butterflies to children at play. But she couldn't stand there idling all morning, not with the *Larkspur*'s garden requiring her almost constant attention.

She turned and began to retrace her steps, humming the chorus of "She Wore a Wreath of Roses," a song Mrs. Dearing had been trying to master on the piano. But at the sight of a certain man walking in her direction, the tranquillity that had nestled in her mind all morning evaporated.

"Why, is that you, Mrs. Kingston?" Squire Thurmond Bartley called when within range, waving his hand as if he were Caesar returning home victorious from war.

Mrs. Kingston did not consider herself to be in possession of great intellect, but she could be rather shrewd when it came to judging a person's motives, and she knew that this meeting was not accidental. Still, she stretched her lips into a smile over her clenched teeth and returned his wave—albeit with less vigor. That of course motivated the squire to hasten his pace, and the gap between them rapidly closed. Then she let him have it. "You knew very well I would be here, you old blister! Didn't you?"

He froze, openmouthed. "Why, how could I—?"

"You've had me followed!"

"Followed?" The gray eyes, topped by belligerent tufts of white eyebrows, grew indignant. "That's ludicrous beyond comprehension, Mrs. Kingston!"

"Oh, don't play the innocent with me!" She shook the knob of her walking stick at him. "I've seen him darting amongst the shrubbery, that shoe boy of yours."

"Boot boy," he corrected, just before his eyes widened with horror at the slip. "What I meant to say was—"

"Another falsehood, no doubt! I think it would be fitting of a gentleman to admit when he has been caught, Squire Bartley."

He opened his mouth and then closed it a few times, then hung his head. "I was driven to desperation, Mrs. Kingston. You wouldn't accept my gifts."

"You know why, don't you?"

"Why, no." This time his expression seemed sincere. "I haven't the foggiest. I thought we got along nicely when you toured the manor gardens."

He sounded so much like a wounded child that Mrs. Kingston found herself taking pity upon him. She was just about to admit she actually *had* enjoyed his company that day at the manor and that her recent aloofness had only been because she didn't want to be discarded like an old shoe when he grew bored with her affection, but then she stopped herself. He had pursued her, actually sent his boot boy to spy upon her, because her remoteness had worked. She knew next to nothing about fishing but had gathered from overhearing conversations between Philip and his young friends that when a certain bait proved effective, one continued to use it.

Yet she didn't think it prudent to discourage him totally. So it was with

114

a slight softening of the voice that she admitted, "I will confess the day was tolerable."

"*Tolerable?*"

"Very well, then . . . somewhat pleasant."

"Then why do you act as if I've the plague, Mrs. Kingston?" They had started walking slowly back toward Gresham, with the squire on her left. She switched the walking stick to that side too in case he had some notion of seizing her hand.

I have to give him a reason, she thought. But how could she do so without fabricating, which would be terribly shabby behavior after just having spent several minutes in prayer.

"Is there someone else?" the squire asked.

She slowed her steps and thought about what an obliging man he was for providing her with a solution. "What a question to ask," she replied demurely.

He gave her a sidelong look. "Yes, but you didn't answer it, did you?"

"I didn't answer because it's a silly question." She concentrated on smoothing a wrinkle from her sleeve, all the while thinking that dear Mr. Clay would be proud of her performance. "Do you think it will rain this afternoon?"

"I would appreciate an answer to the question, Mrs. Kingston."

"Very well." She sighed. "Yes, I believe it will rain." From the corner of her eye she could see crimson creeping up from his chin to his bushy eyebrows, which needed pruning shears more desperately than her azaleas.

"So . . . you'll see some other man, but not me. Does *he* send you flowers and cheeses?"

"Well, not exactly . . ."

"Is it that Mr. Ellis? A shifty-eyed Lothario if I ever saw—"

"For your information, Mr. Ellis is married and extremely devoted to his wife."

His shoulders slumped forward. "I . . . beg your pardon. But it isn't at all fair of you, Mrs. Kingston, to allow some other suitor the pleasure of your company while refusing mine. Won't you even allow me to prove to you that I can be quite an agreeable companion?"

Pursing her lips and pretending to think the matter over, she allowed several seconds to pass before conceding, "I suppose I haven't been exactly fair."

"Not fair at all, Mrs. Kingston," he agreed stoutly.

"Very well, then. You may call upon me occasionally."

Finally some life came back into his face. "Indeed?"

"But please bear in mind that I'm a busy woman. What with the gardening and charity work—"

115

"And that other fellow . . ." he interjected, causing Mrs. Kingston to send him a disapproving look.

"Jealousy does not become you, Squire."

"Forgive me—I could not stop myself." A hopeful note crept into his voice. "Will you take my arm, Mrs. Kingston?"

She considered his question and supposed that it wouldn't hurt. *But if he attempts to kiss me, I shall clout him with my stick.* "The road surface *is* rather unstable," she said, surrendering her walking stick to him and resting her left hand upon the inside of his crooked elbow.

"Frightfully unstable," he agreed but smiled as if the instability of the road was a source of great happiness to him. But the smile lasted only a moment. "Oh bother!" he said. "Who is that coming this way?"

"Why, I haven't the faintest." Mrs. Kingston removed her hand from his arm, lest this stranger form the mistaken opinion that she was a woman of dubious morality.

"Sir?" the man addressed them when in range enough not to shout. Tall and muscular-looking, he wore the clothes of a gardener or groomsman, yet seemed too pale to be employed in those capacities. "Squire Bartley?"

"Yes!" her companion snorted. "What is it?"

The man caught up with them and took the cap from his head. "My name is Seth Langford," he said, clearly sensing that his presence was not welcome. With an apologetic look at Mrs. Kingston he said, "Forgive me for disturbing your walk, but I'm interested in the place on Nettle Lane."

"Fine. Come by the manor and my bailiff will draw you up an agreement."

Mr. Langford nodded, but it appeared from his expression that the matter was a bit more complicated. Sure enough, he went on. "I would like to buy the place, Squire Bartley. Would you consider selling it to me?"

"Out of the question," the squire snorted. .

"I can pay with cash."

"You can offer me the Kohinoor diamond and I would not be interested, young man. I do not sell land."

Disappointment filled the stranger's brown eyes, and to Mrs. Kingston he looked like a man who had had more than his share of disappointments. Her heart went out to him. "Why do you insist upon buying, Mr. Langford?" she asked gently.

He gave her a grateful look. "I've never owned a place of my own. And I have to consider the future of my boy."

"How old is your boy?"

"Seven."

By then Mrs. Kingston wanted to tell him he could just keep the land, free and clear, but of course it wasn't hers to give. She rather liked this young man who had the nerve to approach the squire with so brash an offer. She especially admired that while he was obviously quite eager to acquire the cottage and pastures, he did not grovel and scrape to the only person who could grant such a wish.

"Oh, why don't you go ahead and sell him the place," she said to Squire Bartley. "You've more land than you know what to do with, and no one to leave it to but a nephew who hardly ever visits." He had conveyed his disappointment over the sad state of his remaining family to her in the garden the day she had visited the manor. Mrs. Kingston was aware that she was taking unfair advantage by reminding him of such, but it apparently worked, for he didn't look quite so adamant anymore.

"I'm not keen on the idea of the land going to strangers. . . ." he said, a note of unsureness in his voice.

"I'll give you one hundred pounds for it."

The squire's eyes grew sharp again. "Two hundred."

"One twenty-five."

"One fifty. With the agreement that if you ever sell, you must first offer it to me for the same price." His lips tightened. "That doesn't extend to my nephew when I've passed on."

Mr. Langford nodded and reached out his hand. "Agreed, sir. I thank you."

"Then you can show your gratitude by leaving," the squire said testily after they had shook on the agreement. "Again, see my bailiff, and he'll attend to the details."

"Yes, of course. And good day to you." After another grateful glance to Mrs. Kingston, Seth turned and strode quickly out of their morning walk.

"That was very good of you, Squire," she said, taking his arm when he again offered it. "Again, you've proved that you aren't as irascible as people say you are."

He actually blushed. "You seem to bring out the good in me, Octavia. May I address you as such?"

She pretended to think it over. "Very well, Squire."

"Thurmond?"

"Thurmond." But she drew the line at accepting his invitation to supper, figuring that she had allowed their relationship to progress far enough for the moment. When he expressed his acute disappointment, she did take pity upon him and give his arm a pat. "This is too overwhelming to take in all at once, Thurmond. A lady needs time to think over such things."

"Next week, then?"

"Very well," she replied after allowing another hesitation.

It seemed he had been holding his breath, for he expelled a long one. "I'll have cook prepare *Foie de Veau Gratiné.*" He glanced at her. "You do like calf's liver, don't you?"

"I'm terribly fond of it, but I was of the understanding that your digestion forbade such delicacies."

Gallantly he replied, "It doesn't forbid me from watching you enjoy them." He knitted his brow. "Some *Pommes de Terre aux Cèpes* would go nicely with the liver."

"Quite nicely. Potatoes are most nourishing, according to Mr. Durwin."

He eyed her for a second, a faint suspicion in his expression. "Mr. Durwin . . ."

"Is all set to marry Mrs. Hyatt next month, and I'm overjoyed for both of them."

The roadway turned into the cobbled stones of Market Lane. They lapsed into a companionable silence, with Squire Bartley adding items to next week's menu, and Mrs. Kingston wondering if a lace collar would look too "youngish" on a wedding gown for a woman of her advanced years.

———

Thomas's slight form looked swallowed up by the stone bench in the *Bow and Fiddle*'s courtyard. Both narrow shoulders were hunched forward, and his hands clasped together upon his knees. As Seth drew closer, he suspected the boy had been weeping. He hastened his steps.

"Thomas?"

"Yes, sir?" the boy answered in a small voice.

Seth squatted in front of the bench. Sure enough, the blue eyes were rimmed with red. "What is wrong?"

"Nothing, sir," Thomas replied, and then to prove his words, the boy stretched the corners of his mouth.

It was the first time Seth could recall seeing him smile, but this was more of a grimace than an expression of happiness.

Giving a sigh, Seth moved himself to sit beside the boy. Raising a child had seemed so easy from the outside. One just told the child what to do, and hopefully the child obeyed. Of course there were measures that must be taken when the child chose not to obey, but he had never thought those through and certainly didn't anticipate needing them with Thomas. Why, the boy had such a submissive nature that he would probably lie down in the lane and allow a carriage to roll over him if ordered to do so.

"Thomas," he began wearily.

"Yes, sir?"

"Have I ever been less than honest with you?"

The boy blinked. "Sir?"

"Have I lied to you so far?"

"No, sir."

"So why are you lying to me right now?"

Another blink, and the bottom lip began trembling. "I didn't lie, sir."

"You did when you said nothing was wrong." Seth touched the boy's shoulder. "Now, why don't you tell me what made you sit here and cry?"

The trembling intensified in between vain efforts to stretch his lips into another grimacelike smile. Finally the child gave in and broke into sobs. After a minute of wondering what to do, Seth draped an arm around his shoulders and pulled him close.

"There, there now," he said gently. Apparently the cry had been coming on for quite some time now, and he reckoned the best thing to do was to allow the tears to run their course. When the shoulders had stopped heaving and the sniffing lessened, he pulled his handkerchief out of his pocket and raised the boy's head.

"What a mess you've made of yourself," he said, wiping the small pinched face.

"I'm sorry, sir," Thomas mumbled and blew his nose.

"Ah well, I'm sure it did some good. Now, I want to know what's been troubling you." He took a deep breath. "Is it the orphanage?"

The boy was quiet for a spell but then mumbled, "Yes, sir."

Even though Seth had already assumed as much, his heart gave a disappointed lurch. "I can't take you back there, Thomas."

"You can't?"

"No, I can't." Seth wondered if he was imagining the relief that washed over the young face, the tension that seemed to leave the narrow shoulders. "Don't you know that you've been adopted?" he asked cautiously.

"Adopted?"

"Why, yes. Why did you think we've been traipsing all over England together?"

"I don't know, sir."

Seth searched his memory, trying to recall the brief span of time between his being introduced to Thomas and then the boy being hurried upstairs to fetch his belongings. Had anyone actually mentioned the word "adoption"? He supposed that everyone, himself included, had taken for granted that the little fellow understood what was happening. But obviously he hadn't, and the poor lad had lived under a cloud of uncertainty for the past five days. *Forgive me, Elaine*, he thought. *I'll do better.*

"Thomas?"

"Yes, sir?"

"You're never going back to the orphanage. Never." He actually heard the boy swallow. "You believe me, don't you?"

"Yes, sir." Timidly he asked, "Does that mean you're my father?"

Now it was Seth who swallowed. Yes, he had adopted Elaine's child and had begun to care for him more than he would have imagined possible, but he had not yet thought of himself as a father. Even now the whole idea seemed staggering.

However, this boy's need to feel that he belonged to someone was more important than his own misgivings over the title. "Yes. Is that all right with you?"

He could again feel the tension leaving the seven-year-old's shoulders. "Yes, sir."

"Well, good." Seth was ready to move on to other things, because so much emotion had nearly drained him. "Now that that's settled, do you feel up to another walk?" He patted the shirt pocket that held his money. "We've a cottage to buy, Thomas Langford."

Late that same morning Andrew arrived at the Burrell cottage as Mr. Burrell and his two oldest boys were packing their meager belongings in Mr. Jowett's wagon. The thatcher had kindly offered one of his sons to drive the family to Shrewsbury. He had some tools to pick up in the city, so the team of four dray horses he would be bringing by to harness up shortly would have been making the journey anyway—or so he had said. Whether that was exactly the case or not was hard to tell. The people of Gresham had gotten into a habit of seeing about the Burrells in the father's absence. Now it almost seemed they held their collective breaths, hoping the family would really mend this time.

"Why, good day to you, Vicar!" Mr. Burrell called down from the bed of the wagon, where he was presently tying down a chair with Mark's aid. If he seemed a bit surprised it was with good reason, for the good-byes had been said yesterday afternoon. That was when Mr. and Mrs. Burrell had shown up at the vicarage to thank Elizabeth for tending to Molly and David and to announce with radiant faces that they were moving. They'd brought the two youngest of their brood so that they could bid Elizabeth farewell. She had governed her emotions admirably, reading to the two on her lap while Andrew was given the details of Mr. Burrell's new position and of their new little cottage that even had a patch of land for a decent vegetable garden.

It was later that his daughter had sobbed against his shoulder. Even Laurel, who had not been entrusted with their care but had managed to spend a good bit of time with them, had shed a copious amount of tears. And after an evening of having to be strong for his daughters' sakes, he had gone to bed with an ache in his own heart.

"Mrs. Paget sent some sandwiches," Andrew explained, indicating the large brown paper parcel under his arm that would likely sustain the Burrells for the next two days. The man raised himself and mopped his brow with a handkerchief. It was of some comfort to see that besides the honest sweat of carrying and loading, he was still as well-groomed as he had been yesterday. No reek of gin drifted Andrew's way, and after over two decades in the ministry, he had a nose for it.

"How good of her to do so . . . and you to deliver them, Vicar."

"I'll pass along your thanks to her."

Mrs. Burrell came out of the cottage, holding little David. She smiled at Andrew and they exchanged the contents of their arms—her taking Mrs. Paget's parcel and him taking the boy. He went into the cottage and said farewells to the remaining children, accepting another kiss on the cheek from Molly. Yet not this, nor the delivery of the sandwiches, was the primary purpose of his call.

He put David to his toddling feet and helped Mr. Burrell and Mark heft up the biggest piece of shabby furniture, a cupboard. When all that was left were small parcels that the children could manage, Andrew drew Mr. Burrell aside. "I realize you have to get on your way, but would you spare me five minutes alone?"

"You?" The man looked as if that were the most foolish question imaginable. "After all you've done for my family?"

They walked together past a little stand of fir trees behind the cottage. When Andrew was sure they were out of hearing range of the rest of the family, he said, "I couldn't live with myself if I didn't tell you my fears concerning your family." Had he more time, he would not have been so blunt. "I should have mentioned them yesterday evening, but your announcement about leaving took me by surprise."

Mr. Burrell nodded gravely. "You're worried I'll start drinkin' again, ain't you?"

"In a word, yes."

"Can't says I blame you. To tell the truth, Vicar, I can't promise that I won't—no matter how much I hate what it did to my family."

"I don't understand," Andrew said. "Why can't you promise to give it up?"

The man seemed to search his limited vocabulary. "Mr. Green—he's the man I work for down to Shrewsbury—says grand promises like that just tempt us to break 'em." His eyes began to water. "Don't you think

121

I've made those sort of promises in the past, Vicar? No man cares to see his children wantin'.''

His explanation struck a chord with Andrew. He had indeed witnessed many a vow to "turn over a new leaf" from drunks, opium addicts, and the like. Most were made with the purest of intentions, and sadly, most did not last. "So how can you give your family any assurance that this time will be different?"

Mr. Burrell ran his hand through his mop of hair. Andrew had been surprised yesterday to notice that the man's hair was actually a light brown color, but then, that had been the first time he had seen it clean. "I can assure 'em of that *today*, Vicar. Because this mornin' I asked Jesus to give me the strength to stay away from the bottle, but only to give me enough for this day. That ways I know I'll have to ask again tomorrow, and the next day. It's kept Mr. Green sober for thirty years now, Vicar."

It seemed too dangerous a way to approach such a serious problem, and Andrew opened his mouth to argue. But his mind could produce no logical words to refute this philosophy. In fact, he found himself reluctantly agreeing. Did not the Scriptures say, *Give us this day our daily bread?* Then how could it be wrong to ask for daily sobriety?

"Just assure me of one thing, Mr. Burrell," he said finally.

"Yes, Vicar?" There was extraordinary strength in the man's expression.

"If this Mr. Green should ever fail you—and I pray he does not—remember for whom you're doing this. Remember the legacy you'll leave to your children, Mr. Burrell. The memories that will come to their minds when they visit your grave."

Mr. Burrell's eyes watered. "Pray for me, Vicar?" he asked huskily. "For all of us?"

Clasping the man's hand in his own, Andrew replied, "Every day, Mr. Burrell."

*T*he first thing Seth reckoned he needed to do was get a team and wagon. Fortunately, Mr. Pool knew of a cheese factory worker who had both for sale. It just so happened that he and his wife had been servants of the woman who had lived in the cottage on Nettle Lane, and she had left them an aged but sturdy wagon and two black dray horses dubbed Bonny and Soot. The couple apparently decided they had no need for either, preferring instead to have the money. It was the factory worker's wife who struck the bargain with Seth. Her eyes teared when she described Mrs. Brent's goodness to her and her husband—*"She were an angel, she were."*—and those same eyes lit up brightly when Seth counted five pounds into her hand.

Fortunately, he had noticed upon his initial inspection that Mrs. Brent's furnishings still remained in the cottage, but he would need such necessities as candles, lamp oil, matches and such, so with Thomas at his side he drove his new team of horses to *Trumbles.*

The shopkeeper filled his order quickly, then asked, "Won't you be needing some food?"

Seth blinked. "Food?"

Mercifully, the shopkeeper did not chuckle. Spreading his hands upon the counter, he said, "The garden's likely gone to seed. Unless you plan on taking all your meals at the *Bow and Fiddle* . . ."

"What kind of food have you?"

"Tinned and dried. Fresh foods you'll have to get from Mr. Sway or Mr. Shelton or Mr. Johnson. They're the greengrocer, butcher, and baker."

Tinned seemed his only option. He did not know how to cook, or even store, anything fresh. "You have oats for porridge?"

Mr. Trumble nodded toward a barrel next to one of the supporting posts. "Scottish oats, my friend. How many pounds?"

Seth gave him a blank look.

"Let's start you out with ten." The shopkeeper took a folded white cloth sack from a shelf. Then he diplomatically mentioned while scooping up the oats, "Now remember, you'll want to have your kettle boilin' before you put in about four fistfuls of oats. Use a spoon, too, or you'll have a mess on your hands."

"Thank you." Seth bought a dozen tins each of beef, pork, and lamb. Having never prepared a meal in his life, he found modern technology quite amazing! Wherein his ancestors had had to take to the woods with bow and arrow for their meat, he would simply have to take it down from a shelf. "But how does it come out?" he asked, holding up a tin of *Sergeant-at-Arms* beef to inspect it.

Mr. Trumble smiled and produced a hinged metal tool with a device resembling a key attached. "Tin opener—just patented this year. Was a time not too long ago we had to use knives." He held up his hand and wiggled a finger. "Got this here scar from tryin' to open a tin of pears."

After an appropriate sympathetic look, Seth said, "You have tinned pears too?"

———

"Is there anything I can do to help?" Elizabeth asked Mrs. Paget and Dora from the kitchen doorway.

Mrs. Paget looked up from the bowl of apples she was peeling. "Eh, miss?"

"I could help."

After sending a curious glance to Dora, who was rolling out a pie crust, the cook said, "There's naught that we can't handle, miss. But thank you kindly."

Elizabeth walked from room to empty room. In the parlor, Laurel sat draped sideways over a chair with Jane Austen's *Emma*, too absorbed to be drawn into conversation that required more than an absent "uh-huh." *I should have gone with Papa*, Elizabeth thought. There were too many reminders of little Molly and David here. *Animals in Rhyme* still lay on an end table. She wished she had thought to send it with them. She could almost hear Molly's soft little laugh as Papa produced a high-pitched voice when reading the part of Frederick The Fearful Field Mouse.

She realized then that Laurel had spoken to her. "What?" she asked.

Her sister gave her a sympathetic smile. "We can visit them sometime. They haven't moved to Mars, you know."

It won't be the same. But it was *something*, and it had been kind of Laurel to mention it. Forcing enthusiasm into her voice, Elizabeth responded, "Wouldn't that be fun?"

———

The unmistakable sound of guineas being tormented drifted to Mercy's ears as she prepared supper. She hastened to the front, wiping her hands with her apron. Sure enough, Jack was chasing the birds around the yard as if he hadn't been scolded twice this week for doing the very same thing.

"Jack!" Mercy shouted from the doorway. "Stop that!"

He obeyed reluctantly, panting like a piston as he leaned down to rest his hands upon his knees. "I—was—just—running," he said between breaths. The guineas took off in the direction of the barn, making indignant little clucks along the way.

"I'm going to have to tell Papa this time," Mercy said, frowning. It was a threat without teeth, she realized, because unless a matter *directly* inconvenienced their father, he seldom wanted to be bothered with administering discipline.

Jack realized it, too, because when he had caught his breath, he thrust his tongue out at her and began running down the same path the guineas had taken.

"No blackberry cobbler for you tonight if you bother them again!" Mercy called after him. Her threat seemed to work. He turned to give her a cherub smile.

"I weren't gonter chase them."

"Then go find something useful to do."

She was about to go back to her cooking when the rattles and grinding squeaks of a wagon met her ears. She cocked her head to listen and could soon hear dull hoofbeats upon the dirt lane. It was inconceivable that someone should be calling on them, and equally inconceivable that someone would be calling at Mrs. Brent's, so she waited, curious. All she could see was the dust of the lane rising above the hedgerows, but two seconds later Mrs. Brent's wagon and horses came into view beyond the drive. It moved out of sight behind the hedgerows again before Mercy could even discern the two faces on the bench.

They weren't Janet and Elliott. Had they lent the horse and wagon so that someone could move into the cottage? *Surely not this soon,* she thought with a fair amount of bitterness. Was there no respect for the dead? Of course she couldn't expect the cottage to sit empty forever, but she was still used to thinking of it as Mrs. Brent's. Just yesterday she had walked the half mile simply to gaze at it for a little while.

————

It was only after the tins and assorted supplies from *Trumbles* were stacked in a heap on the front parlor floor that Seth realized his mistake. The supper hour was upon them, and he hadn't planned for it. *We should have gotten something at the inn or bakery*, he thought. Thomas was thin enough already—he couldn't afford to miss too many meals—and Seth himself was feeling some hunger pangs. *Small wonder!* he thought. In all of the activity of the day—buying the cottage and supplies—he had forgotten about lunch, and bashful Thomas would starve to death before reminding him. *At least we've food.* He took a tin of beef and the can opener into the kitchen. An apple crate of kindling sat on the stone floor next to the stove, and he stashed a handful in the opening.

"Thomas, I need matches!" he called to the boy whom he had already put to work looking for soap among the supplies. While he waited he went outside the kitchen door to the wood stack and took up a log—surely one log would be enough just to warm the beef. Then he remembered tomorrow morning's porridge and took up another larger one to set inside the door to keep it dry just in case of rain during the night. Thomas caught the door for him on his way inside and handed him the tin of matches when he was ready for them. The boy leaned closer, watching Seth take one out of the box.

"You've never lit a match?" Seth asked him.

"No, sir," he replied. "But I've seen it done."

"Would you like to?" Just as the words left Seth's mouth, he remembered that it had been fire that had robbed the boy of his parents. Perhaps he shouldn't have offered. But Thomas, who likely had no memories of that fateful night, responded with an eager nod. Seth put his big hands over the boy's small ones and showed him how to hold the match and strike it against the side of the box. With Seth still guiding his hand, he lit one of the kindling splinters and then another before having to blow out the match.

The log took longer to catch, and by the time the beef was warm enough to eat—or at least warmer than room temperature—Seth's stomach was sending up rumblings. Thomas, having dispatched their belongings to two bedrooms, had assembled the remaining tins at the end of the table. "Hungry?" Seth asked while spooning beef onto two plates.

"Yes, sir," Thomas replied, pulling out two chairs. The meat was stringy and the gravy clotted with grease, but surely it would be tastier than any meal he had received at Newgate or that the boy had received at the orphanage. Remembering the pears—he had bought two dozen tins because he was particularly fond of them—he opened a tin and dished them up too.

At the table, Seth lowered his head for silent prayer, as was his habit, but raised it again and considered the bowed head across from him. He had heard or read—he couldn't recall which—of fathers who said grace aloud before meals. Now that he actually owned his own cottage, it seemed fitting that he should establish that custom.

"Father, thank you for this food and for our home," he said, wishing he could be more eloquent. "In Christ's name, amen."

When he had tasted a bite of the beef, Seth thought it a good thing that mealtime prayers were said *before* and not after eating, for he would have had a harder time being sincere. The stringy, mushy texture was not as disappointing as the strange aftertaste it left on the palate. *I suppose it just takes some getting used to*, he thought. At least he couldn't complain about the convenience. He certainly didn't have time to learn how to cook with all the patching and repairing that needed doing.

The pears, though also mushy, helped temper the aftertaste of the beef. "Well, what do you think?" he asked Thomas.

"It's very good, sir."

Seth smiled to himself. He imagined that he could serve dirt and earthworms and the boy would not find fault with it. While he heated up some water and washed the few dishes and kettle, Thomas stacked tins in a cupboard. He had to use a chair for a step stool and could only carry two tins at a time. When chores were finished in the kitchen, Seth lit a lamp, as the light coming in from the windows had almost completely faded. They headed upstairs next to arrange bedding in the two rooms across the landing from each other.

"When will you buy more horses?" the boy asked as they tucked the sides of a sheet into the mattress that would be his.

"Not until next summer," Seth replied. "The haying season is past, and the horses would need food over the winter."

"Won't they eat oats?" he asked almost apologetically.

"Oats are good for them now and then, but too rich for every day. Besides, we'll need the time to make repairs."

"I can help you?"

Seth smiled while slipping a pillowcase over the pillow. "I'm counting on it." The bed finished, he looked around. "Will you be afraid in here by yourself?" He was surprised when the boy, who had yet to complain, gave a hesitant nod.

"I've never slept in a room by myself, sir."

"Would it help if we kept both doors open?"

"Oh yes, sir," he replied, but with uncertainty in his eyes.

"Of course, I'll be sitting up with you for a while," Seth added, as if he had simply forgotten to mention that part of the plan.

Relief eased across the boy's face. "You will, sir?"

Later, when Thomas had washed up, cleaned his teeth, and changed into the nightshirt purchased in Shrewsbury along with some other new clothing, Seth brought the chair from the room that was to be his and placed it near the bedside. The air drifting in through the window was pleasant but would likely become chilly before morning, so he tucked the sheet and quilt about the boy's shoulders. He sat in the chair, leaving the lamp burning on the bedside table. The boy looked so small in the big bed that Seth found himself saying impulsively, "Would you like me to listen to your prayers?"

"My prayers?"

"Yes." In whatever way he'd discovered that good families prayed over meals, he'd also learned that good parents listened to children's prayers at bedside. Though he still had difficulty thinking of himself as a father, that did not excuse him from the duties of one. "Didn't you say prayers at the orphanage?"

"Oh yes, sir. We recited the Lord's Prayer before meals, and the Twenty-third Psalm at bedtime."

"Well, you could do that now if you like. Or you could just pray."

"Like you did at supper?"

"Yes. But you might want to leave out the part about the food, since that was already mentioned."

"What should I say then?"

Seth thought for a minute. "You could thank God for our house, and ask Him to watch over us during the night."

"Yes, sir." He closed his eyes and pushed his fingertips together under his chin. "Thank you, God, for this house. Please watch over me and . . ." There was a long pause while the muscles of the boy's face worked. He finally finished with, ". . . Mister Langford. Amen."

The formality didn't offend Seth. How could it, when the notion of being a father still seemed to fit him like an ill-cut suit of clothes? He couldn't help but wonder what the village people would think if they had overheard Thomas's prayer. They both had a fresh new start here in Gresham, and even though they had settled down in a secluded spot, they could not totally isolate themselves. For one thing, he should send Thomas to school. And he could imagine what the other children would say if they learned he had been raised in an orphanage and now lived with a former convict.

"Thomas?"

"Yes, sir?" Thomas turned on his side to watch him.

"I think it best if we not tell people that you're from The Whitechapel Home."

"Yes, sir" was the predictable reply, though again with uncertainty in the young voice.

Seth wished he could explain, but how could he expect a child to understand that some might assume he'd been in an orphanage because he

was ill born? "There is nothing to be ashamed of being raised in an orphanage," he reassured the boy. "But I don't want to encourage people
to ask too many questions. If anyone asks about our pasts, we'll simply tell
them that we lived in London." Which was the truth, of course, though
they hadn't lived there together.

"Yes, sir."

He felt compelled to go on to a more difficult subject. "And if you're
asked why you haven't a mother, do you know what you should say?"

Thomas shook his head upon the pillow.

Swallowing around the lump that had suddenly risen in his throat, Seth
said, "You should say the truth—that she passed away."

"Passed away?"

"That means she died, Thomas. They told you that in the orphanage,
didn't they?"

"Yes, sir," he murmured. "My father too."

"Yes. He was a brave man and saved your life." He meant those words.
The anger he had felt upon first hearing that another man had married
Elaine was gone, for how could he blame anyone for loving her? "But now
I'm your father, Thomas. So if you tell people that your father died, they'll
be confused and start asking questions."

"We don't want people to ask questions?"

Seth blew out his cheeks. *Forgive me, Elaine, but I just want to protect
him.* "We don't, Thomas, or rather we don't want them asking questions
about how we came to be here together. When you're a bit older, I'll explain it all to you."

———

"I think it's rude, moving into a house so soon after someone has
died," Mercy said the next morning to Violet, one of Mrs. Brent's cows.

The cattle were in the pasture, the morning milking having been finished, and Mercy wanted to escape the heat of the kitchen for a little while.
Violet's gentle brown eyes looked understandingly into hers for a few seconds, then the cow bent her head to pull up another mouthful of grass.
Mercy sighed. The most sympathetic pair of ears on the whole farm happened to be bovine. Getting to her feet again, she brushed loose grass from
her skirt and started back for the house.

Even though breakfast had only been finished two hours ago, it was
time to begin preparations for lunch. Potato-and-leek soup, she decided,
with sausages. She went to the pantry and opened the crock in which she
stored dried apples from the six trees flanking Ward Creek, which ran behind their pasture and caught up with the Bryce to the east. *I should really
use these up before the new ones are ripe*, she thought. *It would be nice to*

have cake after lunch. Mrs. Brent had loved her apple cake, declaring it the best she had ever tasted.

She thought of the new neighbors again and could almost hear Mrs. Brent saying, *It's not being disloyal to make them feel welcome, dear.* Actually, there were more than enough apples for two cakes. And as long as she had to heat the oven anyway . . . *I'll bake them one,* she thought grudgingly. Whoever *they* were. It was the least she could do as a Christian. But she would have one of her brothers deliver it, as she wasn't up to seeing someone else answer Mrs. Brent's door just yet.

"Would you take this to the new family down the lane?" she asked Fernie later, indicating the basket in her hands as her father and brothers left the lunch table.

"Aw . . ." Fernie whined. "It's too far."

"It's not. I used to walk there all the time. But take the wagon if you don't feel up to walking." She caught Oram by the arm as he attempted to pass. "You'll need to go and hold it for him. It'll be dashed to crumbs in the wagon bed."

"I don't want to," Oram protested, shrugging his arm away. "I was gonter ask Papa if we could go bathing in the creek."

Fernie's mouth was opened to protest too, but then comprehension filled his green eyes. "Dashed to crumbs? You mean there's another cake in there?"

"You had three slices at lunch. This one's for the new family."

"Why do you have to give away a whole . . ." Oram began, but Fernie silenced him with a punch to the arm.

"Stop yer blubberin' and let's get the wagon hitched. Like Mercy said, it won't take long."

Oram looked at his brother as if he'd lost his mind, but then some silent communication seemed to pass between them, and he nodded. It was the little lift to the corner of his mouth that made Mercy suspicious.

"Never mind," she said, pulling the basket away from Fernie's outstretched arms. "I'll take it over there myself."

"We weren't gonter eat it!" Oram said in a panicked voice. "Was we, Fernie?"

"Shut up!" his brother whispered through clenched teeth, then he smiled at Mercy, as if to say, *Isn't he just the silliest fellow?* Patting his stomach, he said, "I had so much after lunch I couldn't eat another bite. That's a nice thing to do, sendin' a treat to the neighbors."

The pleasantness of his voice was even more suspicious than Oram's little smile had been. "Just go away," she told them. She took off her apron and, taking no chances, brought the basket upstairs with her while she brushed her hair.

130

She could hear the sounds of hammering long before the Brent cottage was in sight. At least it seemed that whoever had moved there was taking some initiative about making repairs. She could tell as she opened the gate that the sounds were coming from the milking barn. But the woman of the house would likely be inside, so she went to the front door and knocked. When there was no answer, she waited a few more seconds and knocked again, just in case whoever was inside had been upstairs. Again, no answer.

I'll just leave it on the table, she thought, reaching for the doorknob. She could send one of her brothers for the basket in a few days, and she certainly wasn't going to go trudging out to the barnyard. Movement attracted her attention at the corner of her eye. Mercy turned her head to see a small boy had rounded the corner of the cottage and was walking toward her. He was so slight that he almost looked fragile, and he wore a brown cap too big for his head.

"Hello, miss," he said softly.

"Oh, hello." Embarrassed that her hand was on the knob, Mercy allowed it to drop to her side. "I was just going to leave this inside. It's an apple cake."

He gave a timid smile. "Thank you, miss. Would you like to speak to my father?"

Mercy noticed a curious hesitation before the words "my father." She glanced in the direction of the milking barn. "Why, no thank you. Isn't your mother inside?"

"My mother passed away."

"Oh!" Guilt came over her, replacing her earlier bitterness toward these people twofold. "I'm so sorry."

"Thank you." While his little face was somber, he didn't look stricken, as if the death had occurred recently. "Would you want to put that inside?"

Mercy glanced down at the basket in her hand. "All right. Then I could take my basket back home and not trouble you about it later."

He opened the door and then led her through the front parlor to the kitchen, as if she hadn't been in the cottage a hundred times already. She took the cake out of the basket and put it in the pie safe. "There's no hurry for the plate," she told the boy. "What is your name?"

"Thomas," he replied, returning her smile.

"I'm Mercy Sanders." She reached out to shake his hand. "I live in the next house." She started to mention that she had brothers he might like to play with sometime but sadly realized that this boy could not hold his own against even her youngest brothers' aggressive natures. "Have you brothers or sisters?"

"No, miss."

"Oh. Well, I'll be going now."

He thanked her again, and she marveled that someone his age could be so polite. On her way out of the kitchen she happened to glance at one of the cupboards. Two open shelves were filled with rows of tinned goods. *No wonder he's so thin*, she thought, wishing she'd brought something more nourishing than cake.

"Have you seen the apple trees in your back pasture?" she asked as they both walked toward the front door.

"No, miss," he said with an automatic glance in that direction, as if he could see through the cottage walls.

"They grow along Ward Creek. We have some too. Someone planted them years and years ago. They'll be ripe in another eight weeks or so." She restrained herself from glancing again at his thin arms. "They're very nourishing, you know."

"Thank you, miss. I like apples."

Now she had to restrain herself from patting him on the head, for she found his pleasant manner refreshing. But knowing that would only embarrass him, she just smiled and bade him good-day. On her way home she could still hear the ringing of a hammer against nails. It seemed a rather melancholy sound now.

"Did you hear about the new people on Nettle Lane?" Iris Worthy asked Julia that same afternoon. The lace spinners had beckoned to her and Grace on their way back from *Trumbles*. Actually, Julia had heard about this Mr. Langford and son from the shopkeeper but knew that would not make a bit of difference to the Worthy sisters. So she smiled benignly and waited, and sure enough Jewel jumped into the pause.

"Mr. Langford is his name, and he's got a boy," she said. "Real closemouthed about himself and as white as a haunt. We seen 'em both wandering about the lanes the day before yesterday."

Julia turned to Grace and handed her the small package in her hand. "Why don't you bring this cinnamon to Mrs. Herrick?"

"Yes, Mother," her daughter replied. "What's a haunt?"

"A ghost," Julia replied with a meaningful glance at Jewel. "And we know there is no such thing, don't we?"

"Yes, ma'am." As Grace crossed the lane toward the carriage drive, Julia could hear the girl repeating "white as a haunt" over and over to herself. She turned back to the sisters.

"There is no law against walking the lanes, you know," she said gently, for Iris and Jewel had been good to her and meant well in spite of the outrageous things that sometimes came out of their mouths.

"Oh, we know that, but Mrs. Pool says she wonders if the man's been in prison," Iris said in a hushed tone after glancing about her. "That would account for the paleness."

Julia sighed to herself and tried to be patient. "Mrs. Pool shouldn't spread rumors like that. The man could have been ill."

"I'm wondering if that has anything to do wi' his not having a wife," Jewel said in an equally hushed tone.

"His being pale?"

She nodded, her eyes wide, though her fingers never stopped spinning. "He could ha' murdered her and got sent to prison for it."

"You don't actually believe that, do you?"

Even Iris obviously thought her sister-in-law had gone too far. "Yes, Jewel. Besides, they hang people for murdering their wives. It would more likely be for stealing. Didn't Mrs. Pool say he had lots of money?"

Julia had heard enough. With great affection, but just as much firmness, she said, "He's likely someone who needs a fresh start, just as my family did when we settled here last year. If we all gossip about him, he's not likely to have that opportunity, is he?"

The sisters were sufficiently chagrined enough to bob their heads in agreement, but Julia knew as she crossed the lane to the *Larkspur* that the gossip would continue. From what she had heard, this Mr. Langford had moved to a remote farm at the end of Nettle Lane, so perhaps he would not be too affected by it. It was his son who could suffer, though, if he enrolled at the school. She would have to urge Grace and Aleda to be especially kind to him.

She slowed her steps halfway across the courtyard. *The man in the cheese wagon and the Lion Hotel.* He had been unusually pale and had a boy with him too. She had failed to connect the faces with Mr. Trumble's account of newcomers to Gresham, but of course they were most likely the same people. Which meant very little to her, because where anyone chose to settle was none of her business.

The courtyard door opened, and Georgette stuck her bespectacled face out. "Oh, missus. Miss Phelps is in the hall to see you."

"Thank you, Georgette," Julia replied. "Would you see if Mrs. Herrick has some lemonade to bring to my room in a little while? Tea will be fine if she hasn't."

"Yer room, missus?" the maid asked, holding the door open for her.

"Please." Andrew had told her this morning that Elizabeth had been gloomy ever since the Burrell children left, so she was not surprised at this visit. She had entertained the notion of calling upon the girl herself but could ill afford to pop over to the vicarage too often, even if Andrew was not home. As was demonstrated by the Worthy sisters only minutes ago, the villagers loved to talk and weren't always accurate with the details. Propriety was a rigid master, but one that must be obeyed if one wanted to keep a sterling reputation.

She knew having a serious conversation in the hall would prove to be impossible, for Mrs. Kingston liked to pop in from her garden whenever company arrived, and usually one or two other lodgers would be in there reading or busy with needlework. *Or practicing the piano*, she thought as her ears picked up the halting notes of "Beautiful Dreamer."

She found Elizabeth standing at Mrs. Dearing's shoulder at the piano. The girl looked deceptively cheerful in a sunny yellow gown and ribboned silk cap from which ringlets of her blond hair flowed in back. But as they traded greetings, Julia could clearly see loss in the brown depths of Elizabeth's eyes.

Sure enough, Mrs. Kingston had come inside and sat in the sofa across from the one where Mrs. Hyatt and Mr. Durwin were seated. It would have been rude not to chat for a while. Julia knew that Elizabeth, being a vicar's daughter, understood this, so when Mrs. Dearing finished her song, she and the girl took places on either side of Mrs. Kingston while Mrs. Dearing sat next to Mrs. Hyatt.

The chatter ranged from Mr. Durwin's and Mrs. Hyatt's family members who would be filling the *Bow and Fiddle* next month for their wedding, to Mrs. Dearing's piano lessons, and then to Mrs. Kingston's account of a garden she had seen once in Bath that contained a large goldfish pond surrounded by calliopsis the same color as the fish. Thankfully the newcomers to Gresham were not mentioned, and when Julia deemed enough time had passed, she excused Elizabeth and herself and they walked up the corridor to her room.

"Here, you take the chair," Julia told the girl, then pulled out the bench from her dressing table for herself. Georgette, who must have waited outside the hall to see when they left, arrived at that moment with tumblers of lemonade.

"Thank you for seeing me privately," Elizabeth said when the maid had left. "It's so good having an older woman to confide in." A hand went up to her chest. "I don't mean that you're *old*. . . ."

Julia laughed. "I know what you meant, and I'm flattered that you want to confide in me."

Giving her an appreciative smile, the girl continued, "Grandmother was always too busy to listen to us. I'm going to love having a mother again."

"Truly? You don't mind?" It was a question Julia had never gathered up the nerve to ask, though Andrew had assured her many times that his daughters were happy about the upcoming nuptials.

"Oh, I think it's wonderful. Laurel too."

"That's most reassuring to me, Elizabeth." Julia allowed a moment's silence while they both sipped from their lemonades, then said, "Now tell me how you're faring."

Pain washed across the girl's face. "Did Papa tell you about Molly and David?"

"He did. You must miss them terribly."

"Oh, well." She looked away for a second. "We want what's best for the family, don't we?"

"Yes, of course. But I hate seeing you hurt."

"I'm getting used to it, I think. It seems that every time I love someone, this happens."

"I'm sorry." Julia felt so inadequate, attempting to give advice to a practically grown young woman. "But think of the people you love who are still in your life."

"I know," the girl sighed apologetically. "I have a tendency toward theatrics, if you haven't noticed."

"I think you're just perfect."

A faint smile caused Elizabeth's dimples to appear. "You always know just the right thing to say, don't you?"

"Goodness, if you only knew," Julia responded, waving a hand. "I suffer through self-doubts often."

"That's disappointing. You mean I won't know all the answers when I'm older?"

"I'm afraid not, dear. But you'll have experience and maturity to help you. Thankfully, when we allow God to lead, He keeps us from making too many blunders." Returning to the girl's immediate situation, she said, "Perhaps you should find something with which to keep yourself busy so you won't miss the children so much. This is just a suggestion, but there is a teacher's college in Shrewsbury, and you're so good with children. Would becoming a schoolmistress interest you?"

Elizabeth gave an adamant shake of her head. "I know it disappoints Papa that I have no interest in continuing my schooling. I've never been an enthusiastic scholar. It was only to make Papa proud of me that I did so well at Brunswick. I've wanted to be a wife and mother ever since I held my first doll."

"I don't believe your father would ever be disappointed at your becoming a wife and mother, Elizabeth. I think he just wants you to be positively certain that's what you want before you take any irrevocable steps."

"Meaning marrying Paul."

"Marrying anyone, Elizabeth, just for the sake of being married."

"Is that what he thinks?"

Julia sighed inwardly and thought it was a shame that so much confusion was almost invariably tied up with romance. "You keep asking me what your father thinks. You live under the same roof, Elizabeth. Have you asked him?"

"We had a discussion the night you came for supper with the Clays. He says he approves of Paul."

"Then what is wrong, Elizabeth?" Setting her empty tumbler on the scarf of her dressing table, Julia asked, "Is it that he approves of Mr. Treves that's troubling you?"

"What do you mean?"

"Well, when you thought your father *didn't* approve, that was a barrier between you and any future plans of marriage with Mr. Treves. Now that it's been lifted, I wonder if that frightens you a little."

Elizabeth blinked. "Why would that frighten me?"

"Because the only barrier left would be one in your own mind."

"There is no barrier. Paul will make a wonderful husband."

"I'm sure he will," Julia said. "But tell me about the present, Elizabeth. Is he a friend?"

"I don't understand. Are you asking if I love him?"

"No. I'm asking if you and Mr. Treves have the foundation for a true and lasting love—which is friendship. Is he your best friend, Elizabeth?"

"Of course," Elizabeth replied at once, but after a long silence, she lowered her chin to stare at her hands. "I don't know. Sometimes . . ."

Julia allowed her to collect her thoughts for several seconds, then persisted gently, "Sometimes what, Elizabeth?"

"Well, I'm proud of him for giving his life to God, but he can have such hard opinions of people. I wonder sometimes if he thinks I'm frivolous because I occasionally like to talk about things other than the Bible."

"Have you mentioned this to him?"

"Not exactly." She shrugged. "I'm probably just being oversensitive."

"I don't think you're too sensitive, Elizabeth," Julia told her. "But don't you see? If you and Mr. Treves were friends, you would be able to discuss those concerns freely with him—just as you could with a girlfriend. Haven't you ever had a friend you could confide in without having to worry about her forming a lesser opinion of you?"

Again a small silence, and then Elizabeth nodded. "They're all married now, Mrs. Hollis. But I feel that I can tell you anything. You don't mind that I consider you a friend as well as a future stepmother, do you?"

Julia smiled and appreciated Andrew all the more for having such nice daughters. "Mind? Why, you've given me a compliment I will treasure always, and I'll pray that if marriage to Mr. Treves is God's will for you, He will show it to you clearly."

"Thank you, Mrs. Hollis." She rose from her seat and embraced Julia, promising to think over the things they had discussed. As they walked up the corridor, Julia spotted Aleda through the open doorway of the library. Her daughter sat sideways in a chair with her head resting on one arm and her knees draped over the other, a book held out in front of her. Minutes later, when Elizabeth had left, Julia returned to the library and stood in the doorway and watched her read.

Thank God she's still got some years to go before we have to start thinking about marriage. But then she wondered if perhaps the time to instill in a girl what qualities to look for in a mate should be *before* the first flutterings of romance affected her judgment. Julia also wondered if she would have chosen her first husband differently had she any idea of the gravity of committing to marriage. At seventeen she had barely known enough about herself, much less another person. What if her own mother had better prepared her for the second most important decision a woman can make?

There was a rustle of the turning of a page, then as if sensing her presence, Aleda turned her head. "Mother? What are you doing?"

"Just watching you." Julia stepped into the room. "What is that you're reading?"

The girl held up the cover for her to see. "*Little Women*. Helen's aunt sent it from Boston for her birthday."

"Is it good?" Julia asked, sitting in a nearby chair.

"It's wonderful." Aleda turned herself around to sit properly, holding her place in the book with her hand. "But I'm afraid Beth is going to die. Helen wouldn't tell me, and I'm trying not to peek ahead. I hope she doesn't."

"I hope so, too, dear."

"Did I hear Elizabeth a little while ago?"

Glancing automatically at the door, Julia replied, "She just left."

"She must have wanted to talk about Mr. Treves. I hope you told her not to marry him."

"Aleda . . ."

"Well, Laurel says he's too stuffy. And I've never seen him laugh even once."

Julia couldn't help but smile. "So you and Laurel have him all figured out?"

"Well, I don't think someone who likes to laugh should marry someone who doesn't," she said earnestly. "Do you?"

"No, I don't. But that's a decision Elizabeth will have to make. And since she sought my advice privately, it would hurt her if she knew we were discussing the situation. So please keep this to yourself."

"I will, Mother."

Changing the subject abruptly, Julia said, "Would you like to take a walk?"

Aleda shifted in her chair. "Just you and me?"

"If you don't mind leaving your story for a little while."

Obeying, the girl marked her place with a square of paper and closed the book. She eyed Julia cautiously as she got to her feet. "Am I in trouble?"

Julia laughed. "Of course not. It's just I want to spend some time with you before I wake up one morning to find you all grown up."

*F*ridays were when Mercy made her weekly shopping trip for supplies. The arguing among her brothers over who would drive the wagon usually began on Thursday afternoons, if not earlier, for opportunities to escape the morning chores were highly coveted. This morning it was Dale, second to the oldest, who had won the privilege. He had just reined Dan and Bob to turn left onto the northern part of Market Lane when Mercy spotted Mrs. Kingston coming up the lane in their direction, walking stick in hand.

"Please stop, Dale," she said, putting a hand upon his arm. She hopped down from the wagon seat. "Good morning, Mrs. Kingston."

"And good morning to you!" Mrs. Kingston returned, smiling. She wore a calico dress with tiny rosebuds that became her, and her cheeks seemed to have a glow that Mercy hadn't noticed last Tuesday. "Shopping day, is it?"

"Yes, ma'am," Mercy replied. "May we offer you a ride?"

"Oh, no thank you, dear." The elderly woman sent a wave up to Dale, who responded with an unenthusiastic lift of the hand. "I'm out for my usual stroll."

"I've never seen you walk this far north."

"Yes, well . . ." Mrs. Kingston glanced over her shoulder. "Circumstances forced me to plan a completely different route and leave an hour earlier."

Mercy had no idea how to respond. Was this good news or bad? She decided upon a safe, noncommittal, "I see."

"It's such a bother! I despise having to hurry through breakfast, and I'm used to varying my routine, you see. One doesn't get bored that way. But there are only so many roads in Gresham, so I imagine I shall be taking this route every day until I get caught."

"Caught?" Mercy asked, dazed.

"*Discovered* would be a more appropriate word, I suppose."

Mercy glanced up at her brother and noted with satisfaction that he had decided to take advantage of this idle time to loop the reins over the back of the seat and curl up for a nap. Still, she lowered her voice. "Mrs. Kingston—are you in need of help? My father and brothers—"

"Oh my . . . no, dear." Mrs. Kingston also sent a glance up to the wagon seat before leaning closer. "There is a certain gentleman who has joined me on my walks for the past two days now. I wish to convey the message that I'm not so predictable, nor my company so available."

"Why don't you just ask him to leave you alone?"

"Actually I took that very action at first, which is why he finds himself so intrigued with me now. I believe you young girls call it 'playing hard to get.'"

Mercy covered a smile with her hand. She had never heard any woman talk this way. "You mean you're doing this because you *like* him?"

"Oh, very much," Mrs. Kingston answered with a chuckle. "And you know? It's rather fun!"

Warmly they bade each other good-day, and the woman resumed her walk. Mercy climbed back into the wagon and woke her brother. Minutes later they were forced to creep along a herd of cattle being led to the Bryce by a boy. "Why are you doing that?" Dale asked beside her.

"Doing what?"

"Grinning. You look like a dimwit, sitting there grinnin' for no reason."

Mercy had not even been aware that she had been doing so. She turned to him and smiled again. "I enjoyed talking with Mrs. Kingston."

"That old woman?" He snorted.

He could not ruin her day, and she even felt sorry for him. How sad it must be to go through life refusing God's gifts because of scorn for the packaging. "I'll be back," he told her as he pulled the reins to a stop outside of *Trumbles*.

"Papa said not to take too long," she reminded him.

Already on the ground, he set off across the lane for the *Bow and Fiddle*. Mercy realized now why Dale had gone to the trouble of combing his hair. According to Harold, he was smitten with Mary Sloane, the serving girl Mercy knew from the Wesleyan Chapel, and took every opportunity he could to sit at the establishment over a pint of ale. Unfortunately for Dale, his mouth was his most unattractive feature whenever he was in his cups, and the girl sensibly ignored him.

"Have you met your new neighbor?" Mr. Trumble asked as he assembled Mercy's order.

"Only his son. His name is Thomas." Mercy ran her hand over a bolt of raspberry sateen on a table stacked with new bolts of cloth and fought the urge to buy a length. She had two dress-up gowns for church and couldn't justify the extravagance just because a pretty color caught her eye. Besides, Jack and Edgar should have new shirts for school, and she needed to start sewing on those.

"Just came in yesterday," the shopkeeper said. "You would look awful pretty in that sateen, Miss Sanders."

Mercy smiled at him. However he had felt about her in the past, she knew he wasn't flirting, because he was that friendly with everyone. "Just five yards of this, please," she replied, bringing a bolt of serviceable blue cotton to the counter. "And a spool of thread."

"Right away," he smiled, picking up his shears. "He has only that one child, you know."

Mercy stared for a second before realizing he was referring to her new neighbor. "Yes?"

"Polite little fellow," the shopkeeper went on. "Mr. Langford, too, for that matter. But kind of recursive, if you ask me. I suppose that's why he bought that place."

"Recursive?" Mercy blinked.

"You know . . . don't have much to do with other people."

"I see."

The bell over the door jingled. Mr. Sykes, the churchwarden of Saint Jude's, walked inside. He tipped his hat to Mercy and she flushed, recalling how her father had chased away him and the rest of the school board less than two weeks ago.

"I'll have my brother collect the packages," she murmured to Mr. Trumble. But before she could walk to the door, Mr. Sykes stepped up to her.

"Fine decision your father made, changing his mind like that. Please thank him on behalf of the board."

Knowing full well why the board didn't deliver the thanks in person, Mercy managed a smile. "I'll tell him."

"You know that new fellow, Mr. Langford, has a young boy too," Mr. Trumble offered from behind his counter. "You might want to see what his plans are as far as schooling."

Mr. Sykes nodded. "I just spoke with the vicar out in front of the *Larkspur*. He says he was already planning to pay a visit out there this morning and would mention the school."

After bidding the men in the shop good-morning, Mercy ended up having to cross the lane to the *Bow and Fiddle* to fetch Dale. He was well into his second pint in spite of the early hour and shrugged off her attempt to get him to leave.

"Go 'way!" he mumbled while grinning and trying to catch the eye of Mary, who obviously was taking great pains *not* to look in his direction.

Mercy thought that she could not possibly have looked more dim-witted earlier than her brother did now.

"Papa's going to want us back," Mercy leaned down to whisper, for she was highly embarrassed. He waved her away.

"I'll be there directly."

She straightened and gave a helpless look to Mr. Pool, who sent one back to her. Unfortunately none of the villagers cared to risk the ire of the Sanders men. While they bickered among themselves like blue jays, any outsider who dared come against one of them quickly found himself facing a unified front.

It was either stand there in mortification or go back to the wagon. Mercy chose the latter. She sat on the bench with her back rigid and shoulders squared because of the curious looks sent her way from the occasional passerby. Had she yielded to her inner inclination, she would have curled up in a ball in the back. *It's so unfair!* she thought, vexed that she had to wear the reputations of her family like a garment. She had no doubt that if she were to achieve world fame by writing beautiful songs or better yet, discovering cures for every disease, people in Gresham would still remember her as "one of those awful Sanderses."

She felt a tear trickle down the right side of her nose and wiped it with the back of her hand. *Please forgive me, Lord,* she prayed silently. *You're so good to me, and I spend so much time feeling sorry for myself.*

"Miss Sanders?"

Mercy turned to see Vicar Phelps standing at the side of the wagon. Not being a member of Saint Jude's, she had never spoken with him except to return his greetings on the few times she had crossed his path in town.

"Good morning, Vicar Phelps," she managed and was mortified to feel another tear trickle down the same side of her nose. She ignored it and hoped he didn't notice from where he stood on the ground.

"Forgive me for disturbing you, but are you all right, Miss Sanders?"

The kindness in his voice caused another tear to form, this time in her left eye. Mercy blinked both eyes and angled her face away from him. "Yes, sir—thank you." From the corner of her eye she could see him glance over his shoulder in the direction of the *Bow and Fiddle. Of course he knows,* she told herself, for how many other times had Dale or Harold replayed this little drama? She wished she had the nerve to risk Papa's anger by taking up the reins and driving the wagon home herself. It didn't seem difficult, and the horses knew the way. . . .

The kind voice cut into her thoughts again. "You know, Miss Sanders, I happen to be on my way out to Nettle Lane to pay a call on the new family. I'll pass right by your cottage. May I offer you a ride?" He didn't mention her brother, acting as if she were merely sitting there because the horses refused to budge. Such kindness would have moved her to more tears had she not willed herself to keep them from forming.

"Thank you, sir," she replied, still not quite looking at him. "But I have supplies inside *Trumbles*."

"Would they fit in the boot of my trap?"

She opened her mouth for another polite refusal but then told herself, *It's better than sitting here in the middle of town, and you have work to do.* Turning her face and this time making herself meet the vicar's eyes, she said, "I would be grateful, sir."

With Mr. Trumble's assistance, Vicar Phelps soon had her supplies in the trap. The sacks of oats and flour were too heavy for the vicar's lone horse, so they heaved them into the bed of the wagon for Dale to bring home. As the trap moved over the cobbled stones of Market Lane, the vicar did not attempt to engage her in small talk. Mercy was relieved at this, for what could she possibly have to say that would interest someone as esteemed in Gresham as Vicar Phelps?

Mercy could see most of her brothers at their chores when the vicar's trap finally halted in the drive. Or rather, they *had* been at their chores, for now they stared curiously in Mercy's direction. Oram, however, stopped staring and started running toward the barn. *Papa*, she thought. *And he won't be happy that I left Dale.* The worst thing about her father's anger was that it almost always spilled out onto whoever else happened to be in the vicinity. Vicar Phelps was winding the reins around the whip socket—she turned to him before he could hop down.

"Please, sir, may we leave the packages here?"

He gave her a questioning look. "On the ground?"

"Yes, sir. My brothers will carry them inside." She glanced at the barn again. "Please?"

"Of course," he nodded, as if she had made a perfectly rational request. He got to the ground and hurried around to help her alight, then started stacking her packages on the ground, waving away her efforts to assist.

She thanked him after he had set down the last package, a five-pound sack of sugar. "You'd best leave now."

He climbed into his trap, but instead of leaving, he held the reins and directed a fatherly smile at her. Or rather, what Mercy would *imagine* a fatherly smile to be, for she couldn't recall ever receiving one from her own father.

"God sees our good deeds, Miss Sanders, and sometimes other people do as well."

"Sir?"

"Your pastor has told me how kind you were to Mrs. Brent. I feel priv-

143

ileged to have shared your company this morning." With that he tipped his hat to her as if she were a respectable lady. The trap left the drive and moved on toward the end of the lane, leaving Mercy staring in its wake.

"Where's your brother?" Her father's belligerent voice broke into her thoughts. "And why were you riding with thet vicar fellow?"

Mercy turned to meet the glare from his green eyes. "Dale wouldn't leave, and Vicar Phelps offered me a ride."

"Well, if he thinks he'll be allowed to come around here courtin' . . ."

"Papa," she sighed. "He was only being kind. Besides, he's engaged to marry the lady from the *Larkspur*."

That pacified him somewhat, for he let out a snort, albeit a subdued one. "Just as long as *he* remembers that. Why, he's twenty years older than you if a day!"

It was useless to argue, for Mercy was aware that if the most eligible bachelor in the village—and her own age at that—had offered her the courtesy of a ride home, her father still would have complained. *Especially* in that case, for the possibility of losing his unpaid servant to someone in marriage would be an even greater threat.

Oram, Fernie, and Jack appeared then, and after much grumbling, they obeyed their father's orders to carry in the packages.

"Why didn't you have him bring them up to the door?" Jack whined, bent under the load of sugar. "Where's Dale?"

"In town." Mercy picked up the parcel of cloth and started for the cottage.

Still cross, her father admonished her from behind. "You should ha' made him come home. He's got chores to do."

Make him come home? The package in Mercy's arms felt heavier. *I can't even get him to wipe his feet at the door.*

———

Andrew found Mr. Langford balanced precariously on a windowsill in the milking shed while attempting to rake broken shingles from the roof with a hoe. On the ground out of the way, a young boy squatted over an old board and was attempting to remove a nail with the claw of a hammer. Unaware of his presence, both boy and man jerked heads in his direction when Andrew cleared his throat.

"Good day. I'm Andrew Phelps," he hurried on. "Vicar of Saint Jude's. No doubt you've seen the steeple?"

The man clinging with his left hand to the top of the window nodded. "I'm Seth Langford, and this is Thomas." It was said politely enough, but then followed with a dismissive, "We're Wesleyans."

144

"I see. Well, the Reverend Seaton is my good friend. He'll be happy to know it."

"Yes." Again a dismissive tone, while the boy stared.

Andrew offered the boy a smile, which he returned timidly. "I can see that you're busy, Mr. Langford, but might I have a word with you?" He glanced at the white-knuckled grip the man had on the top portion of the paneless window. "And wouldn't you fare better with a ladder?"

"The ladder's rotten."

Andrew looked about him at the shambles that had probably once been a decent building. The hay barn seemed in the same shape. He knew next to nothing about carpentry, but it seemed that it would take one man weeks to render both buildings serviceable again. He was about to offer his apologies for the intrusion and leave, when Mr. Langford tossed the hoe clear to the side and eased himself down from the window. The blisters on the hand he offered to Andrew and the sunburn across his face indicated a man who was unused to heavy outdoor labor despite his muscular build.

"I say, you've taken on quite a job for yourself," Andrew said.

Mr. Langford pushed back the brim of his cap and wiped his flushed brow with a sleeve. "Aye."

"I hear you're planning to raise horses?"

"When the buildings and pastures are ready."

"I wish you well." Andrew looked around. "We've some fine carpenters in Gresham. Forgive me for prying, but wouldn't hiring a couple help?" And according to Mr. Pool, who had offered this bit of unsolicited information, the man had enough money for such doings.

Mr. Langford seemed to consider that for a moment, but then turned to the boy, who was now standing at his side. "Would you fetch us some water?" He gave Andrew a questioning look, to which Andrew replied that he would indeed like some water.

When Thomas was out of earshot, Mr. Langford wiped his brow again. "I appreciate you coming by, Vicar . . ." In the pause he appeared to be searching his memory for the name.

"Phelps," Andrew supplied with an understanding smile.

"Thank you. I hope you can understand that we chose this place for the privacy. I wouldn't care to have carpenters here every day."

"I see." Feeling a little awkward, Andrew took a step backward. "Then perhaps I should take my leave now."

"Wait." Now it was Mr. Langford who seemed to feel awkward. "I wasn't suggesting that you do that, Vicar Phelps."

"Oh." Andrew glanced at the hoe lying amongst a heap of broken slate shingles. "Is there anything I can do to help you?"

145

"No, thank you." But then he followed that with, "Actually, there is."

Thomas returned carrying a pail half filled with water. Judging from the wetness of his trouser legs, Andrew imagined that it had been full when he left the pump. Mr. Langford insisted that Andrew take the first dipperful.

"Thank you," Andrew said afterward to the boy.

"You're welcome, sir," he replied.

He in no way resembled his father, but Andrew gathered no implications from this—he had lived long enough to know that sometimes that happened. *Thank God my girls look more like their mother* had come to his mind more than once over the years.

It took three dippers of water to quench Mr. Langford's thirst, and when he had finished, he wiped his sleeve again and absently put a hand on the boy's head. Thomas looked up at him with something close to awe across his young face. "Why don't you set that in the shade?" Mr. Langford told the boy. "We'll likely want some later."

Thomas obeyed immediately, looking back for approval when he had found a relatively clear spot beside an outer wall.

"That's fine," Mr. Langford said, then turned to Andrew again.

"I'm having some lumber and shingles delivered tomorrow," he said, then gave a sheepish little shrug. "And a ladder."

"Fine enough. Now, how may I help you, Mr. Langford?"

The man glanced again at his son, who had returned to digging at the nail with the hammer. "I noticed there was a school in Gresham, but I was too concerned about acquiring this place to make inquiries. Is it possible for Thomas to attend?"

Andrew smiled. "That's actually the second reason I came here. The first being to snare you for my congregation, of course."

For the first time, Mr. Langford's face eased into a smile. "I'm sorry about that, Vicar."

Waving a hand, Andrew said, "We've some fine Wesleyans in Gresham. As to the school, Thomas is more than welcome to attend. In fact, a member of the school board asked me to speak with you about it."

"That's good—thank you." And then the man's face took on a thoughtful cast. "I suppose there are supplies he'll need? And lunch . . . should he bring one, or am I supposed to fetch him at noon? I've horses. . . ."

He spoke like someone with no experience with the schooling of his child, and yet the boy looked old enough to have had at least a year or two behind him. *Perhaps the boy's mother tended to all of that in the past,* Andrew thought. Obviously Mr. Langford was a widower, and perhaps a recent one. Andrew's heart went out to the man.

146

"Thomas's teacher will tell him if there are any supplies required. And yes, most of the students bring their lunches. Fact is, one of my daughters will be attending boarding school this fall, and I'm sure her lunch pail has been consigned to the cellar by now. Why don't I bring it to you one day when I'm out making calls?"

It seemed almost as if a curtain was drawn across Mr. Langford's expression. "It's very kind of you to offer, but that won't be necessary." He sent a glance toward the roof of the milking barn, a signal that was not lost on Andrew.

"I'll leave you to your work," Andrew said, stretching out his hand again.

Mr. Langford seemed almost apologetic as they shook hands. "I do appreciate you seeing about us. . . ."

He did not finish his sentence, but Andrew supplied the rest silently as he sent a farewell wave to the boy. . . . *but please don't come around again.*

He could not blame Mr. Langford for not displaying the warmest of hospitality. He could recall the days immediately following Kathleen's death, when he would have gladly consigned himself to the confines of his house. However, duties to his parishioners, and particularly to his daughters, had forbidden such self-indulgence.

As his trap began to move back up Nettle Lane, Andrew thought it good that at least young Thomas would have the companionship of other children when school began. Which would leave Mr. Langford with even more hours of isolation. It was none of Andrew's business, and if solitude was what he wanted, then there was no one to say he shouldn't have it. But Andrew knew that God wasn't only referring to Adam when He said, *"It is not good for man to be alone."*

————

From his perch on the windowsill, Seth ventured a look at the cloud of dust raised by the retreating trap. No doubt the vicar had thought him ill-disposed, as likely did the whole of Gresham by now. He sincerely regretted that, but better to be considered unsociable than to have Thomas suffer once the truth were to be known.

"Sir?" the boy called from below. He had finished pulling the nail from the board and had now taken it upon himself to collect the loose shingles that lay on the ground.

Seth looked down at him. "Be careful not to get in the way," he warned.

"Yes, sir."

"Now, what did you want?"

"What's a vicar?"

"A minister, Thomas." Seth stretched out the hoe to rake another shingle. "From that big church we saw Wednesday."

"Will he come visit again? Or the lady?"

"What lady?"

"The cake lady."

A smile came to Seth's lips at the boy's wording. How could he have forgotten? The apple cake had saved them from a breakfast of tinned meat—which he was already beginning to think of with faint revulsion— and enough cake still remained to last a few more days. "I don't think so, Thomas," he replied. "But we'll need to return the plate when the cake is gone, so perhaps you'll see her again."

*T*hat new schoolmistress is here," Iris Worthy said to Julia as the sisters spun their laces on Saturday morning. "Miss Clark is her name, but of course we knew her as 'Lydia' when she was a girl. She must be going on thirty-two by now."

"Real daydreamer she were back then," Jewel said, her face crinkling pleasurably with the memory. "Always a book in her hand. Why, just like your Aleda."

"I'm looking forward to meeting her," Julia told the two.

"Well, you can do that this very morning," Iris said. "She passed by here not more than an hour ago on her way to the schoolhouse."

Pointing with her chin over her left shoulder as her fingers continued to spin, Jewel said, "Lives back on Walnut Lane with her folks again. Her brother Noah married in the spring of '61."

"Spring of '62," Iris gently corrected, but Jewel would have none of it.

"It were '61, because that were the year Abram Summers' roof burned."

Iris, usually the milder of the two, set her jaw adamantly. "His roof burned in '62, Jewel. I remember Mr. Derby saying he felt wretched, because his broken arm prevented him from joining the bucket brigade." She looked up at Julia. "I'm sure you know that they've been friends since boyhood, Mr. Derby and Mr. Summers, so naturally Mr. Derby would have wished to help."

"But he did take the Summerses into his home until the roof could be rebuilt," Jewel said, then, in a tone as adamant as the thrust of her sister's jaw, added, "in '61."

"No, Jewel. You're remembering '61 because that was when Mrs. Perkins' cat fell in her well. Mr. Derby helped get her out, and how could he do that with a broken arm?" To Julia she said, "Whiteface was her name—the cat, not Mrs. Perkins. She was so named because she was completely gray except for her face."

Jewel was working her mouth into a rebuttal when Julia stepped in. "Both years sound perfectly dreadful, if you ask me," she quipped, smiling to show she meant no offense. "You say Miss Clark is at the schoolhouse?"

Both heads nodded, and she took her leave. She had not gone more than ten feet when she heard Jewel say grudgingly to her sister, "Well, maybe it were '62. But everybody knows that little Horace threw his mother's cat down that well."

As expected, the schoolmistress was in the main classroom, bent over some papers on her desk, when Julia paused in the doorway. "Miss Clark?" she said softly.

Miss Clark looked up, a pen poised in her fingers. "Yes?"

"I'm Julia Hollis. You'll be teaching my two daughters this year."

"Indeed?" With a welcoming smile she rose from her chair. "Please, do come in."

Julia could see that she favored her father physically, for she had to be almost six feet tall. Light brown hair was drawn back severely into a knot, revealing ears that stuck out just a bit. Her face wore a welcoming, pleasant expression. "I won't stay long and keep you from your work," Julia said on her way to the front of the classroom.

"I would enjoy the company, Mrs. Hollis." They shook hands over the desk. "Let's see . . . your daughters are Aleda and Grace?"

"I'm impressed. You've learned your students' names already?"

"Don't forget, I was raised here, so most of the last names are already familiar to me. It's only a matter of learning the given names and a few new ones." She then nodded toward the door. "Would you mind if we sat out on the steps? Saint Margaret's was like a mausoleum—damp and cold, even in the summer. Between my teaching and housemother duties, I had very little time to enjoy the outdoors. I'm charmed with the idea of having a school yard."

"Is that why you left Saint Margaret's?" Julia asked when they had settled on the steps and arranged their skirts to cover their ankles.

"Not exactly. I was content there, in spite of the overwhelmingly Gothic atmosphere. But my parents are growing old, and it struck me once during my morning prayers that I couldn't take for granted they would always be here. Then later that same day I received two things—a letter from my mother expressing the desire that I would come back home, and a wire from Mr. Sykes concerning the position here. That night I asked God for direction as I was opening my Bible for my nightly reading. I looked down to see the passage where Jesus looked down from the cross and asked Saint John to care for his mother. I just can't believe that was all coincidence."

Julia rubbed her arms over her sleeves. "That gives me chill bumps just to think of it."

"Me too." The teacher smiled, green eyes soft. "Anyway, I'm happy to be back home and am looking forward to next month."

"I believe the children are too. No doubt you've heard about the merry-go-round?"

"My parents told me. I've never seen one. Have you?"

"In London," Julia nodded. "We lived there until just last year."

That led to the schoolmistress asking how Julia had turned the *Larkspur* from an abandoned coaching inn to a lodging house. Julia told as much as she could of the story without going into detail about her late husband. When she rose to leave almost an hour later, she apologized for staying so long.

"I'll forgive you if you promise to do it again sometime," was Miss Clark's gracious reply.

Julia smiled back. Any doubts about the teacher who would be replacing Captain Powell were gone. She left the schoolhouse and was on her way back to the *Larkspur* when a familiar voice called to her above the rattle of carriage wheels.

"My dear Mrs. Hollis!" Ophelia Rhodes called from her runabout, flagging an enthusiastic hand beside George Sykes, the churchwarden's nephew. The gray cob was soon pulled to a halt, and Mrs. Rhodes spilled out of the carriage. "Drive on back, will you?" she said to her assistant. "I'll be along shortly."

"It's so good to see you!" Julia said as the two linked arms and walked up Church Lane.

Bonnetless as usual, Mrs. Rhodes smoothed some graying strands of hair away from her ruddy face and tucked them behind her ear. "And you as well, Mrs. Hollis. I've been so terribly busy these days that it seems I rarely see my own husband. I'll be happy when Grace is able to share my practice."

Julia smiled. While it was true that Grace loved animals and had taken to wandering over to the Rhodeses' cottage to watch Mrs. Rhodes in the surgery, she was only seven years old. If indeed Grace did decide to study veterinary medicine, she would not be ready to practice for a good many years. But Julia had a feeling that her friend would still be involved with her practice, for she was one of those ageless individuals who thrive upon keeping busy.

"Where have you been this morning?" asked Julia.

"We treated a colicky horse on the Towly farm east of Gipsy Woods and then on to Clive to remove an impacted tooth from a pig."

"That sounds dangerous."

"But for chloroform, my dear, it would be." Her face grew sober. "Which reminds me—I treated a pig for hoof rot near Alveley a fortnight ago."

Unsure of how she was expected to respond to this, Julia simply said, "Yes?"

The *Larkspur* was in sight now. Julia could see Mrs. Kingston puttering about in the garden. Mrs. Rhodes had noticed, too, and lowered her voice. "The owners of the pig were parishioners of Saint Matthew's."

"Where Mr. Treves is curate?"

"Yes." She studied Julia's face. "I'm not sure if I should tell you this. I don't wish to cause trouble."

"Is it concerning Mr. Treves?"

Mrs. Rhodes nodded. "It's far from scandalous, so don't get that aghast look on your face, and perhaps my fondness for animals has caused me prejudice."

"I think you should tell me," Julia said, slowing her steps.

"Very well, then." She glanced again at the *Larkspur*'s garden. "I'm not sure if you're aware of this, not having been brought up rural, but the small farmers around here are quite dependent upon their pigs for winter meat."

"Yes, I know that." Julia could not help but be aware, for even the meanest cottage usually had a pigsty out back.

"Well, regarding the pig in Alveley, it seems the owner—a Mr. Sims and his wife—had asked Mr. Treves to pray that their pig would recover. Whereupon Mr. Treves lectured them that God's time was not to be wasted with prayers over animals."

"Truly?"

"I see no reason that the Simses would make up the story. They weren't even aware of my indirect acquaintance with the young man."

Julia frowned. "That seems so insensitive. While Mr. Treves isn't overly warm, I can't imagine him saying such a thing." But even as she spoke, she recalled his remark about poor people last week at Andrew's house.

"He wouldn't be the first young man to put aside his true nature for the benefit of his fiancée's family," Mrs. Rhodes was saying. "Of course we're only hearing one side of the story. And you know Mr. Treves far better than I do—"

"I feel I hardly know him at all."

"Mmm. Should you tell Miss Phelps?"

"I'm not sure, but I'll certainly tell Andrew."

Andrew, walking with Julia in the *Larkspur*'s garden after he and his daughters had enjoyed supper with Julia's family and the lodgers, was quite pensive. "I shall have to tell her, of course. But I don't care for the idea of interfering in their courtship over a remark that can probably be attributed to the ignorance of youth."

"Do you think that was all it was?"

He shrugged. "How can we know? Young curates are notorious for being full of themselves, you know. It's likely that ten years from now Mr. Treves will shudder at the memory of his callousness."

They were both quiet for a spell as they strolled around the gray forms of flower beds, trellis, and shrubbery, illuminated by light spilling out from the inn's windows and the evening's earliest stars.

"Elizabeth received a letter today from one of her former classmates," Andrew told her presently, breaking the silence. "She wed last year and is now expecting a child. I'm sure I don't have to tell you it put Elizabeth in a somber mood."

"The poor dear. She wants to be a wife and mother so badly."

"Of course marriage was created by God, so there is absolutely nothing wrong with that. . . ."

"As long as she doesn't marry just for the sake of marrying," Julia finished for him.

"Exactly." He smiled and patted the hand she had resting upon his arm. "I'm glad I didn't allow my mother to talk me into doing the same thing, or I would have missed out on having you in my life."

"You mean you almost married someone in Cambridge?"

"Not quite." Feigning a little shudder, he replied, "A Mrs. Keswick had set her cap for me. I can't see why, unless her eyesight—"

"Oh, stop that," Julia told him.

"Stop what?" He appeared genuinely puzzled.

"You make harsh comments about your looks, so I'll contradict you and tell you how handsome you are. Why, I believe you're vain, Vicar Phelps."

"Vain?" Andrew touched the cloth of his coat over his chest. "You cut me to the quick, Julia Hollis. I'm well aware that you say such things out of pity."

"I say nothing out of pity." Reaching up to touch his bearded cheek, Julia said, "Handsome is as handsome does, Andrew. And that makes you the most handsome man in Shropshire."

Sunday morning Seth woke even earlier than usual and went to the north window, as was becoming his habit. The view from his barred cell window in Newgate had been simply of another building. How welcome to his eyes were the sedate greens and blues of pastures and hedgerows and sky. How blessed he was!

With that awareness came again a stab of guilt. His mind was weary from wrestling over the matter of the Wesleyan Chapel. Reverend Seaton, who had called yesterday, seemed a decent fellow. But again came the uncomfortable thought of having to leave the blessed seclusion of his farm. *And I've no Sunday clothes.*

But there was Thomas to consider now, and none of his arguments justified raising the boy as a heathen. "Forsake not the assembling of yourselves together," Reverend Mercer had often reminded his small congregation of prisoners. Now Seth understood the reason. He was probably not the first convict faced with the temptation to seclude himself on the outside.

He sighed, realizing that he would spend the whole week carrying a weight of guilt upon his shoulders if he didn't go to chapel. Ten minutes later he was in the kitchen, brewing up some tea and dividing the remains of the apple cake onto two dishes. He put the plate carefully into the metal dishpan. Hot water he would add later, when breakfast was finished and his teapot was free again.

He went back upstairs to fetch Thomas. The boy lay on his side, his ash-colored hair in disarray, a hand cupped under one cheek and his mouth parted slightly. It was a shame to disturb such peace, Seth thought, touching a narrow shoulder.

"Thomas?"

Both blue eyes opened and blinked. "Yes, sir?"

"Breakfast is ready." *Such as it is,* Seth thought, though three-day-old apple cake was more appetizing than tinned meat. He supposed he needed to buy a milking cow as soon as possible. *And perhaps some chickens.* Surely fresh eggs and milk every day would put some flesh on the boy's bones.

They breakfasted in silence, then cleared away the dishes together. As Thomas went to his room to wash and dress himself, Seth shaved at the washbowl in his bedroom. Working out in the sun for the past three days had put some color to his face, he was glad to see. Not that he was vain, but one didn't care to go about looking like a ghost. "Put some water on your hair before you comb it," he called out to Thomas, then yelped as the razor took a bite of his chin.

"Are you hurt?" the boy asked a second later from the doorway.

"Just nipped myself, thank you." Seth pressed a towel to his chin with one hand and continued to shave around it with the straight razor, aware

154

that he was risking another nip. He knew life would be easier if he grew a beard, but he had never had one, not even in Newgate where they had been forbidden, and didn't care for the thought of hair upon his face. "Mind you wash the sleep from your eyes."

When he had donned a clean set of work clothes, he found Thomas waiting at the bottom of the staircase. *At least one of us is dressed properly*, Seth thought, though the sleeve of the boy's coat ended well above his narrow wrists. Why hadn't he noticed that before? He remembered then Mr. Trumble mentioning something about there being a tailor in Gresham. He would have to take care of that tomorrow, and as long as Thomas needed to go to the tailor, he reckoned it wouldn't hurt to order himself a decent suit of clothes for church at the same time.

There was so much to do, and he hadn't even started purchasing horses yet! A far cry from how his life had been less than two weeks ago with every hour of his day planned for him by others.

"Should we bring the plate to the lady on the way?" asked Thomas while Seth straightened the boy's collar.

"Why, I don't know. Her family could be at chapel, too, you know, and not be home when we stopped." Seth took his watch from his pocket and snapped it open. They needed to hurry if they were to be on time. He quickly hitched Bonny and Soot to the wagon. The air smelled of dampness, and back behind him, over the Anwyl, he could see dark clouds. Hopefully the rain would wait until they arrived back at home.

A half mile up the lane they came to the next cottage. Seth regretted not bringing the plate along, for there were two boys with straw-colored hair playing "catch" with a ball out in the yard. As the horse drew closer, Seth could see they were much older than Thomas. The two ran to their garden gate to stare, and Seth reined the horses to a halt and bade them good-morning. He thought it unconscionable that he should pass without at least sending thanks to the lady of the house for the cake and an assurance that he would bring the plate by soon. The boys mumbled what appeared to be greetings, directing their most curious stares at Thomas.

"Is your mother at home?" Seth asked. Being late for chapel was beginning to look rather attractive to him, for if he and Thomas could slip in the back after the services had begun and slip out early, perhaps they could avoid being subject to sociable inquiry about their private lives.

The two gave each other quick glances, then one of the boys shook his head while the other said, "No."

"Oh. Well, please thank her for the cake," he said. "I'm Seth Langford."

"Oh," one boy replied flatly, then turned away from the gate.

Sociable creatures, Seth thought to himself and lifted the reins to continue on his way. Just then a flock of gray speckled birds caught his attention, pecking and scratching the ground near a vegetable garden. Even with his limited experience, Seth could tell they weren't chickens. But they seemed to be domesticated.

"Excuse me," he said to the boy remaining at the gate. "What kind of birds are they?"

He glanced over his shoulder and then back at Seth. "Guineas."

"Yes?" The horses paced and snorted, ready to be on their way, but Seth was intrigued. "Do they lay eggs?"

Now the boy looked at him askew, as if he thought him ignorant. "They do."

"The kind you can eat?"

The boy's brother returned to the gate, and both exchanged deep-lidded glances. "We eats them every day, mister," the taller one said. "Want to buy some?"

"Some eggs?"

"No, some guineas. We've too many."

"Why, yes," Seth replied. Mindful of the minutes ticking by, he said, "I'll stop by and speak with your father after chapel."

Again there was an exchange of glances. "Our papa's gonter be busy all day. They're mine and my brother's guineas, so we're allowed to sell 'em."

"We sells 'em all the time," said the shorter. "We sold a half dozen just yesterday."

"We'll even bring them to your place while you're gone," offered the taller boy. "That way they don't get scared and run away. How many do you want?"

"Would two be enough, you think?" asked Seth. After all, that would mean one egg each for him and Thomas. "They do lay every day, don't they?"

"Well, most days. So you'd best get another."

"All right." Seth dug into his pocket. "Three, then. How much are they?"

At the sight of Seth's purse, both boys spilled out of the gate and came up close to the horse. "Half a crown each oughter do it," said the shorter boy.

"Half a crown?" That sounded expensive, and he hadn't asked around to see if any could be had more cheaply. He drew his purse back toward his pocket, a motion that wasn't lost on the two in the lane.

"Excuse Oram, mister," said the taller boy. "He was kicked by a horse when he were small, and he don't know about money."

His brother looked puzzled for just a second, then bobbed his head up and down. "I don't know about money."

"Four-bob for three birds," the taller boy went on. "How about it?"

Seth supposed it was reasonable, and the idea of having them delivered was appealing. "Very well, then," he said, counting out four shillings. "By the way, what should I feed them?"

The boy closed his hand around the shillings and looked back up at him. "They'll scratch for bugs and such. But you should throw them a little corn every morning too. Sell you some for another couple o'bob."

———

. . . by grace the Comforter comes nigh;
and for thy grace our love shall be
Forever, only, Lord, for thee.

It was while she was standing at front singing the final stanza of "We Bless the Name of Christ the Lord" to the piano accompaniment of Mrs. Jones, the postman's wife, that Mercy watched a man clad in a Fustian shirt and corded trousers lead a boy through the tiny vestibule and to a back pew. The boy she recognized at once as Thomas Langford and so gathered that the man was his father.

The boy's eyes widened in his delicate face as if he were surprised to see her. By then her song was over, and Mercy returned to her pew, having had only enough time to assess that Mr. Langford felt ill at ease. When the last stanza of the final hymn ended at the close of the service, the two were already gone.

———

Seth knocked upon the Sanderses' door two mornings later, the cake plate tucked under his arm. He and Thomas were on their way to town to have their measurements taken for Sunday clothing and to inquire about who would be willing to sell a cow, but it would be unthinkable not to thank the woman of the house for her kindness.

The door was opened by the shorter of the two boys he had spoken with on Sunday. When no greeting was forthcoming, simply a stare with slackened jaw, Seth asked, "Is your mother at home?"

"No," the boy replied.

"Oh." Seth gave a questioning glance to Thomas, who of course was too young and inexperienced to advise him of proper etiquette in this case. There were so many things required of him at his farm that he simply could not continue showing up at the neighbor's cottage in the hopes that the woman who brought over the cake would be present. Letting go of Thomas's hand, he took the plate from under his arm.

"Would you mind thanking her for the cake?" he said, handing it over. Again the boy did not reply as he took the plate from him, but all Seth could do was trust that the message would be conveyed. *I should have written a note*, he told himself. "Thank you and good day," he added to the boy who had resumed his slack-jawed stare.

The boy mumbled something in reply.

There was nothing more that could be accomplished here, so Seth took Thomas's hand and was turning both of them to leave when Thomas whispered, "The birds, sir."

The door was almost closed. Seth reached a hand to stop it. "By the way, those guineas haven't laid any eggs yet."

Now an almost fearful expression came over the boy's face. "Wait here." He actually shut the door. Seth shifted his weight on his other foot and looked at Thomas.

"A strange family, I think," he whispered.

"Yes, sir," the boy whispered back with eyes wide just as the door was opened again. Now present were both boys who had sold Seth the guineas. The taller at least had the social grace to stretch his lips into something resembling a smile.

"The guineas ain't used to their new home yet," the boy said matter-of-factly.

"Well, how long will it take?"

He chewed on his lip. "Maybe a week. Do you need some more corn?"

"No, thank you." Seth figured he would get some at a better price in Gresham, and that his trading days with these two were best brought to an end.

———

"Did I hear a horse out front?" Mercy asked, returning downstairs from making beds.

"Yes," Fernie replied. He was tossing a folded pocket knife up and down in the air. "Have you seen Oram's knife? We want to play mumblety-peg."

Mercy fished in her apron pocket among the candle stubs, then tossed it over to him. "It was under his pillow. Tell your brother if it ever gets in the wash, he'll wish he'd been more careful."

"Uh-huh." Fernie went to the back door and called, "Oram! I've got it!" That was when Mercy noticed a plate sitting on the table top.

"Was that Mr. Langford who was here?"

"Who?"

She sighed. "Our neighbor."

158

Oram came inside, slamming the door behind him. "It was him," said Fernie.

"Well, what did he say?"

"Say?" He tossed the folded knife to his brother. "Nothing as I can recall."

"Who?" Oram asked.

"That man from down the lane."

Oram scratched his head. "But he said—"

"That's right," Fernie interrupted quickly. "He did say something. I forgot."

Mercy folded her arms and looked at the two suspiciously. Fernie had ordered Oram around ever since they were little, and it seemed he was doing so now. But for what purpose? "Well, what did he say?"

"He said 'here's your plate.' "

"That's all?"

"Yes." Fernie looked at Oram. "Ain't that right, Oram?"

"That's right," Oram agreed. " 'Here's your plate' was all he said."

"He's a grumpy sort," Fernie went on. "Didn't even smile. If I was you, I wouldn't go over there bringin' him any more cakes."

Whether this was the truth or not was impossible to tell, but the fact that Mr. Langford had slipped in and out of church before anyone could meet him lent *some* credibility to their account. Shooing her brothers out of the house, she said, "Off with you, then. You've put enough marks in the door posts with those knives."

"But we wanted to play—"

"Play somewhere else. And while you're in the yard, see if you can find out what happened to those three guineas."

————

"Miss Clark will be very good for the children," Mrs. Dearing remarked at the *Larkspur*'s table that evening. "I had a long discussion with her in the lending library this morning. She's impressively well schooled in classic literature."

"Indeed?" Mr. Durwin buttered a slice of bread. "I'm all for the study of literature, but not at the expense of arithmetic and history."

"From what I hear, she is more than competent to teach all subjects," Julia said from the head of the table.

Mrs. Kingston looked up from helping Grace cut up her roast beef and nodded. "She has a calm way about her that the children will respond to. That's so important for maintaining discipline, don't you think?"

"Discipline is essential," Mr. Durwin agreed. "One cannot learn in an environment of chaos." Looking over at Julia, he said, "I don't think I ever had a proper potato until I moved here, Mrs. Hollis. Mrs. Herrick is indeed an artist, and the kitchen is her canvas."

Julia smiled. "Thank you, Mr. Durwin. She'll be pleased."

"He compliments her all the time," the usually quiet and reticent Mrs. Hyatt said. "Why, if she weren't married, I believe Mr. Durwin would ask her hand." This caused some laughter around the table and Aleda to put a hand over her mouth to cover the shock. With their wedding date only five weeks away, both Mr. Durwin and Mrs. Hyatt had become positively lighthearted.

Love does wonderful things to people, Julia thought and smiled at the wink Mrs. Kingston sent her.

"That's not so, Mrs. Hyatt," Mr. Durwin was protesting. "But I do appreciate a cook who can do justice to a potato. And the Irish, of course, for contributing them to civilization."

Mr. Pitney, who seemed to be turning as introverted as Mrs. Hyatt was outgoing lately, lifted a finger. "I beg your pardon?"

All eyes shifted to his end of the table, which of course caused a blush to stain his cheeks. "Yes, Mr. Pitney?" said Mrs. Dearing.

"The potato." He dropped his fork on the floor, bent to pick it up, and emerged more red-faced than before. "Oh . . . thank you," he said to Sarah, who appeared at his side to supply a clean fork. Everyone else at the table busied themselves with their food, pretending not to notice while still maintaining a posture of alertness.

"What about potatoes?" Mrs. Kingston asked kindly. "Are you fond of them too, Mr. Pitney?"

"Why, yes." He looked at Mr. Durwin. "But, begging your pardon . . . they're actually indigenous to South America, or more specifically, Chile and the Andes."

"Do tell, Mr. Pitney?" This came with raised eyebrows from Miss Rawlins, who seldom spoke to the young archeologist.

"Why, yes, Miss Rawlins," he replied, straightening in his chair. "They were brought back to Spain by explorers in the late 1500s."

"Mr. Pitney is indeed correct," Mr. Ellis said while chewing.

Philip leaned closer to Julia and whispered, "Mother, may I ask a question?" When she nodded, he turned back to Mr. Pitney and said, "But how did they get to England?"

Mr. Pitney smiled at the boy. He was clearly more at ease speaking with Philip than with Miss Rawlins, in spite of Mr. Pitney's obvious infatuation with her . . . *or perhaps because of it*, Julia thought.

"Sir Francis Drake brought them over from Colombia. What's interesting is that the Spaniards most likely had introduced them there from their explorations in Chile. So the potato has a history of crossing the ocean more than once."

"Fascinating," Miss Rawlins declared, and others murmured agreement. The bliss on Mr. Pitney's face caused Julia to fiddle with her napkin in order to hide a smile.

Later in the hall, though, when Mr. Ellis and Mrs. Kingston had persuaded Mr. Pitney to expound on the methods used by the Romans and Celts for baking bread, she noticed Miss Rawlins cover a yawn—and then another. Mr. Pitney must have noticed, too, for he excused himself to go upstairs as soon as possible. *And then again, love can be a real burden sometimes*, Julia thought.

*T*hree weeks later on Monday, August twenty-ninth, Jonathan Raleigh sat in the back of a hired coach and chewed on a fingernail—a nervous habit he had acquired of late. *I should have written first*, he thought. But of course he had no doubt that the letter he had sent last year had ended up in Reverend Phelps's fireplace. *And how can I blame him? I would have done the same had I a daughter so mistreated.*

"Elizabeth, please don't hate me," he said under his breath, staring vacantly out the window at the passing countryside. *Hate the man who chose the cesspools of life over your love, yes, but understand that man no longer exists.*

He picked up a Bible from the seat beside him. His Grandfather Hastings had presented it to him only seven months ago, and the leather cover was already showing signs of wear around the edges.

"*He will have compassion upon us; He will subdue our iniquities; and thou wilt cast all their sins into the depths of the sea*," Jonathan read silently from the seventh chapter of Micah. It was of great comfort to him that God had consigned all memory of his earlier wicked ways to ocean's depths on the day he committed his life to following the Lord. But of course the consequences of his past actions still remained to haunt him.

Perhaps she's married now, he thought, and not for the first time. She would deserve an honest, God-fearing man with no vile past to come between them. But he was selfish enough to hope that wasn't so and that she still harbored some love for him.

Cottages and gardens began to take the place of pastures, and the surface of the road changed abruptly. All too soon the coach came to a halt. "The *Bow and Fiddle*, sir," the driver said, opening the door. "Gresham's onliest coaching inn."

Jonathan was led to an upstairs room by an innkeeper who identified himself as Mr. Pool. "We don't get many overnight patrons," the man said, pausing at a door and opening it. "From this room you can look out at th' Anwyl."

"The Anwyl?" Jonathan asked.

"Yes, sir." Mr. Pool pointed toward a window at the far wall. Even from the doorway Jonathan could see the greens and brownish-reds of a steep hill. "Didn't you notice it on your way up?"

"I'm afraid I didn't," Jonathan replied, but then circus elephants could have passed by his coach's window without his notice. "This room will be fine."

"Care for some tea whiles you unpack? Ale, perhaps?"

Nervousness and the strain of his travels had brought on a great thirst. For just a split second the thought of downing a mug of ale was tempting. But he had only to recall the night that Vicar Phelps had caught him inebriated and in the company of a sergeant's wife in Cambridge, and the tea suddenly sounded better. "I'm in a bit of a hurry, so I'll have some tea in your dining room instead. Could you tell me how to locate Reverend Andrew Phelps?"

"The vicar? Just look for the steeple of Saint Jude's when you're outside. The vicarage is but a stone's throw behind it."

The tea was served to him by the innkeeper's wife, a thin, sharp-featured woman. "Paying a call on the vicar, are you?" she asked while pouring milk into his cup.

"Yes," Jonathan replied. He sipped his tea, then assumed the reason she was still hovering at his table was to see if it was satisfactory. "It's fine, thank you."

"You must not be a relation, or you'd be stayin' at the vicarage."

Her tone of voice made it more of a question than a statement. Jonathan didn't rise to the bait but gave her a slight nod before taking another sip of tea.

"I s'pose you know he's got two daughters—one about your age."

Pushing out his chair, he said, "I'm sorry I haven't time to finish the rest, but it was good." He noticed from the inn's courtyard that indeed the steeple of a church rose above the treetops. Heading toward it down a road that went east, he happened upon a school building where two workmen were constructing something of metal piping and wood in the yard. A dozen or so children and adults had gathered to watch. Jonathan returned the nods of greeting some gave and searched the faces. He was relieved when none proved familiar. Though he had dreamt of this day for a year now, he still had to fight a strong impulse to turn and sprint for the safety of the *Bow and Fiddle*.

Please give me a chance to have my say before he slams the door, Father, Jonathan prayed silently. *And please . . . if I could at least see Elizabeth's face today.*

He turned up a lane and a pleasant cottage came into his sight, settled on a knoll behind a wooden fence and garden shaded by a couple of giant oaks. With his stomach in knots, he crossed the garden to the porch and knocked on the door. It was answered by a young maid wearing a brown dress, white apron, and frilled cap. "Yes, sir?" she said with a welcoming smile that reassured him a little.

Jonathan cleared his throat and fought the temptation not to give his name. "My name is Jonathan Raleigh. May I speak with the vicar and Miss Phelps?"

"I'm sorry, sir, but the vicar is out making calls. But he shouldn't be away too long on account of Miss Phelps being ill."

His heart lurched in his chest. "What's wrong?"

"Oh, just a head cold, sir. Mr. Raleigh, is it?"

"Yes," he said after a sigh of both relief that her illness was not serious and disappointment that he would have to wait still longer to see her. "But of course I'll call again when Miss Phelps is well."

"Is there any message you'd like me to give her?"

"No, thank you. Just that I called."

The maid disappeared from his sight, leaving the door partly open. Jonathan stood there wondering if she had misunderstood him. He was just about to turn to leave when the space was filled with Elizabeth's form.

"Donathan?" she called in a clogged nasal voice. Her nose was red, her eyes puffy, but she could have smeared her face with mud and looked beautiful to him. Jonathan's knees turned to butter, while his voice betrayed him and would not function.

Elizabeth seemed to be battling some emotion herself, for she stared for several seconds before speaking. "What are you doing here?"

"I came to tell you how sorry, how much I wish I had never—"

"You hab to go."

"Elizabeth, please . . ."

"My father will be home any minute. Go back to Kensington, Mr. Raleigh."

"I live in Cambridge again. My uncle's law firm—"

"Cambridge, then." Her brown eyes filled with recrimination. "You should nebber hab come here. Go away now."

It was no different than what he'd expected, but disappointment still surged through him like a fever. Raising a hand in the hopes that she wouldn't close the door until he'd had at least enough time to plead his case, he said, "I'll leave if that's what you really want, Elizabeth. Just tell me . . . is that what you want?"

"Yes," she said without hesitation.

The word was like a knife through his heart. *What are you doing here?* he asked himself, suddenly aware that he must be the most foolish man in

England. "Very well," he replied in a thick voice. He had traveled so far and still possessed just enough feeble hope to add, "But your name has been in my prayers every day for the past seven months, Elizabeth. If you could see my heart, you would know how truly sorry I am . . . and how much love I have for you."

He became aware sometime during the course of his impassioned words that his eyes were wet. He did not move to wipe them for fear that she would think he was attempting to manipulate her with theatrics. But amazingly, he could see tears quivering upon her bottom eyelashes.

"Elizabeth?"

She looked away for the briefest of seconds. "My father would die before allowing me to see you. Go away, Jonathan."

When Jonathan found himself facing a closed door, he stared at it until he realized it wasn't going to open again. With a heavy heart he turned. It was as he walked across the garden that he found a small measure of encouragement. *"My father would die before allowing me to see you,"* she had said. The focus had shifted away from *her* not wishing to see him to her father's wishes. Did that mean she still felt something for him?

Please, God, let it be so. Even if she did still care and could see her way to forgive him, there still remained a formidable obstacle in the form of her protective father.

————

"Are you all right, miss?"

Elizabeth opened her eyes and focused them upon Dora, then moved away from the door upon which she had been leaning. "Yes, I think so."

The maid stared skeptically. "That man—he upset you? Shall I send Luke to find Vicar?"

"No. Please." She blew her nose into the handkerchief. "I just need to lie down for a while."

With Dora's assistance Elizabeth went upstairs to her room. She lay on her side on top of her bed, insisting that she did not need cover. Seconds later, though, she felt a quilt being smoothed over her. Elizabeth curled up under it and tried to forget that her first instinct had been to fly into Jonathan's arms. *Paul is a decent man, and I love him. It's the future that I have to think about, and he can provide a stable one for me.*

Just a short while later she heard footsteps bounding up the stairs. "Elizabeth!" came Laurel's voice from the doorway. Elizabeth opened her eyes reluctantly.

"Yes?"

Her sister hurried to the bedside. "I just saw Jonathan Raleigh outside the *Bow and Fiddle*!" Leaning closer, she said, "You've been crying?"

"Miss Laurel!" Now Mrs. Paget stood in the doorway, her arms folded across her ample chest and Dora looking over her shoulder. "Let your sister rest. She's not feeling well."

"It's all right, Mrs. Paget . . . Dora," Elizabeth told them, raising her head and smiling weakly to show her gratitude at their concern.

"Shall we bring you up some broth, miss?"

"No, thank you. Really, I'm fine now."

Laurel watched this exchange with mouth gaping, and when the two servants were gone, she said, "You mean he came *here*?"

"Yes." After blowing her nose again, Elizabeth moved the quilt aside and swung her feet over the side of the bed. "I sent him away."

"You did? Does Papa know?"

She rubbed an eye with the heel of her hand. "He's out making calls."

Taking a seat beside her, Laurel said, "Why did Jonathan come here? Is he in love with you again?"

"Laurel . . ."

"Well, is he?"

"I don't know." Elizabeth tried to recall what he had said. "He claims to be."

"Well, do you love him?"

"No."

"Then why were you crying?"

"I just didn't expect him to show up at our door. Even if I did care about him, too much has happened."

"But if he's sorry . . ."

" 'Sorry' isn't enough sometimes, Laurel."

"What did he do that was so terrible?" Laurel went on before Elizabeth could answer. "And please don't tell me that I'm too young to know. I'm old enough to go off to school, so I'm old enough to not be treated like a child."

"Yes, you are, aren't you?" Elizabeth touched her sister's dimpled cheek. Just four more days and she would be gone.

"What did Jonathan do?" Laurel insisted.

Before she could reply, Elizabeth had to swallow over the lump that had welled up in her throat. "Another woman—a married one. Papa saw them together."

This was met with silence, until her sister said, "Maybe they were just friends. You know . . . and happened to be walking together?"

Elizabeth shook her head. "It wasn't like that."

"They were in love?"

"It wasn't like that either."

"Oh," Laurel said, her cheeks flushing with understanding. "I liked

166

him. He was funny, not stuffy like Mr. Treves."

"Don't say that, Laurel. Paul is a good man."

She didn't argue, nor did she take back the statement. "Will Papa be angry?"

"Oh, I've no doubt about that." After all, Elizabeth had never believed that her father gave up his prestigious position in Cambridge because he longed for a more simple life. Perhaps that was what he had convinced himself, but she had never doubted that it was to lessen any chance of her and Jonathan happening to cross paths again. *And now it's happened.* "But hopefully he's on his way back home by now."

Suddenly she felt drained of strength. "I think I'll lie down a while longer," she said, sinking sideways back onto her pillow.

Laurel moved to make room for her feet. "Would you like me to stay with you?"

"No, thank you."

The expression on Jonathan's face, the way he had raised his hand pleadingly, came back to Elizabeth. *Why did he have to come now?* Just a few more weeks—just a little while longer—and she was positive she could have forgotten him entirely.

"I'll miss you too," Philip said, caught up in his mother's embrace as the last boarding whistle sounded. And he meant it, even as excited as he was about going away to school. Which was why he had requested that only his mother and sisters see him off at the Shrewsbury station. The memory he wanted to carry with him to Worcester was of the three people who meant more to him than anyone else. They had come through some unsure times when his father passed away, and he was learning that adversity caused people who truly loved each other to grow closer.

Yesterday had been his time for farewells to the people outside his family. Ben had been a good sport about it, handing over a new cricket bat. "In case you get to play at school," he said. There was affection mixed with envy in his eyes, and Philip had had to restrain himself from embracing his friend instead of shaking his hand.

Jeremiah had presented a gift as well in his own practical manner. "Candy for the trip," he had said of the tin of chocolates he presented. "I ate three to make sure they wasn't spoiled."

From Vicar Phelps and his daughters he received a handsome Bible of his own, bound in fine kid leather with gilded pages. The lodgers and servants had presented little gifts as well. Mrs. Kingston and Mrs. Herrick had wept copiously, which caused him some sadness until he reasoned with himself that while it was true they would miss him, they had other loved ones in their lives and would settle back into their routines when he was gone.

It had come as a relief, the realization that he wasn't the center of anyone's universe, not even his mother's. Though she, too, would miss him far more than would anyone else, she had two daughters to tend, and of course would be gaining two more, as well as a husband soon. She would carry on without him, just as she had carried on without Father when he passed away.

It was still a comfort to know that he would be missed. After embracing his sisters and reminding them to study hard in school, he took from his mother's arms the heavy parcel Mrs. Herrick had packed, bade them all farewell again, and boarded his day coach. A conductor came by, took tickets, and shut the door. He found a place overhead for his basket and satchel, then went to the window and waved at his mother and sisters until the train started moving and they were out of sight. It was only then that he settled back into his seat and thought to notice his fellow passengers.

Across from him sat two women—probably mother and daughter, considering the similar structure of their faces. An elderly man with a thick red beard and balding head shared Philip's seat. He was reading from a book he held about six inches from his eyes.

"Leaving home for the first time, are you?" asked the older of the two women when Philip gave them a shy smile.

"I'm going to school in Worcester."

"My son left for Eton yesterday. Been there two years now."

Finally the man looked up from his page. "You ever read any of Pope's writings, young man?"

"Yes, sir," Philip replied. Mr. Hunter, his tutor back in London, had been fond of Alexander Pope and had occasionally read to him and his sisters from *The Dunciad*.

The elderly man moved the book away and closed his eyes. In a surprisingly crisp voice, he quoted:

"Happy the man whose wish and care
A few paternal acres bound
Content to breathe his native air
In his own ground."

He gave Philip a meaningful look. "Food for thought, eh, young man?"

"Yes, sir," Philip said uneasily. The women across from him smiled and nodded agreement, then exchanged puzzled glances when the man had returned to his reading. Philip felt relieved when no further comment was directed his way. *Something to write home about*, he told himself. He had

168

promised to write his mother weekly and could imagine her sharing his written adventures with his sisters around the breakfast table. That he would not be there with them caused just the tiniest pang, but he ignored it and it went away. He was almost a man now, and let Alexander Pope say what he will—men were supposed to go out and conquer the world.

$\mathcal{T}$he guineas Seth bought had yet to produce an egg. "You got to build 'em a coop," one of the Sanders boys had instructed when he came across them on another trip to church. "They won't lay unless they've got a coop. Didn't you know that?"

He had begun to suspect that the boys had cheated him, especially after finding out that he had paid them four times as much as Mr. Trumble charged for a gallon of corn. But the animals were his responsibility now, so the next time he drove his wagon to the lumber mill, he bought extra lumber for the project. Chores elsewhere on the place, however, had kept his hands busy. Meanwhile, the guineas roamed the yard clucking *pot-rack!* and feasted upon the corn without a trace of guilt over not earning their supper.

At least Florence, the cow he had purchased from a Mr. Putnam, was doing her part. The dairy farmer had kindly given Seth a milking lesson, so now he and Thomas had something to supplement the tinned meals. He imagined that the boy was looking just a bit healthier—at least there was some sun on his cheeks. Every morning Thomas had asked, "Will we build the coop today?" Finally Seth figured out the reason for his eagerness. All of the work they had done on the place had been repairs—they had never built anything from scratch, and the boy was becoming quite a craftsman for his size. Besides wanting to provide a home for the guineas, which he practically regarded as pets, Thomas most likely wanted the satisfaction of seeing their labor transform a stack of lumber and nails into something useful.

Seth had chosen to begin the project today while Thomas still had a week before school would begin. They chose a spot outside the barnyard— near the gardening shed—and measured out a square of eight-foot boards. Seth measured and hammered while Thomas sawed. Sweat bathed both their faces as they erected a six-foot-tall frame.

"Hand me that hammer, son," Seth said around a nail between his teeth while holding a roofing board. He froze. Never had he addressed

Thomas that way. He was almost embarrassed to see what the boy's reaction was, yet he couldn't bring himself *not* to look. And when he did, taking the hammer from the small hands, he observed an expression of such affection and gratitude that it caused his eyes to sting.

I'm going to miss him while he's at school, Seth realized. How strange and wonderful that a good deed he'd performed grudgingly at best, taking Elaine's child from the orphanage, had turned out this way. Seth was beginning to believe that he himself benefited more from the arrangement than did Thomas.

As content as he was to occupy a world that included only the two of them, he knew that Thomas needed the companionship of other children. It was too bad that the Sanders boys had proved to be so irascible. He had been forced to reprimand a couple of them, who looked younger than the two who had sold him the guineas, for aiming slingshots threateningly at his horses from their gate as he drove by on his wagon just last week. Then from out of nowhere a man he rightly assumed to be Mr. Sanders appeared, ranting and railing that Seth had best go on his way and leave his sons alone.

"I got enough boys here ter whip you good!" the man had shouted, with some expletives thrown in for good measure.

Recalling that incident, Seth wondered how it was that the cottage that housed such characters could also produce someone kind enough to bring cake to new neighbors. He hoped that the woman's sons had relayed his gratitude to her.

"They're going to like their new house, aren't they?"

Seth turned his attention back to Thomas. "The guineas?"

"Maybe they'll start laying eggs in the morning."

Slowly and with just a bit of bashfulness, he reached out a hand to tousle the boy's ash-colored hair. "I wouldn't be a bit surprised."

Thomas grinned. "Yes, sir, we wouldn't be a bit surprised."

Jonathan jumped at the sound of a knock. He rose hurriedly from his chair, from which he'd been staring out of the window for the better part of an hour. It was only when his hand touched the knob that he hesitated. "Please give me the chance to prove to you that I've changed, sir," he rehearsed under his breath.

As much as he wanted to get the confrontation with Vicar Phelps over with, he couldn't help but feel some relief when it was only Mr. Pool on the other side.

"Wouldn't you be wantin' some lunch, sir?" he asked. "It's half-past twelve."

"No, thank you," Jonathan replied. He'd only had toast and tea at the railway station this morning, but he couldn't have eaten had his life depended upon it. When the door was closed again, he took off his shoes and lay across the bed. If he could just make himself rest for a little while, perhaps he wouldn't be so jumpy. But that proved worse, for he worried about accidentally falling asleep and facing the vicar with his wits in a fog.

So he returned to his chair and resumed his watch out of the window, reminding himself that Elizabeth Phelps was worth putting himself through this torment.

" ' . . . and Cornelius said, four days ago I was fasting until this hour; and at the ninth hour I prayed in my house, and behold, a man stood before me in bright clothing,' " Andrew read loudly into the silver-haired woman's ear horn as she sat propped upon her pillows.

"Yes?" she said, her faded brown eyes wide. "Who was the man in bright clothing, Vicar?"

"He was an angel, Mrs. Cobbe. Remember how he told Cornelius to send men to Joppa?" he fairly shouted so the poor woman could hear.

"Yes, for Simon Peter." The woman gave him a grateful smile. "I remember now. Go ahead, Vicar."

Andrew called at the cottage on Thatcher Lane weekly to deliver a condensed version of the sermon that Mrs. Cobbe and her daughter, Mrs. Ramsey, missed at church each Sunday—and to pass along news of the parish. It was a strain to have to speak so loudly, but he enjoyed his visits with the two. They were so appreciative and drank up news like sponges.

If he had not insisted that Elizabeth stay home and nurse her cold, she would have entertained the two with descriptions of what the ladies had worn to the service. Gresham was by no means a fashion Mecca, but to Mrs. Cobbe, who never left the confines of her bedroom, it was an opportunity to participate vicariously in village life. Mrs. Ramsey was almost as reclusive—she left her mother only when it was necessary to go to *Trumbles* or the bakery, or to tend to her vegetable garden. A combination of the wages the widow earned as a seamstress and parish assistance kept the two alive.

Andrew had to be careful how he offered this assistance, for both women were proud. He had learned that it was easier to purchase staples with their portion of the poor box proceeds and casually set them inside the door on his Monday visits than to attempt to press money into Mrs. Ramsey's hands.

"Will you have a bite of lunch with us?" Mrs. Ramsey asked when Andrew rose from the bedside chair. She was a plain woman with a pockmarked complexion, but the flowers set about in every conceivable container proved she had a love of beauty.

"Thank you," Andrew replied, "but I should see about Elizabeth."

"What did you say, Ruth?" asked Mrs. Cobbe.

"I asked the vicar for lunch, but he has to leave," she said loudly.

"Well, perhaps next week," her mother said sweetly, nodding her understanding.

Sometimes Andrew accepted their offer of a meal in spite of their limited means, because he had learned over the years that poor people did not feel so poor when allowed to give occasionally. He was startled to discover his pocket watch read almost one o'clock when he stepped out into the sunlight again. Today's calls were within walking distance, so he had left Rusty and the trap at the vicarage. *Those poor women*, he thought, chiding himself for running behind on his calls and staying so late. They would starve before interrupting the sermon.

He knew he was in hot water with Mrs. Paget, whom he had advised he would be home for lunch. So when he approached the back of the *Larkspur* from Church Lane and spotted Mr. Herrick helping Julia and her girls from the landau, he exchanged quick greetings with the Worthy sisters and turned into the carriage drive. He would stop for just a minute to see how she was coping with Philip's departure.

"Tell me again he's going to be all right," Julia said after Aleda and Grace had greeted him and gone inside. Andrew sat with her on a bench in the courtyard, the west wing shielding them from the ever vigilant eyes of the Worthy sisters.

"He's going to be just fine," Andrew replied, raising her fingertips to his lips. It was obvious from the look of her green eyes that she had shed some tears earlier. He understood. He certainly wasn't looking forward to Laurel's departure next Monday, and *she* wasn't even going very far and would be home every weekend. "He's an intelligent boy, and this will be a good experience for him."

"Of course it will." She mustered up a smile for him, though it was clear to see that it took some effort.

"And it's a blessing that he can come home once a month, you know?" Andrew reminded her. "Most lads in boarding schools see their families only on holidays."

Grasping at that, she added, "And we stay so busy around here that a month will pass before we know it."

"There, you see? He's practically on his way home already."

Now her smile became more genuine. "Thank you, Andrew." She glanced back at the door. "Mrs. Herrick will be holding some lunch for us. I should go in now. Would you care to join us?"

"No, thank you. I told Mrs. Paget I'd be home at noon. She'll have some cold shoulder waiting for me."

"I see. Then you should hurry—" She stopped, suspicion narrowing her eyes. "Some cold shoulder? I've had to say good-bye to my son today, and you're making a *joke?*"

He grimaced. "Forgive me, dear. It just slipped out."

Julia stared at him for several long seconds, while Andrew, feeling miserable, chided himself for his lack of sensitivity. No doubt she was wondering why she ever agreed to marry him. Just as he was considering throwing himself upon his knees and begging for one more chance, she smiled.

"I never realized it before, but you're just alike, you and Philip."

"You're not angry?"

She shook her head. "I *should* be, you know. But I suppose one woman giving you cold shoulder is enough for today." Allowing him to assist her to her feet, she said, "Why isn't Elizabeth making calls with you today?"

Relieved that she held no grudge, he replied, "She has a head cold."

"Oh, I'm sorry. Is it a very bad one?"

"Not too bad, but I didn't think people like Mrs. Cobbe should be exposed."

He said good-bye with just a squeeze of her hand. Only a boorish fellow would expect a kiss from a woman who had so recently shed tears over her son's departure.

But she surprised him by standing on her toes and leaning forward. "Thank you for being such a comfort, Andrew," she said, just before planting a soft kiss upon his lips.

It put him in such a pleasant mood that he hummed all the way up Church Lane. Even the prospect of facing Mrs. Paget couldn't take the bounce out of his steps. When the vicarage came into view, he noticed Laurel seated on the top step of the stoop with an open book in her lap. She looked up when the garden gate let out its usual squeak.

"Hello, Pet!" he called.

"Hello, Papa!" Apparently she had been waiting for him, for she put the book aside and jumped to her feet. "I thought you'd never get home!"

"Why, what's happened?" he asked, sending a worried glance up to Elizabeth's window. "Is your sister—"

"She's upstairs, most likely crying her eyes out again."

––––––––––

When the next knock came, Jonathan knew in his heart it was the vicar. He had expected it to be louder, more forceful, perhaps hard enough to rattle the windowpanes. With legs that seemed to have turned to wood, he rose from the chair by the window and opened the door.

"Good afternoon, Mr. Raleigh," Vicar Phelps said.

He was the same as Jonathan remembered, from the broad shoulders to the neatly trimmed beard. "Won't you come in, sir?" It was then that Jonathan realized he was still in his stocking feet, as his shoes were still at the side of the bed. He felt embarrassed about that, but it was too late to do anything about it now.

"Yes, thank you," the vicar replied and walked into the room. From the tone of his voice it appeared he was taking great pains to keep himself under control.

Realizing he was wringing his hands like an underclassman before his orals, Jonathan wiped his palms upon the front of his pants and motioned to the only chair. "Would you care to have a seat?"

The vicar closed the door behind him. "I prefer to stand, thank you."

It was ludicrous, the two of them exercising such courtesy as if they were just about to discuss favorite novels over tea and shortbread, when Jonathan was sure that his visitor would have much preferred pouncing upon him and ripping out his lungs. He stood there awkwardly while the pair of hazel eyes studied him. It was a relief when the vicar brought up the subject on both their minds.

"I will not ask you why you came here, Mr. Raleigh," he said in a well-modulated voice.

Jonathan could imagine him using the same tone to explain the parable of the wheat and the tares to his congregation.

"I can only assume you still fancy yourself to harbor some feelings for my daughter."

Jonathan straightened. "I love her, sir."

"No doubt it seems that way to you." Taking a step closer, Vicar Phelps clasped both hands behind his back and said, "You are still quite young, Mr. Raleigh. Oftentimes it takes years for a man to discover his true nature. Shall I save you some time and tell you something about yours?"

"Sir, if you would just allow me to—"

"You are shallow, Mr. Raleigh." He took another step closer until they stood only two feet apart. "And just as an infant sits in the midst of his toys and frets for the one forbidden to him, you desire Elizabeth because she has no use for you."

"That's not true." Swallowing hard, Jonathan said, "Perhaps it was true at one time, but I've changed, Vicar Phelps. I've become—"

"You've changed? I could preach a sermon on the likes of you." He drew his lips sarcastically. "One about a leopard changing its spots comes to mind right away."

I know that verse, Jonathan realized. If only he could recall from where, surely the vicar would understand. *Isaiah? Ezekiel?*

"So as you can see, Mr. Raleigh, your journey here has been—"

"Jeremiah!"

The vicar blinked, his sentence left hanging in the air. "I beg your pardon?"

" 'Can the Ethiopian change his skin, or the leopard his spots? Then may ye also do good, that are accustomed to do evil.' "

It was almost comical, how Vicar Phelps gaped at him. Jonathan gave a self-conscious shrug. "My grandfather, sir. He encouraged me to memorize scripture since I was a boy. But I confess it never meant anything to me until last January."

Vicar Phelps's eyes widened. "You've come to personal faith in Christ?"

"Yes, sir—in my grandfather's parlor. I was practically suicidal with self-loathing. Please believe me, sir. I wouldn't lie about something so serious."

The face across from him actually paled. Jonathan couldn't help but feel disappointed. He had not expected the vicar to shout with joy and *embrace* him, but surely a man of the cloth would take the news of a conversion without appearing as if suddenly stricken with a stomach ailment.

"Vicar Phelps?"

Without asking, Vicar Phelps moved to the chair and sat down. "January?" he mumbled, scratching his blond beard.

"I should think you would be pleased, sir."

"But of course . . . ." He gave another sigh and then studied Jonathan in thoughtful silence.

Jonathan waited, resisting the compulsion to plead his case further. Presently the vicar straightened his shoulders.

"Of course I'm pleased at your news, Mr. Raleigh. But I can't help but wonder if your *conversion,* if you will, was for the purpose of finding your way back into my daughter's good graces. People don't always follow Christ for the right reasons. Look at Judas Iscariot."

So now you're comparing me with Judas? Jonathan thought but managed to hold his indignation in check. He had only to recall a certain evening last year in Cambridge to remind himself that he could expect no less than the rough side of the vicar's tongue. Still, he had the right to defend himself.

"I would rather look at Saul of Tarsus, sir," he said respectfully. "As you know, he had a wretched past as well, but the other disciples managed to forgive him."

Vicar Phelps looked as if he would choke, and sure enough, he lowered his head and started coughing. *Water,* Jonathan thought, padding across the carpet to the door and pulling it open. He jumped back as the inn-keeper's wife stumbled into the room.

The vicar raised his head to stare at her. "Mrs. Pool?" he said between coughs.

She smoothed her apron and raised her chin. "I were just wonderin' if the young man wanted an extra blanket. The nights are turnin' chilly." This was said with a straight, albeit crimson face, in spite of the fact that daylight still poured through the window—and that there was no blanket in her arms.

"No, thank you," Jonathan told her. "But may we have some water?"

"That's not necessary. I'm fine now," the vicar said from behind him. "Good day, Mrs. Pool."

"Good day, Vicar." Gathering her bruised dignity around her like a cloak, she gave Jonathan a crisp nod on her way to the door. "Mr. Raleigh."

Jonathan turned back around as soon as the door snapped shut. Both sets of eyes met, and both men burst into laughter. Vicar Phelps laughed hardest, until he had to take out a handkerchief and wipe his eyes. "I suppose you've heard that 'a merry heart doeth good like a medicine,' " he said.

"Proverbs, sir," Jonathan said, smiling himself. The shared merriment put him at ease enough to sit upon the foot of the bed.

"This doesn't change a thing, you know."

The smile froze upon Jonathan's face. "It doesn't?"

"Oh, I confess my opinion of you has gone up several notches. But as far as stability goes, Mr. Raleigh, frankly your faith has not been tested. I can't risk my daughter's future in the hopes that you won't grow bored one day with living a decent life and decide debauchery was more appealing."

"But that's the very reason I didn't come here as soon as I committed my life to Christ," Jonathan argued. "I wanted to make sure I wasn't just a flash-in-the-pan."

"Very wise of you," the vicar said and gave him a sad smile. "But six . . . seven months? Give yourself another year or two to grow spiritually before thinking about such things as courting."

"Another year—"

"Or two."

"But Elizabeth could be married by then." Something passed across the man's expression that told Jonathan that was more than a possibility. Rising from the foot of the bed, he said, "She's seeing someone, isn't she?"

"Well, yes."

"Does she plan to marry him?"

"She does, Mr. Raleigh. I'm sorry, but—"

"When is the wedding, Vicar Phelps?" While he didn't believe the vicar would lie to him, there had been some hesitancy in his tone, enough to give Jonathan some hope.

The vicar sighed. "That hasn't been decided yet."

"Have the banns been published?"

"No, but it's only a matter of . . ." A little of his former attitude showed itself. "This has nothing to do with you, Mr. Raleigh. The man has dedicated his life to the ministry and will make a decent husband. If you care about Elizabeth as much as you say, you'll want her to be happy."

"And this man makes her happy?"

"Yes, Mr. Raleigh." The vicar rose from the chair, walked toward Jonathan, and offered his hand. "It does my heart good to see the change in you." Again the sad smile appeared. "Forgive me if I've been unduly harsh, but I pray you'll take to heart what I've told you. Elizabeth has been through much heartache and deserves this opportunity for a good life. Sometimes we show our love best by letting go."

Jonathan could only nod stupidly as he and the vicar shook hands. Here was an older, wiser man, whom he respected almost as much as he respected his own grandfather, finally displaying some warmth toward him. *I'm confident you'll do the honorable thing,* the eyes that stared into his said. It was enough to raise doubts within himself. He had spent most of his life acting selfishly. Had his coming to Gresham merely been more of the same?

When the vicar was gone, Jonathan went back to his chair and slumped into it. He propped his elbows upon his knees and cradled his head, wishing his grandfather were here to counsel him. Then the thought dawned upon him. *If she had no feelings left for me, her father wouldn't be so adamant that I leave. It wouldn't matter.* And shouldn't Elizabeth have some say in whether he should disappear from her life forever?

If there were only some way he could prove to her—and her father, for he was sure that she would not marry someone of whom he strongly disapproved—that he could stay on the course. As it was, he wasn't sure if he could prove it to himself. The vicar was correct in stating that his faith had not been tested. Aside from aching to see Elizabeth again, his few months as a new believer had been easy. But what was he to do?

Show me how to prove myself, Father, he prayed. *And then please help me not to fail you.*

*T*he man who had quoted Alexander Pope to Philip left the train at Birmingham Station, leaving Philip feeling guiltily relieved. In his place boarded a boy wearing the same brown tweed Norfolk jacket and trousers that were the uniform of the Josiah Smith Preparatory Academy. At least the boy attempted to board, for his weeping mother clung to him at the open door of the compartment and cried, "Don't make him go!" over and over. At her side stood a stern-faced man in a gray top hat and coat.

"Let him go, Helen," he said, looking much embarrassed.

This scene continued for about a full minute, until a ticket taker came to collect tickets and close the door. On the platform Philip could see through the window that the man had put an arm around the woman's shoulder—whether to comfort her or to keep her from flinging open the door to the compartment, he couldn't tell.

Finally the train began rolling. After the boy had waved to his parents until they were out of sight, he turned to look at Philip. He was rather stout, with full cheeks and light brown hair. It was clear that he was embarrassed. "My mother," he said, his face crumpling a bit as if he would weep himself. "My older brother died in a typhus epidemic at boarding school in Gloucester."

Philip gave a sympathetic nod, and the women across from them made sympathetic little sounds. "She's afraid it will happen to you?"

"Or something just as bad."

Philip felt pity for the mother now. As worried as his own mother had been about him, at least she had not experienced the loss of another son. "Aren't there preparatory schools in Birmingham?" At least he *assumed* the boy was from Birmingham.

It turned out he was right, for the boy shrugged. "Father says I'm too sheltered, and that it will be better for me to get away. Are you going to the Josiah Smith Academy?"

"Yes. And you?"

The boy smiled. "My first time away from home."

"Mine too." Philip extended a hand and they shook. "Philip Hollis."

"Gabriel Patterson."

They exchanged particulars about their homes and families, and Philip discovered that Gabriel's father was also a surgeon, as his had been.

"Only I'm not so keen on becoming a doctor," the boy confessed in a lower voice, as if he feared the two women, who had resumed chatting about a cousin they were on their way to visit, would overhear and shame him.

Philip's wish to become a doctor was so strong that it was hard to imagine anyone with the opportunity to do so *not* having that same desire. But he sympathized with the boy again. "What do you want to do?"

Gabriel Patterson hesitated before replying. "I like to write stories."

"Yes? Are they any good?"

"I hope so. I once had one published."

Now Philip was impressed . . . and a little skeptical. "You did, truly?"

His new traveling companion smiled and stood, then brought down his satchel from the overhead compartment. "I keep it with me constantly," he confessed, handing over a copy of the March issue of Beeton's *Boy's Own Magazine*. "It begins on page thirty-one."

Reverently Philip opened up the magazine and found a five-page story titled "The Dagger" by Gabriel Kendrick Patterson.

"They don't usually print stories by children," Gabriel explained. "But there is a yearly competition for boys."

"And you won?"

"Yes," the boy replied with a modest flush.

"You say you write other stories?" This came from the younger of the two women, who had ceased their conversation when Gabriel brought down his satchel.

He nodded. "But none that have been published. I usually just show them to my mother and my tutor."

Both women agreed aloud that he was a bright boy and went back to their chat. "Would you like to read it?" Gabriel asked Philip.

"Yes, of course." Philip began to read, aware from the corner of his eye that his new friend was watching expectantly. He soon forgot about Gabriel as he became immersed in the story of two children who find a small rusty, blunt dagger which they almost discard, until accidentally discovering it has the power to cause people to tell the truth when pointed in their direction. When he was finished, Philip remarked, "Why, this is very good."

"Thank you."

A discussion ensued over favorite novels. Philip found that in spite of

Gabriel's not wanting to be a doctor, being the youngest child in his family, and having never gone fishing, they had much in common. In fact, by the time the train steamed into Worcester Station, Philip felt as if they had known each other for years.

A man holding up a placard with the hand-lettered words Josiah Smith Preparatory Academy directed Philip and Gabriel to a waiting wagon and team of four horses. At least a dozen boys ranging in ages from thirteen to seventeen came from other parts of the train, tossed gripsacks and portmanteaus in the middle, and took places on benches built into both sides. The older boys were obviously familiar with the routine and fell to chatter and laughter as they bounded up into the wagon bed. The younger ones, like Philip and Gabriel, were intimidated into silence.

They were carried down some six miles of gently undulating road—past shops, a cathedral, and many half-timbered houses. Knuckles became white from gripping the edges of the bench, and the older boys, who had managed to seat themselves along one side, laughed every time the wagon hit a bump. They also laughed for other reasons unclear to Philip until he realized it was he and his fellow younger students who were providing the source of levity. *Why?* he wondered, but a glance at his bench mates told him they were too absorbed with simply holding on to the side of the wagon to engage in any clowning.

Finally the wagon turned into a gravel drive lined with copper beeches and lime trees. Philip caught glimpses of a river off to the north and assumed it to be the Severn because it appeared to be much wider than the Bryce. Presently they passed iron gates and a cricket field, then came to a four-story building of brown brick, its roof hidden by a parapet. Wide portico and steps led up to a wooden door carved with what Philip assumed to be the Smith family's coat of arms. Flanking this main door and some feet away on either side were two plain doors at the tops of steps with iron balustrades. It was in front of one of these that the driver reined the team to a halt.

There was a mad scramble for satchels and cases—at least among the older boys. The younger sat and stared. "If this were the first day, we'd have to carry their things upstairs," the boy on Philip's right, obviously a returning student, said in a low voice.

"You're serious?" Philip whispered back.

"Upperclassmen have the right to order the younger students about. They can make us carry their food trays and make their beds too."

Vicar Phelps's warning about bullies came back to Philip. "And if we refuse?"

The boy shrugged. "They actually *like* it when you refuse, if you understand my meaning, so it's best to go along. You wouldn't want your shoes to end up in the lavatory, or horse dung smeared into your hair while you're sleeping."

Philip was stunned. "How can they get away with that?"

"Easy. They don't get caught—even if others see them. Talebearers get tormented worse than anyone." Another shrug. "But at least we'll have our chance too in a couple of years."

I can hardly wait, Philip thought, frowning.

"What did he say?" Gabriel asked from his left.

Philip hesitated because his traveling companion already had expressed misgivings about coming here. But he supposed a warning was necessary. "We're going to have to carry things for the upperclassmen and make their beds and such."

Panic flooded Gabriel's face. "But I don't know how to make up a bed."

"Don't worry. I'll teach you." He thought back to the days when his family had moved to the *Larkspur* after it had been abandoned for several years. There was so much work to do that his mother had insisted he and his sisters learn to make their beds. Even to this day, they continued the chore. He had occasionally grumbled about it to himself then but was grateful now he had the experience.

The older boys had jumped down from the wagon with their belongings and were disappearing through the door, leaving the others to retrieve their own scattered belongings. It was then that Philip noticed a man standing at the foot of the wagon, wearing an old-fashioned frock coat and holding a pad and pencil.

"Good afternoon, gentlemen," he said with a welcoming smile. He seemed to be about Mr. Pitney's age, though the top of his scalp was visible through thinning strands of brown hair. "I'm Mr. Archer, housemaster for third form students. I lecture on chemistry as well."

Philip found himself relaxing, for he had begun to wonder on the journey from the station if any friendly faces were to be found at the school. A boy of about sixteen came out of the door and joined Mr. Archer. He wore the same Norfolk jacket, but it was clear from his stance at Mr. Archer's side that he carried some authority. *Josiah Smith's son?* Philip wondered half seriously.

"May I have a show of hands of those in the third form, or perhaps new students in higher forms?" the housemaster asked. Philip lifted his hand, along with Gabriel and two other boys. Mr. Archer nodded. "Wait here and I'll give you instructions. You who are returning students may go on up to the dormitories. Rooming lists are posted in the corridors."

The remaining students climbed down from the wagon, leaving Philip and the other three.

"You'll be welcomed formally at the assembly before dinner," Mr. Archer said, "but I would like to take this opportunity to welcome you myself. May I have your names now?"

As they gave their names, the housemaster ticked them from his list. It turned out all four were third form students. "That's good," he said, then nodded toward the boy beside him. "I'd like to introduce Quinton Westbrook. He's a student prefect and will be rooming in your dormitory as my representative. If you have any concerns or difficulties, Mr. Westbrook will assist you. By the way, students address each other by last name only, no matter what rank. Mr. Westbrook will show you to your dormitory now."

Silently the four students followed Westbrook up three flights of stairs. Elsewhere in the huge building were sounds of laughter and camaraderie from students who clearly thought the Josiah Smith Preparatory Academy a home away from home. *I'll feel the same one day*, Philip assured himself, though that day seemed far off in the future.

They were led up a long hardwood floor corridor. Most doors were open, and Philip could see boys making beds, unpacking satchels, or just visiting. Westbrook stopped at the last open door on the left and turned to face the four. He was not much taller than himself, Philip realized now that he wasn't looking up at him on the staircase or down at him from the wagon. He had coal-black hair, brows, and lashes, oddly mixed with eyes so light blue that they almost looked transparent. And unlike Mr. Archer, he had yet to smile.

"You will store your immediate belongings in the trunk at the foot of your bed. A lavatory and water closet are at the end of the room. Wipe the sink out after you use it, and if you haven't experience with hot water faucets, see me before taking your first bath, which are only allowed on Saturday evenings, by the way."

He recited this litany with little inflection, as if he had said it hundreds of times. Then he stepped into the room with Philip and his group following. Three boys were already unpacking and stopped to stare with unsure expressions. Eight narrow beds, iron railed and painted dull brown, stood out against each of the two long walls. There was a space of not more than three feet between the sides of each bed, and a corridor of about six feet ran between the two rows. Westbrook went over to the nearest bed and took a sheet of paper from the top.

"Are you Barnhart?" he asked, looking over his list at a boy with hair as carrot red as Ben Mayhew's. The boy nodded, causing Westbrook to bark sharply, "Answer yes or no!"

"Uh, yes."

The prefect pointed to the farthest bed on the opposite wall. "Last bed."

You know, it would help a lot if you would smile, Philip thought, but of course he didn't feel the liberty to say.

"Lowry?" Westbrook said.

Another boy, the smallest of the lot so far, raised a hand but then checked himself midway and jerked it back to his side. "Yes?" he replied in a voice that cracked in the middle.

"You don't wet the bed, do you?"

"Uh . . . no."

Westbrook jabbed a thumb in the direction of the bed nearest to the lavatory. "Over there. Just in case." This remark was followed by his first smile—only the mocking look in his pale eyes made it more of a smirk.

"Smith," he said next, but there was no Smith yet among the old or new arrivals. He frowned at his list. "Patterson."

Gabriel Patterson took a step forward. "Yes?"

The smirk spread across Westbrook's face again, even more pronounced. "I had you assigned in the bed next to mine, but I didn't realize you were such an elephant."

There was a titter of laughter from one of the boys. Gabriel smiled, too, as if trying hard to pretend that the joke wasn't on him, but his eyes gave evidence that he was on the verge of tears. *Is being obnoxious a prerequisite for becoming a prefect?* Philip wondered.

"Take Barnhart's," Westbrook continued, nodding toward the farthest bed. "You move up here, Barnhart. I don't care for my first sight every morning to be a mountain of blubber."

More chortles came from a couple of the other boys. Gabriel's face assumed a blank look, as if he had retreated somewhere safer inside himself. Philip had had enough. "There's no call to be so rude, you know," he told Westbrook. Silence immediately followed as stunned faces were whipped in his direction.

"What did you say to me?" the prefect demanded, his washed-out eyes now slits.

"I said there was no call to be rude. He hasn't done anything to you."

"Philip, don't—" Gabriel began but was pushed aside roughly by Westbrook, who stepped up to Philip's face and assumed the smirk again.

"Because this is your first day, I'm going to be agreeable and forget I ever heard your squeak, little mouse," he said in a controlled voice, as if he were enjoying himself. "But you'd best do yourself a favor and never cross me again."

What am I, in the army? thought Philip, whose previous educational experience had been with his tutor in London and Captain Powell in

184

Gresham, both whose authority had been tempered with kindness. Something inside told him that reasoning with such a beast would be futile, but his emotions were so charged that he ignored it. "Do you consider a simple request to be civil to be 'crossing you'?"

Now the slits that were Westbrook's eyes opened to the point of bulging. Still the volume of his voice never increased as he said, "I've got to go downstairs to meet another group, Hollis. You *are* Hollis, aren't you?"

"Yes."

He pointed to a bed in the center of the opposite wall. "Over there, Hollis. But before you make your bed, change into knickers and give me four laps."

Philip didn't understand. "Four laps . . ."

"*Running*, you half-wit. Around the building, then the tennis courts and cricket field. Cross me again and you'll spend your lunch breaks running around in circles."

———

It was not until Laurel had gone to bed that Elizabeth came down from her room. Her blond hair was a mess about her shoulders, and her dress rumpled as if she had slept in it all day—and according to Dora, she had.

"Hello, Papa," she yawned in the doorway to his study.

Andrew rose and hurried around his desk. "Beth . . . I've been so worried."

"Oh, I'm—" she said, but then assumed a pinched expression. She held up a hand bearing a handkerchief more crumpled than her gown.

"You're what? Should I call for Dora?"

She shook her head, her expression growing more pinched. Then the handkerchief flew up to her face and she sneezed violently into it. "I'm all right," she said when she could speak again.

"I can see that," Andrew said, taking her by the arm and leading her down the passageway. "Mrs. Paget left some soup on the back of the stove."

"But I'm not hungry."

"Then have some just to humor me." In the kitchen the kettle was lukewarm to the touch, but it only took Andrew a minute to figure out how to light the gas jet with a match. He soon dished her up a bowl of beef-and-cabbage soup and sat beside her at the table. For someone who had declared herself not hungry, she ate well, finishing that bowl and asking for a half serving more. And then it was time to talk.

"I called upon Mr. Raleigh today," Andrew said. His daughter nodded. He couldn't discern any emotion in her expression, perhaps because of the cold.

"I assumed you would."

"Laurel says he came here to see you."

"We spoke in the front doorway." She blew her nose. "I didn't ask him in, of course."

Andrew felt some relief upon hearing that. "So you won't care if he leaves town?"

"Care? I insisted upon that very thing."

Good for you! Andrew thought. It was on the tip of his tongue to tell her that Jonathan Raleigh now claimed to be a Christian, but he thought better of it. No sense in muddying the waters. Days from now Mr. Raleigh's visit would be just a memory. "Now, let me help you upstairs," he said, rising to take her empty bowl. "You'll get over that cold much sooner if you have enough rest." *And as soon as she's well, we should have Mr. Treves over for supper again.*

He felt a little guilty when he recalled praying about a month ago that he wouldn't influence his daughter in the wrong direction in the matter of choosing a suitor and potential husband. But he was only trying to influence her in the *right* direction, he told himself. Even if he wasn't sure exactly where that path happened to lie, he was more than certain it wasn't in the direction of Jonathan Raleigh—converted or not.

What should I do? Jonathan asked himself as he shaved his face in the water closet of the *Bow and Fiddle*. Yesterday's prayer for discernment had not been answered—or perhaps God's silence on the matter *was* the answer. Did that mean he was supposed to go back to Cambridge?

Grandfather had said that it sometimes took years to recognize the stirrings of God in the heart, that he mustn't be discouraged. Jonathan wasn't discouraged about his newfound faith, because he still had it in him to appreciate feeling clean after so many years of self-centered, self-destructive behavior. Yet he could not help but wish that, until he grew in wisdom, he had more concrete directions from God for matters not directly spelled out in his Bible. There was no chapter or verse to tell him whether he should leave Gresham today.

His stomach, however, was sending up a clear message, reminding him that he hadn't eaten since the toast and tea yesterday morning. Mrs. Pool took his order for bacon and eggs as if she had never stumbled into his room yesterday, and she didn't ask prying questions beyond, "Will you be stayin' another day?" Which of course she had the duty to ask, being the innkeeper's wife.

"I'm not sure," he replied. "May I tell you in a little while?" Perhaps some more prayer was in order after breakfast.

"Certainly," she sniffed and moved on to the next table. There sat three men with long faces, close enough for Jonathan to overhear their conversation. Not that he was purposely *trying*, but he couldn't very well stop up his ears.

"Doctor Rhodes says it's pleurisy all right. She likely had it for a while and didn't know it until it came upon her so intense late last night."

"That school in Scotland is to blame. You can't house people in tombs without expecting their lungs to be affected."

"What are we going to do? Don't see how we can find someone to take her place in just six days."

A collective sigh came from all three as a serving girl brought Jonathan his food. Now he found himself listening on purpose, even though he had no idea who was being discussed and the significance of six days.

"I wonder if Miss Hillock could be persuaded to combine both sections—just until Miss Clark recovers."

The suggestion was silently considered, but then one man shook his head. He was white-haired and older than the rest and seemed to be the head of what Jonathan now realized was the local school board.

"There would be forty-five students if we combined them—too many for one woman. And I don't know if Miss Hillock is competent enough in the subject matter of the older sections. She's been more than able with the younger children, but as you know, she never went to college."

The three talked on of their problem and considered—and discarded—several suggestions. Meanwhile, a wild idea was beginning to form itself in Jonathan's mind. If the town was in dire straits and he could possibly offer some assistance, he would have a reason to stay in Gresham.

Extending his leave of absence from his position in Cambridge was no problem. Even though he had his degree, he couldn't become a solicitor until he had articled himself to a practicing lawyer—in this case his father's brother—for five years. But they weren't required to be *consecutive* years, and the firm was already saturated with attorneys. He was aware that his uncle had taken him on only out of family courtesy, yet for him to have applied at any other firm would have offended both his father and uncle. But this . . .

"I wonder if we should delay school for a month or so?" he heard from the table beside him.

What do you know about teaching? Jonathan asked himself.

"What about one of the students who graduated last term? That Mayhew boy is bright."

Graduated last term? Too young, Jonathan thought.

"Too young," someone said.

Suddenly it hit Jonathan like a slap in the face that his prayer had been answered after all. Grandfather was a devout man and undoubtedly correct in saying that most of God's answers took the form of stirrings of the heart. Some, however, apparently took the form of three men having breakfast. *Thank you, Father*. He cleared his throat and turned to the table beside him.

"Excuse me, gentlemen," he said. "I wonder if I might have a word with you?"

———

It was not enough that Philip had been forced to carry the tray for

Tupper, a hulking figure with teeth as crooked as an old picket fence, but to amuse his friends, the boy wanted his eggs and bacon cut and his toast buttered. From bits and pieces overheard as Philip performed the task, he became aware that his present taskmaster was in the fifth form. Which meant that Tupper had himself been the object of overlording upperclassmen just last year. Philip would have thought that having suffered such treatment would cause a person to be less prone to inflict it upon others, but the older boys seemed to revel in their new authority.

Finally Tupper was too busy forking down breakfast to make sport of him, and Philip was able to get his own tray. He sat down at a third form table next to Gabriel Patterson, who, like the rest of the third form, had carried trays for older students.

"I didn't think you were going to have time to eat," Gabriel whispered.

"Me neither," Philip answered. They were forced to whisper because at the head of the table sat Westbrook, who seemed in an even more vile mood today than yesterday. It seemed wise to take for granted he could silence all conversation at the table with the bark of a command and would do so if they appeared to be enjoying themselves *too* much. "But it isn't so bad. My father once told me that he used to get caned by his prefect at Rugby."

"He did?" Gabriel's face clouded. "I don't think I would be able to bear it! The mocking about my size is bad enough!"

"I'm sorry" was all Philip could think of to say.

The boy's bottom lip trembled for a second, but then he shrugged with an obviously forced casualness. "It's not your fault, Hollis. In fact, if you hadn't befriended me, I think I would have thrown myself out of a window last night. I'm sorry you had to run around the school."

Philip leaned closer. "Don't tell Westbrook, but I'm very fond of running."

"You are?" Gabriel said with conspiratorial delight.

"Oh, very much." And he meant that, even if he was saying it mostly to reassure his new friend. But what he didn't say was that while he indeed enjoyed a good run, there was a profound difference between racing his friends across the village green and skipping lunch to run around a school building.

The thought of Gresham gave him a little stab of homesickness, but he comforted himself by thinking about his upcoming classes. *One can find a bright side to almost any situation if one looks hard enough*, he had heard Mrs. Dearing say at the supper table recently. It was a good bit of advice and worth repeating to himself now and then, given his present situation.

Something flew past his shoulder and hit Lowry, who was seated across from him, squarely in the forehead. The missile turned out to be a crust of well-buttered toast, and it fell to the lapel of the boy's jacket. It left a greasy smear even after he wiped the spot with a napkin. Philip felt sorry for the boy, who was now staring down at his plate so as not to provoke the thrower into further action, but he didn't think consolation in the form of Mrs. Dearing's philosophy would be welcome at the moment.

"You did *what*?"

Elizabeth and Laurel exchanged looks upon hearing their father's agitated voice. "Who's in the vestibule?" asked Elizabeth, who reclined against the arm of the sofa wrapped in a blanket. She felt better today, likely because of Mrs. Paget's soup, but was still forced to keep a handkerchief in hand.

Laurel put aside the copy of *Little Women* she'd borrowed from Helen Johnson on recommendation of Aleda Hollis and rose from her chair. "I'll go see." She edged over to the door and peered out, but by then it wasn't necessary because Mr. Sykes's voice carried clearly.

"We thought you'd be pleased, Vicar."

Laurel turned to whisper loudly, "That was Mr. Sykes. The school board is here."

Elizabeth nodded.

"Well, you could have at least asked me for a character recommendation!" their father's voice thundered. "The young man led me to believe he was leaving town!"

He had decided to forgo any calls today to tend to Elizabeth and write his Sunday morning sermon. As she didn't have a temperature, she wondered if the possibility of Jonathan reappearing on the porch today had anything to do with it. "You have to undo all of this now! What in the world were you thinking?"

"We can't undo it, Vicar, and we had no other choice. He has a degree from Cambridge, and he's wiring for references from his minister there." Mr. Sway was speaking quite defensively now. "Besides, we didn't even know you were acquainted with him."

"And Mr. Pool vouched he was a good customer," added Mr. Casper.

"Mr. Pool?" their father said, his voice dripping with sarcasm. "The *same* Mr. Pool who has known Mr. Raleigh all of twenty-four hours, if that long? The Mr. Pool who will be collecting lodging fees from him for as long as he stays in Gresham?"

Laurel turned to Elizabeth. "Can you hear all of this? They've hired Jonathan!"

Elizabeth nodded again. "You don't have to stand there. You can hear

190

every word sitting down." But her sister waved her away and resumed her post. *Why did you allow him to come here, Lord?* she prayed as the argument went on in the next room. She meant no disrespect, but it seemed to her that after all the times she'd asked God to help her forget Jonathan Raleigh, He wouldn't allow something like this to happen.

Now it was Mr. Sykes who spoke again. "We're sorry you ain't pleased, Vicar, but what's done is done. It was nothing short of a miracle, his falling into our laps two hours after we find out Miss Clark was ill."

There were more words and then the sound of the door closing. Laurel hurried to her chair just as their father stalked into the room. He dropped into his chair, planted both elbows upon his knees, and cradled his head with his hands.

"What's wrong, Papa?" Laurel asked innocently.

He gave a low groan. "We're going to have to move again."

Intercepting the panicked look her sister threw her, Elizabeth realized at that moment from whom she had inherited her tendency toward theatrics. "We can't go traipsing all over England just to hide from Jonathan, Papa. Besides, you have to consider the Hollises now too. Do you plan to break off your engagement?"

"No, of course not," he sighed, looking up at her with the saddest of expressions.

"You can't shield us from life, Papa."

"I know." He sighed again, then straightened in his chair. "I'm just so afraid."

So am I, Elizabeth thought. Of what, she wasn't quite sure. "Doctor Rhodes is extremely competent," she told him. "Miss Clark will probably be on her feet in a couple of weeks, then Mr. Raleigh will have no excuse to stay in Gresham."

Then the absurdity of the whole matter struck her. *Jonathan Raleigh teach school?* The mental picture alone was enough to cause her a bit of a smile just before another sneeze seized her.

"Laurel, fetch your sister another handkerchief," their father said, getting to his feet. "I want to see how Miss Clark is faring." Whether he had decided Elizabeth's reassurance had merit or his innate sense of duty had taken over was unclear, but he seemed relieved to have something constructive to do.

And since the *Larkspur* happened to be on the way to the Clarks' cottage, she had no doubt that he would call upon Mrs. Hollis. If anyone could coax him out of a foul mood, she could.

———

Dear Uncle Everet ... I've completely lost my mind, Jonathan thought,

191

holding his pen above the page as he struggled for words.

"It's not too late to back out," he mumbled and entertained the thought of looking up the school board members and confessing that youthful impulsiveness had rendered him temporarily insane. Or better yet, asking Mr. Pool to procure a coach or carriage so that he could put Gresham to his back as soon as possible.

But then he would be giving up any chance, however slim, of winning Elizabeth back, which would prove to her—and her father—that his word was no better than it had been before. *How difficult can it be?* he asked himself. He'd sat under schoolmasters for most of his life, and they hadn't appeared to be under any great strain. *Just a matter of organizing the lessons.* The members of the school board had informed him that he could avail himself of the school building at any time. He had only a few days to plan a schedule, but as long as he stayed a week or two ahead of the students, they would learn. It was like walking down a road after dark. If one could see to the edge of his lantern's light, he could go on for miles.

He didn't have to go miles—just until this Miss Clark was well again. *And you're fond of children.* On second thought, he couldn't recall any he actually had held a *conversation* with in the past five years besides Laurel Phelps. But one of his uncle's solicitors had a three-year-old, Hannah, whose lisping voice made everyone in the office chuckle whenever her mother brought her around. *And I gave her that paperweight.* It had been a cross-section of topaz stone that everyone who passed his desk would pause to admire. He hadn't *had* to give it to her, which must prove he had a soft spot for children.

He was beginning to feel better about the whole idea and decided that as soon as he finished writing letters and had a quick lunch, he would go over to the school and prepare lessons. *Whatsoever thy hand findeth to do, do it with thy might* he had read somewhere in the Scriptures. Ecclesiastes, he believed.

"I've just finished visiting the Clarks," Andrew told Julia in the *Larkspur*'s library. He had asked to speak with her privately, but of course that was now impossible in light of their engagement. With Mrs. Kingston tending the flower garden out front and Mr. Herrick the vegetable garden in back, the best she could offer was the library with the door open wide so that anyone who passed down the corridor could see that they sat in chairs some two feet apart. "I suppose you've heard about Miss Clark's pleurisy?"

"Yes," Julia nodded. "So sad. Were you able to speak with her?"

"A little. They're treating her with steam. If you've an abundance of mint in your kitchen garden, you may wish to send some over."

"Yes, of course. I'll see to that as soon as you leave."

"Thank you." He was studying her face now, as if trying to decide whether to say something.

"What is it, Andrew?" Julia asked.

A pained look came into his hazel eyes. "You haven't heard the rest, have you?"

"About Miss Clark?"

"Jonathan Raleigh is in Gresham."

"No . . ." Julia breathed. "Has he attempted to see Elizabeth?"

Andrew's lips tightened. "Thank God she had the good sense to send him away. But the school board members apparently had something stronger than tea with their breakfast this morning. They've hired him as a temporary replacement for Miss Clark."

"But they can't do that—can they?"

"Apparently they can. We did elect them, you know."

"But his morals . . ." Now it was Julia pressing her lips together. "I'll not allow someone like that to teach Aleda and Grace, Andrew. Didn't you tell them about that woman in Cambridge?"

He closed his eyes and rubbed his forehead. "I was so vexed I can't recall exactly *what* I told them, Julia. I was fairly certain that Laurel could overhear us, so I couldn't go into too much detail."

"You *will* tell them now, won't you?"

"Yes . . . of course."

The hesitancy in his reply made Julia suspect there was more to this than he had divulged so far. "Andrew?" she said. "What haven't you told me?"

Andrew's shoulders rose and fell with a heavy sigh. "Mr. Raleigh claims to have been led to Christ by his grandfather."

"He has?" It took Julia a second to digest this bit of information. "And now he comes here to win back Elizabeth? How convenient. Surely you don't believe him."

"No . . . yes." He shook his head. "I don't know. But he had the audacity to bring up how the disciples eventually forgave the apostle Paul of his past. His grandfather has encouraged him to ground himself in the Word, and it's quite obvious that he has been doing so."

"Oh." Julia was struck by how odd a picture they made, she and Andrew. They were discussing a young man's conversion in somber tones that would have been better suited for a funeral parlor. "Could it be that he's sincere, Andrew?"

"Not knowing that is what troubles me the most, Julia. As much as I tell myself he's only acting sincere in the hopes of winning back Elizabeth's affections, there is a part of me that believes him." His expression darkened again. "But that doesn't change my conviction that he's totally unsuitable for Elizabeth. My daughter deserves better than a husband who'll be comparing her to every strumpet who walked the streets of Cambridge."

It was in that glum mood that he took his leave. Julia went to her office and attempted to tally last month's receipts but gave up. She missed Philip terribly, and now there was Elizabeth to be concerned about, not to mention some anxiety about Mr. Raleigh becoming schoolmaster, however temporary the arrangement. If indeed the young man had become a Christian, that was wonderful news. But until she was convinced of that fact, she would not compromise her daughters' welfare. *If Andrew can't talk the board out of hiring him, I'll sit in that classroom myself.*

*T*he next morning after having tea with Andrew, who still wore a long face, Julia walked to *Trumbles* to post the letter she'd penned to Philip last night. She had filled her letter with little tidbits of news about the lodgers, servants, and neighbors, avoiding any mention of their latest worries. There was not much to tell, with his having been away only three days now, but she was of the mind that the contents of a letter from home were not nearly so important as the overall message—that the receiver of the letter is loved and missed.

"Ah, a letter to young Philip, eh?" said Mr. Trumble, holding up the envelope to the window's light. He had no timidity about reading the addresses of envelopes handed to him in his official role of postmaster.

Julia had once heard Ophelia Rhodes declare that if it weren't for seals, Mr. Trumble would likely open the letter in front of the bearer and peruse its contents. But Mr. Trumble was such an engaging and affable fellow that no one really complained.

"Did you tell him that the merry-go-round was finished yesterday?" he asked.

Julia let out a sigh. How could she have forgotten, when her two daughters practically had to be tied to their chairs at breakfast in their haste to go to the school yard? "It didn't even cross my mind, Mr. Trumble."

"Ah well . . . then you'll have some news for your next letter. Give him my warmest regrets, will you?"

Julia smiled at the man's blunder and assured him that she would. Then she walked on to the school yard, where it seemed half the village children had assembled. Amazingly some of the older children, Aleda and Laurel included, had persuaded the younger ones to form a queue so that turns could be taken in an orderly fashion. Six children at a time would assemble on the merry-go-round, with the younger children holding on to its posts for dear life and older boys pushing until it went fast enough for them to jump on for a while. While squeals came from the blurred images of passengers, equally enthusiastic squeals and handclaps came from the children

195

waiting their turns. Finally after about three minutes, the merry-go-round would slow to a halt, and the six disoriented children would weave their ways to the back of the queue, while others scrambled for seating on the contraption.

"You'll stay and watch us, Mrs. Hollis?" Laurel called as she and Aleda prepared to board.

"I would love to," she replied with a smile, moving over to sit at the top of the steps. It looked like great fun, and as Julia returned Grace's wave, she wished she could be a child again—at least for this morning. Sometime later she heard a noise from behind her. She turned to look up over her shoulder.

"Excuse me," said the young man standing in the doorway. "I hope I didn't startle you."

Of medium height and build, he was well-dressed in a gray frock coat, black trousers, and paisley silk cravat. His hair was as black as his trousers, with side whiskers extending only an inch below his ears. Dark lashes fringed eyes that were shades of gray and green. Julia needed no introduction and could see how Elizabeth could have fallen for such a person. *But only God sees the heart. Please help us to see it, too, Father, before Elizabeth gets hurt again.*

"You didn't startle me, Mr. Raleigh."

He gave her a searching look. "I'm sorry—you have me at a disadvantage."

And I'm sure that's a rarity for you, Julia thought cynically. But she rose to her feet, ignoring the hand of assistance he offered. "My name is Julia Hollis."

She was surprised to see recognition flood his eyes—and fear. "You're engaged to marry Vicar Phelps?"

Before Julia could ask him how he had known that, he gestured in the direction of the *Bow and Fiddle*.

"The landlord's wife . . ."

"Yes, of course." He didn't have to explain. "Has she informed you that I have two daughters who will be in your classroom?" *If Andrew hasn't convinced the school board to send you packing before school begins.*

He looked out at the assemblage of children. "I wasn't aware of that." The fear seemed to intensify in his expression. Still, he motioned toward the door behind him. "Would you care to come inside, Mrs. Hollis? I'm sure there are things we should discuss."

As Julia went through the door he held open for her, she grudgingly allowed him credit for not attempting to evade what promised to be an unpleasant conversation. Mr. Raleigh hurried to the desk, which was covered with papers and textbooks, pulled out the chair, and brought it over to a clear area near the blackboard. He waited until she had seated herself, then pulled out a smaller chair from the nearest student desk. There were larger chairs in the back rows, but apparently he didn't think of that. He looked rather comical with his knees jutting up into the air. Julia would have smiled to herself if Mr. Raleigh had been anyone else.

It seemed he was waiting for her to speak, watching her cautiously with his gray-green eyes. When she declined to do so, he cleared his throat.

"I'm going to take for granted that you know everything about my past, Mrs. Hollis," he said, avoiding her eyes now.

Such frankness in the face of obvious discomfort gave Julia still more reason to wonder about the young man. She had long held the opinion that he was a rogue with no conscience. And from what she had heard about such men, she knew that they were adept at evading accountability for their actions. "Only the part that concerns Elizabeth, Mr. Raleigh," she replied.

He actually winced. "I see."

"Can you understand how I would have reservations about your teaching my daughters or any other children here? A schoolmaster cannot help but flavor the lessons with his own morality . . . or lack thereof."

"Yes," he replied, nodding somberly. "I don't know how I can reassure you, Mrs. Hollis. I assume that Vicar Phelps has told you I've become a believer."

"He has."

"But of course *anyone* can say that," Mr. Raleigh said, voicing her very thoughts. He wrapped his arms around his raised knees, a posture that made him seem more a boy than a man of twenty-two. "Perhaps it was wrong for me to come here—I don't know. It just seemed that God allowed everything to fall into place, especially with my being offered this position."

There was such misery and confusion in his expression that Julia found her opinion of him softening in spite of her determination otherwise. *If this is all an act, he's a very good actor.* "Mr. Raleigh," she sighed. "I wish with all my heart to believe that you have found Christ, and that your commitment is real."

He gave her a grateful, if somewhat ironic, look. "But you don't care to have the children be the testing ground."

"Can you understand that?"

"I can, Mrs. Hollis. But what would you have me do? I gave my word to the school board. Until they see fit to release me, I'm bound to it."

"And I appreciate that commitment." She lapsed into silence, recalling the thought that had occurred to her yesterday. Dare she mention it without offending him? *Who cares if he's offended?* she told herself. *The children are more important.* "Mr. Raleigh," she said. "I have a suggestion."

He released his knees from his arms and straightened as much as possible. "Yes?"

"Would you allow me to sit in your classroom for the first few days—or weeks?"

Tilting his head as if he hadn't heard clearly, he said, "Sit in the classroom?"

The Larkspur practically runs itself anyway. "Without drawing attention to myself, of course." She peered over her shoulder and then pointed at a back corner. "Over there would be out of the way. I could even mark papers if you'd like."

To her utter surprise, he expelled a long sigh that sounded suspiciously like relief. "You wouldn't mind?"

"Why, no," Julia replied. The smile upon his face confused her. "Mr. Raleigh, you do understand my motive for doing this, don't you?"

"Of course, Mrs. Hollis. You're not certain if I'll be a good moral influence upon the children."

She wouldn't have put it quite so bluntly, but as it was the truth, Julia nodded.

His smile did not fade. "You'll be most welcome here. And I thank you."

———

After walking Mrs. Hollis outside, Jonathan stood in the doorway and watched the children at play. It was odd how in the space of a few minutes the headache that had gripped the top of his head had vanished. *I won't have to be alone with them.*

A small boy looked up and waved an arm from the merry-go-round that had come to a halt to exchange passengers. Jonathan smiled and returned the wave. He had arrived early to have more time to spend at preparations—even so, there had already been a handful of children in the school yard playing with the new device. Earlier, when from inside the schoolroom he had heard the sounds escalating—meaning the crowd outside was growing—he had begun to experience a gnawing sense of panic. How could he, with no experience with children, hope to direct such youthful vigor in the direction of learning? He was a stranger in Gresham and not very long out of childhood himself. Why should they pay attention to him?

Looking out past the row of elder trees, he caught sight of Mrs. Hollis walking along the lane back to wherever she lived. Surely the presence of a woman—especially one with children—would have a calming effect upon the students.

198

He felt almost giddy with relief. So giddy that on impulse he took off his coat and hung it on the railing, then bounded down the steps and crossed over to the merry-go-round. "Get on," he told the two boys who were waiting to push. "I'll push it."

They jumped on immediately, and Jonathan shouldered a rail and sent six squealing children spinning. Of course when their time was up, another six ran to the contraption and asked that he spin them as well. Even Laurel Phelps, whom he understood was going away to school soon, piled on with the others, and while she did not smile at him, she didn't frown either.

Finally he had to plead weariness and shook his dizzy head at the children's pleadings. "I've work to do inside," he explained, mounting the steps again.

"Will you come out later, sir?" a young voice called.

"Perhaps," he sent back with another wave. He smiled all the way back to his desk. *They like me*, he thought. And with Mrs. Hollis unwittingly supplying moral support, how could he fail to be a good teacher? Why, he was actually looking forward to the first day of school.

On their way back from town, Seth Langford smiled at the boy beside him on the wagon seat. Thomas sat with a serene smile, clutching his newly purchased lunch pail, slate, and tin of chalk as if they were made of gold. Mr. Trumble had advised against the slate and chalk, saying that the squire had donated some to the school, but Seth thought he should have some supplies with which to practice at home.

The Sanders cottage loomed ahead in the distance now, and Seth could see a woman out tending the vegetable garden. *Mrs. Sanders*, he thought, feeling a tinge of guilt. He had some misgivings over whether her sons had relayed his thanks for the apple cake—no doubt she thought him ungrateful. *Should I stop?* he wondered, then reminded himself that almost a month had passed. It seemed better to go on his way than to experience the embarrassment of having delayed gratitude after so long.

As the wagon drew closer, the woman straightened to look curiously in their direction. She was much younger than he had first thought. Long curly brown hair was bound in a ribbon or comb, but some tendrils had escaped to dangle in her face, for she was pushing these aside. *She's the one who sings*, Seth realized. He had never caught her name because he and Thomas had fallen into the practice of slipping into chapel late and leaving early on Sunday mornings.

She's a Sanders? he thought with wonder. He had seen none of the rest of the family at chapel—and he thought he could recognize all of the males now after passing their place every now and then. Perhaps she was married

199

to one. That had to be it, he told himself, for a family of antisocial scowlers surely couldn't produce someone with such a lovely voice and pleasant demeanor. But then it was even harder to imagine someone such as she actually *choosing* to marry one of their ilk.

"There's the cake lady," Thomas said, finally looking up from his bounty.

"The cake lady? You mean she's the one?"

The boy nodded, but by then the young woman had gone back to her gardening. *Surely someone thanked her for me,* Seth thought. Every time he had stopped in front of this cottage he had ended up regretting it, so it seemed best just to turn his eyes back to the road ahead.

––––––––

Two days later, Dale was finally allowed to drive Mercy to town for supplies. It had been four weeks since his last turn, and he had had to promise his father within an inch of his life that he would not set foot in the *Bow and Fiddle*.

But that was exactly where he headed as soon as he had tied the reins to the hitching rail in front of *Trumbles*. "Dale, Papa will be furious," Mercy warned his retreating back as he crossed the lane.

Her brother waved a hand, still walking. "I'll only be gone long enough for a swallow or two, and he'll never know unless you go takin' another ride home." Of course he knew she wouldn't do that, for their father had grumbled on for days about her riding in a trap with Vicar Phelps, engaged or not.

"Good morning, Miss Sanders!" Mr. Trumble greeted from behind his counter. "And what might I do for you today?"

She smiled and gave him the list she had made. "It's mostly the usual, Mr. Trumble, and we'll need two lunch pails for Jack and Edgar."

"I'll get right to it. I'm afraid we're out of sugar, though. But I expect some in on Monday morning."

"We aren't completely out yet," Mercy reassured him. And Oram and Fernie had robbed a honey tree just last week. Papa didn't care for it, but when given a choice between cakes and pies sweetened with honey or no sweets, he preferred the former.

"You know, I've gotten in another shipment of cloth. There's a bolt of organdy that would suit you right fancy."

"I don't think so, Mr. Trumble." But while he gathered the items on her list, Mercy found herself moving over to the bolt table. The organdy was indeed soft and fine, a lovely shade of blue. *Wedgwood Blue,* said the lettering on the end of the bolt.

"You know what they say, don't you?" Mr. Trumble said from behind his counter.

"I'm afraid not, Mr. Trumble."

"He who hesperates is lost. Or *she*, being in your case. I don't think that bolt is goin' to last long."

Maybe it will go to someone who has someone special to dress up for, she thought. The bell over the door tinkled, and suddenly Mercy was face-to-face with Mrs. Kingston.

"My dear Miss Sanders!" the elderly woman exclaimed. She was splendidly dressed in a gown of rose and beige silk that brought out the high color in her cheeks and a straw bonnet trimmed with lace and silk flowers. "How good to see you!"

"Mrs. Kingston." Mercy smiled. "I haven't seen you out walking lately."

Mrs. Kingston sent a wave and greeting to Mr. Trumble, then drew Mercy off toward the front corner of the shop, beside the window. Lowering her voice, she said, "I walked twice yesterday to make up for today, because I'm leaving town in another hour or so. I've been forced to alter my route again, after a certain person 'happened' to cross my path last Monday morning. I had dined with him a few evenings earlier, you see, and I'm afraid that encouraged him all the more so."

Even though Mrs. Kingston had used the word "afraid," she didn't seem very fearful to Mercy. In fact, her blue eyes shone with what appeared to be pure enjoyment.

"But won't he become discouraged eventually?" Mercy dared to venture.

Mrs. Kingston didn't seem insulted but did change the subject abruptly. "Did your brother accompany you here?"

Mercy shifted her eyes uneasily away from the woman's face. "He's at the *Bow and Fiddle.*"

"I see. Then you have time for a little visit, don't you?" She moved over to the counter, opened her beaded reticule, and handed over a coin. "I would like a dozen peppermints, Mr. Trumble. And you won't mind holding Miss Sanders' purchases, will you?"

"Of course not, Mrs. Kingston," he replied, setting down Mercy's list long enough to wrap some candies in brown paper.

"When her brother returns, please have him stop by the *Larkspur.*"

"The *Larkspur*?" Mercy asked, for if Mary was snubbing Dale again at the *Bow and Fiddle*, he would be in no mood to do anyone any favors.

"Just the garden, child. We'll spot him as he comes up the lane."

Before Mercy had time to think, she was being escorted arm in arm with Mrs. Kingston up Market Lane. She had admired the *Larkspur*'s garden many times upon passing. What a treat it was to be seated upon a willow bench near a rose of Sharon hibiscus with flowers still a deep pink even with autumn approaching.

"Miss Sanders," Mrs. Kingston said after offering her a peppermint, which she was too nervous to accept. "May I call you Mercy? It's such a lovely name."

"I would be honored, ma'am."

"Very well, Mercy. God has brought you to my mind many times since we spoke last month. May I ask how you are faring?"

"Faring?" Mercy fidgeted under the scrutiny of the penetrating blue eyes. "Very well, Mrs. Kingston. Thank you."

"Are you quite sure?"

"Yes, ma'am." *Compared to those without food or shelter, or suffering from some disease, I live a charmed life.* She had to remind herself of that often lately, lest God think her terribly ungrateful.

"Well, I'm glad to hear it," Mrs. Kingston said. "But I wish you to know that I'm very moved by what I've heard about your tenderness toward your elderly neighbor, may God rest her soul. Most young people don't seem to have time for those of us who are getting along in years. If there is ever any way that I can help you, will you promise to tell me?"

It was staggering to think that God cared enough about her to move upon another woman's heart, as He had Mrs. Brent's, to offer some maternal solicitude. Mercy's heart felt as if it were welling up in her chest. "I will, ma'am. Thank you."

"My pleasure, dear child." She touched her wrinkled cheek. "Oh . . . but I should tell you that I'll be away for almost a fortnight. Vicar Phelps will be here to borrow the landau shortly. He's bringing his daughter Laurel to school in Shrewsbury and will drop me by the railway station. I'm going to visit my son and his family in Sheffield."

Now Mercy recalled her saying she was going out of town. "You must be looking forward to it."

"Oh, very much. It's been over a year since I've seen them. I expect my grandchildren have sprouted like weeds. My son asked me to come three or four months ago, but I was afraid it was too soon."

"Too soon, ma'am?" Mercy asked and then regretted it, for a shadow crossed the woman's face.

"I used to be quite . . . overbearing." She shook her head to ward off Mercy's protest. "It's true, Mercy, though it pains me to admit it. Thank God I was brought to realize what a tyrant I had become before I lost my family altogether."

Mrs. Kingston then waved a hand. "But life is learning, is it not? And there is a secondary purpose to my journey. I want a certain gentleman to see that just because I allow him to call upon me occasionally doesn't mean I pace the floor waiting for his next visit."

Mercy had to smile. She almost felt as if she were chatting with Mrs. Brent again. "Is this the same gentleman who caused you to alter your walks?"

"The very same." Mrs. Kingston leaned closer, a conspiratorial glint in her eyes. "Are you good at keeping secrets? I'll tell you his name if you'll keep it to yourself."

"Cross my heart," Mercy said solemnly and did so.

"Squire Bartley."

Eyes widening, Mercy breathed, "The squire?"

"He doesn't look the romantic sort, does he? But I tell you there is some poetry behind that grumpy facade. He just needs the right woman to bring it out." She actually winked. "And I perceive myself to be that right woman."

Feeling she would be doing the dear woman disservice if she didn't voice the little nag of doubt that tugged at her mind, Mercy said respectfully, "You don't worry he'll become discouraged, do you? With your leaving and all."

"That's a very good question, my dear. It could happen, but I'm willing to take that risk. I have come to realize that there is nothing more attractive to a man than a woman who is comfortable with her own company and isn't dependent upon him as her only source of gratification."

"Yes?"

"But of course." Mrs. Kingston sat back and folded her arms. "Yet here I am rattling on about myself and my plans. Please forgive my self-centeredness."

"Oh, but you've been very kind to me," Mercy assured her.

"It isn't kind to cultivate a friendship just so one will have an audience. Now, tell me what is going on in your life."

"My life? Why, nothing." Actually, her life was busy from sunup to sundown, but with nothing that could remotely be considered interesting to someone as worldly wise as Mrs. Kingston. She was saved from having to reply by the sounds of Dan and Bob pulling the wagon up Market Lane. She rose from her seat, smiled, and said, "My brother's on his way. I pray you have a pleasant journey, Mrs. Kingston."

Mrs. Kingston returned her smile. "It was most pleasant chatting with you, Mercy. Please remember that you've a friend here at the *Larkspur*."

As the horses paused in the lane, Dale screwed up his face and growled out to her, "Papa's gonter be sore about you visitin' that old woman and making us late like that."

Mercy, lifting the latch to the gate, winced. *Maybe she didn't under-*

stand him. After all, the time he'd spent in the *Bow and Fiddle* had put a slur to his words.

But then an indignant voice remonstrated from behind her, "It wasn't your sister who caused you to be late, young man! And if you blame her I'll come out there and tell your father the truth!"

Dale flicked the reins with a vengeance the second Mercy was in the seat beside him. She just had time to give Mrs. Kingston a grateful look before the horses started trotting up the lane.

How did she come to have so much courage? Mercy wondered. Not just to reprimand her brother or to face her father about the boys' schooling, but also to act upon her convictions, for it certainly took courage to risk losing the affection of the squire by leaving town.

Mrs. Brent had courage as well. She faced dying without a whimper. That caused her to wonder if age had anything to do with it, but then she considered her father. For all his bluster, he was a coward. As sad as that realization was, it gave her some hope. If courage wasn't a standard result of aging, it meant that the young could somehow acquire it as well.

Oh, Father, she prayed meekly, for it was still an incredible thing to her that she could approach the throne of God. *Please grant me courage.*

Their father was working in the back pasture, so there was no ranting at either of them for keeping the wagon so long in town. Smug with having gotten away with something, Dale called Fernie and Oram over to unload the wagon while he slipped inside the cottage for a smoke on his pipe before returning to chores. He was full of himself and information at the lunch table later.

"You know that fellow at the Brent place? Folks say he broke out of prison and is hidin' from the law."

Harold grinned and opened a mouth already stuffed with pork pie to say, "I heard that too."

"Did anyone offer any proof?" Mercy asked while slicing bread.

"Proof enough." Dale held up tobacco-stained fingers to count his arguments. "He was all doughy-lookin' when he got here, like he ain't seen the sun in a long time. And he had a lump of money in his pocket, the likes of which that Mrs. Pool ain't never seen." Holding up a third finger, he said, "And last of all, he buys a place way out of the way. And he don't go anywhere."

"He goes to chapel," Mercy argued. True, Mr. Langford wasn't the most sociable neighbor, but this was ridiculous. "How many escaped prisoners go to church?"

But that argument apparently fell on deaf ears, for the next comment, which came from Oram, had nothing to do with church. "He's a stupid 'un, that's for sure."

This brought chuckles from Jack and Edgar, and a smirk from Fernie. Mercy, weary of attempting reason, shook her head. It was her father who asked, "Why do you say that?" He spoke not in the manner of one who is defending an innocent person, but with the anticipation of one who is hoping for more gossip.

"Oh, I can just tell," Oram replied after receiving a warning look from Fernie.

Those two have been up to something, Mercy thought.

"He's gonter raise *horses*," Harold snorted, rolling his moss green eyes. "That oughter be proof enough. And with a cheese factory in spittin' distance buyin' up all the milk!"

"Stupid," Fernie laughed.

"Yeah, stupid," Edgar echoed.

God help us, Mercy prayed.

$\mathcal{W}$as she excited?" Julia asked Andrew in the garden that same Friday afternoon. They sat in their customary places at either end of a willow bench, as if the tea tray still occupied its proprietary spot between them. Having delivered Laurel to school, Mrs. Kingston to the railway station, and then Elizabeth back to the vicarage, he had come straight over to the *Larkspur*. Julia suspected he needed some consoling, but after having reasoned with her that she should allow Philip to grow up, he was reluctant to admit it.

"Oh, you know Laurel," he replied, returning the wave of Mr. Blake, the Rhodeses gardener, who passed pulling a hand cart of firewood. "Eager for a new adventure."

"Just like Philip," Julia said.

"They're cut from the same cloth, those two." But then Andrew's hazel eyes filled with sadness and he mumbled, ". . . from the same cloth."

Julia reached over to touch his sleeve. "It'll be all right, Andrew."

"It will?"

He looked so much like a small boy who has just been reassured that Father Christmas would not forget his address that Julia had to smile. It would be pointless to remind him that she would see her son only once monthly until the Christmas recess—the fact that her situation was more severe did not make his any easier to bear. "She'll be home next weekend."

"Yes. Thank you for reminding me. But I'm afraid Elizabeth will be lonesome for her during the weeks to come. I don't like the idea of her being lonely when Jonathan Raleigh is in town."

That reminded Julia of something. "Perhaps if she stays busy she won't have time to think about Mr. Raleigh. I must tell you what Mr. Ellis asked me this morning."

"Yes?"

"Because of some of the artifacts Mr. Ellis and Mr. Pitney have uncovered, the Archeological Society has upgraded the importance of the Anwyl's ruins. They're to receive funds to hire a secretary to organize their notes and catalogue their findings. Mr. Ellis asked if I could recommend anyone, and I mentioned Elizabeth."

Andrew arched a doubtful eyebrow. "Elizabeth? A secretary?"

"Women are being hired as secretaries all the time these days, Andrew. Or at least they were before I left London, and I doubt if that has changed."

"The world is changing too fast for me," he sighed but smiled. "She might find this interesting work. It won't require her actually climbing the hill every day, will it?"

"Not at all. In fact, she would be doing this at home. Why don't you and Elizabeth come for supper, and you can both discuss it with Mr. Ellis?"

"Thank you, Julia. It would be good for her to have something to do besides pay calls with me."

The sound of hooves clattering upon cobblestone drew their attention to the lane, where a carriage was slowing to a halt outside the gate. It was Squire Bartley's barouche.

"I thought the squire held a grudge against you for stealing his cook," Andrew leaned closer to whisper as they watched a footman in full livery hop down from the back to assist the elderly passenger.

"I didn't steal his cook," Julia whispered back. "It's not me he's here to see."

"Oh?"

They both got to their feet as the squire swept through the gate held open by that same footman. He held a bouquet of pink hothouse roses in one hand, a silver-tipped cane in the other. The well-cut black double-breasted jacket and top hat were far too elegant for the simple tastes of Gresham's inhabitants, but none would have expected any less of their squire.

"Mrs. Hollis," he said, hooking his cane over his left elbow to take her offered hand and bow over it.

"Squire Bartley," Julia replied. "How are you?"

"Most excellent, thank you."

"Will you join us?" asked Andrew as the two men shook hands.

"Actually, I'm here to see Mrs. Kingston. I assumed she would be tending the garden this time of day."

After exchanging a quick glance with Andrew, Julia said, "She left for Sheffield this morning."

"Sheffield?" He could not have looked more stunned had she slapped him. "What for?"

"She has family there," Andrew answered for Julia.

"I'm well aware of that," the elderly man said, a bit testily. His brow

207

was so furrowed that both bushy white eyebrows had blended into one. "How long will she be away?"

"A fortnight, Squire," Julia replied.

A pink stain, almost the color of the roses he held, was beginning to spread upward from the squire's collar. "Well, why didn't she inform me? Was it a family emergency?"

Recalling that Mrs. Kingston had spoken of her plans to visit her family no less than a week ago, Julia began to suspect that Mrs. Kingston was being coy with Squire Bartley so he wouldn't take her for granted the way he had the women of his younger courtships. But she certainly couldn't tell that to the elderly man in front of her. Before she could offer some meager reply, Andrew came to her rescue.

"Perhaps you should ask her when she returns," he said.

"I certainly intend to!" the squire snapped, then turned to stalk back up the path toward his waiting carriage. He jerked his arm away from the footman's assistance and sprang up into the seat himself, barking an order to the driver to get on the way.

"Whew!" Andrew blew out his cheeks. "Did you understand any of that?"

"Every bit of it." Julia sat down on the bench again, and Andrew did the same. "He's fond of Mrs. Kingston."

"Yes? Well, surely she doesn't return that sentiment. During the flower show she had not one kind word for him."

"Oh, but that was because she wanted to win the blue ribbon. Now that it's hers, she can afford to be magnanimous."

"You mean she likes him too?"

"Very much so. They've been seeing each other quite a bit lately."

Now Andrew's forehead was as drawn as the squire's had been. "But if she's fond of him, then why would she leave without telling him?"

Julia gave him an affectionate smile. He was completely without guile, so naturally he wouldn't understand the games that women sometimes felt compelled to play to advance a courtship. "I'm afraid I can't tell you, my dear. Loyalty to my gender forbids it."

"Loyalty to your gender?"

"Yes. It's one of those secrets among women. Will you forgive me?"

His eyes crinkled at the corners as he raised a hand to touch her cheek. "With you smiling at me like that, Julia Hollis, I could forgive Napoleon."

———

Being prepared for the next day's lectures was vital if one was to succeed at the Josiah Smith Preparatory Academy for Boys. The students were

208

reminded often that in the headmaster's office was a waiting list of over thirty boys who would gladly trade places with any of them—and the list grew longer every week.

The gaslights were shut off promptly at nine o'clock every evening, and so a student had to learn to manage his time wisely and complete his studying before then. This was not difficult for Philip, who went to the library with Gabriel Patterson as soon as classes were finished for the afternoon. Neither had any desire to join the boys at play on the lawn. Even Philip's love of cricket wasn't strong enough to compel him to spend any more time than necessary with the older students.

He was certainly getting enough exercise, having been ordered by Westbrook to spend his lunch break running around the grounds three times since Monday. On Saturday, after a morning devoted to transcribing a chapter from his Latin text and then lunch, there would be intramural competitions of cricket and tennis. Although Gabriel dreaded the thought of tomorrow because of his inexperience with sports, Philip was reassured that at least housemasters would be present to keep score and hopefully would keep bullying to a minimum.

The best thing about getting at their studies as soon as lectures were finished was that the library was practically empty. Most students waited until after supper to open their texts. By then, Philip and Gabriel would be in their dormitory room, settled on one or the other's bed lost in novels. Occasionally they gave their eyes a rest and talked quietly so as not to disturb those who studied in their beds, describing for each other their homes and families.

"You should be the writer," Gabriel said that evening. With a plump hand he marked his place in the pages of *The Moonstone* by Wilkie Collins. "I can almost see Gresham and the *Larkspur* from the way you describe them."

Philip smiled, ignoring the lump of homesickness that had settled in his chest since waking. *You haven't been here a week*, he reminded himself. *It'll get better.* "That's because you have a writer's imagination, Gabriel. Your mind paints pictures."

"Well, doesn't yours?"

"Yes, but only of people I want to cut open and make well."

This brought a rare grin from Gabriel. Glancing at the prefect's empty bunk, he whispered, "I wonder what you would find if you cut Westbrook open?"

"Snakes and lizards, I would guess. I wonder how he got to be a prefect?"

"The work-study program. That's how a few of the older ones can earn their tuition, if they were students here as underclassmen. Didn't you know that?"

Philip shook his head.

"I'm sure that's why they hate us—because they think we're rich."

"*I'm* not rich," Philip protested.

"But you're not poor either. Westbrook most likely is." Gabriel sighed. "The prefects hate us because we're not poor, and the upperclassmen hate us because we're not older."

"And the teachers likely hate us because we're not Newton or Pasteur. Do you ever wish you could wake up and discover this place was all a bad dream?" At first Gabriel didn't reply, making Philip wonder whether he'd understood the question. But then he noticed the sheen that had come to his friend's eyes.

"Every day," Gabriel finally mumbled after an audible swallow. Because of his size and meekness, he presented more of a target for ridicule than any of the other underclassmen.

"It's going to get better, Gabriel. I mean, it can't get any worse."

"Yes, thank you." His friend gave him a grateful smile and they returned to their novels.

Philip became so caught up in Mark Twain's *Innocents Abroad* that he was totally caught off guard when Westbrook's sharp voice declared, "Lights out in ten minutes."

It was a scramble to ready himself for bed, for the fifteen other residents of the room had the same intention. He accomplished everything but cleaning his teeth, and by the time he had a turn at the lavatory basin, Westbrook had extinguished the gas lamps. He had to find his way back by touching and counting trunks at the ends of the beds.

"Is that you, Hollis?" Milton Hayes' voice came from the bed on his right. He was a quiet boy of medium height. It was likely his ordinary, nondescript features that saved him from the intense bullying that Gabriel Patterson suffered, for he seemed to fade into the background.

"It's me," Philip answered, pulling his blanket up to his shoulders. He listened for the boy's response but there was none save a sniff. *So he doesn't have it so easy after all.* "Sleep tight, Hayes," he whispered.

"And you," the boy whispered back.

But there was no sleeping tight for anyone just yet, for at that moment a noise came from the door. Philip raised his head to see four boys enter the room, two bearing candles. Even in the muted light it was obvious they were upperclassmen. They walked over to Westbrook's bed and there was a low mumble of voices. When Westbrook got to his feet, Philip's stomach began to feel queasy as the group approached his bed. He dropped his head

210

to his pillow and closed his eyes, barely daring to breathe.

"Hollis!" came Westbrook's loud whisper.

Ignore him and he'll go away, Philip told himself.

A hand seized his shoulder and shook it roughly. "Hollis!"

"Huh?" Philip muttered as if just waking. "Westbrook?"

"Get up."

There was nothing to do but obey, not if he didn't want to run laps tomorrow with the whole school outside at intramurals to jeer him. He got out of bed and stood there in his nightshirt on the cold quarry tiles.

"Put your slippers on," Westbrook ordered. Philip would have been grateful for the consideration coming from anyone else. As he felt with his feet under the bed for his slippers, he could see Hayes' dark outline. The boy wisely lay as still as a corpse.

Westbrook motioned for him to wait at the foot of the bed while he roused another student. It was Sydney Jenkins, who had gotten into some trouble with Westbrook earlier today for balking when ordered to shine the prefect's boots. When Jenkins was close enough to Philip so they could see each other's faces, they exchanged worried looks while silently following Westbrook back to his bunk and into the dim light.

One upperclassman briefly held a candle up to inspect both faces. Philip recognized him as Tupper, the upperclassman who had ordered him to cut up his food on the first morning. To Westbrook he said, "They'll do fine. Here's your two-bob."

This was too much. Philip turned to Westbrook, who stood there with folded arms. "What is this all about?"

"You'll find out soon enough, Hollis," the prefect sneered. "Any more questions and I'll have ten laps from you tomorrow."

After a fraction of indecision Philip decided that, ten laps or a hundred, he wasn't going anywhere with this lot. "You can't make us go," he said, backing away.

A hand clamped on his arm. One of the upperclassmen said, "We aren't going to hurt you, infant. We just have a chore for you."

"I'll report you to the headmaster. There aren't any rules about your paying Westbrook for us to do chores."

"You will, will you?" Westbrook stepped up to where their noses were an inch apart. Flickering candlelight was mixed with immense dislike in the prefect's pale blue eyes. "I wouldn't advise that, Hollis. You think you've got it tough now? Besides, you'll have no proof."

"No proof?" Philip turned and made a sweeping motion with his hand, for he was well aware that fourteen sets of ears were listening from beds. "We'll all go to the headmaster."

"Will you?" Westbrook's face assumed its usual smirk as he took the candle from the other boy and held it out toward the rest of the darkened room. "So how many talebearers have we in here? Come forward and let us have a look at you."

There was no response, not even the creak of a mattress. He shoved the candle inches away from Jenkins' face. "You?"

Jenkins took a backwards step. "N-no, sir."

Just yell, Philip told himself. *You'll wake one of the housemasters*. But his vocal cords wouldn't obey, and he found himself being led roughly out the door. The candles caused strange shadows to dance upon the paneled walls of the corridor. They passed several doors and then entered one leading into another dormitory. Two more candles burned atop trunks, and combined with the candles the boys leading Philip and Jenkins held, there was a little more illumination.

"We play *Commerce* on Friday nights," one of the older boys explained while another spread a blanket in the middle of the floor.

Philip could see that less than half of the beds were occupied with sleeping boys. Others milled about visiting in small groups. None seemed surprised at seeing them there.

"But we haven't candlestands and daren't turn the gas back on. Last year Barnes burned a hole in his blanket, so we daren't keep the candles on the floor either." He spoke in the tone one would use when addressing a servant who must take care of a situation, not a boy who had been dragged out of a warm bed.

"So you're to be our candlestands," Tupper explained, wearing an expression that dared him to argue. "It's quite simple, really."

It's quite ludicrous, really, Philip thought. But he actually felt some relief, for he had halfway feared they would be beaten for sport. Two hours later, when the candles in both his and Jenkins' holders had been changed, he wondered if a beating might have been preferable. At least he would be back in bed now, bruised but allowed to sleep. His arms ached, for the six involved in the card game were not content that the candles be simply held motionless. With Jenkins behind the three boys on the opposite side of the blanket, they were supposed to stretch out the arm holding the candle in order to provide as much direct overhead light as possible. This necessitated switching arms constantly while holding the same position. If they shifted their positions too much, their naked shins became the targets of the nearest elbows.

For almost three hours they stood in this manner, while below the six upperclassmen dealt cards and cursed and gambled for pennies. Sometimes boys drifted over from their beds to watch. As long as they performed their duties correctly, Philip and Jenkins were ignored, as any other article of furniture might be. When the game was over the candles were taken from them while one of the boys nodded toward the door. They had to feel their way along the corridor, but it was such a relief to be heading back toward his bed that Philip thought he would gladly walk over hot coals to get there.

*B*ut the horses will have the stables," Thomas said Saturday morning while holding the reins stiffly. Seth was teaching him how to drive the wagon as they hauled lumber and tools out to the back pasture to construct three-sided field shelters. "Why do they need shelters too?"

"They'll need places to get in from sudden rain or wind storms," Seth replied. "Sometimes there isn't time to herd them all to the stables. And if we're in town or at chapel, we won't have to worry."

"What if it snows?"

"A little snow won't hurt them." He smiled and gave a playful tug to the bill of Thomas's oversized cap, which the boy had grown accustomed to and declined his offer of a replacement. "But now a *hailstorm*, well, that's another story."

"Have you ever been in a hailstorm, sir?"

"Once or twice."

The boy was full of questions now that he had gotten over some of his initial shyness, but Seth wasn't annoyed. It was, in fact, rewarding to him that Thomas looked to him to explain so many things.

It was also good to see some color in his cheeks. He even seemed heartier, though Seth couldn't imagine how that could have come to pass on a diet of cheese sandwiches, porridge, and tinned beef. Of course having fresh milk helped. *I need to ask Mr. Trumble where I can buy chickens*, he reminded himself as he directed Thomas to a high spot in the pasture. They still needed eggs. He had come to accept that he had been cheated by the Sanders boys regarding the guineas, but now the boy had become too fond of them for him to consider giving them back. Even now, they hurried behind the wagon, clucking and clattering their *pot-rack!* calls.

It would be a welcome change to have a meal at the *Bow and Fiddle* once in a while, but he had only to remember Mr. and Mrs. Pool's inquisitiveness to put that notion to rest. Sometimes when passing cottages on the way to town, he would get a whiff of roast beef cooking or some savory stew that made his mouth water. If his business turned out to be profitable, he could hire a cook and perhaps a housekeeper, but he couldn't risk Thomas's future now on any unnecessary expenditures.

They would be in that spot in the pasture for the rest of the morning, so Seth unhitched Bonny and Soot from the wagon and allowed them to wander. Thomas scrambled back into the wagon bed without being asked and began hefting one oak plank at a time and handing them over. Seth could have unloaded them in a third of the time by himself, but he wouldn't have caused the boy's expression of pride to be hindered for anything in the world.

God has been better to me than I ever deserved, he reminded himself while taking another board from the boy. So his meals were less than desirable. Food wasn't everything. He had the companionship of a little fellow who trusted him completely for his every need. The only thing that would make life completely perfect would be to have Elaine here with them, but that wasn't going to happen. When thoughts like that came around, he forced himself to think of something else. Sometimes it actually worked.

———

Of all days . . . Andrew thought from the pulpit the next morning upon catching sight of Jonathan Raleigh's face in the back row. *Why didn't I consider that he might come to church?* He knew the answer to that one. He was still skeptical of the young man's professed conversion, no matter how many Bible verses he had memorized. Even Satan could quote the Bible, as he had while tempting the Lord Jesus. If Mr. Raleigh had truly become a Christian, the fruits were surely lacking. Wouldn't a true Christian heed the counsel of a man of God?

Andrew realized at that moment that while he was staring toward the back of the church, his congregation had begun to direct curious stares in his direction. Bringing himself sharply back to the duties at hand, he cleared his throat and looked down at the text he had announced seconds ago. It was only because he had already announced this particular chapter and verse that he didn't switch over to something safe, such as the feeding of the five thousand or perhaps even Joshua and the battle of Jericho.

Clearing his throat, he began to read from the eighteenth chapter of Matthew: " 'Then came Peter to him, and said, Lord, how oft shall my brother sin against me, and I forgive him? till seven times? Jesus saith unto him, I say not unto thee, Until seven times: but, Until seventy times seven.' "

His sermon revolved around the servant who was forgiven by his master of an overwhelming debt but then turned around and threw into prison another who owed him a pittance. He kept his eyes averted from the back row as he delivered it. Just the sight of a smug look on Jonathan Raleigh's face, and Andrew feared he would lose all control of his temper, stalk down the aisle, and seize him by the throat.

It isn't a matter of forgiveness, he reminded himself as the words of his sermon hopefully found their way into the hearts of his congregation. But a little part of him was aware that it was. During the closing hymn he slipped away to the vestibule and front door, as was his custom, to bid farewell to the parishioners as they left. Because Mr. Raleigh had been seated in the back, he was one of the first to come through. Andrew girded himself mentally for the triumph that would surely be in his expression— after all, not only had the young man refused his request that he leave town, but he had wormed his way into a teaching position.

But curiously, Mr. Raleigh merely shook his hand, gave a respectful nod, and then walked across the green toward the *Bow and Fiddle*. He did not even look back, Andrew noticed between shaking other hands. Grudgingly he felt grateful that Mr. Raleigh at least had the decency not to linger in the hopes of a chat with Elizabeth.

"Would you come to visit Stanley this week?" Mrs. Croft, the joiner's wife, asked as they clasped hands. "His bunion's giving him horrible fits."

"Of course, Mrs. Croft," Andrew answered. "I'll come tomorrow. But don't you think Doctor Rhodes should have a look at it?"

"Ooh . . . he's afeared the doctor will go at it with a knife."

All he could do was reassure her again that he would come, hoping he could talk some sense into the man. Just then he caught sight of Elizabeth, who had slipped through the door behind Mrs. Croft and was standing off to herself. His lips tightened at the realization that she was staring in the direction of Mr. Raleigh's retreating back.

———

"Good morning, boys and girls," Jonathan said the next morning, hands clasped behind his back. "I am Mr. Raleigh, your schoolmaster."

"Good morning, Mr. Raleigh," the children replied in perfect unison—or they *would* have replied in such a manner had they been present in the rows of empty desks that Jonathan addressed.

"Just as a ship raises anchor and sets forth to discover new lands, we will embark upon a journey of learning," he went on and then shook his head at the pompous way that sounded to his own ears.

"We will learn many things together," he said next. *Too casual and too bland*, he thought. *And the older children will think I'm talking down to them.*

"It was Aristotle in the fourth century who said, 'The roots of education are bitter, but the fruit is sweet.' " Frowning, Jonathan mumbled,

"What if they only consider the *bitter* part and get discouraged?"

"I don't think that will happen," came a voice from the doorway. Jonathan jerked his head in that direction and felt his face flush at the sight of Mrs. Hollis.

"Mrs. Hollis," he said. "When did you get here?"

She walked inside the room. "Just as the ship was raising anchor, Mr. Raleigh."

After a stunned second he could do nothing but smile sheepishly, and she smiled back. She was an attractive woman with rich auburn hair and a gracious manner. Jonathan felt happy that Elizabeth would be gaining such a person as a stepmother, for once during their earlier courtship she had confided in him a longing for a maternal presence in her life.

"I decided to come early," she said. "In case you needed some moral support on your first day."

"How thoughtful of you." As he shook the hand she offered, he held up his other hand for her to see. "I've been shaking since last night."

"You'll do fine." A childish whoop sounded from outside. "It looks as if the merry-go-round has drawn some other early arrivers."

"Yes, more early arrivers," Jonathan echoed. The sound of a flesh and blood child, as opposed to the invisible ones in the desks, intensified his panic. Yes, he had played with them in the school yard, but then he hadn't been burdened with being in a position of authority. What if they figured him out for the phony he was? *Whatever makes you think you can teach anyway?* he asked himself for the hundredth time.

Apparently reading his thoughts, Mrs. Hollis remarked gently, "No one ever died from teaching school, Mr. Raleigh."

"Now, remember to mind your schoolmaster," Seth told Thomas as they stood beside the wagon in the lane facing the school yard. He was aware that such a reminder was unnecessary for someone as obedient as Thomas, but having never gone to school himself, he wasn't quite sure what it was that parents were supposed to say.

"Yes, sir." Thomas smiled back at him. With his lunch pail on one arm, he looked eager to begin the day.

"And take your cap off when you're inside." Seth gave the bill a tug. "I'll be out here when it's over."

"Yes, sir."

"All right, be off with you then," Seth said with a gruffness that belied the sudden thickness of his throat. The boy turned and walked toward the school yard. He paused only once to send back to Seth a nervous little smile.

217

I should go with him and take him inside to meet the schoolmaster. But he didn't see any other fathers around. Again, he had to consider Thomas's relationship with his schoolmates. Some teasing was inevitable because of the boy's small size. Even though he was filling out a bit, he still looked younger than his seven years. But there was no sense in providing those who were so inclined to tease with further ammunition.

Just drive away, he thought as Thomas appeared to be conversing with a little girl with curly brown hair. There was work to be done, and he would sure enough subject Thomas to ridicule if he sat staring from the wagon all morning. Giving the reins a twitch, he forced himself to keep his eyes on the lane ahead.

He needed to get some things from *Trumbles*, so at the crossroads he reined the horses to the left. The bell above the door gave its usual tinkle after he had tied the reins to the rail outside. To his right a middle-aged woman turned her head briefly from a table piled with bolts of cloth to give him a timid smile, and Seth nodded back. She held a blanket-swathed baby up to one shoulder and a small package tucked under the other elbow. Seth thought no more about her when Mr. Trumble bade him good day from behind the counter.

"How may I assist you this morning, Mr. Langford?"

"A needle and some thread, please," Seth replied, reluctantly adding, "and half a dozen tins of beef."

"Got some mending to do, eh?"

"Some," Seth admitted. The repairs on the outbuildings were wreaking havoc with his clothing, and now two shirts and a pair of trousers had rips, as well as one of Thomas's shirts. He had sewn a button on a shirt once years ago and thought surely he could learn to mend as well.

The shopkeeper spread his hands authoritatively upon the counter. "May I offer you some advice, Mr. Langford?"

Seth wasn't sure he wanted advice this morning but nodded.

"You need more than one needle. They're easy to lose, you see. One falls between the cracks of a stone floor, and you'll be hard pressed to find it."

"How many would you recommend?" Seth asked, relieved that it was nothing more personal.

"Smallest pack is a half dozen. That oughter do you rightly for a couple o' years." The shopkeeper's walrus mustache widened over a grin. "Unless you're particular clumsy. I have a cousin over to Horton who can't tie his own cravat without gettin' a thumb caught in the knot."

Seth had to smile at the mental picture that evoked. "A half dozen, then."

"They're in a rack over by Mrs. Kerns if you'd care to get them whilst

I fetch some more tins from the back. Just got a shipment in early this morning, and I ain't had the chance to uncrate it all yet. Thread's on the same rack, by the way."

While Mr. Trumble disappeared behind his curtain, Seth went over to the rack near the draper's table and perused the display of needles. But making a selection wasn't as easy as he would have thought, for some packages contained the words "darners" and "quilters" and "upholstery." Mr. Trumble still hadn't reappeared, so he considered asking the woman standing at the table for advice. Had she looked up at him, as she did earlier, he would have felt no shyness in speaking to her, but she seemed to be unaware that he stood only three feet away.

There was something about the way she stared longingly at a bolt of blue cloth that touched him. He began to watch her while pretending to examine packages of needles. The green dress she wore was exceedingly faded and bereft of any lace or trim. Her straw bonnet, frayed at the edges, was trimmed with a limp red ribbon. Clearly she could not afford the cloth, but she could not tear herself away from it either. But soon he noticed the resignation alter her face—an expression that suggested there were very few pretty things in her life. She turned from the table, murmuring soothing noises to the infant on her shoulder as she made her way to the door. Mr. Trumble reappeared at the same time the bell jingled with her exit.

"Got your beef here." Mr. Trumble raised eyebrows at the sight of the woman passing on the other side of the glass shopfront but said nothing about, her and came around the counter. "I take it you're havin' trouble findin the right needles?"

"Yes," Seth replied. "I didn't realize there were so many types."

The shopkeeper picked up a red paper package. "*Sharps* is what you want."

"But aren't they all supposed to be sharp?"

"That's a good one, Mr. Langford!" Mr. Trumble declared, slapping a knee.

Seth, who had not meant to make a joke, smiled. Then he sobered at the memory of the woman. "She's poor?"

Mr. Trumble did not ask of whom he meant but glanced at the empty window and sighed. "No poorer than any of the factory workers' wives. But her husband's wages have to stretch to provide for nine children. I offered to let her have that bolt at cost, but I take it she decided against it."

For once there was no levity on the good-natured face. "I do all I can to help folks, but I have to stay in business."

"Yes, of course." An impulse took hold of Seth. "I'd like to buy the cloth."

"You? Didn't know you was that serious about learnin' to sew."

"Not for me—for that woman. At your regular price, of course. Will you deliver it?"

"Why, I'd be happy to!" the shopkeeper declared, grinning widely.

"But you mustn't tell her who bought it."

"No, of course not." Mr. Trumble cocked his head to study Seth. "You're sort of like that Robert Hood, ain't you?"

"Who?"

"You know—that fellow from up to Nottinghamshire. He gave lots of money to poor folk. And he had a fondness for green clothes."

"Oh." Now embarrassed, Seth decided to hurry the process along. Reaching for the first spool of thread that caught his eye, he made a move toward the counter. Mr. Trumble hurried back behind the counter and tallied up the purchases, including the bolt of organdy, with a pencil and paper.

"That'll be four and sixpence," the shopkeeper said, turning the paper so that Seth could see his ciphering. Seth gave it a cursory glance out of politeness and paid. He was on his way through the doorway a few seconds later, his needle and thread tucked into the pasteboard box containing the tins, when he noticed the young woman who sang hymns at chapel alighting from a wagon right behind his. A boy of about fourteen sat at the reins. Seth recognized him right away as one of the guinea sellers.

Seeing the boy reminded him that he hadn't asked Mr. Trumble about purchasing chickens, but he was loathe to go back into the shop with one of the Sanderses present, even if she was so kind as to give them a cake.

But he was gentleman enough to wait and hold the door open for her. She thanked him and they exchanged unsmiling nods as she went through it. On to his wagon he went, storing his box in the bed. He was just about to give the reins a twitch when from behind him came a curious sound.

"Pot-rack?"

Seth twisted around to peer at the wagon behind him. The boy seated at the reins was working hard at studying the facade of *Trumbles*. But there lurked just the hint of a smile on his lips. Pressing his own lips tightly together, Seth snapped the reins a little more sharply than he had intended. As Bonny and Soot broke into an immediate trot, he heard it once again.

"Pot-rack?"

This time Seth did not look back.

————

"I knew everybody had that Langford fellow figured all wrong," Mr. Trumble told Mercy as he scooped out and weighed five pounds of sugar.

"Yes?" Recalling the face that had practically glared at her at the door,

220

she thought, *Has he only murdered five people instead of ten?*

She wasn't in the best of moods anyway. Jack and Edgar, nervous about their first day at school, had traded cuffs and jabs and kicks all the way. They were too far away in the bed of the wagon for her to seize them by the collars, as she had a mind to do, and they ignored her orders that they stop. To make matters worse, Fernie had egged them on by mugging faces at them over his shoulder.

" . . . paid for it himself, he did."

Realizing she had fumed through the first part of Mr. Trumble's sentence, she begged his pardon.

"Mrs. Kerns." He lowered his voice. "Do you know the Kernses?"

"I don't believe so."

"Poor as last year's corn, bless their souls. Well, Mr. Langford, he sees Mrs. Kerns starin' at that bolt of organdy you so admired . . . you know, the Wedgwood Blue?"

"Yes, that was the one."

"When she left here, he tells me to send it to her. Paid full price for it too. He didn't ask for any discount. Then he says not to tell her who it's from."

"He did?" Mercy asked, even though Mr. Trumble had the reputation of being truthful and surely wouldn't make something like this up.

"Aye, right in front of my eyes. Everybody has him pegged for a rotten apple and turns out he's a phlebotomist."

Fernie was looking especially pleased with himself when Mercy climbed up in the wagon seat. She didn't care to know why but spent most of the trip homeward wrapped up in a pleasant daydream about how surprised the poor woman Mr. Trumble had mentioned would be. *You just can't tell about people*, she thought. It was reassuring to know that someone with the capacity for kindness occupied Mrs. Brent's cottage, even though he clearly wanted no contact with anyone else.

Of course if I lived next to my family, I don't think I'd care to be neighborly either, she thought, feeling an immediate stab of guilt for her lack of loyalty. She was as much a Sanders as any of them, and that's how it would likely stay for the rest of her days.

Why, this is going just fine, Jonathan told himself after having each student introduce himself or herself to the others. He had been told that there would be ten new students, not counting the three graduating from Miss Hillock's class in the next room, so it seemed that they should get to know one another. It would certainly help him to attach faces to the names he had memorized.

Even his welcoming speech—he had chosen the one about the ship after all—was received well by them. Only two children, brothers with hair the color of straw, had looked at each other and snickered behind their hands. Jonathan had decided to allow it to pass as if he hadn't noticed. There would be ample time to assert his authority in the coming days, and he hadn't wanted to mar the morning with a reprimand.

Presently, Vicar Phelps would be arriving to conduct Monday morning chapel. That thought made him anxious, and surely the minister had qualms about being anywhere where he was present. But there was nothing he could do about that.

The former schoolmaster, a Captain Powell, had drafted a comprehensive daily schedule, so Jonathan knew that it was time for Aleda Hollis to go to the piano in a back corner of the classroom and accompany the students in the singing of hymns. He took up a hymnal Mr. Sykes had allowed him to borrow from the church, for having been a believer for only six months, he was unfamiliar with many of the hymns on Captain Powell's list. He had never stood in front of anyone, much less a roomful, and led singing, but he looked to Mrs. Hollis at her desk in the opposite corner, and sure enough she sent back a reassuring smile that helped considerably.

"We will sing 'Abide with Me,' " Jonathan announced. He gave a nod to Aleda at the piano, and the first chords were struck, followed by youthful voices joining in.

> *Abide with me: fast falls the eventide;*
> *The darkness deepens; Lord, with me abide:*

When other helpers fail, and comforts flee,
Help of the helpless, oh, abide with me!

Even as he directed and sang the first verse, Jonathan noticed that some students were as unfamiliar with the hymn as was he. They were supposed to sing three hymns, but he wondered if perhaps the time would be spent more productively at learning only one thoroughly. On impulse he raised a hand to signal for Aleda to cease playing. "Why don't I read each line twice and then you repeat after me? That way those of us who aren't familiar with it can learn the song."

Six hands shot up. "But Captain Powell never did it that way," a girl with brown braids said when Jonathan called upon her. The other five bobbed heads vigorously in agreement.

"Well, that's fine, but we've several new students, and I'm not familiar with this hymn myself." Heads swiveled in all directions to gape at each other, as if he had announced he didn't know the alphabet.

"But you're the schoolmaster!" one boy called out.

Jonathan was again tempted to allow the indiscretion to pass without comment just this first morning, but he happened to catch Mrs. Hollis's concerned expression. *If you allow control to slip away, you'll never regain it,* seemed to be the silent message she was sending.

"You must raise your hand, Mr. Casper," he said, then noticed a relaxing of Mrs. Hollis's posture.

The boy obeyed and lifted his hand.

"Yes, Mr. Casper?"

"But you're the schoolmaster."

"That's correct." Jonathan gave a helpless smile. "But you see, this is my first day as a schoolmaster. So I'm learning as you learn."

Heads again turned in all directions as students sought one another's faces. Somehow, Jonathan felt he had made an error, but he was compelled to be honest, so what was he to do? Fortunately, the students obediently echoed the lines of the first verse. They had gone through it twice and were singing it along with the piano again when the door opened and Vicar Phelps walked in. He stood against the wall and listened to the singing, his face expressionless except for a softening when he glanced over at Mrs. Hollis. There was nothing in Captain Powell's notes that told who was supposed to greet whom on Monday mornings, so Jonathan cleared his throat and said, "Good morning, Vicar Phelps."

"Good morning, Mr. Raleigh," the vicar replied, not quite meeting his eyes. It was the first time he had spoken to Jonathan since his visit to the *Bow and Fiddle*, and it was painfully obvious that the man took no pleasure in being in his company. Jonathan moved several feet aside as the man strode to the front of the classroom. He was a commanding presence, and even the new students seemed to sit a little straighter. "And good morning to you, students."

"Good morning, Vicar Phelps," they replied with a fair degree of unison.

"Let us bow our heads for prayer." The vicar prayed for the children, that they would learn much during the coming school year, but that they would also remember that knowledge without godly wisdom always led to folly.

He smiled then and relaxed his posture, causing the students to do the same. He gave an inspiring little sermon on how Daniel practiced his faith even knowing it would lead to the lions' den. "He cared more about pleasing God than protecting his life, and God gave his life back to him."

Even Jonathan found himself engrossed in the story. He had heard of Daniel and the lions as a boy, but the story had never meant anything to him until he came to faith himself. Now he was in awe of such courage. He doubted he would have the same fortitude if put to the same tests Daniel or any of the great biblical heroes had faced, and it made him ashamed. Perhaps Vicar Phelps was right about his lack of character after all.

He realized his thoughts were drifting and turned his attention back to the sermon.

"Was Daniel afraid of being put in the lions' den?" the vicar was asking. There were almost unanimous negative shakes of heads save one of the brothers with straw-colored hair. That one nodded until noticing that he was alone in doing so, then switched to headshaking like the others.

"Then does having strong faith in God mean you're *never* afraid?"

Now only half answered in the negative. The other half looked unsure, glancing at Jonathan for help. Jonathan couldn't provide any, as he was caught up in wondering that same thing himself.

The vicar smiled at the students, as if he realized he was making them too anxious to risk an incorrect reply. Softening his voice, he said, "I'll ask you one more question that may help us understand how Daniel might have felt. Some of you older students will know the answer. Was Jesus Christ afraid to go to the cross?"

Aleda Hollis, seated again in her desk, was the first to raise a hand. "Yes, sir," she replied.

"How do you know that, Miss Hollis?"

"Because of how He prayed in the garden the night before."

"Very good. So it's possible that Daniel was afraid of the lions?"

The nods this question produced were finally confident and enthusiastic.

"Then why do we always speak of Daniel's great courage?" the vicar asked.

A silence settled in the room as thirty-two students contemplatively screwed up their foreheads, chewed pencils, fingernails, or their bottom lips. Finally, one tall fair-haired young man in the back row raised a timid hand.

"Yes, Mr. Keegan?" the vicar said, smiling again.

In a strong Irish brogue, the boy replied, "Because he acted rightly in spite of his fearin', sir?"

Now it was Vicar Phelps who nodded. "Very good, Mr. Keegan. So we see that true courage doesn't mean the absence of fear. Perhaps Daniel even trembled as he was being led to the lions. But his willingness to please his Father was stronger than his fear."

Absently Jonathan fingered a button on his coat. It had never occurred to him that the giants of the faith had possessed the same human frailties as himself. Even while reading of the failings of such as David and Moses, Abraham and Peter, he had still regarded them as almost superior beings who just happened to stumble occasionally. Vicar Phelps had put flesh and blood to someone whose presence Jonathan wouldn't have considered himself worthy of being in had he appeared in front of him today.

Jonathan realized something that he had missed in seven months of intensive Bible study—that God didn't expect His followers to be anything more than human here on earth. How could they be? But if they would be obedient and faithful, He would supply what was lacking when it was needed. That gave him great hope.

"Before I leave, I've a scripture verse for you to think upon," the vicar went on. For the first time he looked directly at Jonathan. "Will you read it to them, Mr. Raleigh?"

"Yes, sir." In an effort to be helpful, Jonathan almost leapt to his desk to scoop up his Bible.

"Thank you, Mr. Raleigh. It comes from the book of Saint Matthew, chapter seven and verse six."

He quickly flipped through the fine pages and found the passage. Clearing his throat, he began to read, "Give not that which is holy unto the dogs. . . ."

Jonathan looked over at the vicar again, thinking there must be some mistake. He had expected something related to the sermon on courage. But the man merely nodded him on.

Again Jonathan cleared his throat. ". . . neither cast ye your pearls before swine, lest they trample them under their feet, and turn again and rend you."

"Thank you, Mr. Raleigh," the vicar said. "There is something we can all learn from this verse." He bade them farewell and moved to the door without a backward glance.

When the door clicked shut, Jonathan, who had been stunned into a near stupor, snapped back to his senses and realized he was clenching his teeth together so tightly that they ached. For two shillings he would leave this town, he told himself, even walk the twelve miles to Shrewsbury if he had to. *Let them find another schoolmaster!*

Only he hoped the school board would have enough integrity to inform any new applicant, "Oh by the way, the vicar will pop in every Monday to spear covert insults at you, and one of the mothers will sit in the back to make sure you don't teach the children how to smoke cigars and tell bawdy jokes, and some of the children will snicker at your introductory speech while others remind you that you aren't Captain Powell."

He became aware then that thirty-two sets of young eyes were trained upon him, as were Mrs. Hollis's. She also had a little crease between her brows, as if she were wondering whether to send for medical assistance. Jonathan let out a sigh and then nodded lamely at her. He couldn't really fault her for being here. If he had children, he supposed he would do the same thing. And of course her very presence gave him courage to face these children, no matter what her reason. As for the vicar . . . he started to grind his teeth again but then stopped. *He'll change his mind about me one day. But there's no use thinking about that now.*

"Students in the sixth standard," he announced, drawing up his notes from memory. "Take out pencil and paper and supply the answers to the grammar exercise on the third page of your text. Remember to use complete sentences." He raised an eyebrow. "Can anyone—from any standard—give me the definition of a complete sentence?"

———

"Please, don't get up," Julia told the young man as he turned to look up over his shoulder from his place on the steps. He held half of a sandwich in one hand, and the other half rested upon the brown paper wrapping upon his lap. "I'll join you."

He sent her a grateful look and moved over to give her room. "Would you care for half of a roast beef sandwich? It's very good."

"No, thank you." She sat and unwrapped her own lunch, which also contained a roast beef sandwich, this one prepared by Mrs. Herrick and likely far superior to the one produced by the *Bow and Fiddle*. But of course she didn't point this out to Mr. Raleigh. There were only twenty children in the school yard—Mrs. Hillock's students ate in their classroom and would come outside later, and a dozen students walked to their cottages nearby for lunch. The boys who remained found patches of grass upon which to plop themselves down, and the girls had discovered the temporarily idle merry-go-round a convenient place to sit with lunch pails at their sides and their feet dangling over the edge

"Mrs. Herrick—she's our cook at the *Larkspur*—packed an extra fig pastry." Julia held out a smaller paper-wrapped bundle to the young man. "Would you care for it?"

Now surprise crossed his well-sculptured face as she put the wrapped pastry in his hand. "I thought you disliked me, Mrs. Hollis."

Julia could hear the dejection in his voice. *That was wrong of Andrew to do that.* She certainly intended to speak to him about it. In the first few seconds after Mr. Raleigh had read the verse aloud, she had seen signs of a struggle within him and had almost expected him to leave the classroom. He certainly deserved some credit for tenacity, if nothing else.

"I don't dislike you, Mr. Raleigh." Julia thought for a minute. "Surely you've read Shakespeare during your years of schooling?"

"Why, yes." He blinked uncertainly at her change of subject. "In fact, I enjoy reading him even now."

Wouldn't Andrew be thrilled to hear that? she thought. It appeared the two had something in common, besides a mutual dislike for each other after all. "I am not so well acquainted with his works, although in boarding school we were required to read *Julius Caesar, King Lear,* and *Macbeth.*" She smiled. "We would have much preferred *Romeo and Juliet,* but the founders assumed it would put romantic notions in our young heads. And *Hamlet* was considered totally unsuitable—for what reason I've yet to understand."

"Yes?" he said while unwrapping his pastry, leaving his sandwich half eaten.

"There is a scene where Brutus speaks at Caesar's funeral. Do you recall it?"

"Very well." A third of the fig pastry was now a bulge in his cheek. "This is very tasty, Mrs. Hollis."

"I'll relay that compliment to Mrs. Herrick. But be forewarned, she'll consider that as permission to send more."

"How nice to hear," he said, finally smiling back. "I'm sorry . . . you were saying something about Brutus?"

"Yes." For a second Julia tried to recall where her train of thought had derailed. When clarity returned to her, she continued, "Brutus says something to the effect that if any demanded to know why he rose against his friend, it was not because he loved Caesar less, but that he loved Rome more."

"I remember."

"Well, Mr. Raleigh, that's why I'm here. I wouldn't purposely offend you. But my love for my daughters is greater than my reluctance to offend anyone. Can you understand that?"

He nodded and gave her a sad smile. "Well said, Mrs. Hollis. And please allow me to say, in spite of the reason for your being here, your presence has helped calm my nerves tremendously."

They sat in silence then, watching the children who had set their pails on the side of the steps and now played. Miss Hillock's class came outside, and Julia and Mr. Raleigh moved farther apart to allow them to pass on the steps, and then for Mrs. Hillock to sit between them. The merry-go-round was put to use again. Mr. Raleigh squinted toward the elms at the edge of the school yard.

"Is that a child I see?"

Julia and Miss Hillock looked in that direction. "I don't—" Julia began but then caught a flash of motion. A boy, she realized, wearing an oversized cap. "It is, Mr. Raleigh."

He was off and away at once. He caught up with the lad as he was midway across Church Lane. Both of them stood there—Mr. Raleigh looking down and the boy looking up. Presently Mr. Raleigh took him by the hand and they both walked back toward the steps. Now that she could see his face, Julia recognized the boy as Thomas, son of the reticent and somewhat mysterious Mr. Langford. His cheeks were splotched and the rims of his waifish blue eyes red.

"There, there . . . what's wrong with the little fellow?" Miss Hillock clucked as soon as they were near enough.

"Oh, just a matter of someone saying something he shouldn't have," Mr. Raleigh replied.

Julia was grateful that he didn't go into detail, for the boy had flushed even deeper at being referred to as a "little fellow."

"Have you had a ride on the merry-go-round yet?" he asked Thomas.

The boy sent a somewhat longing glance past him and shook his head. "No, sir," he replied in a voice that matched his slight build.

"Well, let's see what we can do about that." When the merry-go-round paused to discharge its present load of squealing children, Mr. Raleigh, still holding the boy's hand, stepped up to Rory Keegan, the first student waiting to board. He was a quiet child, the same age as Thomas, though a little taller. "Mr. Keegan, is it?" the schoolmaster inquired.

Rory nodded back, openmouthed at being singled out.

"Mr. Langford here hasn't had a turn yet. May he ride with you?" Rory nodded again, and before anyone else in the queue could protest, Mr. Raleigh turned to the rest and said, "I'll push." The change was instantaneous. Giggling and chattering children clamored on the contraption, and Mr. Raleigh indeed gave them a good spin. But since it only held six safely, he found another queue already waiting when he was finished with the first group. He came over to the steps only long enough to hang his coat over the railing and give Julia and Miss Hillock a helpless shrug.

By the time recess was over, some of the older boys were clapping Mr. Raleigh on the back as if he were one of them. And actually, only about ten years separated him from the oldest student. It was obvious Mr. Raleigh enjoyed the acceptance that was demonstrated.

But as much as she enjoyed the sight of teacher and students at play, an old saying came to Julia's mind. *Familiarity breeds contempt.*

When the last of his calls had been made, Andrew reined southeast toward Alveley. He could still hear the children at recess as the wheels jolted from the change of Church Lane's cobbled stones to macadamized roadway. It had crossed his mind after sharing Scripture and prayers with Mrs. Ramsey and Mrs. Cobbe that some five or six weeks had passed since Paul Treves had joined them for supper at the vicarage. He frowned at the memory of how he had corrected the young curate in front of Elizabeth and his other guests. It was foolish to treat a potential son-in-law that way. What if the young man had gotten discouraged and given up on courting Elizabeth?

What if, indeed? Andrew shuddered, lifting a hand to wave at a passing farmer in his wagon. That would have been a fine situation—Jonathan Raleigh showing up in Gresham just after Elizabeth's heart had been broken again. Thankfully, she had received a letter from Mr. Treves recently and had seemed in no lesser spirits for it.

A nagging guilt occupied the back recesses of his mind over his actions at the school this morning. *If he only would have left town, I wouldn't have been forced to do it*, Andrew reminded himself and felt a little better.

Would that be quinarius with an "n" or quimarius with an "m," Elizabeth wondered that same afternoon, holding her pen poised above the journal. All she could tell from Mr. Pitney's notes was that he had been listing some types of coins uncovered in the excavation. And all she could do in this case was to leave a space to be filled in later after consulting with the archeologist.

Just two days into her work, Elizabeth found that she enjoyed her new secretarial position very much. It was a lonely occupation, performed at an old desk in a quiet corner of the upstairs sitting room, but interesting. Her job was to combine the notes taken from the archeologists the day before and enter them into the pages of a monthly journal that would be sent to officials of the British Archeological Society. It was a challenge at times to decipher Mr. Pitney's scribbling and Mr. Ellis's surprisingly poor spelling. But that made the work all the more interesting, and she was more than a little proud when she could turn it all into uniformly penned lines of facts, measurements, and dates.

The thought of earning wages of her own was also appealing. Papa was exceedingly generous, but a village vicar only earned so much, and she hated asking him for spending money. Now she would be able to put aside savings for Christmas gifts. With the family more than doubling in size by then, the extra funds would certainly come in handy.

Also in the back of her mind was the thought that she should put some away for when she and Paul married. There was plenty of time to accumulate a good-sized nest egg, what with his waiting until he became a vicar to propose. Even then they would have to plan an engagement of at least six months. Any shorter and the local gossips tended to speculate about certain things, vicar's daughter or not.

She had wondered more than once why he didn't formally ask her to marry him now, so that when he did become a vicar they would have the waiting behind them. Of course that was too forward a question for a young woman to ask her intended, but it would seem that such a notion would occur to Paul. Surely he was as eager to marry her as she was to marry him. She supposed it was pride that made him wait. He would not approach her father for her hand until he could face him as an equal.

A soft knock sounded just as Elizabeth was refilling her pen. "Yes?" she called.

The door opened and Dora entered the room. "The vicar's askin' for you, Miss Phelps. He's in the parlor."

"He is?" A glance at the clock upon the chimneypiece told Elizabeth that the better part of the afternoon had passed. But her father sending someone to fetch her was odd. Usually when he wanted to speak with her while she was working, he just came upstairs himself. She started emptying her pen back into the bottle, managing to stain her thumb and forefinger with blue ink. "Is there anything wrong?"

"Wrong, miss?" Dora shook her head, a decided glint in her eyes. "I'm not supposed to tell you anything more. Your papa says it's a surprise."

"Yes? What kind of surprise?"

The maid grinned coyly. "That's why they call it a surprise, miss."

Grumbling to herself about being interrupted with still a good two hours of work to finish, Elizabeth nonetheless managed to feel some curiosity and anticipation. She rose from her desk and went downstairs. From the parlor doorway she could see that the surprise turned out to be Paul Treves, seated on the sofa and conversing with her father over affairs of the church. He looked as handsome as ever in a gray wool suit, white shirt, and an aquamarine silk cravat that brought out the blue of his eyes.

"Why, good afternoon, Paul," she said, ignoring the unsettling little twinge of disappointment that had nudged its way into her mind.

Smiling back, he replied, "Good afternoon, Elizabeth."

Her father beamed indulgently from his chair. "I realized it has been too long since we had Mr. Treves over, so I persuaded Vicar McDonald to give him the rest of the afternoon off. I owe the vicar a game of chess for it, but he plays poorly, so I got the better end of the bargain." He insisted then that Paul and Elizabeth go out for a stroll. "You've still a couple of hours until supper."

And so it was that within ten minutes of attempting to figure out if Mr. Pitney had scribbled an "n" or an "m," Elizabeth found herself walking with Paul along the edge of the green among the willows that flanked the River Bryce. The shouts of boys at an informal cricket match at the center of the green filled the air, and at times she could hear the faint and awkward strains of a violin being practiced in someone's garden. Ahead, the sun streaked the sky orange from atop its perch on the Anwyl's crest. She was truly happy to have him here now that the surprise had worn off. He seemed happy to be with her as well, which made the afternoon all the more pleasant.

"You've ink on your fingers," he said, scooping up her hand to look at it. It was as close to holding hands as they could come, out here in the waning light of day, and he gave hers a squeeze before letting go. "Writing letters?"

The little sign of affection warmed her, and she smiled up at him. "I was working when Dora came to fetch me."

"Working?"

She told him all about her new job. "This is only my second day, but I find it fascinating."

Paul nodded thoughtfully, both hands in his pockets. "When you say you organize the notes from the day before, does that mean they excavate on *Sundays*?"

"No, of course not. The notes I have today are from Saturday's excavation." She smiled. "Mr. Ellis and Mr. Pitney don't expect me to work on Sunday either."

"That's reassuring." Still, there was a puzzling little dent between his eyebrows.

"What is wrong, Paul?" she asked.

He gave her a tight little smile that did nothing to smooth his forehead. "Nothing. Have I mentioned that Vicar McDonald's son and family are visiting from Yorkshire?"

It seemed as though Paul's mind wasn't really on the vicar's son, but Elizabeth shook her head and asked, "For how long?"

"Only a week. His son is rector at Saint Bartholomew's and can't leave his duties for much longer. And, of course, there is the traveling time to consider."

"Of course," Elizabeth agreed. To her left she could see the roof of the schoolhouse and found herself wondering how Jonathan's first day had been. It was odd that her father hadn't mentioned it, considering that he had been there to conduct Monday chapel. But then she reminded herself that she hadn't seen her father since this morning, and he surely wouldn't be bringing up Jonathan's name in front of Paul. In fact, it was highly doubtful that Papa would want to talk about Jonathan at all.

Why are you even thinking about him? she asked herself, irritated that he kept popping into her thoughts. She had only to remind herself of the humiliation and grief he had caused her in Cambridge, and suddenly Paul seemed all the more dear to her. She was aware, as they neared the bridge, that some five minutes had passed since either of them had spoken. He still walked with his hands thrust into his pockets, his expression thoughtful.

She was about to ask him what had him so absorbed when he stopped and turned to her.

"Elizabeth . . ." He hesitated, as if weighing his words.

"Yes, Paul?"

"It's not my place to pry, but did you seek your father's counsel before taking on that position with the archeologists?"

"Seek his counsel?" Elizabeth shook her head. "It was Papa who brought me over to the *Larkspur* to speak with them."

Both eyebrows shot up. "He did?"

"But of course." Now she was feeling just a little impatient. He quite obviously had misgivings about her new position and expected her to pry them out of him. Well, she wouldn't, she told herself, pointedly staring in the distance south of Market Lane and attempting to identify the person driving the approaching carriage. *It's either Doctor or Mrs. Rhodes out on a call*, she guessed, which meant that somewhere either a human or animal was in need of mending. Elizabeth felt a touch upon her elbow and looked at Paul again. He motioned in the direction of the vicarage.

"It'll be dark before too long. We should start back." They walked quietly for a minute or two, then Paul halted and blurted out, "Elizabeth, I must tell you that I don't approve of women doing men's work."

She was stunned. "Men's work?"

"You're a secretary, aren't you? You may as well pull on boots and drive cattle to market. I cannot imagine what your father was thinking."

The comparison of driving cattle with what she actually did was so ludicrous that Elizabeth laughed. That was the wrong thing to do, for Paul's cheeks flamed red. She had forgotten how much it humiliated him to be corrected and sobered again.

"Paul, I sit alone at a desk and copy notes and scribbling neatly into a journal," she said calmly. "That's all there is to it. Mrs. Hollis says there are hundreds of women secretaries in London."

"This isn't London, Elizabeth. You have to remember that as a vicar's daughter, you set an example for the rest of the women here."

"I don't think my example—"

"It's bad enough some are working in the cheese factory and that you've a woman veterinarian running the roads from one farm to another. It's just not natural, I tell you, and blurs the rightful line between the two sexes."

"But what else would you suggest I do with my time?" she asked, becoming increasingly frustrated with his unwillingness to see reason. *Especially when you're in no hurry to marry me*, she thought. "I've no children to tend, and Papa is out making calls every morning. Dora and Luke and

233

Mrs. Paget have been running the vicarage since before we came and certainly don't want me in the way."

After staring back at her for a second or two he nodded, as if she had explained her situation in such a way that he finally understood. Elizabeth relaxed and let out a quiet sigh of relief, but the whole effect was spoiled when he said in what he probably meant to be a helpful tone, "Couldn't you embroider or something?"

"I don't *like* embroidering!" she replied through clenched teeth.

The heat in her voice accomplished what reason could not, for he blinked as if he had just been jerked out of a heavy slumber. "I didn't intend to make you angry, Elizabeth. I was just expressing an opinion."

"Well, you've expressed it. So may we talk about something else now?"

He nodded miserably. "Yes, of course."

And then, to Elizabeth's amazement, he looked about them, took her by the elbow, and led her into the shade between two willows. Before she could think to ask what was going on, her shoulders were seized, and he pressed a kiss upon her lips. *My first kiss* went through her muddled mind as he raised his head again, for even Jonathan had not taken that liberty back in Cambridge. "Paul," she breathed, touching her burning cheek.

He eased his hands away from her shoulders. "Don't be angry at me, Elizabeth. I care for you so much."

"I care for you too, Paul." And she meant it. What was a little disagreement between two who planned to build their lives together? Even Papa and Mrs. Hollis did not hold the same opinion about *everything*.

As they started back to the vicarage, she only wished that instead of backing away from his argument simply to appease her, he would have made an attempt to see her point of view. While she couldn't expect him to know how it was to be female, surely he could imagine himself with time weighing heavy upon his hands. Then he might understand that even a vicar's daughter has a need for something interesting with which to fill her days.

Seth and Thomas had settled comfortably into a supper routine during the month they had occupied what townspeople continually referred to as "the Brent cottage." Seth had even begun to think of it in that way, for reminders of the elderly woman's former life were everywhere. Her needlepoint samplers hung on the walls; the same woven cloth rugs were upon the stone floors; and items such as the chipped blue vase containing a geranium in the front window and the porcelain figurine of a shepherdess atop the chimneypiece were still just as Mrs. Brent had left them. At times he felt guilty that the belongings she had acquired over a lifetime were now a stranger's, who had no idea of the memories behind them that must have made them special to her.

Seth did feel some sentiment for Mrs. Brent's things. The little touches here and there gave the stone cottage an almost nurturing atmosphere and were a softening to the days spent outside with hammer and nails. More than once, when smoothing the quilt over Thomas's shoulders at bedtime, he had wondered what the woman would have thought had she known that her handiwork would one day provide warmth for an orphaned boy.

But this evening as he heard Thomas's prayers and tucked him in for the night, his thoughts were taken up with what was troubling the boy. He claimed to have had a good first day at school the three times Seth had inquired. Each time he had responded with the same hollow inflection in his voice and the same unconvincing smile. Across the table from him at their usual supper of tinned beef and pears, the boy's eyes had rarely met his.

This left Seth in a quandary over what to do. While common sense told him that children were entitled to moods too—he certainly had his own struggles with them, especially when thoughts of Elaine drifted through his mind—he didn't like the idea of leaving the boy alone in that big bed with such a haunted look in his blue eyes.

He decided to make one more attempt and this time not ask the same question in the same way. "Thomas," he said, seating himself on the side of the bed.

"Yes, sir?" answered the small voice.

As usual, Seth felt a little pang at being referred to as *sir* instead of *father*, as he himself had come to think of the boy as his own son. But he would never allow Thomas to know. There were some things that shouldn't be forced. "I want to know what happened at school today."

Whether it was because of the insistence in Seth's voice or because he could no longer bear the burden of his thoughts alone, Thomas gave a truthful reply. "Some boys said you killed someone and stole his money."

The answer was so unexpected and delivered with such seriousness that Seth gave a chuckle. *So that's all there was to it!* "Oh yes?" he said, raising both eyebrows. "And who is it that I'm supposed to have killed? Did they tell you?"

"No, sir." Relief mingled with the worry in Thomas's expression. "You didn't?"

"Of course not." Smoothing some ash-colored hair back from the boy's forehead, Seth replied, "Did you really think it was true?"

After a fractional hesitation, the boy shook his head.

"Well there, now you have it," Seth said, reaching for the lamp.

"Then you didn't go to prison?"

235

Heaviness from within suddenly pulled at Seth's chest. How foolish he had been, he told himself, to assume that moving far away from Newgate would ensure that this question would never be asked. It was even more painful to have it come from the lips of the person who mattered most in the world to him! His immediate thought was to deny it, but he found himself unable to give voice to a lie. He straightened again and let the lamplight be.

"I've been to prison, Thomas," he replied softly, watching for any sign of waning of affection in the boy's face.

"Why?"

Seth blew out his cheeks and figured he may as well tell the whole story now and be done with it. "I was accused of stealing a piece of jewelry. I spent ten years in Newgate Prison. Have you heard of it?"

"No, sir."

"And you never would have had someone not said such a thing to you. I was innocent, Thomas. When the person who accused me confessed, I was set free. That's how I came to have enough money to buy this place."

"He gave it to you?"

"Yes. Now, do you think any less of me?"

The boy blinked again, his blue eyes serious. "I never did, sir."

Studying the young face, Seth said, "Not even when you worried that they might have been telling the truth?"

Now his bottom lip trembled a bit. "You're good to me, sir."

How overwhelming, to be the recipient of such blind devotion, when just seconds ago Seth had fretted inwardly over being addressed as *sir*. He could have robbed and murdered someone, and Thomas would still want to be with him! While he would have much preferred that his past had never been mentioned, the heaviness in his chest lifted, replaced by a great warmth.

Finally a question occurred to him. "Which boys said this to you, Thomas?"

"Jack and Edgar."

"Who?"

"They live in that house with the cake lady."

"Oh . . ." Now it was becoming clear to him. He could see now that the prison talk was simply a weapon with which to goad someone smaller and more naïve. Perhaps he himself had helped to foster such notions, keeping their lives as private as possible and spending so much money upon his arrival in Gresham. How ironic that the very actions he had taken to keep his past from being discovered were used to spin fabrications that were painfully close to the truth.

"Well, next time you hear such talk, just ignore it," he told the boy.

236

"If they can't get a reaction from you, they'll soon tire of trying."

"They will?"

Smiling, Seth smoothed back hair that really didn't need smoothing, just to have an excuse to touch the boy. "Yes, they will—unless boys have changed a whole lot since I was one."

"You seemed preoccupied at supper last night," Elizabeth's father commented over breakfast the next day. "Did you not enjoy Mr. Treves' company?"

"We had words earlier," Elizabeth replied truthfully.

Her father's bearded face became anxious. "I'm sorry. Perhaps I shouldn't have invited him without consulting you."

"It was kind of you to invite him, Papa. It was just a small disagreement."

"Well, that's good. I was thinking we should have him over every Monday evening—a standing invitation."

"That would be nice," she replied, picking up her fork and knife to cut her bacon. *Men's work!* As if God made only the male fingers capable of grasping a pen! She had assumed she was over her irritation, but as she recalled their walk late yesterday afternoon, her pulse quickened, and it wasn't because of the kiss.

"Beth?"

She looked up at her father. "Yes, Papa?"

"You're overdoing the bacon a bit, aren't you?"

It was then she realized that she had sawed the strip into tiny pieces, bearing down so hard that her knife scratched the china. Sheepishly she met her father's hazel eyes again. They were filled with concern or sadness—she couldn't tell which. Perhaps both.

Hours later, after Andrew had retired to his study to write his sermon and Elizabeth had penned several pages of notes into the journal, her father came into the upstairs sitting room to remind her that they were invited to have lunch at the Sykeses. "He's trying to make it up to me," he grumbled but did not elaborate.

Of course Elizabeth knew exactly what he meant. She couldn't help but smile a little. "Would you mind going without me?"

"Not if you would rather stay. Are you all right, Beth?"

"Yes. Just not in the mood for company."

He nodded understandingly. That was the good thing about her father. While he insisted that she and Laurel live their lives according to biblical, moral standards, he seldom obligated them socially. His way of thinking was that *he* was the person the church had assigned to Gresham, and his girls were just as entitled to lives of their own as were the cobbler's or smithy's daughters. "Shall I ask Mrs. Paget to send up a tray?"

"No, thank you," she replied, stretching in her chair. "But if she wouldn't mind making a sandwich, I'll come down later for it. It'll be good to have an excuse to move around for a few minutes."

Some ten minutes later, she found herself on her way downstairs to the kitchen. "Miss Phelps," the cook said, looking up from the potatoes she was peeling at the worktable. "The vicar said you wasn't in no hurry for the sandwich. If you'll sit a minute I'll make one right away."

Elizabeth shook her head. "Thank you, but I'm not hungry yet, Mrs. Paget. I just thought I'd get some fresh air. Would you care for anything from one of the shops?"

"We'll be needin' more silver polish soon!" Dora called from the scullery.

The cook pursed her lips thoughtfully. "I could use a pound of salt. And Luke was sayin' this morning he was almost out of harness soap. Can you manage that, Miss Phelps?"

"Of course." She was taking her everyday straw bonnet from the rack in the vestibule when it occurred to her that one of her nicer hats upstairs would best accent the burgundy-and-cream gown she wore. She chose a narrow-brimmed hat of fine burgundy felt, trimmed with a velvet band and a cluster of ribbons at the side. And as long as she was in her room, she sat briefly at her dressing table and decided to twist her straight, wheat-colored hair into a chignon before angling the hat upon her head.

"Why, Miss Phelps, you look like a princess!" Dora said, appearing just as Elizabeth reached the bottom of the staircase for the second time. "If Mr. Treves could see you now, eh?"

Elizabeth thanked her but flushed guiltily, for Paul had been the last person on her mind. She wished now that she hadn't committed to making purchases. Her place was upstairs penning archeological material, not strolling by the schoolhouse in the hopes of seeing Jonathan Raleigh while the children were at recess.

There was no use in denying it to herself. Somewhere in the back of her mind, she had known all along her reason for offering to shop for Mrs. Paget. *Why do you even care about seeing him? He made a fool of you.* She decided that since she couldn't very well tell the cook she had changed her mind, she would send not even a glance toward the schoolhouse. If Mr. Raleigh happened to be outside, there was nothing she could do about that, since he had ensconced himself into a position of importance in the village. But there was no law that said she had to look at him. As she unlatched the garden gate, harness soap, silver polish, and salt were the only thoughts occupying her mind—at least for a while.

From the schoolhouse steps, Julia was the first to catch sight of Elizabeth. She lifted a hand to wave, but the young woman did not turn her face to the left. In fact, she walked on the opposite side of Church Lane, as if trying to distance herself as far from the school as possible.

Julia was not tempted to call out to her. For one reason, she would have to screech like a fishwife to be heard over the squeals and shouts of the children at play. And her main reason was that if Elizabeth did not want to look in this direction, then she would respect that. She had no doubt that the reason was sitting near her finishing up the square of shortbread Mrs. Herrick had sent him.

"She's beautiful, isn't she?" she heard Mr. Raleigh say softly beside her. She turned to look at him. He was staring off at Elizabeth, his gray-green eyes sorrowful.

"Yes, Mr. Raleigh," Julia replied, grateful that Miss Hillock had not appeared with her students yet, for only a handful of people in Gresham knew of Elizabeth's and Mr. Raleigh's past courtship. "Her character as well as her looks."

"I only cared about the looks before," he admitted. Then he turned to Julia. "You know, that's not entirely true, Mrs. Hollis. As wicked as I was, I always respected the goodness in her. I never tried . . ." His voice trailed off and he stared out again at Elizabeth, now shielded from sight every few feet by the row of elder trees.

He does love her, Julia thought. But she agreed with Andrew. Love without commitment and moral standards was shallow and ultimately damaging. That she knew from personal experience.

*T*his is nice, isn't it?" Andrew said to Julia as they sat in the *Larkspur*'s garden Friday afternoon. September breezes eddied pleasantly about them, stirring the fringe upon Julia's forehead and wafting over the scent of the Worthy sisters' white jasmine. "I've seen so little of you this week."

"Next week will be a little less hectic," she smiled. She wore a chartreuse silk gown that made her hair seem as russet as changing leaves, and she could see in his eyes that he liked the effect. "I've told Mr. Raleigh that I won't be back in the classroom."

"You did? I suppose he was happy about that."

"Actually, he seemed a little distressed." The memory of the anxiety on the young man's face brought a small pang, and again Julia questioned if she should have offered to stay another week. *But he assured the school board that he was capable of the position. And without me looking over his shoulder, perhaps he'll have more confidence in himself.*

Andrew's voice nudged her out of her thoughts. "Julia, are you sure you're ready to trust him with Aleda and Grace? I'm certainly not ready to trust him with Elizabeth."

"I trust Mr. Raleigh as their *schoolmaster*, Andrew. It's not the same as with Elizabeth."

"Yes, I suppose so . . ." His broad shoulders moved with a sigh. "Life was so much easier before *he* decided to come here."

"Easier for us, Andrew," Julia said. "But what about for Elizabeth?"

"Why, she was happily planning a future with Mr. Treves."

"I don't know about the 'happily' part."

He looked shocked. "What are you saying, Julia?"

"Something you've pointed out to me yourself. It doesn't seem she's totally committed to Mr. Treves."

"Well, that does seem the case," he conceded heavily after a thoughtful hesitation. "Even more so lately, I'm sorry to say." But then his jaw tightened. "Surely you're not suggesting I allow Mr. Raleigh to court her. Because it'll be a cold day in July—"

Leaning over the tea tray to raise fingers lightly to his lips, Julia said, "I'm suggesting no such thing, Andrew."

Miffed as he was at Mr. Raleigh, he still managed enough ardor to catch up that same hand and plant a quick kiss upon her fingertips. "Then what *are* you suggesting?"

"That you do nothing at present. Mr. Raleigh isn't staying here *just* to prove to you and Elizabeth that he has developed some character. I believe he wants to prove it to himself as well." She narrowed her eyes suspiciously. "And I sincerely hope you won't be needling him at chapel anymore. It's quite beneath you."

Andrew grimaced. "I had hoped you'd forgotten about that. I suppose he has sulked over it all week?"

Julia smiled to herself at the faint hope in his tone. She could appreciate how hard this was on him—how torn he was between protecting his daughter and attempting not to influence her plans for the future too strongly. "He hasn't sulked at all, Andrew."

———

Saturday morning, Andrew borrowed the *Larkspur*'s landau so that he and Elizabeth could make the trip to Shrewsbury to collect Laurel from school. "If you'd like to wait here, I'll go inside," Elizabeth told him after he had reined Donny and Pete into a circular drive crowded with other carriages in front of Saint Julien's Academy.

"That might be best," Andrew told her, leaving the reins long enough to help his daughter from the landau. *How blessed I am!* he thought as he watched Elizabeth weave her way around waiting carriages to walk into the red brick building. He had seen more cases than he cared to recall during the years of his ministry of children from all social levels who had grown up only to bring sorrow and shame upon their families. While his daughters were often an enigma to him, he was immensely proud of the women they were becoming. The thought of seeing Laurel again after a week's absence brought sunshine into an overcast September morning.

"Why, good morning there, Vicar Phelps!" From Andrew's left boomed a voice as familiar and as bothersome as a recurring toothache. Andrew turned his head as Vicar Nippert and his wife and daughter sent threefold grins at him from a carriage facing the opposite direction only two feet away. "Fetching your daughter, eh?"

"Good morning." Andrew tipped his hat to Mrs. Nippert and the young Miss Nippert. "How are you today?"

"Oh, most excellent as usual, what ho? Ernestine here tells us that it looks as if she'll be the head of her class again this year. Good thing your daughter's in a lower form, eh? Wouldn't want to have hard feelings among friends, would we?"

"Laurel happens to be very bright," Andrew replied, still smiling but with an edge to his voice. Which was of course lost on Vicar Nippert, because he opened wide his mouth and rolled out a thunderous laugh.

"Spoken like a true father, eh? Well, no doubt she'll do fine, won't she?" That last question was directed to his wife and daughter, who both bobbed heads in agreement.

Andrew detected an underlying smugness in the looks they sent to each other, and it irritated him. However, he was determined not to allow Vicar Nippert to spoil the day he had looked forward to all week, so he allowed the smile to stay upon his face and sent a meaningful glance to their two horses in harness. "I suppose you have a long drive ahead of you?"

None of the Nippert smiles wavered. "And it isn't getting any shorter, is it?" replied the vicar. "As pleasant as it is chatting like this, you will excuse us, won't you? Ernestine here is teaching our chancel choir an arrangement she composed over the summer this afternoon."

"By all means." Now Andrew's smile required less effort. Tipping his hat again to the female Nipperts, he bade them all good day.

"And to you as well, eh?" Vicar Nippert returned as he lifted the reins and his horses began to move. "Why, with our fetching and delivering our daughters here every week, we'll soon be as tight as Jonathan and David, won't we?"

"Hello, Papa!"

At the sound of Laurel's voice, Andrew turned his face quickly to the right. With Elizabeth at her shoulder she stood there, grinning and looking much older than he had remembered her. "So our Pet is coming home for a little while!" he said, jumping down from the landau. He embraced his daughter and thought that this was worth even bearing the company of Vicar Nippert every week.

———

Cricket was so important an extracurricular activity at the Josiah Smith Academy that it was said the reason enrollment was limited to sixty-six students in each of the four forms was so teams could be divided evenly. And Philip's latest problem began that Saturday when Mr. Morley, one of the two mathematics lecturers, counted out twenty-two students for the first match of the day. He chose two captains, upperclassmen by the names of Quain and Whitby, and instructed them to divide their teams from the remaining twenty.

It was a gray day that smelled of rain, but the weather didn't matter to

242

Philip. He loved the game second only to fishing, so much so that he thought he would play in a deluge if the choice were that or not playing at all. The upperclassmen had all been chosen by the captains, and now players were being taken from the underclassmen. Philip straightened and attempted to look as capable as possible.

"They'll fight over having to take me," Gabriel Patterson whispered nervously from his side.

There was no use denying it, because that was likely what would happen. But in an attempt to bolster his spirits, Philip said in a low voice, "Just give it all you've got, and you'll show them."

"I've never played."

Philip looked askew at Gabriel. "Never?"

Staring down at the ground, Gabriel replied shamefacedly, "There was never really anyone to play with."

They're going to torment him, Philip thought, grateful that his own mother had allowed him to experience the everyday things of life. "Do you know the rules?" he whispered.

"Yes." For a second Gabriel looked hopeful, as if this would indeed save his day, but then he bit his lip. "Most of them."

"Well, just do the best you can. If we get on the same team, I'll try to explain them as we go along."

"You there!"

He became aware then that he had just been chosen for a team. Glancing helplessly back at Gabriel, Philip walked over to join the boys assembled behind Whitby. Soon afterward there were only two boys remaining—Billy Lowry, the smallest boy in the third form, and Gabriel. It was Quain's turn to choose, but before he could do so, Whitby became indignant.

"You're not going to leave me with the fat one, are you?"

"I won the toss. I can choose whomever I want," Quain shot back.

"But you've got Clayton!" Whitby said, indicating an upperclassman head and shoulders above his teammates. "You ought to have to take the last one."

"That's not in the rules and you know it!"

Faces became red as the argument escalated between the captains, with several older team members joining in from each side. But Gabriel, standing off to himself and staring at the ground again, had the most crimson face of all.

Don't cry, Philip silently urged, for even from several feet away he could see a suspicious tremble to his friend's bottom lip. That would be the ultimate humiliation, one Gabriel would never live down.

"The rules don't say anything about having fat people on teams,"

Whitby persisted. He turned long enough to send Gabriel a glance of ultimate scorn. "It isn't fair."

"Hey, perhaps we could use him for the ball!" one wag offered, which brought roars of laughter from both camps.

As Philip watched Gabriel's face flush even deeper, he reminded himself of what had happened the last time he'd taken up for him. He wanted to play cricket, not run laps around the grounds.

"You'd break your arm tryin' to bowl that one!" another hooted.

"But I'll wager he's a good roller. Hey, walrus boy. Show us how you can roll, will you?"

With that insult Philip reached his saturation point. Fists clinched at his sides, he stepped out between the two opposing captains, and when the laughter sputtered down enough for him to be heard, he said, "He's not an animal, you know."

A stunned silence fell. "What did you say, boy?" Whitby, his own team captain, demanded.

"He's brighter than the lot of you." The stares and smirks of those surrounding him were intimidating, but Philip did not back down. "He hasn't done anything to any of you, so why don't you leave him alone?"

In no way did Philip believe his admonishment would be seriously considered, so he was quite prepared for the laughter that began all over again. What mattered was that Gabriel no longer stood alone in the dubious spotlight, and that Philip wouldn't have to be haunted with guilt days later over not having done anything to help his friend.

One boy stepped over, his face full of venom, and shoved Philip's shoulder. "He ain't brighter than me, infant!"

"What's going on here?" came the adult voice of Mr. Morley. "Why aren't you ready to start?"

"Just choosing sides, sir," Whitby replied with a look daring Philip to add anything. Not that Philip would. It was one thing to threaten to tell the headmaster about being dragged out of bed to hold candles so Westbrook could line his pockets, but this incident wasn't worth getting the reputation as a taleteller. "You there!" Whitby called to Gabriel, as if that had been his plan all along. "You're on my team."

It would have been an outstanding turn of events, Philip thought later as he washed his face in the lavatory, if Gabriel would have turned out to be the best player on either team. Or even a capable one. But nervousness and inexperience combined caused him to be put out both times at bat. Their teammates had treated the loss of the match as if it were Philip's and Gabriel's fault, even though Philip had scored sixty points, and Lowry, on the opposing team, turned out to be no more skillful than Gabriel.

"They're only words," Philip reminded Gabriel as they studied later that afternoon on Gabriel's bed. They were the lone occupants of their dormitory. On the grounds another cricket match was going on between two more new teams, but neither boy had any inclination to attend and be subject to more derisive comments from their own teammates. "They can't hurt you if you don't allow them." Even as he spoke he knew that wasn't true. Words could indeed sting and bite, but he had no other consolation for his friend. A tentative smile then came to Gabriel's round face.

"You were so brave out there," he said admiringly. "I wish I could be like you."

"And I wish I had your writing talent," Philip returned, steering the subject away from what he had done on the cricket field, for the scorn of his teammates didn't serve as a pleasant memory. "Are you working on anything right now?"

"A short story." He held up his notebook briefly. "It's another fantasy. About three cousins who lose their way in some dense woods and stumble upon a field in which air currents lift them up and they can fly. Only no one believes them."

"No one ever believes children in stories. I wonder why?"

"I don't know, but their grandfather is the most critical of all. He's bitter and unpleasant to be around, you see, because he was an army officer and lost both legs." His forehead furrowed. "I'm not sure where, though. The Crimea?"

"That war started about seventeen years ago, so it would fit. Are you going to have them bring their grandfather to the field?"

"In his wheelchair. And against his will."

"I like that," Philip nodded. "Will he scold them the whole way there?"

"And threatens to box their ears and all sorts of other punishments," Gabriel answered. "But he forgets about that when they reach the field and he discovers he can fly. His legs won't grow back, of course, but he has his grandchildren bring him there almost every day."

"Will the other adults believe them now?"

Gabriel smiled again. "They think the grandfather has gone senile. So now the cousins and the old man share a secret, and he loses his bitterness."

"That's a good story," complimented Philip. "May I read it when you're finished?" He wondered if perhaps the reason Gabriel liked to write fantasies was because his own life was so restricted. It was good, he thought, that his friend had that means of escape, if only in the mind.

"I would be honored." Gabriel was fairly glowing now. "Perhaps I'll even copy it again, and you can bring it to your sister Aleda when you visit home."

"She'd like that." The mention of Aleda's name led to talk of Gresham. Having seldom ventured from the walls of his family estate, Gabriel drank in stories of village life like a thirsty wayfarer. And it did Philip's heart good to relate them, for they lessened the pangs of homesickness for a little while. He told of fishing with Ben and Jeremiah, of watching the Irish children gather reeds along the shallow shoreline of the Bryce, of his collection of ancient marbles from atop the Anwyl, the upcoming marriage of his mother to the vicar, and even of the night Mr. Clay dressed up as a ghost to cure the Sanders brothers of tipping over the Keegans' shed.

"I wish I could live there," Gabriel said dreamily.

I wish I could too was Philip's immediate thought.

"Let's go," Seth whispered to Thomas on Sunday when the last strains of the closing hymn, "There Is a Fountain," had been sung. After discovering that speculation over his past was providing fodder for the village rumor mill, he was more determined than ever to guard their privacy zealously. At the door he gave a quick handshake to Reverend Seaton, again politely turning down his invitation to have supper one night with his family. "We're still quite busy fixing up the place," he explained, for the reverend was a good sort and Seth didn't want to offend him.

He and Thomas were headed for the wagon when a male voice from behind called, "Mr. Langford?"

Seth turned and recognized one of the elderly men who had been in the *Bow and Fiddle* his first day in Gresham. He had noticed him occasionally in the congregation, but since he always left early they had not spoken. "Yes?"

Skirting a puddle from yesterday evening's rainstorm, the white-haired man caught up with him. "Are you finding your new home to your liking?" he asked.

"Yes, very much," Seth replied, anxious to be on his way because now more people were outside, and he certainly didn't want to be drawn into any conversation. But manners and a respect for the man's years constrained him to ask how he was fairing.

"Good, now that the rain is let up." The man tapped his knee. "Hard on the rheumatism, you see."

"I'm sorry." He really was.

"Oh, could always be worse, couldn't it?" Reaching out a gnarled hand, he said, "By the way, I'm Amos Worthy."

"Seth Langford," Seth said, although unnecessary because Mr. Worthy had called him by name. "And this is Thomas."

The weathered face creased with a grin. "And a fine boy too." To Seth

246

again, he said, "I wonder if I might have a word with you privately."

Oh no . . . what's happened now? Seth looked down at Thomas. "Go wait in the wagon, will you?" When the boy was gone, he asked, "What's wrong, Mr. Worthy?"

"Wrong? Why, naught that I know of." The elderly man glanced toward the wagon and lowered his voice. "I seen you taking the boy to school mornings and bringing him back afternoons. Just wanted to see if you're in the market for a pony. Didn't want to get his hopes up if you wasn't."

Seth rubbed his chin thoughtfully. He had never even considered that Thomas could bring himself to and from school, because he thought the boy still too young to manage a horse. But a pony, well, that was worth thinking about. "You've one for sale, Mr. Worthy?"

"Not me, but my nephew. Good gentle animal. His son outgrew him and now prefers a horse. Why don't you give 'im a look after you take the boy to school tomorrow?"

"I'll do that." After finding out the location of the farm where the animal was for sale, Seth reached out to shake the man's hand again. "Thank you."

"Oh, ain't nothing." Now Mr. Worthy looked a little embarrassed. "That time you was in the *Bow and Fiddle* . . . you knew we was just havin' some fun with you, didn't you?"

Seth smiled. "I was pretty ignorant, wasn't I?"

"Oh, we're all green at some time in our lives. It's good to hear you ain't gave up on a horse farm. Just 'cause folks been getting them from Wolverhampton all these years don't mean they *like* havin' to go there. You'll have yourself a tidy business one day."

That was the most encouraging news Seth had heard in weeks. If anyone knew about what would be successful in Gresham, it would be someone who had lived here for decades. When they had parted company, there was a lightness to his step as he went to join Thomas. The boy did not ask why he had been sent away, and Seth was grateful for that. He didn't want to get his hopes up before having a look at the animal, and besides, it would make a nice surprise.

He had taken up the reins when he noticed that most worshipers had left the tiny stone church. "There's the cake lady," the boy said in his ear.

In spite of wanting nothing to do with the Sanderses, Seth looked. The young woman sat in Reverend Seaton's carriage on the other side of his wife. *They're bringing her home,* he realized. Because he was the last to arrive and the first to leave, he had never noticed. Not that he cared anyway, he told himself, but he did feel a bit guilty knowing that the good minister had to make the weekly trip when he himself lived only a stone's throw away from her cottage and could easily bring the wagon to and from chapel.

It has nothing to do with me, Seth told himself, flicking the reins so as to put some distance between them and the carriage. He had no desire to stare at their backs all the way home. But even when they were out of sight, his conscience refused to ease up on him.

An hour later, he and Thomas cleaned the kitchen after a lunch of tinned pork and fried eggs. When Seth recently discovered that the green-grocer also sold eggs, he had decided he was not so eager to purchase chickens and possibly repeat the guinea mistake. After mulling it over, he reached a reluctant compromise with himself. Nothing on earth could persuade him to call at the Sanderses, but he would not leave quite so early next Sunday after the service. If it appeared that Miss Sanders needed a ride home, he would offer it. And then they could discuss his collecting her on Sunday mornings as well—as long as she waited outside, where he wouldn't be forced to have contact with any of her family.

*T*here, now! Let's have some order, shall we?" Jonathan Raleigh addressed the boys in the back row of the classroom, who continued with their conversation as if he had never spoken. He raised his hands and his voice. "Silence, if you please!"

The classroom chatter ceased—for all of two minutes. *If only you were here, Mrs. Hollis!* He wished now that he had gotten on his knees and begged her not to desert him, but his pride had gotten in the way of his good sense, and now he was reaping the consequences.

Even some of the younger students, not so bold as the fifth and sixth standard boys but impressed with how they were getting away with misbehaving, began whispering behind hands to their neighbors.

"Would you *please* stop talking!" Jonathan couldn't imagine what had happened to the nice young children who had clapped him on the back and joked with him just last week. Above the din came the sound of the door opening. The noise abated by the time Vicar Phelps had taken five steps into the room. Deeply embarrassed, Jonathan nonetheless managed to feel some relief. From the astonishment in the vicar's expression, it was obvious he had heard the disorder from the other side of the door. The children respected the vicar. No doubt he would give them a stern lecture on obedience, and order would be restored.

But he did not. After leading the children in prayer, he delivered a sermon about putting on the whole armor of God and then turned to leave. He paused at the door long enough to send Jonathan a look which clearly said, *And you fancy yourself a schoolmaster?*

The unspoken insult stung. Still Jonathan wanted to shout after him, "Please stay!" But the door clicked shut and he was in charge again. Dismally so, for the talking began anew.

He managed to accomplish some teaching by finally threatening to withhold recess privileges. Thankfully, the merry-go-round was a sufficient carrot to dangle in front of any miscreant's nose. But any change in routine, such as his dropping a piece of chalk or a student's loud belch, caused giggles that turned into whispers. By the end of the school day he was happy to see them leave. He dropped down into his chair, nursing a throbbing headache and fighting a renewed temptation to leave Gresham.

————————

"The teacher hollered at us today," Edgar said at the supper table after his father and brothers had exhausted the subject of how Squire Bartley was a stingy old coot for not raising the price he paid per gallon of milk during the past eight years, and of how they should show him up one day by building another cheese factory and driving him out of business.

"Why did he holler at you?" Mr. Sanders asked, his weathered face indignant. "I don't send my boys to school to be hollered at."

On her way to refill the serving bowl of smothered marrow and onions from the kettle on the stove, Mercy said, "They probably deserved it."

"But we wasn't doing nothing."

"The teacher's face got red, just like a apple," Jack threw in, grinning, when Mercy had returned to the table. "Edgar burped out loud three times."

Mercy sent Edgar a severe look. "You should be ashamed." He merely spooned another heap of peas into his mouth while looking very pleased with himself. After she had cleared the table and washed the supper dishes, Mercy sought her father out as he sat by the low parlor fire sharpening his pocket knife on a whetstone. "Shouldn't you talk with the boys about their misbehaving at school?"

He shrugged, his forest green eyes indifferent. "Why?"

Mercy pulled up a footstool and sat near his knees. "Because you're sending them there to learn, Papa, not to give their schoolmaster grief."

"I'm sendin' them because thet woman made a bargain with me. I don't want her coming here and taking thet heifer back before it's old enough for milking."

"But since they have to go to school anyway to keep your end of the bargain, wouldn't it be better if they actually *learned* something?"

Her father stopped sharpening and frowned. "Mercy, it ain't proper to speak ill of the dead, but you let that Brent woman put grand ideas into yer head. I can't even write my name, and I manage to keep the seven of you fed and clothed proper. If thet teacher can't get Jack and Edgar to learn, then I don't know what you expect I can do."

"You could order them to behave. They'll listen to you."

"But I can't go sit with them in thet schoolroom." He resumed moving the knife across the whetstone in a fluid motion. "If they act up too much, maybe thet teacher will send 'em home. Thet Kingston woman can't say I didn't keep our bargain then."

So that was it, Mercy realized. Her father still couldn't see the use in educating boys who would follow in his footsteps and become dairymen. He would just as soon have them here at their chores. But fear of Mrs. Kingston's appearing and taking that heifer away—which would most likely happen, though Mercy couldn't imagine what she would *do* with the animal—compelled him to send Jack and Edgar to school every day. If they were *expelled*, however . . .

Any more conversation along that line was futile, she realized, and since her father's face had assumed the same look of irritation it would have worn should a persistent fly buzz about his ears, she got up from the stool and went upstairs to her room. She went to the window and opened the curtain. Off in the distance burned two lights at the Brent cottage. Upon more thorough scrutiny, she realized one light burned in what was at one time the milking barn. Mr. Langford's reclusiveness was almost bizarre, and he had yet to thank her for the cake. But ever since learning about how the man had sent the bolt of fabric to that poor woman, she found herself wondering at times about him and the boy, Thomas. It seemed a little sad, the two of them living on tinned foods, without a wife and mother to care for them.

———

"Why do we leave food if she's just going to sleep?" Thomas asked, brushing Lucy's gray coat with long strokes as Seth had taught him. Seth had surprised him by showing up on horseback after school, leading the Welsh mountain pony so that the boy could ride her home. At only ten hands tall, the little mare was perfect for Thomas, and the sheer joy in the boy's face was worth even twice what he had paid for the pony and saddle.

He looked up from using the hoof-pick on Lucy's left forefoot and answered the question. "Because she won't sleep the entire night, like we do. She'll wake two or three times and want to eat."

"Will she lie down, sir?"

"Probably not for a few days." Seth moved around to the right forefoot. The pony blew out its nostrils nervously, but the soothing effect of the brush upon her coat probably was what kept her from panic. "She'll need some time to get used to her new home before she feels safe enough to lie down. But in the meantime she'll rest all right standing."

"Perhaps I should stay out here with her . . . just for tonight? In case she gets lonesome?"

Seth smiled at the hopefulness in the boy's voice. "You'll need your sleep too. She'll have Bonny and Soot in the next stalls, and you can see about her in the morning."

"May I ride her to school by myself?"

251

"Well, I'll go with you for a few days until you've had more experience. And I'll need to find a place for her to wait for you." He had been told by Mr. Worthy's nephew that the *Bow and Fiddle* had a paddock and stable, hardly used by customers since the decline of the coaching trade. For a small fee the few students who rode horses to school could keep them contained there. Seth wanted to look over the situation and make sure no aggressive animals would be penned in with her.

He got back to his feet and hung the hoof-pick high on a post, then leaned against the inside of the stall and watched Thomas groom his pony. It was the boy's bedtime, but he hated to tear him away from the animal. Seth seldom thought about the distant future except to make plans for the boy's security, but now his mind painted a picture of himself as an old man, perhaps seated by a fire and wearing a shawl as he thought back on the events of his life. This night with Thomas would be one memory he would smile over and savor always.

———

"It was kind of your father to have me here again," Paul told Elizabeth as she accompanied him through the garden after supper. "I had a most pleasant time."

"I'm glad to hear it," she replied. "Because you seemed a little preoccupied."

"I did? It wasn't the company, I assure you." He held the gate open for her, and when they reached the tethered horse, he turned and glanced over at the vicarage. "I wish to apologize for my . . . behavior last week. I pray you don't think any less of me, Elizabeth. A minister is supposed to hold himself to a higher standard, and I sadly allowed my emotions to overrule my self-control."

"Less of you? For what, Paul?" She knew exactly to what he was referring and would have been amused had she not so many other perplexing feelings struggling within her.

Shifting upon his feet he said, "What I did . . . down by the river."

Now a definitely recognizable feeling surfaced. Irritation. "Was it *that* unpleasant for you, Paul?"

In the moonlight she could see his eyes widen. "Unpleasant? Why, no."

"Then why are you apologizing?"

"Elizabeth. . . ." Again he glanced over at the house. "I don't feel comfortable discussing it with you like this. We both know what I did, and until we're officially betrothed, I haven't the right to take such liberties. Will you just accept my apology?"

She folded her arms. "If you'll tell me why you can't say the word 'kiss.'"

The shock upon his face could not have been greater had she spat out an oath. "Elizabeth, it doesn't become you to talk this way. There are certain things an unmarried man and woman shouldn't discuss."

"Of course there are," she agreed. But this particular instance seemed quite silly to her. They had already *done* the deed, as dastardly as he now considered it. Which was worse—doing it or saying it?

It didn't vex her that his standard of morality was obviously higher than hers, for she had thought nothing wrong with the kiss and even had enjoyed it a little. What was so troublesome was that the few times they had attempted to discuss anything deeper than the usual daily incidents in each other's lives, they found little mutual agreement. For months she had told herself that marriage would change all that, but now she wondered if that change might be even worse. Would she be expected to surrender every opinion she had that was incompatible with his?

She would have to take those thoughts inside now, because surely the lamp would appear in the window any minute. Paul was looking at her with such worry on his handsome face that she gave him a reassuring smile. "I forgive you, Paul."

"Thank you, Elizabeth," he said, his posture easing. "I couldn't bear the thought of you being disappointed in me."

"I'm not disappointed in you." Seconds later, when he had swung into the saddle and was headed for home, Elizabeth stood just inside the gate and told herself she had spoken truthfully. He was a good man, full of integrity and a diligent worker for God. But disappointment of another source lay heavy within her. Her hopes and dreams for a perfect marriage seemed to be fading as rapidly as the sound of hoofbeats in the distance.

If Philip had been unpopular at the Josiah Smith Academy before Saturday's cricket match, he was now the equivalent of Guy Fawkes in the minds of most upperclassmen. Being held in such low esteem by fellows he considered to be Huns in Norfolk jackets did not trouble him nearly as much as the thought of what those same fellows were capable of doing to make his life even more miserable. After stepping into a shoe Monday morning that contained a raw egg, he had acquired the habit of overturning and shaking his shoes before slipping his feet into them, of hiding his toothbrush under a corner of his mattress, and taking other similar precautions.

He had Gabriel doing the same, for even though he hadn't Philip's reputation of being a "bad sport," he was still an object of scorn because of his size and gentle nature. It also didn't help Gabriel's case that he was Philip's friend, but when Philip had mentioned that perhaps for his own protection he should distance himself, Gabriel refused to hear of it. "I'd rather have the worst done to me and still have your friendship than have it lighter and be alone," he insisted.

So they took to watching out for each other. They were especially cautious this particular Wednesday night, because the students in the fourth form had caught frogs along the River Severn that afternoon for dissection in class tomorrow. Philip had just come from washing up in the lavatory, when Gabriel approached him.

"There is a lump under your covers," he whispered.

Philip groaned. While he didn't share Aleda's repulsion toward amphibians and reptiles, the idea of having a slimy creature between one's sheets didn't appeal to him.

"What's the matter?" Smith, one of their dormitory mates, asked as Philip and Gabriel walked toward Philip's bed.

"We think there's a frog in Philip's bed," Gabriel replied.

"Oh, nasty!" The boy said, making a face. He fell into step with the two and was soon joined by three others. Sure enough, there was a lump in the center of the mattress, one that was too large and well-defined to be caused by a wrinkle in the sheets.

"What's going on?" This voice came from Westbrook, standing four feet away and sending his usual scowl in their direction. "You're supposed to be dressing for bed."

"There's a frog under the covers, sir," Smith replied.

"I think it just moved," Lowry declared.

"That's ridiculous," said Westbrook. "Nobody brought frogs in here. Hollis was too lazy to make up his bed proper."

Then what do you call this! Philip thought, grabbing hold of the edge of his blanket. It was almost worth having a frog soil his sheets, to prove Westbrook wrong. He threw back the blanket and top sheet and sure enough, the lump quivered slightly. But it was brown, not green, and revealed itself on closer inspection to be a pair of woolen stockings rolled up in a ball.

Laughter erupted around him, and Philip had no choice but to smile sheepishly, though he wished the incident had not drawn an audience. *But they're not my stockings*, he protested silently when Westbrook railed him out about staging a stunt to get attention. It was better to swallow the accusation and run his laps tomorrow than to risk making the prefect despise him even more.

The next morning a small frog happened to show up after all—not in Philip's sheets or shoes, but smashed flat between the pages of his Latin text. Seated in his Latin lecture, he quickly turned several pages and pretended that he hadn't made the grisly discovery. There were a handful of older students who had failed the subject in previous terms, and he could feel their eyes upon him.

The deaths of small animals had never before affected Philip. Many a worm, cricket, and minnow he had impaled upon a hook and afterward gutted his catch without a second thought—other than how tasty his supper would be. But this disturbed him for reasons he could not quite fathom.

"Say, Hollis . . . you look a bit peaked," Quain, the captain of Saturday's opposing cricket team, commented as students filed out of the room on their way to their next classes.

"Maybe you should *hop* on over to the infirmary," his companion grinned just before Philip lost his breakfast on his shoes.

After seeing her daughters off to school Thursday morning and having tea with Andrew, Julia walked over to the town hall with Mrs. Hyatt and Mrs. Dearing. Mr. and Mrs. Sykes met them there, and they spent an hour deciding how the room should be arranged for the Hyatt-Durwin wedding reception a week from Saturday. Four ancient serving tables were brought from the storage room and inspected for stability. Table linens were inspected for holes and then sent to Mrs. Moore's to be laundered.

Soon members of both the Hyatt and Durwin families would be arriving in Gresham and lodging at the *Bow and Fiddle*, which accounted for the bounce in the innkeeper's step as he dashed from greengrocer to butcher to baker, making plans for the flood of guests. Julia, Mrs. Beemish, and Mrs. Herrick were making plans for the *Larkspur*'s dining room as well. On the eve of the wedding there would be a supper for the family members and lodgers, and, of course, Andrew and his daughters, since he would be conducting the ceremony. *And Philip will be here that weekend,* Julia thought, holding up two corners of a long tablecloth while Mrs. Sykes held the other end for the other two women's scrutiny. *I wonder if he's as eager to come home as we are to have him.*

Mrs. Sykes caught her eye and sent her a sentimental smile.

"I can read your thoughts, dear, by the look in your eyes."

Julia returned the smile. "Can you, now?"

"You're thinking it won't be long before we'll be doing this for your wedding."

"And I think you're a very wise woman," Julia told her, causing the churchwarden's wife to flush with pleasure. It would have served no purpose to reply that, while she spent a good amount of time thinking about her own wedding, her thoughts at that moment had centered around her son.

When everything that could be done at the hall that day was finished, Julia did not accompany Mrs. Hyatt and Mrs. Dearing back to the *Larkspur*. During their brief morning tea together, Andrew had asked her if she would see about Elizabeth while he was out making calls. She seemed to be quietly wrapped in melancholia lately, and he feared asking her what was wrong. "If it turns out that her mood has anything to do with Jonathan Raleigh, I'm afraid I'll lose my temper and make matters worse," he had confessed.

At the vicarage, Dora led Julia upstairs to the sitting room. Elizabeth looked up from her desk and immediately pushed out her chair. "What a pleasant surprise!" she declared, crossing the carpet for an embrace. "I thought of visiting you this morning but was afraid to interfere with the wedding plans."

"You should never worry about that," Julia admonished lightly. "You're practically my daughter."

"I like the thought of that." Elizabeth led her over to the desk and showed her how she went about her duties. It was easy to see why Mr. Ellis and Mr. Pitney now considered her an integral part of their team. On the left of the desk top sat a stack of papers torn from a notebook. Some of the pages were creased from having been folded; some were marked with dirty fingerprints, and Elizabeth even brought out one smeared with something resembling quince jam. The girl had meticulously transformed all of this into lines of neat, uniform words and spaces. "I was afraid it would become boring, but I'm enjoying the challenge of making order from chaos."

"And from quince jam," Julia reminded her.

Elizabeth giggled. "Yes . . . and from quince jam."

When the giggles intensified into laughter, Julia grew alarmed. She had not thought her own remark *that* amusing. She put a hand on the girl's shoulder. "Elizabeth?"

Now the laughter turned into sobs, the girl's breath coming in spasmodic heaves while tears spilled from the brown eyes. After a second of stunned immobility, Julia gathered Elizabeth into her arms and patted her back as she continued to sob upon her shoulder. "There, there, now," she soothed while wondering if she should call out for Dora. She decided that such action might make Elizabeth more agitated. To wait this out until she could compose herself would be best. *This either has to do with Mr. Treves or Mr. Raleigh,* Julia thought. *Or more likely, both.*

It took some five minutes for the sobbing to cease, during which time the shoulder of Julia's burgundy gown became soaked. When Elizabeth raised her head and realized the mess she had made, she appeared on the verge of bursting into tears again.

"It's poplin, dear," Julia reassured her. "It'll wash."

"I've some handkerchiefs here," the girl sniffed, her face mottled with red splotches. She leaned down to open the top drawer of her desk and pulled two squares of linen from an orderly stack. Handing one to Julia, she used the other to wipe her eyes and blow her nose. "I seem to be crying a lot lately, so I keep them close at hand."

"You poor child." After the words left her mouth, Julia realized they were the wrong thing to say, for misery washed across Elizabeth's face again, and her bottom lip began to tremble. Taking the girl by the elbow, she started leading her to the settee. "Let's sit, shall we?"

"Your gown . . ."

Julia dabbed at it with the handkerchief when they had seated themselves. "See? No harm done. Now, why don't you tell me what's wrong, Elizabeth?"

Closing her eyes, Elizabeth sighed and then said in a voice strained from weeping, "I don't love Paul, Mrs. Hollis. I don't know if I ever did."

"I see." The question had to be asked. "May I ask you, Elizabeth, how much this has to do with Mr. Raleigh?"

The girl nodded, as if she expected the inquiry. "I've asked myself that a hundred times. It's likely that Jonathan's arrival in Gresham caused me to think more about my relationship with Paul, but to the best of my knowledge, I've never compared the two of them. Or if I have, it has been to Paul's favor because of his stability."

How hard it is to be young, Julia thought, taking up her hand. So many life-altering decisions had to be made by young men and women without the life experience to understand them fully. She herself had been no more competent to choose a marriage partner at the age of seventeen than she was to teach architecture.

"I know Paul is a good man," Elizabeth went on, as if she feared Julia would argue. "But remember when you asked me if he was a friend? I told myself that he was. But would a friend constantly make you feel that your thoughts and opinions are inferior to his? I've been hoping marriage would change all of that, but what if it doesn't?"

"Perhaps if you spoke with him about this?" Julia suggested. "Put off any talk of marriage for a while and give him an opportunity to decide if he is willing to change?" It was not that she felt Elizabeth should marry or *not* marry Mr. Treves. But surely she should explore all avenues before making any sort of monumental decision.

Elizabeth thought about this for several seconds but then shook her head. "I don't want someone I have to try to change, Mrs. Hollis. If he doesn't see the need to do so on his own, then he would be doing it just to keep me from leaving. And what if he slipped back into his old ways after we were married?"

"That's something to consider."

"The early days of our courtship were exciting," she said miserably. "But I can see now that it was having a new, handsome beau to pay attention to me that made them seem that way. Our personalities are too different. Now all I feel for him is pity."

"Pity?" Julia asked.

Her chest rose and fell with a deep breath. "Pity for the hurt I'll cause him if I break off our courtship."

Julia sighed too. "You're positive about this, Elizabeth?"

"Very positive . . . *most* of the time," she confessed. "It's so frightening, the thought that I may be wrong. What if I look back years later and realize I've thrown away my only chance for happiness?"

"Your *only* chance?" Squeezing the girl's hand, she said, "Do you think when God created you, He designed that your only chance for happiness would be wrapped up in one particular person?"

Again several seconds of thoughtful silence passed. "No, of course not," she said presently, then leaned her head upon Julia's shoulder. "I'm so glad you came. My thoughts seem much clearer when I can talk them over with you."

"Thank you, Elizabeth. I'm glad I could help."

"I suppose I should get this over with as soon as possible."

"I don't know," Julia replied uneasily. It was a frightening thought that she had perhaps exerted undue influence over the lives of two young people. "Since you expressed some misgivings, would it hurt to wait at least a couple of weeks, just to be sure?"

"Yes, that makes sense," Elizabeth sighed.

"I should let you get back to your work. Will you be all right if I leave now?"

The girl smiled. "I feel much better, Mrs. Hollis. God must have sent you here today."

"Actually, it was your father. But since his steps are ordered by the Lord, we could say both."

"Papa." Elizabeth grimaced as they both got to their feet. "He'll blame this on Jonathan, won't he?"

"No doubt that will be his first reaction," Julia admitted. "You'll just need to remind him that he had misgivings about your relationship with Mr. Treves before Mr. Raleigh ever came here."

The mention of Mr. Raleigh brought another question to Julia's mind, but now was not the time to ask it. While Elizabeth had declared that Mr.

Raleigh's having settled temporarily in Gresham had nothing to do with her decision concerning Mr. Treves, she wondered how the girl felt about the young man.

She found that she herself rather liked him, but of course that had nothing to do with whether he should be allowed to court Elizabeth again. She had come across Mr. Raleigh at *Trumbles* Tuesday afternoon, looking worse for the wear. Even though Aleda maintained that the new schoolmaster had to keep on his toes constantly to keep order in the classroom, Mr. Raleigh had not complained when Julia asked how he was faring.

If he has indeed given up his old ways for good, and it's your will that they be together, please, God, let it be clear to them was included in Julia's prayers of late, in addition to, *And if that be the case, please show Andrew as well.*

Back at the *Larkspur*, she met postman Mr. Jones at the gate and was pleased to be handed a letter from Philip. She hastened to her bedroom to read it:

> *Dear Mother, Aleda, and Grace,*
> *I hope you are all well. One of the boys in our dormitory contracted a fever yesterday, but I have gotten lots of fresh air and exercise, so my health is good. The food is not nearly as good as Mrs. Herrick's, but the lectures are interesting. I have become friends with a boy named Gabriel Patterson. He writes very good stories, and I will be bringing home a copy of one on the twenty-fourth for Aleda.*
> > *Yours affectionately,*
> > *Philip*

The letter said nothing about how he was coping with living away from home, but it seemed positive enough. *And he's already made a good friend.* She read it two more times, then put it on her night table, for she knew she would want to read it again before going to bed.

Boys go away to school all the time, she reminded herself, for a hollow ache had centered itself in her chest. *Many younger than Philip. Besides, he'll be leaving for university in three years anyway.*

It was the way it was, and the way it would be for years to come. If it seemed terribly unnatural, it had to be because she was a neurotic mother who couldn't let go.

"*P*apa doesn't make us comb our hair," Edgar whined to Mercy on Friday morning after popping the last piece of sausage into his mouth. His eyes darted over to the head of the table, where their father was busy sopping the egg yolk off his plate with a slice of bread. "Do we have to comb our hair just to go t'school? We're in a hurry."

"No," their father grunted.

"But, Papa," Mercy protested. "Just look at them."

Pointing the remaining crust of bread at her, he did not even look over at the two heads of straw-colored hair that stuck out in all directions like hedgehog quills. "Quit tryin' to make girls out of 'em, Mercy. Now get on—all of you. And don't forget my tobacco."

Jack and Edgar left the table immediately and went out the front door with Oram, who would be driving them today. Pressing her lips together, Mercy took her basket from the hook that hung in the kitchen. "We've plenty of time," she grumbled to the two waiting impatiently in the bed of the wagon. "You could have combed your hair ten times and still gotten there early. Why are you in such a hurry?"

"Teacher won't allow us to play on the merry-go-round at recess," Jack replied, pulling a sour face. "But we can play on it before school."

Mercy climbed up into the wagon seat next to Oram, held on to the edge of the seat as the wagon jolted into movement, then turned. "And why won't he allow it?"

The lightning-quick glances Jack and Edgar exchanged were long enough for them to coordinate identical shrugs of the shoulders.

"Have you been misbehaving again?" Mercy pressed.

"Weren't just us," Edgar replied defensively.

Jack nodded. "If you talk during lessons, you have to sit on the steps with teacher at recess."

"Well, how many people have to sit out during recess?"

Jack shrugged again, but Edgar stared down in concentration at his fingers for a second, then replied, "Four yesterday."

"But he makes *us* sit every day," said Jack.

"So that means you *talk* every day, yes?"

The brothers threw accusing looks at each other. "Not as much as *he* does," Edgar said, only to receive a blow between the shoulder blades from Jack's fist. Honor compelled him to return the blow and then some, so by the time the horses turned onto Market Lane, both boys were rolling on the boards trading oaths and jabs.

"Stop right here," Mercy told Oram.

"They ain't hurtin' nothin'," he replied, grinning, but pulled the reins to a stop so that Mercy could step back into the wagon bed and pull Jack and Edgar apart. By the time they reached the schoolhouse she was exhausted and had yet to do her shopping. Her two brothers had obviously not been affected by the rough start to the morning, for they jumped off the wagon and raced toward the school yard, where a half-dozen children were playing on the merry-go-round.

"Your lunch pails!" Mercy called, but they did not turn. She was about to have Oram bring them to Jack and Edgar, but an impulse seized her, and she told Oram to wait in the wagon. Crossing the school yard, she set the lunch pails on the ground near the steps and motioned to Jack that she had put them there. She stared up at the open doorway long enough to gather her courage, for she was aware that in her slightly faded blue gingham she was not dressed appropriately for addressing the schoolmaster. But if she waited until her next trip to town, that would be one more week of Jack and Edgar causing trouble at school.

Taking a deep breath, she mounted the steps. She stopped in the open doorway, unsure if she was required to knock since the door was propped open. Then her eyes caught sight of Mr. Raleigh, seated behind the desk. He was much younger than she had expected—in fact was probably her age. He certainly looked more pitiable than the ogre Jack and Edgar had reported him to be. Both shoulders were slumped forward slightly in a rather dejected posture. His hands were clasped upon the desk in front of him, his eyes were closed, and his lips were moving silently.

Why, he's praying! Mercy thought. She was just about to back away when the man's eyes opened and looked at her.

"Excuse me," she said. "I didn't mean to disturb—"

"Please . . . do come in." Mr. Raleigh stood. The elegance of his black suit and pearl-colored silk cravat made him appear every bit as elegant as Squire Bartley. He gave her a weary smile that did little to lighten the shadows in his handsome face. "Do you wish to speak with me?"

"If you're sure it's no trouble."

"Not at all. Please come in."

Mercy walked into the schoolroom for the first time in her life, and Mr.

261

Raleigh, pulling the chair from behind his desk, asked if she would like to have a seat.

"No, thank you." With great reluctance she introduced herself as Jack and Edgar's sister. "I have to apologize for their misbehavior, Mr. Raleigh."

He did not contradict her. "Your brothers aren't the only ones, Miss Sanders. I blame myself. A teacher should be able to command respect. I haven't quite figured out how that works, to be honest."

"Keeping them off the merry-go-round works, doesn't it?"

"Barely. They have the opportunity to ride it before and after school, so recess is just one portion of their day."

Timidly, for she knew next to nothing about schooling, she asked, "Should you make them stay off in the mornings too?"

Mr. Raleigh's tight smile held no mirth. "Punishment is supposed to come *after* the crime, Miss Sanders. There's always the hope that one will tire of spending recesses sitting on the steps and decide to behave. And it happens occasionally."

She felt so sorry for the part her family played in adding to the young man's troubles, especially when it was his first experience teaching. She knew speaking to her father again would do about as much good as speaking to one of Mrs. Brent's cows. So all she could do was apologize for taking up so much of his time.

"On the contrary, it was a pleasure to meet you," he replied warmly. "And I do appreciate your concern."

"I just wish there was something I could do."

Mr. Raleigh glanced over at the open door, from which the sounds of children at play could be heard along with metallic squeaks made by the merry-go-round. Mercy could see him draw in a deep breath before he looked at her again.

"Are you a believer, Miss Sanders?"

"Why, yes."

"Then I would appreciate your prayers."

He escorted her to the door, and she thanked him for his time. As she turned to descend the steps, she glanced across the school yard and spotted her neighbor, Seth Langford, between two elder trees, holding the reins to his horse and a pony as he spoke with Thomas. It was touching how his hand rested on the young shoulder as the boy looked trustingly up at him. She had never witnessed such a display of mutual affection at home, and it struck her to wonder if the lack of such was why her brothers were so fractious. Of course there had to reside *some* love in her father's heart for his children, but obviously there were degrees to love. Whatever people chose to whisper and speculate about Mr. Langford, Mercy knew two things that were certain—he had a kind heart, as proved by his sending the bolt of cloth to Mrs. Kerns, and he loved his son. What did it matter if he never thanked her for the cake? It had probably slipped his mind with so much to do when he moved in.

Mrs. Brent would have been so pleased to know that such nice people lived in her cottage, she thought on her way across the school yard. And then it occurred to her that, knowing how close Mrs. Brent had been with the Lord, perhaps He had given her an inkling. Why else would she be content leaving her household treasures to strangers?

Now, if I've played my cards right . . .
Fresh from a fortnight with her family in Sheffield, Octavia Kingston peered through the window of her first-class compartment as the train chugged to a halt at the Shrewsbury station. That a certain face was not conspicuous among the others upon the platform did not put a damper upon her hopes. Thurmond Bartley could not abide crowds and naturally would be waiting somewhere off to the side. *But then, so would Mr. Herrick.* Being a dwarf, he found it difficult to negotiate when surrounded by heads taller than his. If indeed it was Mr. Herrick waiting, then her strategy had failed.

She pressed her lips together and forced that thought from her mind. It *had* to be Thurmond out there.

"It was pleasant chatting with you," the young woman who had sat across from her said after her husband appeared at the door of the compartment. She had boarded at Buxton with her two little daughters after having spent a week with her family.

"And you, too, my dears," Mrs. Kingston said after tearing her attention away from the window. She patted both little girls on the tops of their bonnets and smiled at the look of pure affection the young woman and her husband exchanged. *How nice to be missed by someone that badly!*

"Shall I assist you, madam?" asked a courtly old porter at the door after the family had left.

"Yes, please," she said, taking his arm and stepping down to the platform. While he set out to collect her trunk, she discreetly brushed crumbs from the seed cakes she'd brought from Sheffield off her skirt. Then she heard her name.

"Octavia!"

She immediately subdued the little smile that had sprung to her lips and turned. In spite of the press of people, he was standing there staring at her, his black suit almost as elegant as her hunter green cashmere traveling costume. His arms were folded across his chest, his head tilted and

263

expression almost comically stern. If he was so cross at her, Octavia reminded herself smugly, why had he bothered to come here?

"Why, Thurmond!" she said, extending a gloved hand. "How good to see you! Are you traveling somewhere?"

"You know good and well why I'm here, Octavia Kingston!" he snapped. His gray eyes blazed under their thatching of white brows.

Mrs. Kingston gave him a blank look, extending the coyness for just a bit longer. "I do?"

Now he rolled his eyes and opened his mouth for another retort but squelched it when Mrs. Kingston's porter reappeared pulling her trunk upon a cart. "Where shall I carry this, madam?" he asked.

"My carriage is out front," the squire replied for her, handing the man a coin. Then taking her by the elbow, he escorted her across the platform. He waved away his driver's efforts to be helpful, assisting Mrs. Kingston into the landau himself. As the pair of black Cleveland bays pulled the barouche north, the two sat in silence—the squire, because he obviously intended to nurse his grudge a bit longer, and Mrs. Kingston, because she wasn't quite sure that it was incumbent upon her to say something at this point. She owed him no apology, for until he decided to pledge his troth to her, she was her own woman, not answerable to anyone but the Almighty.

But the sulking silence was becoming uncomfortable and more than a little silly. She turned to him with a smile. "It was such a delight to see my grandchildren again, Thurmond! Why, it seemed I couldn't sit down without one climbing into my lap."

"Yes?" The face he turned to hers looked as if he'd been weaned upon quinine. "Well, I haven't any grandchildren, so I wouldn't know about that, would I?"

And whose fault is that, you old coot? Yes, she was pleased that he had obviously been shaken by her unannounced departure. But enough was enough. In a calm, frank voice she said, "Squire Bartley, it was thoughtful of you to meet my train. But you shouldn't have bothered. I somehow doubt Mr. Herrick would have been such unpleasant company."

He gaped as if she had slapped him. "Octavia, I certainly didn't—" Both hands lifted helplessly from his knees and fell again. "When you left without warning, I wondered if I had imagined the . . . affection that seemed to be developing between us."

It took great effort for Mrs. Kingston to keep from smiling while she touched her chin and assumed a thoughtful pose. "Why, Thurmond. I do apologize. I had no idea it would affect you so." Which was the truth, because she had left only *hoping* he would see that she couldn't be taken for granted.

264

"Well . . ." he grumbled but then managed a little smile. "You're back now, so that's all that matters."

Settling back contentedly into her seat, Mrs. Kingston agreed. "Yes, that's true."

The carriage reached the outskirts of Shrewsbury. Hedgerows flanked the macadamized road, laden with elderberries, blackberries, and the bright crimson berries of the bittersweet. Mrs. Kingston and the squire chatted amiably—his asking about her visit with her family and her asking about goings-on in the village while she'd been away. "Oh, the *Bow and Fiddle* is filling up with relatives of Mr. Durwin and Mrs. Hyatt," he replied. As if to prove his point, a hired coach drawn by four horses raced by, the driver tipping his hat to them from his lofty perch.

After the dust had settled, Squire Bartley went on. "I suppose they're being ridiculous."

"Who, Thurmond? The relatives?" Mrs. Kingston asked, though she knew perfectly well of whom he was referring.

"No, Mrs. Hyatt and Mr. Durwin. Carrying on with a huge wedding at their age. Why, they're even planning to sally off to Scotland afterward for a honeymoon!"

He expects me to argue and protest that romance is appropriate for even old people, she told herself. She could tell by the way his eyes studied her, how he seemed to be holding his breath while waiting for her response. But if she *did* respond in the manner he expected, it would be tantamount to hinting that she would not be opposed to a proposal and such goings-on herself. And while that was very true, at this point it wouldn't do to have him deciding she was no different from the women of his earlier courtships.

With drama worthy of Mr. Clay, she replied casually, "I haven't given it much thought, but it does seem that way, doesn't it?"

"It does?" He cocked a busy eyebrow. "But don't you think they're entitled to this late happiness?"

"Mrs. Hyatt and Mr. Durwin? Oh, but of course. They're both such dears, aren't they?" Mrs. Kingston pointed to a tall chestnut tree on his right, shading a herd of resting cattle with its branches. "The chestnuts should be plentiful now, shouldn't they? I'm so very fond of them, especially roasted at the fireplace. And, of course, Christmas wouldn't be the same without them."

The squire stared at her, clearly more than a little befuddled. "Ah . . . that's very true, Octavia."

———

" . . . and so by assigning to hydrogen the atomic weight of 'one',

Gabriel Dalton was then able to calculate the relative atomic weights of other elements. Hence, a precise quantitative value could be assigned to each atom."

The wall clock was only seconds away from striking noon when Mr. Archer concluded his chemistry lecture. Philip slowly closed his notebook and gathered his pencils as students hurried past his desk in pursuit of lunch. When the classroom had emptied, he walked up to the lecturer's desk.

"Yes, Mr. Hollis?" Mr. Archer looked politely up at him over spectacles worn on the bridge of the nose.

Shifting his weight from his right to his left foot, Philip asked, "May I speak with you, sir?"

Mr. Archer sat back in his chair. "Of course."

"It's Gabriel Patterson, sir. He's in our dormitory and sits in your earlier lectures."

"I'm aware of the young man."

Philip drew in a galvanizing breath. "Are you aware that students have started 'oinking' at him when he passes by?"

"Oinking?"

"Like a pig, sir." He had no intention of adding that he himself couldn't walk a corridor without someone producing croaking sounds. It wasn't talebearing if it was done on someone else's behalf, and this was about Gabriel.

Lines appeared above the man's brows. "I see."

"He's most miserable. Even some of the underclassmen have started doing it."

Frowning, Mr. Archer said, "I'm certainly disappointed. It's unfortunate that institutional living so often breeds cruelty."

He understands! Philip thought as tension drained from his body.

"But just as unfortunately, there is nothing that can be done about it save advising Mr. Patterson to ignore the insults in hopes that they'll tire of making sport of him."

"Nothing can be done? But—"

The man gave him a frank stare. "Mr. Hollis, if I could put a halt to your friend's ill treatment by ordering it terminated, I would march into the dining room and do so at once. But surely you realize that if we were to order the perpetrators to stop, it would only make them more determined to heap misery upon Mr. Patterson. We cannot be there to protect him all hours of the day."

In his heart Philip knew that was true. But it wasn't right and certainly was not just. What had Gabriel done to hurt anyone?

"You must understand that this behavior has gone on for decades, Mr.

266

Hollis," the man continued. His tone was kindly but lacking the fire that burned in Philip's chest. "I was treated harshly at school myself, as were many of my friends. But one grows up in spite of it. I assure you, one day you and your friend Mr. Patterson will chuckle at the memories."

And that was the whole of it, for Philip could not produce the words to refute such bland acceptance of cruelty. While carrying his lunch tray to join Gabriel at the table, he passed a knot of boys who broke into a chorus of croaking sounds. He ignored them and thought, *I'd rather be made sport of by you than be just like you.*

As regretful as Mercy was over her family situation, she was also aware of the many blessings in her life. She had lost her best friend, Mrs. Brent, but the memories of their many companionable hours were still a comfort to her. Her garden brought her pleasure, for the work of her hands combined with a miracle of God turned dry seeds into abundant food for the table. Even her singing voice was a continual source of wonder.

Until attending the Wesleyan Chapel, all she had known of music were the bawdy songs her older brothers sometimes bellowed out in slurred voices after acquiring a bottle. She did not know how it was that she could sing unwaveringly every note of her beloved hymns, even when Mrs. Jones' piano accompaniment struck an occasional raw chord. There were some people in the congregation who seemed to move their voices at random, with no thought to the placement of the notes upon the scale. If striking true notes could not be accomplished by *everyone* who sang, then Mercy realized it was not a skill that could be learned in every case, but a talent—a gift. Why God had chosen to bless her with such, she had no idea. But she thanked Him for it often and was happy to be able to use her talent to honor the Lord.

Of course she had faltered upon first being asked to sing a solo. But Mrs. Brent had gently reminded her of the steward in the Scriptures who had hidden his talent away. "Why would God have given you such a voice if He hadn't intended for you to use it?" her friend had reasoned. Still, it had taken another three weeks before Mercy could bring herself to deliver a weak-kneed rendition of "Come, Ye Thankful People, Come" in front of the small congregation.

Over a year of singing every week had slowly eased away her shyness, which was another blessing, because now Mercy could concentrate on lifting the words and sentiment of the song up to God instead of dwelling upon the fact that all the eyes and ears of the congregation were upon her. But on that Sunday, September eighteenth, right after Mr. Langford and

Thomas had slipped in through the doorway while she was singing "Christian Hearts, in Love United," she was perplexed to discover that her palms were sweating as in the early days.

She made it through the hymn without looking in their direction and took her usual place on the front pew beside Mrs. Seaton and her three children. Over the rustlings of pages in some fifty hymnals and the clearing of at least half a dozen throats in preparation for congregational singing, a voice echoed through Mercy's mind. *"God told me He's going to send you a husband, Mercy."* Mrs. Brent's voice sounded so clear that the dear woman could have been sitting on her other side.

You're giving yourself ideas, Mercy told herself. Naturally seeing an eligible widower would cause her to recall her friend's prophecy. But why hadn't she recalled Mrs. Brent's words two days ago while talking to Mr. Raleigh, who was also unmarried, more handsome, and certainly more sociable than Mr. Langford?

She realized then that Reverend Seaton could have been reciting nursery rhymes for all the consideration she was giving to his sermon. She straightened attentively and pushed all thought of Mr. Langford from her mind. Which was easy to do, in light of the fact that he had never spoken two words to her.

But an astonishing thing happened after the final congregational hymn. She was just leaving through the front door of the chapel, accompanied by Mrs. Seaton and her charming brood, when she spotted Mr. Langford and his son standing off to the side of the lawn. *He must be waiting to talk with Mr. Worthy*, she thought, for she had seen them together last week. But then he met her eye and began leading the boy toward her.

"Miss Sanders?" he ventured politely.

She exchanged rapid glances with Mrs. Seaton, who then covered her surprise by leaning down to fasten a button on her youngest son's coat. "Yes, Mr. Langford?" Mercy replied in a deceptively calm voice. It helped that Thomas was staring up at her with what appeared to be adoration, and for a second she had the urge to pat the top of his oversized cap.

"May I offer you a ride home? I've brought my wagon today."

Stunned, she sought Mrs. Seaton's eye again, but the minister's wife was still fussing with her son's coat. It would be wonderful not to impose upon the pastor and his family for a change. For the sake of propriety, Mrs. Seaton always had to come along, and because their children were too young to be left alone, they as well.

Janet and Elliott had ceased attending chapel after Mrs. Brent's funeral, and besides, they no longer lived in the cottage nearby. Mercy's father, resentful of the time she spent away from her chores those few hours every Sunday, refused to allow any of her brothers to drive her there or fetch her. "That's very kind of you," she managed.

Five minutes later she was seated next to Mr. Langford with Thomas following on his pony. "He loves to ride any chance he gets," the man explained as they started out.

"Then why did you bring the wagon?" was out of Mercy's mouth before good sense could prevent it. Her face grew warm. "I'm sorry, that's none of my business."

Strangely, he seemed even more embarrassed by her question. Staring straight ahead at the horses, he replied in a quiet voice, "It seems unreasonable for you to have to depend on Reverend Seaton when I pass right by your cottage."

For just a second she was overwhelmed that he should be so thoughtful of her when they were practically strangers, until reason told her he was just trying to spare the good reverend some inconvenience. That did not cause her any disappointment because she was used to being taken for granted.

They rode in silence, with the only sounds being the rattle of wheels and the steady, dull *clip-clop* of hooves upon the road. Occasionally Mr. Langford turned to look over his shoulder at Thomas.

"I can stop for you on Sunday mornings too," he said at length.

This offer almost brought her to tears, even if it was actually to benefit someone else. "Thank you, Mr. Langford. It has been difficult being beholden to the Seatons, even though they insist, when there is no way I can repay their kindness."

"You're welcome." The rugged lines of his face actually softened with a smile for the fraction of a second, though his eyes were still on the road ahead. "Besides, I'm actually beholden to you. The cake you delivered made tinned foods more palatable for a while."

"You mean you liked it?"

"Why, very much." Mr. Langford eyed her curiously. "Didn't your brothers tell you?"

Mercy shook her head.

"Oh." He frowned. "You must think me terribly ungrateful."

Actually, I did, she thought guiltily. "I should have known, Mr. Langford. My brothers . . ." She could not finish without complaining about her family, so she merely shrugged. "I'm glad you enjoyed the cake after all."

"Very much," he repeated. "Thank you."

"You're welcome."

This led to another spate of silence. They were turning onto the dirt roadway of Nettle Lane when Mr. Langford asked, "Did you know Mrs. Brent?"

Now Mercy smiled. "Yes. She was my friend."

"She left so many of her belongings in the cottage." He paused briefly, as if considering if he should continue. "I feel a little guilty using them. Had she no family?"

The world was her family, even though she saw so little of it, Mercy thought, her throat thickening with remembrance. "Her husband passed away fifteen years ago. They had no children." Impulsively she added, "You mustn't feel guilty, Mr. Langford. She left those things for you."

He looked at her. "For me?"

"And Thomas."

The mention of the boy's name caused Mr. Langford to send an instinctive glance back over his shoulder. Then his eyes settled upon Mercy again. "But she didn't even know us. Or that we were coming, for that matter."

"I know." Mercy absently lifted a hand in an attempt to explain. "Mrs. Brent was closer to God than anyone I ever knew. She was convinced that God had instructed her to leave most of her belongings for the people who would live in her cottage after she was gone."

"I don't know what to think," he said after a thoughtful hesitation. "She must have been a remarkable woman."

"Very remarkable." Mercy felt tears sting her eyes and turned her face from him to blink them away. The silence resumed, and soon Mr. Langford was reining the horses to a stop outside her cottage. Before she could tell him that it wasn't necessary, he had hopped down and was walking around to her side of the wagon.

Leaving a wagon was quite different from exiting a carriage, especially for a woman. One had to step into the back and then over the side to the top of a wheel, using the spokes as a sort of ladder. Mercy had just stepped over the side, keeping her skirts modestly around her ankles, when she felt his hand clasp her elbow while another took her hand. With his support, her descent was much more graceful than usual, and she thanked him when both feet were secure upon the ground.

"You're welcome, Miss Sanders." Another smile softened his expression while Thomas, who had been waiting behind, nudged his pony closer. Mercy took a step forward to stroke the animal's muzzle.

"She's all mine," the boy said, pride overcoming his timidity.

"She's very nice," she told him. "What's her name?"

"Lucy. When I can ride a little better, I'll be taking her to school myself."

"How wonderful."

For those few seconds Mercy forgot that she was standing in front of her father's cottage. It seemed as if the space surrounding the boy and

271

pony had become an entirely different world—a comfortable one where people said gentle things to each other. But reality invaded that world in the form of a slamming door. She glanced to the right and saw Harold heading in their direction.

"Papa says we're waitin' on dinner, Mercy!" he called.

Mercy sent him a nod, and he headed back for the house, his innate laziness dictating he walk no farther than necessary. Turning back to Mr. Langford and Thomas, she said, "Thank you again. I'll be waiting out here next Sunday so you won't have to come to the door."

To her relief, he didn't argue. "Good day, Miss Sanders." Thomas sent a wave from the back of the pony, which Mercy returned. She could hear them both making their way home as she walked to the cottage. The door jerked open when Mercy was only three feet away from it and out stalked her father. He snatched his pipe from his mouth at the sight of her.

"What's this I hear about you ridin' home with thet Langford fellow?" he demanded, sending a hard look toward the lane. "What happened to thet preacher?"

"Nothing, Papa," Mercy reassured him as the last remnants of the serenity she had felt minutes ago dissolved. "Mr. Langford offered me a ride home, since he had to pass by anyway."

His green eyes narrowed. "I'll not have it, girl!"

"Not have what?"

"Thet Langford fellow thinkin' he can court you!"

This was too much, even measured against her father's past outrages. "It was just a ride home, Papa. And his son followed on his pony."

"I tell you, I'll not have it, Mercy! Thet man ain't the sort decent folk keep company with."

"That's ridiculous, Papa!" she protested, standing her ground. "Mr. Langford is a decent man. And he goes to *chapel*, which is more than I can say for some people!"

"And if I'd escaped from prison and stole some money, I'd do the same. Who'd think to suspect—"

"I can't believe I'm hearing this." She tried to move past him, but he sidestepped to block her way.

"Don't you walk away from me, girl!" he said, grabbing her arm. Even though she could muster up the nerve to argue with him occasionally, Mercy dared not shake her arm loose. Abruptly his voice became solicitous, and his forehead furrowed with what appeared to be concern. "I'm just lookin' out for you, Mercy. Talk is he won't tell nobody what happened to his wife. He could ha' kilt her, for all we know about him."

The charge was ludicrous, but it was pointless to attempt to reason with him. The best thing she could do now was to steer the subject away from

Mr. Langford and hope that her father's anger would cool down during the coming week. "I still have to cook dinner, Papa," she said calmly.

He released his grip upon her arm. "All right, then. But you can forget about riding around with thet Langford fellow. If you're so determined to go to thet church and leave yer chores, one of your brothers'll deliver and fetch you."

We'll talk about it later, Mercy consoled herself as she replied with an affirmative nod. Tomorrow evening perhaps—after she had baked his favorite blackberry tarts for dessert. For now she had kitchen duties to attend. She had learned long ago to prepare quick dinners on Sundays after chapel. If her father became *too* cranky at having to wait for his meals, there was always the chance he would forbid her to attend the services at all. She quickly pulled on an apron and put on some sausages and cabbages to boil. She sliced some cold roasted potatoes to fry in a pan with a little bacon grease, and an apple pie she baked yesterday was ready for dessert. She had also learned long ago that the barest meals would be forgiven if the dessert was ample. Thirty minutes later the table was set, and seven hungry—if somewhat reproachful—faces were busy with the task of devouring forkfuls of cabbages, sausage, and potatoes.

She noticed the unusual quiet a little later when she went outside to toss out the pan of dishwater. Sunday was another workday to her father and brothers, yet she could neither see nor hear any sign of them.

Just then her ears picked up a recognizable sound—her guineas in a state of agitation. Propping her dishpan against the base of a young plum tree, she hurried around the side of the cottage. Jack and Edgar had stationed themselves at opposite ends of the yard and were chasing them back and forth, flapping their arms and roaring like wild animals. *There'll be no eggs tomorrow!* Mercy thought.

"Edgar! Jack!" she called above the din. She was forced to call twice again before they noticed her and ceased. She did not ask them why they delighted in causing such torment, for what reason could they give? At least she had given the birds a chance to escape in the direction of their coop, where no doubt they would huddle for the next couple of hours.

Her brothers, both red-faced and panting, only looked annoyed at having their sport interrupted. This infuriated Mercy even more. "You just remember how spiteful you were when you're eating porridge at breakfast in the morning!" she scolded.

"Aw, Mercy," Edgar whined between puffs of breath. "I don't like—"

"Then it'll be a good lesson for you. Why should you get eggs when you mistreat the guineas?" Before either could protest further, she looked around and asked, "Where is Papa?"

Pulling a sour face, Jack replied, "He said we had to stay here. That weren't fair!"

"The others got to go," Edgar grumbled.

"Go where?" asked Mercy as foreboding began to chill her skin.

"We ain't supposed to tell you," he replied, but the glance he sent to the east, in the direction of the Brent cottage, told the whole story.

"But I *do* like tinned beef, sir," Thomas insisted as Seth handed him a pewter tumbler to dry. "We had it every Sunday at the Home."

"And you're not tired of it by now?" Seth asked. He rather liked sloshing the dishes from breakfast and lunch around in hot sudsy water and the exchange of conversation the task provided as they worked together. For some reason he was in an especially cheerful mood today. "Be honest, now."

The boy looked up at him while waiting for another dish. Though his face had filled out a bit and he had acquired some color, it still wore traces of the waif he had been. "Not at all, sir. Especially with that . . . red gravy."

"Ketchup," Seth corrected, smiling as he handed over a fork. Thank God for Mr. Trumble's pointing out the jars of red sauce upon one of his shelves—six pence each with the buyer's word that the jar would be returned. A dairyman's wife had started her own enterprise, allowing Mr. Trumble to sell her excess canning on consignment, and he had said it was catching on because the recipe was so time consuming. It did mask some of the tinny flavor of the beef and pork. "Well, now that we know we like it, we'll stock up—"

His words were cut short by a pounding on the front door that rattled the windowpanes even in the kitchen. Giving Thomas a curious look, Seth took the towel and dried his hands. "You'd best stay in here," he ordered on his way through the door leading into the parlor. The pounding did not abate until he swung open the door and found the Sanders clan scowling on the opposite side.

Or at least most of them. "Well, what is it?" he demanded. Such pounding and sour faces couldn't expect to be met with any warmer hospitality.

Mr. Sanders, with a scowl that would curdle milk, placed a foot upon the threshold. "You'll stay away from my daughter!" As if to provide emphasis to their father's words, the four sons narrowed their eyes and bobbed their heads behind him.

"I'm sure I don't know what you mean," Seth replied. "If you're referring to my offering her a ride home from chapel—"

"There'll be naught of thet." The old man's fists raised just enough to deliver their threatening message. "You're a big feller all right, but there's more of us. Me and my boys'll make you sorry."

I already am sorry, Seth thought. His cheerful mood of just a few minutes ago was left behind in the kitchen. "Fine, then."

The old man blinked. "What?"

"I won't offer her a ride."

"Well, good," he huffed, lowering his fists. He seemed disappointed that there had been no altercation. "See thet you don't forget it."

"Will there be anything else?" Seth asked impatiently. This crew had worn out their welcome long ago.

"The guineas," the oldest-looking boy mumbled to his father.

The man turned. "What?"

"There's three of 'em."

Mr. Sanders turned back to face Seth, his face crimson with new indignation. "We just now seen three guineas runnin' about in your yard. Seems sort of queer, the same number disappearing from our place the week you moved in."

Folding his arms and narrowing his eyes, Seth replied, "Why don't you ask the two behind you? They're the ones who sold them to me."

"What?"

"For four shillings. Didn't they tell you?"

"He made us sell 'em, Papa!" one boy yelled after his brother had been cuffed over the ear. His attempt at feigning innocence didn't spare him and, in fact, caused him to receive two cuffs—one on each side. It seemed even Mr. Sanders recognized a lie when it was thrown at him.

The boy who had initiated the transaction with Seth, holding his sore ear, attempted to redeem himself by blurting, "But, Papa, they was all roosters!"

"Roosters?" the man asked after a moment of perplexed silence.

"He didn't know the difference."

This brought a snicker from one of the two older sons. "All three?"

The boy nodded, pride creeping into his expression.

Now snickers rippled through the group. The other older son cuffed the boy playfully on the shoulder. "You sold 'im roosters!" Forgetting about Seth, who stood with cheeks burning in the doorway, the five turned and began walking toward the gate. Unfortunately, the guineas chose that moment to flutter across the footpath in front of them. The last sight Seth saw, before slamming the door, was of the Sanderses slapping their knees and guffawing with laughter.

And I had to settle next to them! Seth thought on his way to the kitchen. If his cottage and land were paradise, they were the serpent. He reassured Thomas, who had finished the dishes and stood at the door with an anxious expression, by saying, "It's just the neighbors."

Fortunately, other than having to pass by their cottage to go anywhere, he was able to avoid them for the most part. He truly felt sorry for Miss Sanders, who seemed to be several cuts above her kin and would again have to depend upon the pastor for transportation to church. But he had learned his lesson. Getting involved with the Sanders family in any capacity would only bring more aggravation.

The next morning, Mercy moved woodenly through the motions of preparing breakfast. She had barely slept last night, but the weariness that slogged through her limbs had more to do with the hopelessness of her situation than her physical condition. A dreadful mental scene of her father and brothers descending upon Mr. Langford and raising the kind of commotion she had seen all too frequently over the years repeatedly assailed her mind. How could she ever face him again?

She spoke in monosyllables only when necessary as she served the seven Sanders males their breakfast, but no one noticed. If she would have scorched the porridge or burned the bacon, that would have brought immediate attention. But they munched contentedly—except for Edgar, who whined that he hated porridge—pleased that the minor threat to the continuance of their routine had been quelled.

After breakfast she cleared the dishes from the table and poured a pot of boiling water over them in the dishpan. "Come on!" she heard Fernie shout from outside to her youngest brothers, who could have been anywhere, since she had not even the will to hurry them along in their preparations for school. She looked at the dishpan of soiled dishes and sighed.

And then a notion seized her. Untying her apron, she went to the door and opened it. "Fernie?" she called to the boy, who waited at the reins of the wagon in the drive.

"Where's Jack and Edgar?" he called back.

"I don't know. But wait for me."

"What?"

She held up a palm. "Wait." Turning, she raced up the stairs, meeting her brothers on the way down. "Don't let Fernie leave without me," she told them.

"Aw, Mercy," said Edgar. "We want to ride the merry—"

"Wait for me or it's porridge again in the morning." She did not turn to see if her threat was being taken seriously but went into her room and shrugged out of her faded green house dress and into the more presentable blue gingham. There was no time to do anything about her hair, so she wound it into a chignon that would probably shake partly loose on the way to town.

Her brothers were waiting in the wagon. Jack and Edgar called to her to hurry, but she motioned for them to wait. There was one more thing she had to do.

A series of frantic *moo*s led her behind the milking barn, where her father, with the assistance of Dale, Harold, and Oram, was attempting to put some of Doctor Rhodes' salve upon the nose of an unwilling heifer who had gashed herself on a bramble bush. "Papa," Mercy said, not stalling lest her courage fail her.

He turned an impatient eye toward her. "What, Mercy?"

"I've an errand in town. I'm riding in with the boys."

"Well, go about it then," he barked, waving her away while turning his attention back to the heifer. For a fraction of a second Mercy could only gape at his back. It had been *that* simple? Then she turned and hurried to the wagon before he could realize what he had said and change his mind. She would have to endure a tongue-lashing later, to be sure, but she would worry about that when the time came. She sat resolutely in the wagon, hands folded in her lap, not even bothering to admonish Jack and Edgar for mooing at the tops of their lungs at the cattle as they passed.

Near the end of Nettle Lane, Mr. Langford and Thomas passed the wagon on their horse and pony. Mercy only glanced at them long enough to return Thomas's friendly wave and to ascertain that the boy's father had no intention of looking in their direction. "Stop here," she told Fernie minutes later as the wagon drew abreast of the *Larkspur*.

"Here?" he asked, confusion filling his face. "But—"

"Stop now."

He pulled the reins to a halt. "Where you going, Mercy?" Jack asked from the back.

"I want to talk with Mrs. Kingston." To Fernie, she said, "You go on home after you drop the boys off. I'll walk back." It was worth the long walk, for if she didn't receive some kind counsel, her soul would shrivel up and die.

A maid in black alpaca, white apron, and cap answered her determined tug of the bell. She appeared to be Mercy's age, and the smile she presented made the huge house seem a little less intimidating. "Yes, miss?"

Hearing a noise behind her, Mercy looked over her shoulder. Her three brothers still gaped at her from the wagon. *Go away!* she motioned, then turned back to the young woman. "Is it possible that I could see Mrs. Kingston?"

"Why, yes, miss. Might I ask who's calling?"

"Mercy Sanders."

If the maid recognized the surname, thankfully she showed no sign of revulsion. "Mrs. Kingston is just finishing up breakfast, miss. Would you care to wait in the hall?"

"Please."

She was led to a brown horsehair sofa in the cavernous front room. A good-sized fire, which would have overheated a more modest room, kept the morning chill at bay. The maid offered tea or coffee, which Mercy was too awed by her surroundings to accept. "I don't mind waiting here alone," she answered timidly. Ever mindful of chores that must be done from sunup to sundown, she worried that she was keeping the young woman from hers.

"Very well, miss," the maid said with a smile. "There's bell cords against the far wall. Ring if you'll be needing anything."

Mercy was grateful for the time alone. She had left in such a rush that she had not actually planned on what to say to Mrs. Kingston. *Don't let me sound like a featherbrain, Lord,* she prayed. Some ten minutes later, Mrs. Kingston appeared in the doorway, a figure of feminine strength and formidability.

"Why, Mercy!" she said, hurrying on into the room. "Sarah was waiting for me outside the dining room with the news you were here. How wonderful to see you!"

Mercy stood as the woman rushed into the room and found herself smothered in a rosewater-scented bosomy embrace. "H-how was your trip?" she asked when she could breathe again.

"Oh, delightful! Will you have a seat, dear? Some tea?"

"No, thank you." Hearing voices in the corridor from which Mrs. Kingston had entered, she felt a rising panic. "Will other people be coming in here?"

"Why, yes." Before Mercy had to explain, a knowing look came into the woman's expression. "You wish to speak with me alone?"

Mercy shifted her weight. "If you don't mind?"

"Of course not." Mrs. Kingston seized her hand and led her to the library, a room lined with shelves of books and giving off the pleasant odor of leather bindings and beeswax candles. When she had closed the door behind them and waved Mercy into a chair, she sat down herself. Studying her with penetrating blue eyes, Mrs. Kingston said, "Now tell me what's happened."

Tears gathered immediately on Mercy's bottom lashes. "Oh, Mrs. Kingston. Forgive me for troubling you, but I've no one else. Mrs. Brent is in heaven, and Mrs. Seaton has all she can do to tend her children. If I don't—"

She choked off her words at the sight of Mrs. Kingston's palm, raised as if to restrain her torrent. "Mercy," she said flatly, though her expression was filled with compassion. With her other hand she held out a handkerchief she had withdrawn from her sleeve.

Mercy took the handkerchief and wiped her eyes. "Yes, ma'am?"

"I want you to take three deep breaths."

"Breaths?"

"Fill your lungs until you feel they'll surely burst and then slowly allow the air to escape. Thrice." She folded her arms. "Now, dear."

Under the gaze of those commanding eyes, there was nothing she could do but obey. When she was finished, Mrs. Kingston smiled and nodded.

"Do you feel calmer?"

Actually, Mercy did. "Yes, ma'am."

"Now, what is it that has brought so much sadness to such a lovely face?"

Blushing at the compliment, Mercy still managed to answer, though she couldn't quite meet Mrs. Kingston's eyes. "I'm in love with Mr. Langford."

"Indeed? You mean the man who's going to raise horses?"

Mercy nodded as new tears stung her eyes, and the calm abandoned her. "But Papa says I can't even ride to chapel with him" came out in a torrent of words. "He says it's because Mr. Langford is likely a murderer or a convict, but I know it's because he can't abide the thought of having to hire someone to do the cooking and cleaning. He wants me to stay there and take care of them until I'm old, Mrs. Kingston. I'll never have a husband or home or children of my own."

Raising a hand to her generous chest, Mrs. Kingston "tsked" and shook her head. "You poor, poor dear. But surely Mr. Langford's love for you will be strong enough to overcome your father's objections."

Mercy looked away again miserably. "Mr. Langford doesn't love me. We've only spoken once."

"Indeed?" Mrs. Kingston said again.

"But I do love him, Mrs. Kingston. He's so kind to his son, and he sent Mrs. Kerns a bolt of cloth. He comes to chapel too." She swallowed. "And God told Mrs. Brent that He would send a husband for me. But if it's really supposed to be Mr. Langford, my father is determined to chase him away."

"I see."

"Please forgive me for going on like this, but I didn't know where else to turn."

"My dear, you did exactly the right thing." Leaning forward briefly in her chair, Mrs. Kingston patted her hand. Then she sat back and pursed her lips thoughtfully. After a space of several seconds, she continued. "But a monumental situation such as this is going to require some thought and much prayer. Will you be attending to your shopping this Friday?"

"Yes." A second thought squashed the bit of hope that had begun to rise in Mercy's chest. "If Papa allows me to leave the house after this. He'll be furious."

"Hmm. Well, we can't have that, can we?" Mrs. Kingston pulled herself to her feet. "Well, come along, child."

"Ma'am?" Mercy said, rising.

"We must get you on home and appease your father or there's no sense in our making any further plans. You'll be needing a ride, won't you?"

Mercy hung her head. "I planned to walk back."

"Ah, but we can't have that. Mr. Herrick is a lamb. I've saved him hours of gardening labor, so he's always quite willing to return the favor." She led her through the huge house, down one long corridor, and then turned left through a short one. They exited into a flagstone courtyard and passed under the wide branches of a towering oak to a gravel carriage drive flanked by outbuildings. Mr. Herrick, amiable and courteous, indeed agreed with no hesitation to the favor. He hitched two horses to a landau with considerable speed for someone hampered by a lack of height, and minutes later Mercy was being assisted into the seat directly behind the driver's bench. She turned to thank Mrs. Kingston, but the woman had held out her hand to Mr. Herrick and was soon seated beside her.

"You didn't think I would allow you to face your father alone, did you?"

"But your walk—"

"Will have to be postponed until this afternoon, won't it? No doubt the earth will continue to revolve around the sun, my dear."

While they rode, Mrs. Kingston chatted about her recent visit with her family. That made Mercy recall the primary reason her new friend had left. "Did your leaving get the squire's attention?" she asked shyly.

Before she even said a word, Mrs. Kingston's answer could be seen upon her face. "My, yes," she grinned. "He met me at the station, most put out!"

"He was angry?"

"Until I told him enough was enough. Then he mentioned the upcoming wedding of two of the *Larkspur*'s lodgers, Mrs. Hyatt and Mr. Durwin, in a hinting sort of way."

"How did you reply?" Mercy asked with eyes wide.

Lifting her chin, she said smugly, "I rather ignored the hint and started talking about chestnuts or some such. Hints aren't enough, my girl."

In spite of her anxiety about her father's temper, Mercy found herself smiling. "Aren't you afraid of anything?"

Mrs. Kingston turned a serious face to her. "Oh, I was once quite the coward. And not too long ago."

"*You*, Mrs. Kingston?"

"Absolutely. But one day I realized that most of the things I had worried over for sixty-some-odd years had not come to pass. So all the time I had given over to imaginary troubles-to-be was wasted. And my fretful nature had all but alienated me from my family. I determined I'd not spend the remaining years of my life in that fashion."

"I wish I could be like you."

Sadness briefly passed over the elderly woman's face. "You can, dear, and it would behoove you to start before you've wasted years behind you, as I have. God didn't tell us in Scripture to 'be anxious for nothing' just to have something to say."

Soon the landau was stopped in the lane outside the Sanders cottage. Led by God or at least some survival instinct, Mr. Herrick had wisely passed up the drive. From her carriage seat, Mercy could see Oram was running across the yard toward the barnyard, most likely to fetch her father. Her sense of dread returned twofold as Mr. Herrick assisted first Mrs. Kingston and then her to the ground. Mrs. Kingston brushed the folds from her skirt and turned resolutely toward the cottage. "Mr. Herrick, if you'll be so kind as to get the gate . . ."

"Shouldn't I accompany you?" he asked with a shade of reluctance in his tone.

"That won't be necessary, thank you. Come along, Mercy."

Mercy followed, dreading the scene that was sure to occur. Sure enough, her father appeared on their right, pushing his way through the barnyard gate with Dale and Fernie flanking him. He turned to growl something at the two, who made unintelligible replies but then skulked back through the gates to whatever chores they had sought to abandon.

There was nothing to do but wait on the path to the cottage with Mrs. Kingston at her side. When her father was close enough to fix them with his intimidating stare, he stopped in his tracks. "Well, Mercy. What have you got to say for yourself?"

"You said I could go to town, Papa."

He crossed his arms, pointedly ignoring Mrs. Kingston. "No, I didn't. Oram says you ain't even touched the breakfast dishes."

Mercy glanced at the woman beside her, who stood with a pleasant expression as if absorbed in deep thought. *I should have walked*, she thought, for it was embarrassing to have her witness this exchange. As calmly as possible she said, "If you'll just allow one of the boys to help

282

me, I'll have the kitchen clean and dinner on time."

"One of the boys?" He gaped as if she had just suggested one of her brothers wear a frock.

"They have much more free time than I have, Papa. It wouldn't hurt—"

"Boys don't wash dishes!" he cut in with finality. He decided to vent his spleen on Mrs. Kingston next. "You can go on home to your fancy inn now, Mrs. Kingston. I ain't got nothing to trade with you this time."

"Do tell?" The pleasant smile never left her face. "I didn't come to trade, Mr. Sanders. I came to thank you."

He angled his head suspiciously. "For what?"

"For allowing your lovely daughter to spend a little time bringing cheer to an old woman. I had mentioned some weeks ago how good it does my heart to be in the company of young people. And what a wonderful surprise to have Mercy show up for a little visit!"

"She left chores behind!" he snapped, albeit with a little less heat.

"Oh, but you know what a capable worker she is. She's never gone to bed with her chores undone yet, I'd wager—if I were inclined to gamble. Has she?"

"Well . . ." He scratched the stubble on his chin. "We work hard around here. We need our meals on time."

"Why, of course you do . . . strong men that you are." Mrs. Kingston's smile was positively coquettish now. "I'm sure there is more to dairying than milking cows. Those barns didn't raise themselves, did they?"

"They didn't, indeed," he said, his face assuming an almost pleasant demeanor. "I built 'em all myself years ago, with the aid of Dale and Harold. My two oldest."

"My, my!" She shook her head, as if staggered by the whole concept. "And how sturdy they still seem!"

"Well, they need just a touch with a hammer and nail onest in a while," he admitted with a shrug. Turning toward the young plum tree just at the end of the drive, the trunk of which seemed to have grown a pair of shoulders, Mercy's father called, "Fernie!"

Nothing happened for all of three seconds, and then a head appeared. "What, Papa?" asked an innocent voice.

"Go inside and help Mercy wash up."

"Aw, Papa . . ." the boy replied, his face full of horror. "Me and Oram got to clear the brambles out o' the pasture. You told us to."

"Go tell Harold to help Oram. And then you get in thet kitchen or I'll take a bramble bush to your hide!"

As the boy sprinted toward the barnyard, Mercy's father turned back to Mrs. Kingston. "Won't hurt him to learn a few kitchen chores," he explained gruffly, as if the idea had been his all along. He kicked a small rock with the toe of his boot. "Mercy's allus been a strong girl, but even healthy folk do take ill sometimes."

"That's so true, Mr. Sanders. And sometimes when we least expect it."

"I had a uncle who died in his sleep when he was thirty-eight. Weren't nothing wrong with him either. Just didn't get up."

"Life is so uncertain," Mrs. Kingston nodded. She gave a sigh and glanced over her shoulder at the gate. "And upon that note, I'm afraid I must bid you both farewell. I mustn't keep Mr. Herrick from his duties too long." She took a step forward and extended her hand. "It was so good to chat with you again, Mr. Sanders. I can see where your daughter acquired her amiable nature."

"Well . . ." They shook hands, and then he kicked the rock again. "Don't hurt to be reasonable."

"Indeed not, Mr. Sanders." Facing Mercy next, Mrs. Kingston said, "Thank you again for visiting me, Mercy. Don't be a stranger."

"I won't," Mercy replied, smiling. "Thank you."

The older woman gave her a conspiratorial wink, then turned with a rustle of purple silk and made her way down the path toward the gate, where Mr. Herrick waited and was already swinging it open for her.

"Thank you for letting Fernie help me," Mercy felt compelled to say before starting for the cottage. But her father had obviously not heard, for he still stood staring at Mrs. Kingston being assisted into the landau on the other side of the gate.

"Thet's a right handsome woman, when she ain't being so bossy." He looked at Mercy. "She married?"

Oh no, Mercy winced inwardly. The last thing Mrs. Kingston needed was for her father to decide to court her. It was a disloyal but realistic thought. "Not yet . . ." she hedged, for surely the squire was as good as caught.

"Has a beau?"

"She has."

Her father shrugged, and for a fleeting second Mercy felt sorry for the crushing of his romantic feelings, however brief. "I'm thinking about baking some blackberry tarts for dessert," she said.

"Blackberry tarts?" He raised an eyebrow approvingly before turning back toward the barnyard. "You'd best get on with it, then. I don't expect Fernie has started without you."

As she showed a sullen Fernie how to light the stove to heat some more dishwater, she thought again about Mrs. Kingston. What comfort she had provided today! And she had no doubt that come Friday her new friend would have some suggestions regarding her dilemma.

Mrs. Kingston's words about worrying came back to her. She recalled the sadness that had come to the woman's face over the sixty years she had spent allowing worry to consume her. Mercy could clearly recognize the same tendency in herself. *Will it take me sixty years to learn to trust God to take care of me?*

But if Mrs. Kingston had taught herself to "be anxious for nothing," couldn't Mercy learn as well? Did she have to live through decades of anxiety and worry before finally deciding to give it up and have faith? Or could she apply Mrs. Kingston's sad experiences to her own life?

I will try, she promised God. She would concentrate on her household duties and put Mr. Langford out of her mind until Friday. But she couldn't make that promise regarding her heart. She did not know when it was that she had begun to love the man—and even the child. Perhaps as she watched them in the lane in front of the school building. Or one of the times they had slipped into chapel during one of her hymns.

There were many uncertainties in life, but Mercy was as certain of this as the day she was born: God had given Mrs. Brent a vision of Mr. Langford as her husband. And now she prayed that He would give Mr. Langford the same vision.

*A*re you busy?" Elizabeth asked her father Monday afternoon from the doorway to his study. She had never thought about it before, but she liked it that he kept the door open all the time unless counseling a parishioner. Asking him if he was busy wasn't really necessary, for of course he would be busy if he sat behind his desk. In her family, "Are you busy?" actually meant, "Have you time to spend with me?" Her father's answer to that was always in the affirmative.

"Come in," he said, smiling and closing his book of sermon notes. As she settled in the chair facing his desk, he asked, "Have you finished your work for the day?"

"Just now," Elizabeth answered. She held up a hand. "I've still the ink stains on my fingers."

"Not just your fingers," her father said, mischievous humor glinting in his hazel eyes.

"What?"

"Did your nose happen to itch some time today?"

"I don't remember." She rose to peer at her reflection in the glass of his wall clock. Sure enough, a blue stain decorated the tip of her nose. She licked a finger and rubbed at it, then went back to her seat. "Is that better?"

"Not as funny, but better."

Elizabeth smiled. "How were your calls this morning?" As proud as she was of the caring way he had with the people of his parish, his calls were far from her mind now. But she could not yet bring herself to mention the real reason for her visit to his study and was very aware that she was stalling for time.

"A little vexing, I must admit."

"I'm sorry."

"That's all part of the calling. First, the school seems to be suffering from a serious lack of order." There was a curious lack of glee in his expression over Mr. Raleigh's having difficulty. "I heard chaos from the out-

286

side of the door before devotions. When I entered, it was to discover that one of the Sanders boys had brought a small grass snake and put it on Ellie McFarley's back."

"Oh dear." Elizabeth raised her ink-stained hand up to her mouth. The urge to laugh only lasted a second, replaced with sympathy for Jonathan in spite of her ambiguous feelings about him.

"If matters don't improve, I'll be forced to recommend that the board look for someone else to take over the school," he said, rubbing his eyes. "Miss Clark is still too weak." When he opened his eyes again, her father gave her a frank stare. "I know you think I'm being vindictive, but this has nothing to do with anything that happened in the past. I bear a responsibility to the people of this village, and if their children aren't being educated properly, then I can't sit idly by."

"I know that, Papa," she assured him. "But it says a lot that he hasn't given up, doesn't it? He doesn't need the salary."

"It says volumes, I have to admit."

It did not seem right talking about Jonathan in light of what she had come to say, so Elizabeth made an abrupt change of subject. "And your other calls?"

Her father blew out a long breath. "Well, of course Mrs. Ramsey and her mother are always a blessing. But the wife of one of the cheese factory workers had asked me after church to call today. When I arrived, she wanted me to pray over her three-year-old son. She and her husband had just discovered the boy was left-handed, and she wanted a miracle from God to 'set him right.' "

"What did you do?"

"I read to her from the book of Judges about the army made up of seven hundred left-handed men from the children of Benjamin. The part about their ability to sling stones at a hairsbreadth and not miss seemed to console her."

"You always know the wise thing to say, don't you, Papa?"

He gave her a little smile and touched the open Bible upon his desk. "I'm wise enough to know where to look for answers," he replied. Then he cocked his head a little, his hazel eyes studying her intently. "But you didn't come in here to inquire about my visits, did you, Beth?"

"No, Papa." She shook her head. "It's about Paul."

"I see. So you've decided to break it off with him?"

"How did you know?"

"You haven't exactly acted as if you looked forward to his coming tonight."

Elizabeth nodded guiltily. In fact, she'd gone through the whole week with a growing sense of dread. She had agreed with Mrs. Hollis that she should wait two weeks to allow herself enough time to think, but she could not be more certain than she was now. The thought of having supper with him tonight as if it were any other night was too much. She would only be delaying the inevitable. "How do you feel about this?" she asked her father.

"Beth, it's not important how I feel. This is your future that will be affected. I just have to ask if you're sure."

"I'm sure, Papa."

"No regrets later?"

She shook her head.

"Then it's best to get it over with tonight."

Even though she had told herself the same thing all day, the words sounded so harsh. "How should I go about it?"

"I don't know, Beth. I never really courted anyone before your mother. And, thank God, we never wavered in our affection for each other." He paused thoughtfully, scratching his beard. "But I would suggest that you allow him his supper first. It's likely that he won't feel up to eating for a good while afterward. May as well get one of Mrs. Paget's good meals down him."

That plan also sounded cold. "Do you think I'm cruel, Papa?"

A warm smile eased upon his face. "I think you're an angel. This happens all the time, Beth. But if you end up marrying him out of pity because you can't bear to break his heart, you'll be doing him no favor. In fact, you would be cheating him."

"Cheating him?"

"Of a marriage with someone who truly loves him. Some young woman is waiting in his future. While Mr. Treves' pain will be acute, it is nothing compared to the pain of an unhappy marriage. I've seen too many of them."

A great sense of relief came over Elizabeth. Her father understood. She was not a monster for not loving Paul. "Thank you, Papa. Now I just have to think of how to tell him."

He nodded, his expression serious. "I believe tonight the ten-minute rule needs to be waived. You can bring him in the parlor after supper alone. Some things shouldn't be rushed."

Paul arrived an hour later, looking handsome as ever in his gray suit. If he had a clue as to what was coming, it did not show in his face or in his appetite, for he ate heartily of Mrs. Paget's braised lamb. Elizabeth, however, picked at her food, occasionally meeting her father's eyes across the table. When supper was over, her father excused himself, saying he had some things to attend to in his study. He shook Paul's hand outside the dining room door, clapped him lightly on the back, and moved on down the corridor.

"Why don't we sit in the parlor?" Elizabeth asked Paul, who was still staring bemusedly down the corridor at the retreating figure of her father.

"Huh? Oh yes."

The temptation was strong to take one of the chairs when they entered the room, so they would be forced to sit apart. But she wanted no regrets, and just because she didn't love him didn't give her the liberty to treat him like an animal. She took her place on the sofa, and as expected, he sat next to her.

"This is hard to believe," he said with a glance at the door she had closed behind them. "Your father isn't concerned about our being alone in here?"

"No." *Get it over with.* "Paul, I have something to tell you."

"Yes?" Paul studied her face. "You aren't still angry over what we talked about last week, are you?"

"No. I'm not angry at all." *This would be much easier if I were.*

He took the news well, considering that he had planned to spend his life with her. After the initial look of hurt showed in his eyes, he simply rose to his feet and started for the door. "When you come to your senses, you'll know where to find me" were his last words. After the last hoof-beats had faded into the night, Elizabeth went again to her father's study.

"Well, it's over," she said bleakly from the doorway. While she did not regret her decision, it seemed the parting had been more traumatic for her than for him.

"Already?" Her father got to his feet and came around the desk to gather her into his arms. He held her that way for a little while, then stepped back to look at her. "Are you all right?"

"I . . . I think so."

"How did he take it?"

She told him of the initial hurt in his expression and then his parting shot. "It was as if he was more angry than hurt."

"That's to be expected," he nodded. "His pride was wounded."

"Should I write him a letter? Apologize for hurting him?"

"Do you want him back?"

She did not even have to think about it. "No."

"Then let's not rub salt into his wounds," he said gently.

———

"My father is very ill," Jonathan practiced under his breath the next afternoon while slumped at his desk, drained of every ounce of strength. He was grateful none of those little heathens had brought a snake to school today! But as usual, he had had to stay constantly on his toes to maintain even a semblance of order.

His conscience forced him to discard the excuse that involved his father. First, it was a lie, and secondly, it seemed to be tempting fate. "How about . . . my parents miss me?" But they didn't. In fact, his mother's last letter, after several paragraphs questioning his sanity, had made mention of an iminent holiday in Brighton.

"My health is beginning to fail me." That one had a ring of truth, but not enough to keep it out of the "falsehood" category.

"Why not the truth?" he muttered, staring down at fingernails chewed to the quick. "I'm sending my resignation because I'm a failure."

He had conversed in such a manner with himself almost every day lately and knew deep inside that he would stick it out another day. Each day was one more closer to when Miss Clark would be well enough to take over the reins. When she did, he decided he would send her the largest bouquet of hothouse roses ever seen in Gresham. *But then what excuse will I have for staying?*

With the sigh of someone weary beyond his years, he got to his feet and went to a window. Some children still lingered in the school yard, mostly to play upon the merry-go-round. It wasn't that they were all unruly, but the handful that *were* caused an atmosphere of disrespect in the classroom that was becoming unbearable. *How can I get them to respect me, Lord?*

If he approached the school board with the threat to leave unless certain students were expelled, no doubt they were desperate enough to give him his way. But then he would be admitting to the whole village that he couldn't manage children. Pride was a sin, he well knew, and he was finding it a far more difficult one to overcome than his past debaucheries.

Even in his despondent state, he found himself smiling at the sight of two young boys engaged in a pretend battle with invisible arrows and bows of sticks. He could recall the excitement he felt when presented with a real archery set on his eleventh birthday. By the time he made it to Cambridge, shooting arrows was second nature to him, and he was voted captain of the archery team at the start of his second term—the youngest ever to hold that position. It was a shame, he thought, that the school did not have an archery team. It would teach the older children a whole lot more about important things, such as self-discipline and setting goals, than a merry-go-round did.

The idea seemed to seize him from nowhere. Or at least it *seemed* like nowhere for the first few seconds, until Jonathan realized it could have only come from God. Why could Gresham School not have an archery team? True, he would not be schoolmaster for the whole year, but if he got one started, by the time Miss Clark took over, surely there would be enough excitement that someone in the village would volunteer to take his place. There must be at least one person in the whole of Gresham who knew enough about archery to keep a team going. If not, he could train someone willing to learn. Perhaps that would even take several weeks, thereby giving him an excuse to stay in the village longer.

And only the students who could discipline themselves in the class-room would be allowed to join. It would be an honor society, a reward for those students like Aleda Hollis and Ira Johnson, who actually came to school to learn. And hopefully, it would provide motivation for the troublemakers to mend their ways.

He grabbed his hat from a hook on the wall near the chalkboard, brushed off the inevitable chalk dust, and headed for the door. As he walked toward *Trumbles* with his hands in his pockets, he heard whistling and realized a fraction of a second later that it was coming from his own lips.

There were three school children purchasing candy in the shop. They mumbled shy greetings to Jonathan as they turned from the counter to leave. "What might I do for you today, Mr. Raleigh?" Mr. Trumble's voice greeted him above the tinkle of the bell.

Jonathan smiled. He had become fairly well acquainted with Mr. Trumble during his three weeks in Gresham. The shopkeeper was always ready for a chat when the loneliness of living at the inn became over-whelming. "How would I go about getting some archery equipment?"

"Same as you get anything else that ain't right before your eyes. I send down to Shrewsbury for it—for a small commission, you understand."

"I understand. How long would it take?"

"Not more than two days." Mr. Trumble leaned upon his counter. "Plan to do a little hobbying?"

Shaking his head, Jonathan was grateful for the opportunity to get a reaction to his idea. "I'd like to organize an archery team at school. For ages ten and up, I should think."

"Do tell? Sounds intruding."

Does he mean intriguing? Jonathan wondered. "If I give you a list of equipment, will you order it for me?"

"I'll send an order down with one of the cheese wagons in the morn-ing." Mr. Trumble angled his head thoughtfully. "Pardon my acquisitiveness, but don't you have to get the board's approval before you spend that much money?"

"It's my own money." Jonathan shrugged self-consciously. "My family is wealthy."

"Do tell? Then why are you teachin' school, if you'll pardon me again?"

"Sorry, my friend, but that's a long story."

And the principal character in that long story, it turned out, was coming down Market Lane toward the shop when Jonathan walked outside. Though he saw her every Sunday from his back pew at church, this was the closest he had been to her physically since his first day in Gresham. His senses immediately took leave of him, for he stood rooted to the spot as he watched her approach. Her steps faltered, as if she were deciding whether to make a retreat. But then she lifted her chin slightly and continued.

"Hello, Elizabeth," he said when she was some six feet away.

"Good day, Mr. Raleigh." She did not even look at him while giving the cool reply but had fixed her eyes upon the door to *Trumbles* as if it were Mecca and she a pilgriming Arab.

Jonathan's heart became a burning coal in the pit of his chest. "Can't you even talk with me for a moment, Elizabeth? Do you despise me that much?"

Elizabeth halted in her steps, and a second later, met his eyes. "I just can't. There can be nothing between us, Jonathan."

"Not ever?"

Her brown eyes became liquid. "I don't know. Please don't ask me that now."

The reply should have devastated him, but since it was not a definite rejection, he felt a small measure of hope. "I won't then," he told her. "I don't want to say anything that makes you uncomfortable."

"Thank you." She glanced at the door to *Trumbles* and seemed about to continue on her way but then turned to him again. "Why do you stay at the school, Jonathan? You must be miserable."

"I can't answer that, Elizabeth." He gave her a wry little smile. "I just made a promise not to say things that would make you uncomfortable."

"Oh." Whether that meant she understood or not, he couldn't tell. She studied his face for the fraction of a second, then gave a little nod. "Good day, Jonathan."

"Good day, Elizabeth," he replied, when what he really wanted to say would have sent her fleeing through the door of the shop. *I love you, Elizabeth. I always will.*

Wednesday dawned with a warmth that felt more like mid-June than late September. A perfect day for puttering about in the garden, Mrs. Kingston had told the squire during their morning walk, for he still occasionally managed to find her. She had decided it was time to make herself just a little more accessible, but she had declined his invitation to lunch later at the manor. Relatives of Mrs. Hyatt and Mr. Durwin were pouring into town in increasing number, filling up the *Bow and Fiddle*. Some were even staying in the Clays' apartment over the stables. Mrs. Hyatt had asked permission before the actor and Fiona left for London.

Among these family members were a dozen or so children. While Mrs. Kingston adored children, they tended to be hazardous to well-kept gardens with their games of tag and hide-and-seek. She thought it best to maintain a presence in the garden just to remind children—and parents—that while pleasant strolls along the footpaths through the greenery were expected and even encouraged, it was not a park. Besides, there was mulching to do in preparation for the coming winter.

But the foremost reason she chose to devote her day to the garden was that there were certain days when one just *had* to get one's hands dirty. And this was one of them.

Her mind was just as busy as her hands, for Mercy Sanders' dilemma had often consumed her thoughts these past two days. She would have dismissed a less mature girl's declaration of love to a virtual stranger as foolish infatuation. But Mercy had obviously been forced to grow up quickly, with little time for fanciful daydreams. If the dear girl believed Mr. Langford to be the man God intended to be her husband, then that was good enough for Mrs. Kingston.

There has to be a way for them to be together, Lord, she prayed while raking dried and crushed oak leaves around the base of an azalea. *Surely* if God had told Mercy's friend, Mrs. Brent, that He would send a husband, then He wouldn't abandon the plan because of any overbearing Sanders men. "*Where God guides, He provides,*" she had heard Vicar Phelps say from the pulpit.

But did that mean all that was required was to sit back and wait for it to happen? Did not God often use people to carry out His plans? This was something to ponder, for she did not want to step out ahead of God.

Some time later, while taking a rest upon one of the willow benches in the shade of a young dogwood tree, her thoughts inexplicably drifted to the occasion of Jesus Christ's triumphant return to Jerusalem in the hours before His crucifixion. He had not only sent disciples into the city to acquire a donkey when He could have created one on the spot, but

He moved upon the heart of the owner of the animal to release it to the disciples.

And just as that owner, not even mentioned by name in the Scriptures, had felt God's stirring in his heart, Mrs. Kingston felt her heart was also being stirred to help bring Mercy Sanders and Mr. Langford together. "I'll do it, Lord," she murmured. "Now if you'll just show me how. . . ."

She found her answer that night in the pages of the book of Ruth.

———————

Dale wore a particularly forbidding scowl as he drove the wagon up Market Lane after dropping off Jack and Edgar at school and helping Mercy purchase supplies. He had ventured into the *Bow and Fiddle* long enough to realize the tables were full of people at breakfast and that he would have to wait too long to get his pint. This also meant that Mary would have scant time to notice him.

So when in the near distance Mrs. Kingston waved at Dale and Mercy from the *Larkspur*'s garden gate, Mercy could have expected his muttered, "Balmy old woman."

"Please, Dale," Mercy implored, her hand upon his sleeve.

"No."

"Very well." She began bunching up her skirt so it would not fly up immodestly, for she intended to see Mrs. Kingston today no matter what. Her brother's eyes widened.

"You ain't gonter jump!"

"I am, unless you stop."

Growling an oath that was loud enough for Mrs. Kingston and even the lace spinners at the crossroads to hear, he pulled the reins brusquely. "Now what?" he demanded, but before Mercy could reply, Mrs. Kingston was at his side of the wagon.

"I'm so glad to see you, young man!"

"What?"

"I would like to have the dead plants trimmed from my marigold bed. Mr. Herrick assists when he has time, but the poor man is quite busy with the wedding going on tomorrow. Would you be interested in earning a little pocket money?"

"I got to get back with the wagon."

"It wouldn't take more than twenty minutes."

That eased some of the scowl from his face. "How much?"

"Oh . . . three shillings?"

"Four?"

"Three and sixpence," Mrs. Kingston replied with finality. Within seconds, Dale had tied off the reins and jumped from the wagon. By the time Mercy caught up with them, Mrs. Kingston was standing over a flower bed and showing her brother what to do.

"Mrs. Kingston." Mercy tugged at the end of her sleeve.

"Yes, dear?"

She beckoned the woman away from Dale, who had already begun to pull up decaying plants among the bright orange ones. "Papa is strict about how I spend the household money," she whispered. "I can't repay you for this."

Mrs. Kingston smiled. "Mercy, I don't intend for you to repay me."

"But—"

The elderly woman raised a finger to Mercy's lips. "We have only twenty minutes or so to make plans, dear." Sending a glance at the speed with which Dale worked, she raised an eyebrow. "Perhaps less. Now come along and let me tell you what you're to do."

There was no arguing with Mrs. Kingston, who now steered her by the elbow through the gate and up Market Lane. "When you unpack your purchases, you'll find four cans of tinned beef, as well as two jars of spiced plums. Combined with boiled cabbage, which Mrs. Herrick tells me takes hardly any time at all, you'll have a decent meal for your family. Teach the brother who helped you in the kitchen tomorrow how to warm it up. It won't be a feast fit for Solomon, mind you, but we'll buy a nice chocolate cake, and they'll forgive the tinned food."

"But I didn't buy any—"

"My dear, this is going to take a lot longer if you don't stop interrupting. I purchased the tins yesterday and instructed Mr. Trumble to box them along with your supplies."

This was happening all too fast for Mercy to absorb. And where were they walking to now?

"We're going to the bakery for the cake I mentioned," Mrs. Kingston said, as if reading Mercy's muddled thoughts. "And I've ordered a joint of beef from the butcher's, which his son Henry will deliver to Mr. Langford tomorrow at ten o'clock. The cart will stop outside your gate to collect you on the way."

"To collect me? But why?"

"So that you can go to Mr. Langford's and cook the joint of beef. Bring some vegetables from your garden. I should think some new potatoes and carrots would be tasty on the side, cooked in butter. And while we're at the bakery, we may as well get a pie of some sort to bring with you. Men are so fond of pies—particularly apple."

"Mrs. Kingston." It was hard resisting the force that propelled her by the arm, but Mercy ground her steps to a halt. She pulled in a deep breath and faced the elderly woman, forcing her natural timidity below the surface lest she be bullied any further, however kindly her friend's intentions. "I do appreciate all of this, Mrs. Kingston, but I can't allow you to spend so much money on me. And cook for Mr. Langford?" Shaking her head, she said, "For one thing, my father would never allow it. And what would Mr. Langford think if I appeared at his door inviting myself inside?"

Mrs. Kingston's blue eyes strayed impatiently toward the bakery, but she did not attempt to push Mercy onward. "Very well, Mercy," she sighed. "I'll explain it in as concise terms as possible if you will promise to listen attentively, because I haven't time to repeat myself."

"Yes, ma'am."

"First, I have money. More than I'll need in this lifetime. My son is wealthy, too, so he isn't pacing the floor waiting for an inheritance from me." She gave a wicked little smile. "At least I *hope* not, for I plan to live a while longer. One of the many uses of money is to bring its owner pleasure. That is why people buy art and jewelry, take holidays and such. And it will bring me great pleasure to have a hand in your winning the heart of Mr. Langford. Would you rob me of that pleasure, Mercy Sanders?"

Such kindness rendered Mercy temporarily speechless. Mrs. Kingston took advantage of the silence by taking her elbow again. "Now, if we'll just hurry—"

But Mercy pulled to another halt. "Mrs. Kingston, even if I could allow you to spend money on me, what about my father? And again, what would Mr. Langford think?"

Mrs. Kingston sighed, released Mercy's elbow, and stood facing her. The blue eyes regarded her with both frankness and affection. "Mercy Sanders, do you trust me?"

A thickness came to Mercy's throat in the face of such caring. "Of course I do, Mrs. Kingston."

"Then would you just trust that I'm merely acting according to the answer God has given me concerning your problem?"

This request was a little harder, but she had no choice but to be honest. "But why wouldn't He tell me that same solution, Mrs. Kingston?"

The older woman gave her a beatific smile. "He has given us both the solution, dear Mercy. Only He divided it up, just as the head cook might put one maid to rolling out a pie crust and the other to chopping apples. He gave you the first part of the solution, which was to seek my counsel this past Monday. Now I am acting upon the part of the solution He has given me. He chose me to set this part in motion, because frankly, I have

296

the money with which to carry it out."

The thought of God and Mrs. Kingston putting their heads together on her behalf was staggering, to say the least, after twenty-three years of feeling like the most insignificant person on the planet. Mercy could not refrain herself from asking, "Are you *sure* about this, Mrs. Kingston?"

"More than sure, my dear. And now I must ask you this." Her stare became appraising. "Will you have faith that this plan is for your own good and do whatever I tell you to do . . . no matter how difficult it's going to be for you?"

"Yes, ma'am," Mercy answered after only a slight hesitation, for she was just now realizing that the person who has faith only in the things that are sure and certain really has no faith at all. "What do you want me to do?"

Mrs. Kingston smiled. "I'm going to explain that to you, dear girl." She nodded toward the shop. "But after we've made this quick trip to the bakery, and not a minute before."

"Your archery equipment arrived about an hour ago," Mr. Trumble told Jonathan after school that day. It had been a long, hectic day, and this bit of good news lifted Jonathan's sagging spirits considerably.

"Thank you for ordering them," he told the shopkeeper while eyeing the large crate at the side of the counter. "Please take the money out of my account." Like most inhabitants of Gresham with more than two shillings to rub together, Jonathan also banked at *Trumbles*.

"Would you be wantin' it delivered to the *Bow and Fiddle* or at the school?"

"The school." He would have rather taken it over there himself, but it appeared too bulky for one man to heft even that short distance. "I'll go back there and wait." He could always mark papers.

"You know, this archery must be catching on," the shopkeeper mused aloud before Jonathan bid him farewell. "Fellow who delivered this from Shrewsbury said he made a similar delivery to the Prescott School only last month."

"Archery equipment?"

Mr. Trumble nodded. "Aye."

"Where is Prescott?"

"Oh, not more than eight miles to the west, as the bird flies. Road curves a mite, so it's more like eleven to the horse."

"Hmm." Jonathan rubbed his clean-shaven chin as a plan began to form in his mind. "I wonder if this Prescott School would be interested in a little tournament? Later, of course, when we've had a chance to train."

The shopkeeper grinned and cocked his head. "Haven't even opened the crate, and you've such big plans already?"

"What do you think?"

"I think it's grand. A little healthy compensation gives folks something to look forward to."

You've got to do this now, Mercy told herself as she watched her father push away from the breakfast table. Her hands trembled so badly that she had dropped and broken a plate while preparing the meal. *Remember, Mrs. Kingston is praying for you*, she reminded herself. And if she did not take this chance, did not muster up some courage, her life might never change.

"May I speak with you, Papa?" she asked.

He gave her a curious look, though it was clear to see he was anxious as ever to resume his chores. "What, Mercy?"

Glancing at her brothers, who were also getting to their feet, she said, "Alone, please?"

He shrugged and waved an arm at his sons. "Get on out to your chores."

Reluctantly they shuffled from the cottage, as if they sensed there would be a scene between their sister and father and didn't want to miss it. When the door had finally closed behind them, he turned back to Mercy. "What is it, girl? I've got work to do."

Lord, help me do this. "You might want to sit down, Papa."

"Sit down?" His green eyes narrowed suspiciously. "This ain't about ridin' to church with thet Langford fellow, is it? Like I told you—"

"It's not about that." She took a fortifying breath and told herself to look at him, not as her father this time, but as the obstacle to any future happiness she might have. "The butcher's cart is going to pass by at ten o'clock. I'm going to get a ride on it to Mr. Langford's place. His son Thomas will be there, so nothing improper—"

Mercy had to stop because he had been shaking his head adamantly ever since she said the word "Langford." And into the silence jumped her father's stormy voice.

"Over my dead body, you will!"

"I am, Papa, unless you plan to lock me in the cellar. And you'd have to let me out sometime." Recognizing that bitterness had crept into her voice, Mercy reminded herself that this was not the time for dredging up old hurts and lost opportunities from the past. It would only serve to make him defensive and less willing to listen. She could not go to Mr. Langford's without her father's permission, however reluctantly given, or she would have to contend with him and her brothers coming over and causing another scene.

His hands on his hips, he glared at her while an angry flush suffused his face and neck. "You're talking crazy, girl!"

"I don't think so, Papa." She took another deep breath. "I am going to cook dinner for Mr. Langford and Thomas and then come home. I've shown Fernie how to light the stove, and he can easily warm up your dinner."

The graying head began shaking again, but she ignored it. "Papa, ever since Mrs. Brent passed away, you've known that I've nowhere else to go. But I have somewhere now, and if you stand in my way this time, I'll go there."

"I *will* lock you in the cellar before havin' you live in sin right next door!"

It was almost humorous, Mercy thought, how he had winked at his oldest sons' immorality all these years, and yet could be so furious at the thought of her possibly engaging in the same behavior. "I'm talking about the manor house, Papa. Mrs. Kingston says there is a need for another parlormaid, and the squire has agreed to hire me if you won't be reasonable."

"Thet woman!" he seethed, the whites of his eyes visible. "I should have knowed she put you up to this!"

"She's just trying to help me, Papa."

"Help you what! Spit on your family?"

This was going nowhere, Mercy realized, because he didn't *want* to understand. But she was amazed to discover that the fear had left her. In fact, she had never felt more calm. "I love you, Papa. But I want a husband and family of my own, just like other women have. Just like Mother had. In spite of what you've heard, Mr. Langford is a good Christian man, and I want to show him that I would make a good wife."

"I forbid it, Mercy!" he said, though some uncertainty had crept into his voice. "You throwing yerself at a man like that."

"I'm going, Papa. Since I'm not able to be courted like other women, this is how it has to be. And if you don't want me to come back home afterward, I'll walk to the manor house and trouble you no more."

He gaped at her for several seconds, hurt and fury evident on his face, then turned on his heel and left the cottage. As the door slammed behind him, Mercy felt an immediate urge to follow and apologize, but she held herself rigid until it quelled. A step in that direction would be going backward into her same old life. There were things to do if she was to meet the butcher's cart—pack vegetables in a basket along with the apple pie Mrs. Kingston had purchased yesterday, set out her roasting pan, and prepare her family's simple dinner to be warmed by Fernie. She also needed to change into one of her best dresses, put on a clean apron, and attempt to tame her curly brown hair into a chignon.

Read the book of Ruth, Mrs. Kingston had told her yesterday after they visited the bakery, and Mercy had done so in the Bible Mrs. Brent left her. Ruth, under her mother-in-law Naomi's instruction, had taken matters into her own hand and lain down at Boaz's feet in the threshing floor. Scripture did not say if Ruth felt awkward in carrying out these instructions, but Mercy imagined that she did. The result had been a husband for Ruth, a godly man who treated her well, which was also the desire of Mercy's heart.

It would be too much to hope that Mr. Langford harbored the same love in his heart that she felt for him. But if he would treat her with consideration and respect, it would be enough. More than enough.

———

There was still a myriad of things Julia had to do to prepare for the early afternoon wedding. Even though she had no particular role in the ceremony, and last night's formal supper for the Hyatt and Durwin families was now a memory, the girls and she needed to dress in their new frocks. She would also have to use the curling iron on all three heads of hair.

And all of that would have to be done in the space of an hour or so, for now Julia and her daughters were being driven by Mr. Herrick down to Shrewsbury to meet Philip's ten o'clock train. No matter how busy her day promised to be, she had not seen her son in a month, and nothing short of a broken leg could keep her away.

After meeting Philip they would go on to Saint Julien's to fetch Laurel. Andrew loved his daughter as much as she loved Philip, but as his presence at the wedding was secondary only to the bride's and groom's, he had been relieved when Julia had offered.

"Will he still remember us?" asked Grace on the outskirts of Shrewsbury. To her seven years, a month was an immensely long time.

Aleda opened her mouth for what would obviously be a sarcastic remark but then closed it before Julia needed to give her a warning look. "He'll remember us, Gracie," she said instead, causing Julia to smile. "Just like you remember him."

Remember them he did, as he embraced all three on the platform with a surprising lack of self-consciousness. He even wrapped his arms around

Mr. Herrick. "I was hoping you'd all be here," he said.

"You look thinner," Aleda told him on their way to the landau. "Don't they feed you?"

"Of course," he shrugged, then immediately changed the subject to ask her about school and the new schoolmaster.

Aleda replied that he was nice, but that some of the children misbehaved. "Some of the upper standard boys almost bully him."

"Oh."

Julia noticed a cloud seemed to passed over her son's face, but then she admitted to herself that she was just looking for a reason to find something wrong. She sorely regretted allowing Philip and Doctor Rhodes to pressure her into this. Fourteen was too young an age to live away from home, her heart insisted more strongly than ever. Soon enough would come the time to push him from the nest and toward university. *He could have gone to school here in Shrewsbury. I should have insisted.*

"Grace says we're going to get Laurel?" Philip's voice cut into her thoughts.

She forced away the misgivings and smiled at her son. "Do you mind?"

"Not at all. I'll be happy to see her. Will Ben and Jeremiah be at the wedding?"

"I believe so."

"Good." He blew out a breath. "I have a lot of catching up to do."

Only a day and a half, and I have to share him with everybody, Julia thought. But of course it was good for a boy to spend some time with his friends.

The decision for Julia to fetch Laurel had been made just this week, so the girl would be expecting her father and Elizabeth. Her usually reserved demeanor crumbled at the sight of Philip with Julia in the entrance hall of the school. "I've missed you so!" she exclaimed, seizing him by the arm and giving him a rough hug. "Even though you used to torment me!"

"Torment you?" he replied with feigned indignation. "Who taught you how to fish?"

"My father." She made a face and lowered her voice, for other students and parents milled about nearby. "I've not met one girl here who has ever gone fishing—or at least will admit to it."

"Why not?"

"Snobbery, I suppose. Some of these girls are blue-blooded to the last drop. They would get the vapors if I dared mention that I bait my own hooks."

Julia smiled at this exchange while shepherding them out of the doorway to the waiting carriage. Her attention being upon them and not the walk in front of her, she narrowly missed colliding with a man in a dark suit. "Oh, pardon me!" she told him.

He flashed a smile full of ivory. "No harm done, eh?" Looking at Laurel, he said, "Say, you're Vicar Phelp's daughter, yes?"

"Yes, sir," she nodded, suddenly her reserved self again.

"Ah, no doubt you've heard of my daughter, Ernestine Nippert, eh?"

So this is the man Andrew talks about! Julia thought.

"She's a grade ahead of me," Laurel replied.

"Well, isn't that nice? Say, if you ever find yourself in need of some tutoring, have your father bring you over to Prescott, mind you? Ernestine doesn't believe in hiding her talent under a bushel, so she would be more than willing to help you."

"Thank you," Laurel replied with a smile.

"Music is her calling, I'm sure you're aware if you've heard her sing in chapel, but she has a gift for teaching as well," the vicar said proudly. "Why, I daresay she could teach a hog his alphabet!"

"Thank you," Laurel said again, but when the man had entered the building, she covered a giggle with her hand, causing Philip to chuckle.

Julia whispered a scolding to both, for surely the vicar's wife or another family member was waiting in one of the carriages in the circular drive, and she did not want to hurt any feelings.

But once the carriage was a mile from the school, Philip and Laurel repeated the whole exchange to Aleda and Grace, who also burst into giggles. When Philip began snorting the letters of the alphabet, all four were laughing—Grace so hard that she started hiccuping.

Julia turned her face away from them to hide a smile. Guiltily so, for she knew as an adult she should lecture them about making fun of others. *But he brought it on himself*, she rationalized. And it was so good to hear the children enjoying each other's company. Had she ever fully appreciated these special times together as a family?

Seth and Thomas were constructing another shelter—their tenth—out in the pasture when Seth heard the sound of a wagon approaching in the lane. Anyone who came this far down Nettle Lane was either lost, which wasn't likely, or looking for him, which was only a little more likely. "Shall I go see who it is?" Thomas asked.

Seth nodded down from the roof of the structure because his teeth were engaged in holding nails between them. The boy jumped on the back of his pony and headed for the cottage, causing the trio of guineas to scatter out of the way.

Must have been lost after all, Seth thought, for less than a minute later he paused long enough from hammering to listen to the rattle of wheels fade down Nettle Lane. Yet Thomas did not return for another five minutes. When he did, a smile was spread across his young face.

"It's the cake lady!" he called when close enough for Seth to hear. "Miss Sanders."

Seth removed the nails from his mouth. "Miss Sanders?" But what was she doing here? "Has she left?"

"No, sir. She's in the kitchen."

This made no sense at all. "Is there something wrong?" Seth asked the boy.

"No, sir. She said you should keep on working and that she was cooking our dinner."

But Seth could no more work than fly. He eased himself down from the roof of the shelter. "Here, finish putting the lumber scraps in the wagon," he told Thomas and started for the cottage with long strides. The thought of Miss Sanders in his kitchen was an unsettling one, for if her father had gotten so incensed about his giving her a ride home from church, this would make him livid.

It was not that he was afraid of any of the Sanders men, but he was not foolish enough to believe that he could fight a whole gang of them. Besides, his primary reason for moving out to Nettle Lane was to be left alone.

Sure enough, he heard kitchen sounds as soon as he opened the back door. He walked through the pantry and stood for a second, speechless. She was a vision of loveliness, standing at the table, peeling potatoes with her lips set in a straight line of concentration and stray curls forming a halo around her face. It appeared she was so lost in thought that she had not heard him enter the house. On the cupboard ledge sat a pie, and he could feel the heat wafting over from the oven, so he knew something was inside. There wasn't a tin in sight. It was a pleasant, domestic scene that warmed his heart only long enough for Seth to remind himself that she was still a Sanders.

Before he could speak, she looked up at him and started slightly. "Oh. Mr. Langford."

"Miss Sanders," he nodded. He waited for her to explain herself, but she merely went back to work. "What are you doing?" he was finally forced to ask.

"Peeling potatoes."

That riled him just a little, for he had a feeling she knew exactly what he meant and was being evasive. "I mean, here, Miss Sanders. Why are you here?"

She looked up at him, and for a fleeting second, he detected some uncertainty in her expression. "I'm cooking dinner for you and Thomas," she replied softly.

"But why?"

Her lips pressed together, as if she had to gather courage before she could answer. "Because I want to show you that I would make a good wife, Mr. Langford."

"A good—" he began when he was able to speak. "I don't *want* a wife. Thomas and I are getting by just fine. Besides, your father is likely on his way over here now with a gun."

"My father doesn't approve of my being here, correct, but he won't trouble you." Again, that press of the lips while her hazel eyes acquired a luster that could be seen from across the room. "You may not want a wife, Mr. Langford, but you're in need of one. I could tend to your cottage so that you can concentrate on your horse business. I would plant a garden, too, so you would never want for good meals. I have six cows of my own, and I could sell the milk to the cheese factory so that you never have to give me spending money."

She paused, and Seth saw her shoulders rise and fall.

"All I would ask is that you treat me decently and sit with me during chapel so that I don't have to intrude always upon other people's families."

This was too staggering a proposal even to consider. He and Thomas had a pleasant life here. If he felt any temptation at all—for she was a lovely young woman and surely a good-hearted one, judging by the fact that she sang like an angel in church and had tended to Mrs. Brent—it was more than nullified by the fact that she was a Sanders. While she could not be held accountable for her parentage, she certainly could not blame him for not wishing to be involved in any way with her family.

And lastly, she wasn't Elaine.

"Miss Sanders, you're wasting your time," he said, not unkindly, but aware that it would be the greatest unkindness to deceive her into thinking there was a possibility of a future between them just to get a home-cooked meal.

She didn't even appear surprised but gave him a somber nod and resumed peeling potatoes. "Do you understand?" he was forced to ask.

There was a moment's hesitation, when again the uncertainty washed across her face. Then she looked at him again. "I'm willing to take that chance, Mr. Langford."

Seth cleared his throat to argue further. He found himself bereft of the right words in the face of such determination, so he turned and left the cottage. There was nothing to do but return to his work. She would have to realize at one point or another that her effort had failed.

"She's nice, huh?" Thomas asked when Seth returned to the pasture.

"Yes," Seth told him and hefted himself to the top of the structure to finish the roof. "Hand me some more tiles up here, will you?"

They had started another structure when the boy looked over toward the cottage and said, "Here she comes, sir."

Seth paused from sawing a board and looked. Sure enough, Miss Sanders was walking across the pasture toward them. The guineas rustled over to her and flustered around her skirts, either begging for corn or greeting an old friend.

"Dinner is ready," she said when close enough to speak.

"We're not hungry," Seth replied and blew the sawdust from the freshly cut end of a board.

"But I'm hungry, sir," Thomas told him.

Traitor! Seth thought. He shot the boy a warning look that was lost, for the young eyes stared at Miss Sanders with an expression of pure adoration.

"What did you cook us, Miss Sanders?" Thomas asked.

She smiled back. "Roast beef."

"Not tinned?" asked the boy. The hopefulness in his tone cut Seth to the quick. *You said you liked tinned beef!*

"Not tinned" was her reply.

"May we stop and have some?" Thomas asked Seth.

Seth picked up his hammer. "You have some if you like. I'll fix my own dinner later." The truth was that he was ravenous, but it would serve no good to encourage Miss Sanders. While he didn't have the heart to force the boy to stay away from food that was offered, he had no intention of being led into a culinary trap. Not as long as there was ketchup in his cupboard.

Thomas left without a backward glance, leading his pony by the reins as he and Miss Sanders walked together. The guineas even deserted Seth, running ahead of the two. Seth's hammer pounded the nail he was holding so hard and rapidly that it dented the oak wood.

After some time, the boy returned on the back of his pony. He had the satisfied look of someone who had eaten heartily. Meanwhile, Seth's stomach had started growling. "Here, come help me hold this beam steady," Seth told him.

"Yes, sir," Thomas replied, hopping to the ground. They worked silently together for five minutes, and then the boy said, "That was the best food I ever tasted."

"That's nice. Here, brace your shoulder against it while I hammer this nail."

Another five minutes passed before Seth asked, "She's gone, then?"

"Yes, sir."

306

"Oh." Seth had not heard horses or wheels this time, so she must have walked. While the chivalrous side of his nature felt uneasy at that thought, the more rational side of him figured that it would discourage her from ever trying this again. While his two sides continued their debate, his stomach sent up another growl. He set down his hammer. "I suppose I'll go make my dinner now."

Thomas gave him a curious glance. "But it's still on the table."

"You mean she left the food behind?"

"There's enough for tomorrow, too, I think."

"We'll see about that," Seth told him, for he had every intention of packing whatever lurked inside his kitchen and delivering it to her cottage. But before he even reached his cottage, with Thomas at his side, he knew that he could not. She had told him that while her father did not approve of her actions, he would not appear and cause a row. But Mr. Sanders was obviously not the most stable individual in Gresham. It was not that Seth was afraid of what the Sanders men might do to *him*—but what if he took his anger out on his daughter? While he did not want to marry her, he certainly did not want to cause her to be mistreated.

Since he realized he could not return the food without possibly causing her harm, and that it would be a shame to waste it, he resigned himself to having to eat it. The aroma hit him even before he reached the back door and grew stronger and more savory as he and Thomas walked through the pantry and into the kitchen. There on the table sat a platter of roast beef, surrounded with little potatoes, onions, and carrots. Seth went over to it and cut a small slice, just to taste. Juices ran down the side as the knife went through it like butter.

"It's good, huh?" asked Thomas.

"Yes, it is," Seth agreed reluctantly and ate two more slices before remembering his manners and sitting down at the table. "Will you have some more?" he asked the boy as he spooned carrots and potatoes onto his plate.

The boy shook his head. "I'm full, sir. I didn't even have room for apple pie."

"She walked back?" Seth asked him, though he knew the answer.

"She carried her roasting pan too." This was said without a trace of accusation, but Seth felt ashamed at the idea of her lugging an iron pan for half a mile after cooking them this glorious meal—no matter what her motives. "I offered to let Lucy carry it on her back, but Miss Sanders said she would manage just fine."

Seth frowned guiltily but thought, *At least she's not likely to try this again.*

Apparently Fernie had managed the heating of the meal, Mercy discovered when she arrived at home, though he had considered cleanup not to be part of the job. Soiled dishes still sat on the table, the scraps of which had not even been scraped into the hog's slop pail.

She was not a bit surprised at this and immediately stored the roasting pan in the oven and began clearing the table. Tormenting thoughts plagued her as she worked, the most horrendous being Mr. Langford having the opinion that she was a complete fool.

Father, help me, she prayed as another tear dripped from her chin into the dishwater. *Sing* was the thought that immediately came into her mind. She had not walked with the Lord long enough to have the discernment Mrs. Brent had possessed, but she was fairly certain that He had spoken to her just then. And so she cleared her thickened throat and began to sing softly:

> *O thou, in whose presence my soul takes delight,*
> *On whom in affliction I call,*
> *My comfort by day and my song in the night,*
> *My hope, my salvation, my all.*

By the time she reached the fourth verse, Mercy's tumultuous thoughts were replaced by a comforting sense of peace. She did not know all the particulars of the plan God had given Mrs. Kingston, for her friend had refused to reveal the additional steps that would have to be taken. But she understood her role in that plan now, and that was to trust. Just as Abraham had been called to follow God's leading to a place he did not know, Mercy was being called to step out in faith. And she would do so, she determined, even if Mr. Langford thought her the most foolish woman in Gresham.

*T*he wedding was a lovely affair, with most parishioners of Saint Jude's attending, as well as the people of other faiths who were acquainted with either Mr. Durwin or Mrs. Hyatt. It had done Andrew's heart good to stand at the front of the church and perform the ceremony that joined two lives into one, for the affection shining from the bride's and groom's eyes was a reminder that love was important at any age.

He was not the only person to be so moved, for there were quite a few sniffles coming from the congregation, and surely only a few related to head colds. Andrew had even noticed during a glance at the congregation while the chancel choir sang "Christian Hearts, in Love United," that Squire Bartley, seated with Mrs. Kingston, had traded his usual dour expression for one positively glowing with sentiment.

How blessed I am! Andrew thought during the reception as he caught Julia's eye across the floor of the town hall. She was busy assisting Elizabeth, Mrs. Sykes, and Laurel with serving cake, punch, and sandwiches, but she still paused long enough to return his smile. In less than three months, it would be the two of them exchanging vows in front of God, Bishop Edwards, and the congregation. For a man to be blessed with one great love during his lifetime was an incredible thing, and he was twice blessed.

So overwhelming were his feelings that he suddenly felt the need to be alone with God. The day, and even yesterday, had been hectic, so his morning prayers had been rushed—more rote than sincere. He knew he would not be missed with his daughters and Julia occupied and his part of the ceremony finished. Hands in pockets, he strolled out toward the river and ducked under the trailing umbrella of a willow to stand against the trunk. Only the trunk was already taken by Philip Hollis, who turned a tear-streaked face toward him.

"Philip? What's wrong, son?"

Philip wiped his face with his coat sleeve, clearly mortified at being caught weeping. "Nothing, sir."

"Now, you don't expect me to believe that, do you?" Andrew replied gently. "What's the matter—a touch of homesickness?"

The boy didn't answer, but the tremble of his bottom lip told all.

"That's nothing to be ashamed of, Philip. Our homes have a way of attaching themselves to our hearts."

"Yes," he replied with a strained voice.

"You aren't being mistreated, are you?"

Philip shook his head, which was what Andrew would have expected. For some perverse reason, at fourteen there was more shame at *admitting* one was being bullied than the actual bullying itself.

"You can tell me if you are, son. I've suffered through it myself, you know. It might be that I can help you."

There was a lengthy pause, during which Philip stared out toward the Bryce. "It's not just me," he finally said.

"Older boys lording it over the young ones?"

"Yes, sir."

Now Andrew shook his head. "Nothing changes, I'm afraid. But at least it doesn't last forever. You'll be able to stick it out, won't you?"

"Yes, sir." He turned his face toward Andrew. "You won't tell Mother, will you?"

"Of course not." Patting the boy's wiry shoulder, Andrew smiled and said, "Trust me, you'll laugh at it all one day when you're a doctor."

Philip returned his smile, or at least what was intended to be a smile, for it had a suspicious grimace quality to it. This led Andrew to ask again if the boy was *sure* he could manage the schooling, but before he could open his mouth, Philip said, "Thank you, Vicar. I think I'll go find Ben and Jeremiah again."

Later, after the Durwins had left for a honeymoon in Scotland, and the last of the tables had been consigned again to the storage room of the town hall, Andrew accompanied Julia across the green toward the *Larkspur*. He had a sermon to prepare at the vicarage, but the walk would at least give them some time to chat.

"Have you spoken with Philip today?" she asked.

He recognized the concern in her voice and replied, "Actually, I did. While the reception was going on."

She sighed, absently weaving her fingers together. "He tells me that he's enjoying school. But he evades my questions about any specific part of it. He has been so protective of me since his father died. . . ."

"And that proves that he's a strong boy, Julia. Boarding school takes some time to get used to. Just allow him that time, and it'll become old hat to him."

"I suppose you're right." She turned soulful green eyes to him. "But

I'm afraid it's never going to be old hat with me."

———

"Now listen up!" Jonathan commanded his students on Monday morning. "Vicar Phelps will be here any minute, and I'll not have you running about like a cage of monkeys!" To assure himself of that, he had conducted an inspection of the Sanders brothers' pockets and lunch pails for reptiles. Unfortunately, he hadn't counted on Jessie Sykes, one of the fifth standard boys, having a mild stomach ailment and giving evidence of that fact during Jonathan's calling of the role. The squeals and shrieks of laughter had been immediate, with even crimson-faced Jessie grinning proudly as if he had performed an operatic solo.

It was into this atmosphere Vicar Phelps stepped. An immediate silence swept through the classroom, and though that was what Jonathan had been attempting to attain, it nettled him that the vicar was able to do so without uttering a word. The man sent his usual nod to Jonathan and led the class in prayer. He then delivered a short sermon on the value of self-control. Whether that was another barb aimed at his past behavior or not, Jonathan hadn't the strength to care. He leaned against the wall as the devotion went on, worn out though the day had just begun.

By running from one brush fire to another he was able to maintain a fragile discipline as the morning wore on, thus sapping the remainder of his strength. He spent the whole of recess aware that the three miscreants who sat with him on the steps as punishment were making faces behind his back, yet he lacked even the will to turn and glare at them. By early afternoon he had almost decided to save his plan for tomorrow, but then the realization came to him that tomorrow would be no different from today, so he might as well get on with his plan and pray that it worked.

Casually, he stood in front of the students and announced, "We're going to spend the remaining hour and a half outside."

This was greeted with murmurs of pleased disbelief and a few cheers. "Why, Mr. Raleigh?" asked George Temple.

"I want to show all of you something. We're going to go beyond the school yard toward the squire's apple orchard." He assigned four older boys to carry the crate, which had sat unheeded in a back corner but now roused the students curiosity.

"What is it, Mr. Raleigh?" one of the boys hefting the crate asked.

"You'll see" was Jonathan's enigmatic reply. He had almost begun to enjoy himself as the children filed out of the classroom behind him, the boys with the crate bringing up the rear. He led the chattering queue past the backs of cottages toward the drystone wall surrounding the squire's apple orchard. Even though the archery equipment had been purchased with his own funds, he had still felt it wise to consult the school board about starting a team. Fortunately, the three men had expressed enthusiasm for the idea, for he had not thought to ask permission until *after* ordering the equipment. Mr. Sway had even volunteered to stack a bale of hay against the wall, and it was there that Jonathan stopped.

Almost all chatter ceased when he motioned for the boys with the crate to come over. Those few students who continued to talk were, incredibly, shushed by their classmates. When the crate was upon the ground, Jonathan lifted the lid and brought out a square of heavy canvas cloth. There were oohs and aahs as he unfolded it to reveal a painted circular target constructed of rings of gold, red, blue, black, and white. Jonathan smiled and, with a flourish, draped it over the bale of hay.

"We're gonter shoot arrows, Mr. Raleigh?" someone asked, causing an excited murmur to spread through the group.

"*Going* to shoot arrows," he corrected without thinking and told himself wryly, *So there's some teacher in you after all.*

"Are we *going* to shoot arrows?" the same voice queried.

"We are."

"*All* of us?" someone else asked hopefully.

"Today, yes." Jonathan brought one of the three wooden bows from the crate. Today he would string it himself in order to give the children more time to experience the excitement of aiming an arrow at the target. He had a personal stake in making this as pleasant an experience as possible. "But first, I want to tell you about Robin Hood."

———

Philip had run his first lap around the grounds Tuesday afternoon when a familiar shape appeared in the distance ahead. He sprinted to catch up with Gabriel Patterson.

"What are you doing out here?"

Gabriel, who seemed to be concentrating with all his might on staying vertical and in motion, panted in reply, "Pushed Westbrook down."

"No!"

"Didn't mean to." Six gulps of breath issued before he could continue. "Stood in my face . . . and called me hog . . . because . . . I brushed against his trunk." He dredged up and let out another six lungfuls. "Knocked his ink jar to floor . . . was accident . . . everyone laughed at me."

"Oh no." Philip, now used to running fast to get the punishment over with, was finding it difficult to adjust to Gabriel's slower pace. But of course he could not in good conscience leave his friend to lumber along alone. "Well, at least you didn't get caned."

"Want to go home, Philip."

"Then write to your parents, Gabriel. Tell them how miserable you are."

"I told them . . . Saturday at home . . . Father says it'll . . . make a man out of me."

"I'm sorry." For the first time since his return two days ago, Philip was unable to stop himself from recalling the joy and sadness that had infused his soul during his brief stay at home. Joy, because it was the place he loved more than anywhere else, and sadness, because it was no longer truly his.

But at this moment Philip needed to put away his melancholy as Gabriel was in immediate need of cheering. He lightly punched his friend's arm. "Will you grant me one favor, Gabriel?"

"Yes, what?" Gabriel huffed.

"Next time you knock old Westbrook off his feet, would you make sure I'm there to witness it?"

Gabriel, reddened from the exertion of running, actually produced a fleeting smile. "Was almost worth . . . having to run."

"Doctor Rhodes says I should be able to teach school in another month," Miss Clark said to Andrew in her parents' comfortable back parlor, where she sat reclined with a blanket over her legs and a stack of books at her feet. "If I'm careful not to exert myself too strenuously."

"That's too soon if you ask me," Mrs. Clark, the schoolmistress's mother, reproved from her chair. Her hair was light brown like her daughter's, but that was where the resemblance ended, for she was short and as pleasantly rounded as Miss Clark was tall and slender. "Why, you've still got shadows under your eyes. And you've lost a stone's weight at least."

Both charges appeared to be true in Andrew's observation, but who was he to second-guess Doctor Rhodes? Still, he would not wish to cause Miss Clark a relapse by suggesting that one month would certainly be enough time for her to build up some strength.

He had not called upon this household with the hope of hastening Miss Clark's return to the school, no matter how much he desired that Jonathan Raleigh leave Gresham. He had called upon her four times already during the course of her illness without mentioning school. She was his parishioner and he was her pastor, and it was his duty to comfort the sick. It was Miss Clark who had brought up the subject this time.

"I do hate the thought of taking the position from Mr. Raleigh, though," she went on. "He paid a call here last week and seems a decent person."

"Mr. Raleigh took the position with the understanding that it was temporary," Andrew reminded her. And after witnessing another spectacle this morning, he figured it was about time a capable teacher took charge.

The only thing that troubled him was that Miss Clark's only experience had been at a girls' boarding school. If a strong young man had trouble keeping some of the older boys in line, how would a soft-spoken woman—and one recovering from a grave illness—fare? *That's the school board's concern*, he reminded himself. While they were only too happy to ask his assistance when dealing with the likes of Mr. Sanders, they had made it clear that his opinion was not a concern in the hiring of teachers.

Four more weeks and Mr. Raleigh will have no excuse to stay was the comforting thought that accompanied Andrew back to the vicarage. He felt no more animosity for the young man, who had held on at the school for three weeks now. Indeed, Andrew wished him well in whatever endeavors he chose to pursue outside of Gresham. But it would take longer than three weeks to prove that Mr. Raleigh's changed lifestyle would last. And having just broken off her almost-engagement with Mr. Treves, Elizabeth did not need a former beau so close at hand to add to her confusion.

———

On Thursday, the twenty-ninth of September, Jonathan found himself practically having to shout the grammar lesson to the fourth standard students. But not because of rowdiness, for ever since Monday afternoon's practice at the archery target, there had been a noticeable lessening of misbehavior in the classroom. The reason for his strain of voice was a thunderstorm outside, sending rain lashing violently against the windows and pounding the tiles above.

"Will there be no archery during recess?" Alfred Meeks, a timid second standard student who lived up to his name, asked with raised hand as the lunch hour drew nearer.

"I'm afraid not," Jonathan replied, shaking his head regretfully. "We'll have to stay inside."

Another hand went up. "We could practice in here, couldn't we?"

It was something to consider. The equipment, aside from the bale of hay, was in the cloak room. Basic form could be practiced indoors. But it was tedious work and not nearly as exciting as aiming real arrows at targets. He thought it best to warn them of that fact. "Are you sure you wouldn't rather play quietly instead?"

Jonathan smiled to himself at the heads that shook and the eagerness on the faces staring back at him. During recess, after the children had hastened through their lunches, he strung the three bows and formed three queues of students along the aisles between desks. He went from the head of one group to another, reminding students to align their feet properly, to keep their weight distributed evenly, and shoulders squared as they aimed imaginary arrows at a target he had hastily chalked upon the blackboard.

"The V of your thumb and index finger—see?" he showed Edgar Sanders, moving the boy's grimy hand into the correct position. "Now you have it!" For the first time the boy actually smiled at him. *Thank you for this idea!* Jonathan prayed under his breath.

Near the close of recess, he decided it was time to implement the second part of his plan. He collected and unstrung the bows as the children returned to their seats. There was the usual commotion, but it tapered and died down when Jonathan stood at the front and raised a silencing hand.

"Yesterday I received a reply to a letter I sent to the school board at Prescott," he told them. Eight hands shot up right away but lowered again after Jonathan said, "Prescott is a village about eight miles to the west of us."

"The school there founded an archery team just this year," he went on. "With the permission of our school board, I've challenged them to a little contest, to be held in mid-November before the weather turns too forbidding. They have had a three-week head start, so it would require much dedication and hard work upon our part."

There was a collective intake of breath at this, then a burst of applause. Again, Jonathan raised his hand for silence. "But there will be two strict requirements for membership on our team. The first, I'm very sorry to announce, is that in the interest of safety you must be ten years old or over."

As expected, faces in the front two rows fell. While Jonathan felt great sympathy for his youngest students, he had to remind himself that the disappointment was preferable to an injured eye or worse. "But Mrs. Hillock has offered to allow you to stay with her students during recess when the others are at practice, which means you'll have more turns on the merry-go-round. And if you'll attend faithfully to your arithmetic lessons, you can help keep score at the archery contest. Good scorekeepers are very important, you know."

His consolations seemed to help somewhat, for a few smiles were sent his way. An arm shot up, belonging to Willard Kerns, a fifth standard student. "What is the other requirement, Mr. Raleigh?"

Folding his arms, Jonathan leaned back against his desk. "Robin Hood didn't allow just *any* person to join his merry men, no matter how skillful. And the Gresham team will be composed only of those students who complete their school assignments to the best of their abilities and who can control their behavior during class time."

There were murmurs of disappointment among the older students, to which Jonathan queried, "Is that an impossible demand?" No one challenged that it was, and some students even managed to look embarrassed at their complaints.

"Then do you understand what you older students have to do to be allowed on the team?" he asked just to make sure.

Surprisingly, Jack Sanders, who had never yet volunteered an answer, raised his hand.

"Yes, Mr. Sanders?"

"Do our schoolwork and be good?"

Jonathan smiled. "Exactly."

———

"So tell me about your visit to Mr. Langford's," Mrs. Kingston said after hailing Mercy in front of the *Larkspur* after the shopping had been done. This time it was Oram who drove, and a proffered bag of peppermints from the elderly woman's hand was all that was necessary to appease him into stopping long enough for her to draw Mercy aside. "I've been on pins and needles wondering. I was sorely tempted to pay a call but was afraid it would make your father more angry at you for defying him." She narrowed her eyes appraisingly. "You *did* carry it out, didn't you?"

"Yes," Mercy nodded.

"Good! And what happened?"

Glancing back at Oram in the wagon, whose cheeks now bulged, hamsterlike, with peppermints, she told Mrs. Kingston quickly how the day had gone.

"I see," her friend mused, pursing her lips. "I expected that would happen."

"You did?" In spite of her determination to have faith, Mercy wondered why Mrs. Kingston had not shared that same expectation with her.

"Sometimes it takes a while for men to understand what is best for them, dear. But we mustn't give up. I have ordered lamb to be delivered tomorrow. You do know how to cook a lamb stew, don't you?"

Mercy sucked in her breath. "Tomorrow?"

"Why, yes. Haven't I explained all this to you?"

"Not the part about having to go over there again."

"Dear me, child." A hand went up to Mrs. Kingston's wrinkled cheek. "Have you been of the understanding that only once was required?"

"Yes, ma'am," Mercy replied. The edges of her faith began crumbling even more so at the memory of how he had looked at her from his pantry doorway. "I don't think I can do that again, Mrs. Kingston."

"My dear, you must! And not just tomorrow. You must do this six more times!"

Mercy knew her friend had said something, for her lips had moved emphatically, but before her numbed mind could ask Mrs. Kingston to repeat herself, the elderly woman launched ahead.

"You see, that was the answer God gave to me. I had thought it was only because of my money that He chose to reveal the most difficult part of the plan to me, but now I see you would have been too overwhelmed by it to believe it came from Him."

"Six more times?" Mercy could only mumble.

"Which will total seven. The same number of times Naaman was told to dip in the Jordan; the number of days Joshua was to march around Jericho; and the number of seals in the book of Revelation. So many things are done in sevens in Scripture, I'm sure you've noticed."

Indeed Mercy had, but she could not refrain from asking, "Mrs. Kingston, what does that have to do with Mr. Langford?"

A cherubic smile lit her aged face. "My dear, that's how many times God told me that you are to prepare Saturday dinner for Mr. Langford. Your presence in Mr. Langford's kitchen seven Saturdays in a row will constitute a habit for him—one that he will be unaware he has acquired until after you have stopped."

Five minutes later, Mercy sat in the wagon, staring straight ahead with hands folded in her lap as Oram drove home. She did not know quite how Mrs. Kingston had managed to talk her into continuing with this plan. Perhaps it was when she said, "Just think of what would have happened to poor old Naaman if he had decided to dunk himself only once?"

*T*he ancient Egyptians are credited with the invention of archery," Mr. Ellis said at the *Larkspur*'s breakfast table Saturday morning, in reply to the question Mrs. Dearing had posed. With the Durwins away for yet another three weeks and Philip at school, the gathering seemed sadly sparse. Still, conversation accompanied the meal as usual.

"Indeed, Mr. Ellis?" Mrs. Dearing said while passing the cream to Aleda. "Then if they invented it, surely that gave them an edge over their enemies."

"Quite so, Mrs. Dearing. The Persians were doing battle with sling-shots and spears at that time. They were simply overwhelmed."

With her eyes Grace asked Julia's permission to speak. Julia nodded.

"But a spear is bigger than an arrow," she said shyly, as if concerned that the archeologist would think she questioned his authority on the matter.

"But not able to be aimed as precisely, Miss Hollis," Mr. Ellis explained with a smile. Perhaps because he had several grandchildren, he seemed flattered whenever one of Julia's children showed an interest in his profession. "And a spear can only cover a short distance, depending upon the strength of the person throwing it. But an arrow . . . even the weakest archer, if he has skill, has an advantage over someone whose only weapon is a spear."

Table talk had drifted, as Julia supposed was true in many other homes in Gresham, to the archery team Mr. Raleigh had founded. Even Andrew seemed grudgingly interested after learning nearby Prescott had accepted the challenge for a tournament. Both archeologists, who shared an affinity for ancient tools and weapons, considered the idea an excellent way for children to experience a bit of history.

After swallowing a forkful of his coddled eggs, Mr. Ellis nodded across the table at his bashful assistant. "And of course the Romans owed much of their military superiority to the bow and arrow. Correct, Mr. Pitney?"

"Yes," the younger man affirmed, cheeks assuming their usual flush at being the center of attention, especially when in the vicinity of Miss

Rawlings. But as the subject was one close to his heart, he did manage to share in the conversation. "Until the early medieval period, when they were up against the more highly skilled archers of the Huns, Goths, and Vandals."

Mrs. Kingston paused from buttering her toast to ask, "Goths, Mr. Pitney?"

"From a section of what is now Germany."

"Well, if Vandals and Goths ever decide to take on the *Larkspur*," the elderly woman said with a glint of humor in her blue eyes, "I shall be the first to hide behind Aleda."

This brought laughter, and more when Aleda reminded her, "We have to practice a long time before we're any good."

Even the Worthy sisters had something to say on the subject, Julia discovered. She had gone out to the stables to ask Mr. Herrick to assist the maids with moving Mrs. Hyatt's belongings into Mr. Durwin's room. Mr. Pitney, now occupying the room reserved for her former butler Mr. Jensen, would be moving into Mrs. Hyatt's old room in bits and snatches, whenever he wasn't working atop the Anwyl. Julia was heading toward the courtyard when the lace spinners beckoned to her.

Though the wind on this first day of October was strong enough to rattle the gold and red leaves of a maple in their tiny garden, the sisters would continue to work outside until first frost. Mufflers wrapped their gray heads and woolens swathed their thin frames, but still they could witness the village goings-on at the crossroads—a pleasure denied them at their comfortable fireplace. And their work did not suffer, for woolen gloves snipped at the ends allowed their deft fingers the same freedom of movement.

"What's to keep 'em from shootin' each other?" Jewel asked, wide-eyed.

"Or their schoolmaster?" Iris added.

"I'm positive Mr. Raleigh is teaching them to be careful," Julia reassured the two. "Aleda is taking the lessons too, and I'm not worried. They tell me he won't give them an arrow if someone is standing even to the side of them."

"But he hasn't any little ones of his own," Jewel argued. "He don't know how some of 'em is plain mean. Take Horace Perkins, for instance. He pitched his mother's cat down the well in '61."

"It was '62," corrected Iris.

Julia took the opportunity to take her leave politely. She had a ready excuse, for Mrs. Kingston wanted to ask her advice about where to plant some Rembrandt tulip bulbs in the garden for spring blooming.

"I didn't want to say anything at breakfast," Mrs. Kingston said in a confidential tone after they had decided upon a patch of ground between a coralberry shrub and rose trellis. "But I believe Mr. Raleigh is infatuated with Miss Phelps."

"What makes you say that?" Julia hedged, for she and Andrew had managed to keep the reason for the young man's arrival in Gresham a secret so far. There was no sense in having Elizabeth undergo the pressure of villagers speculating as to whether or not he would win her hand, Andrew had wisely said.

"I have eyes, haven't I? And Mr. Raleigh's eyes seem to spend a lot of time fastened upon Miss Phelps's back during church."

"Aren't you supposed to be paying attention to the *sermon* during church?" Julia gently chided.

"Well, yes," Mrs. Kingston huffed, raising her chin. "But one does feel the need to shift one's head occasionally. And besides, he hails from Cambridge. It doesn't take a genius to figure out that he must have come to Gresham in the pursuit of Miss Phelps."

Julia wished just this once, Mrs. Kingston weren't so astute. "If I tell you that you're correct, will you please keep it to yourself?"

"Why, I'll be the soul of discretion." The elderly woman wore a pleased-with-herself expression. "He must be the reason Miss Phelps broke off her engagement with that curate."

"Are there no secrets in Gresham?" Julia sighed.

"Calm yourself, Mrs. Hollis," Mrs. Kingston said, patting her arm. "I happen to be too observant for my own good. I've heard no gossip linking Mr. Raleigh and Miss Elizabeth. Most likely because one never sees them together."

"That's reassuring."

"Perhaps to everyone but Mr. Raleigh. Has she no feelings for him whatsoever?"

"It's not that simple." Julia had to weigh her words carefully, even though she could count on Mrs. Kingston's discretion. "Something happened in Cambridge that is not easy to forgive."

"Ah . . . and so Mr. Raleigh has come to pay penance."

"Something like that."

"Is it working?"

"I don't know," Julia confessed with a shake of the head.

"Well, tell him not to give up." Mrs. Kingston glanced in the direction of the schoolhouse, as if she could see Mr. Raleigh on the steps. "Look at Jacob."

"Mr. Pitney?"

"No, dear. From the Bible. He worked to earn Rachel's hand for fourteen years."

Julia did not think Mr. Raleigh would last fourteen years at Gresham school, archery or no archery, but did not say so. After Mrs. Kingston took up her walking stick and set out on her usual routine, Julia was about to look for Mr. Herrick when she noticed Ben Mayhew on the other side of the gate. He was walking toward the Bryce with fishing pole slung over his shoulder and a basket in the crook of his arm. He stopped when she hailed him.

"Good morning, Mrs. Hollis," the boy said as they met on opposite sides of the gate. The bite of the wind gave his freckled cheeks a rosy glow that almost matched his red hair. "Have you received a letter from Philip since his return?"

"Not yet. I sent him one yesterday, so they're likely to cross." The sight of Ben or Jeremiah usually brought a little pang, since it seemed only natural that Philip should be at their sides. But she gave him an affectionate smile and asked, "Aren't you heading from the wrong direction?"

He smiled sheepishly, indicating the tackle basket. "I had a craving for lemon drops. Would you care for one?"

Julia did enjoy an occasional lemon drop, but the thought of it sharing the same basket, even if wrapped, with a jar of worms or crickets was not an appealing one. "No, thank you." She glanced up at the sky, azure blue beneath white cotton clouds. "At least you'll have no rain, but I hope you'll stay warm."

"Oh, I'm bundled snugly enough," he smiled. "My father's right fond of fish, so he allows me Saturday mornings off."

It was then that Julia noticed the book tucked under the arm that held the fishing pole. "Reading and fishing and lemon drops—you do have a fine morning ahead of you, Ben. May I ask what you're reading?"

The sheepish look returned, but he held the book out over the gate. Julia took it from his hands. It was *Principles of Architecture*, authored by an S.S. Teulon.

"You still want to be an architect." It was a statement, not a question, for of course he did with such a book in his possession.

He shrugged as if it didn't matter, but a shadow passed over his freckled face. "My father doesn't want to spend the money for schooling when he can teach me wheelwrighting for free."

"I'm sorry, Ben" was all Julia could think of to say.

Again the shrug, and he sent a glance up the lane. "I'd best be catching some fish. It was good talking with you, Mrs. Hollis."

"It was good to see you as well," she said, handing back his book. "And Ben . . ."

"Yes, ma'am?"

She had been about to say that surely there was some way he could acquire some extra schooling. If Philip's tuition were not so high—and she did not have Aleda's to plan for in another year—she would have liked to have sponsored him herself. But since she couldn't, it would be cruel to raise his hopes. "I hope the fish are biting well," she said instead. The prayer she prayed after the boy had bade her farewell and started again for the river had nothing to do with fish. *Please show me a way to help him.*

This time Mr. Langford appeared at his door seconds after the butcher's cart bearing Mercy and a lamb roast stopped outside his cottage. He did not step out to offer assistance as Henry unloaded the basket of food and Mercy lifted her iron stewing pot. He merely stood there with arms akimbo.

"It's not necessary to unload all of that, Miss Sanders. Take it back and cook it for your family."

Henry paused to give Mercy an uncertain look, to which she responded with a tight-lipped shake of the head. "You don't have to eat the dinner, Mr. Langford," she told him, not quite meeting his eyes, lest she be intimidated into following his order. "But I'm going to prepare it."

"Miss Sanders, you're wasting your time."

"It's my time to waste, Mr. Langford."

Just then Thomas's face appeared behind the crook of his father's bent elbow. "Miss Sanders!" he said, squirming past him to take the pot from her arms. "You've come to cook for us again?"

"Thomas," Mr. Langford cut in before Mercy could reply. This time he took a step out into the yard. "Miss Sanders was just leaving."

"But she brought her pot, sir."

"Thomas!"

The boy turned to him with a stunned expression, which had an immediate effect upon Mr. Langford. He shrugged, sent Mercy a severe glance, and said in a considerably softer voice, "Bring the pot inside for her, will you?"

Mercy lowered her head as she walked past Mr. Langford with the basket. "I didn't mean to cause disharmony, Mr. Langford," she murmured as the boy ambled ahead of her toward the kitchen.

"But you did, didn't you?" was his icy reply. He called for Thomas, and they resumed the task she had interrupted—the reapplication of pitch to the windows of the house. Mercy unpacked her basket, thankful that they were upstairs, for she was so humiliated by the unpleasantness at the door that she continually had to wipe her eyes with the hem of her apron.

Some time later, as she was chopping leeks to add to the braised meat in the pot, she heard only one set of footsteps on the staircase. She gave

322

her eyes a quick swipe again, just before Mr. Langford walked into the kitchen from the parlor. Mercy only knew it was Mr. Langford by the tread of his shoes, not by sight, for she kept her attention upon the task at hand. "I must ask your forgiveness for my rudeness, Miss Sanders," he said. "I simply don't want to give you false hope."

"I appreciate that, Mr. Langford," she replied softly, still chopping. "But sometimes false hopes are better than no hope at all."

"I don't agree. I have seen men drive themselves mad because they couldn't accept the reality of their situations."

It was a puzzling thing to say, a reminder that she knew nothing of his past besides the ridiculous speculations of her brothers. "So no one should have hope, Mr. Langford?" she asked.

The question apparently took him by surprise, for several silent seconds passed before he answered. When he did, it was to say in a gentler tone, "You deserve a husband who could *love* you, Miss Sanders."

The way he stressed "love" made it clear that he did not, but of course Mercy had never imagined that he did. Now she brought herself to look at him, setting down her knife. He stood with arms folded, his face softened by what appeared to be pity. This alarmed Mercy. While she wished very much to marry Mr. Langford, she wanted no man to marry her out of pity.

"My mother married my father out of love and was treated no better than the livestock in his barn. I am not looking to be loved."

"What *are* you looking for?"

"Respect and consideration, sir. Conversation once in a while that doesn't center around what needs to be cooked or cleaned or mended. A man not too proud to pray before meals and for the safe keep of his family at night."

Surprise again filled his face, and understandably so, for Mercy herself was surprised at the candor with which she was able to reply. But it had taken every ounce of boldness from her, so she dropped her gaze to the table again and began scraping carrots for the stew. He left the kitchen shortly afterward.

When she had finished cooking, she went upstairs to announce dinner was ready. Mr. Langford and Thomas were working at one of the two windows in the room that was once Mrs. Brent's. Mercy had not been up here since the funeral. It smelled of pitch mingled with lamb stew, but everything looked almost the same as it had when illness had confined Mrs. Brent here, even down to the quilt upon the bed. Memories of the woman who had mothered her so lovingly brought fresh tears to Mercy's eyes. She wiped them quickly, but then to her horror she sniffed.

This caused Mr. Langford and Thomas to turn from the window, seeing her for the first time since she had come upstairs. "Miss Sanders?" the man said in a puzzled tone.

"It's the room, sir," she flustered. "It was Mrs. Brent's."

He nodded understanding, and Thomas, as if searching for something that would cheer her, offered, "Now the windowpanes won't rattle so much in the wind."

Mercy smiled. "That's good to know." With forced casualness, she added, "Would you be ready for dinner now?"

"I am!" the boy exclaimed but then turned to his father with an uncertain expression. "May we?"

The man's shoulders rose and fell with what appeared to be a deep sigh, but he smiled at his son. "Very well."

They ate quietly, with Thomas doing most of the chattering. He talked mostly of his pony and of how Mr. Raleigh had said he could be a score-keeper if he studied his arithmetic. Mercy marveled to herself that this was the timid boy who had met her the day she delivered the apple cake. A couple of times her eyes met Mr. Langford's, and they exchanged looks of amusement, only to glance away again immediately afterward. Both males ate heartily of the stew and brown bread, then smiled at each other's teeth—stained from the blackberry cobbler she brought out of the oven when the meal was finished.

Mercy, on the other hand, spoke rarely and ate very little. The courage and faith required of her to carry out this plan were monumental, and she had no resources left to quell her own nervousness.

Mr. Langford insisted upon helping her with the dishes while Thomas went out to see about his pony. "That was a delicious meal, Miss Sanders," he said, his brow drawn in concentration as he scraped at the insides of the iron pot with a knife.

"Thank you, Mr. Langford."

"I want to know how much you spent on both meals so I can repay you before you leave."

She shook her head. "I spend nothing. A good friend insists on paying for the food."

Turning a suspicious eye to her, he asked, "Who?"

"I can't tell you that, Mr. Langford."

And then apparently he realized the full meaning of her previous answer. "*Insists?* You aren't planning to do this again, are you?"

Mercy took in a long breath, and when it was not enough, she took another. Meanwhile, he ceased scraping at the pot and awaited her reply.

"I am."

The scraping resumed with a vengeance. "How long do you intend to keep this up?"

Taking another breath, she replied, "Five more times."

"Five?" An eyebrow quirked as he turned his face to her again. "Did you say *five*?"

Mercy nodded and reached for another plate to dry.

"Is there nothing I can say to stop you?"

"Nothing, Mr. Langford."

He sighed heavily, then, "Why five?"

"That, I cannot tell you."

"You plan to intrude upon my life five more times, and you won't tell me why?" he said incredulously.

To keep from dissolving into tears, Mercy reminded herself that Mrs. Kingston was likely praying for her at this very minute. "I cannot tell you," she repeated.

He shook his head and muttered something under his breath, and the kitchen was taken over by sounds of clinking of dishes and the swishing water. When they were finished, he eyed the pot and sighed again. "You can't carry that home by yourself. I'll walk with you."

Mr. Langford was on his way to the door before she could protest with, "I can carry—"

He did not turn around but raised a hand from his side as if to quell any argument.

"I'm going to walk Miss Sanders home," Seth told Thomas, calling the boy over from the stables.

"Will she come again?" he asked.

There was no mistaking the hopefulness in his voice, and for a second, Seth felt sorry for the boy's motherless condition. *He has me*, he reminded himself with tightened jaw. And no child needed Mr. Sanders as a grandfather or that crew of savages for uncles. The thought alone was enough to bring a shudder.

Thomas was watching him for an answer, so Seth replied flatly, "She will." *At least she's planned a stopping point to it*. She waited outside the door, her arms burdened with her pot and basket.

"How is it that your father allows you to do this?" he asked as he carried the iron pot out toward the lane, with her walking beside him. In spite of himself, he took a glance at the hands clutching the basket. They were work-worn, as Elaine's had been, but also slender and feminine. *What are you doing?* he asked himself and shot his eyes back to the lane ahead of him.

"I told him I would move away if he did anything to prevent it."

"Oh?" This piqued his curiosity. "Move where?" *Surely she doesn't mean with us!*

"To the manor house. There is a position vacant for a parlormaid."

"I see. So the squire is the mysterious person behind all this?"

"No," she replied.

Seth waited for more, but she did not offer it, so he lapsed into silence himself. Just before they reached the cottage gate, Mr. Sanders and a couple of boys could be seen trimming the hedgerow. Curiously, aside from stony glances, they did not stop working to provoke hostilities.

"I'll take it from here," Miss Sanders told him at the gate. "Thank you."

Seth set it over the gate to the ground so one of her brothers could get it for her if so inclined. "I don't suppose it would do any good to ask you one more time not to come next week," he said in a resigned voice.

Uncertainty crept into her hazel eyes, which made Seth feel almost boorish for even asking the question. But in spite of her obvious struggle, she replied before turning toward her cottage, "It would not, Mr. Langford."

After exchanging affectionate smiles with Andrew at the door of Saint Jude's on Sunday, Julia was surprised to see that Mr. Raleigh had not made his customary beeline for the *Bow and Fiddle*. The reason for his delay became apparent after a knot of people moved from her line of vision. Mrs. McFarley, the barber's wife, was speaking with him and, judging by her gesturing, was pleased about something. *Archery*, she told herself, and curiosity to see if her guess was correct compelled her to move a little closer as her daughters scattered to seek out playmates.

"My Robert has ne'er been so eager about school," she was saying, though the Gaelic of her accent caused *about* to come out as *aboot*. "Who would ha' thought that gettin' a chance to shoot arrows would make him get to his homework?"

Mr. Raleigh smiled back, nodding and thanking her. When Mrs. McFarley had turned to leave, Julia walked over to the schoolmaster before he could do the same. "I would like to add my compliments as well," she said, extending her hand. "There is little talk of anything else at the *Larkspur*'s table. What a clever idea!"

"I must confess it came in the midst of a desperate prayer," he said modestly as they shook hands.

"And Aleda tells me that the children have calmed down considerably."

A pleased smile touched his lips. "Considerably, Mrs. Hollis. Why, I find myself at times even *liking* being a schoolmaster." Immediate distress altered his expression. "I didn't mean—"

"I know. It was rough going for you at first."

He sent a breath through his teeth. "Extremely rough."

From the corner of her eye Julia sensed movement. She turned her face to find Elizabeth standing close by, her hand upon Laurel's shoulder. "Hello, Mrs. Hollis," she said and then added as if almost an afterthought, "and Jonathan."

Julia glanced at the doorway of the church after greeting both. Although she doubted her fiancé would come tearing across the grounds to break up their conversation, she was relieved to find him still occupied with shaking the hands of departing worshipers. She respected Andrew's wishes not to allow Mr. Raleigh to court Elizabeth, but as they lived in the same village, it was inevitable that they would speak occasionally.

She would have taken her leave at this time under ordinary circumstances. But these were not, and she knew that, perchance Andrew would glance in their direction, he would be more reassured to see Laurel and her acting as chaperones.

"Hello, Elizabeth." He appeared to be struggling to keep his expression casual. "How are you?"

"Fine." Elizabeth lowered her eyes for a second, perhaps having that same struggle herself. She looked lovely in a simple fawn-colored silk trimmed with dark brown piping. "And you?"

"Fine." The strain seemed to ease a bit when he looked at her younger sister. "Laurel. Are you enjoying school?"

She wrinkled her nose. "Sometimes. My literature teacher went to Queen Victoria's coronation ceremony when she was my age. She's interesting. But my French teacher is boring. She insists we speak nothing but French the whole hour."

"*Oui?*" Mr. Raleigh replied with a cocked eyebrow. Laurel snickered appreciatively at this, and Elizabeth smiled and touched her sister's sleeve. "We'd best be going now."

"Good days" were repeated and the two girls set out toward the vicarage. Mr. Raleigh watched them walk away, then turned to Julia. "May I accompany you part way, Mrs. Hollis?" he asked almost timidly but then sent a worrisome glance toward the church door. "Of course if you'd feel uncomfortable . . ."

"I would feel no discomfort," she reassured him, and they started out across the green. She caught Aleda's eye and motioned that she would be going on ahead. The girls would not be ready to leave, and would either accompany each other or some of the lodgers who usually lingered to chat. When they were out of earshot of any of the other worshipers, she added, "But I'm sure you understand I must respect my fiancé's position concerning you and Elizabeth."

"Yes, of course."

Smiling to herself at the resignation in his voice, Julia went on. "But I must also tell you that I have changed my initial opinion of you."

He turned incredulous eyes to her. "You have?"

She nodded. "Your having stuck it out at the school gives evidence that you have the strength of character to stay on the right path."

"Thank you, Mrs. Hollis! I'm overwhelmed."

"But again, it's not my opinion that matters," she felt compelled to remind him.

A sigh escaped his lips, and they walked in silence, listening to the sociable hum of people still behind them and the caws of rooks winging across the green. "May I ask you something, Mrs. Hollis?" he said when the *Larkspur* loomed in sight.

"Very well, Mr. Raleigh."

There was a pause, and then, "Is it true that Elizabeth stopped seeing the man from Alveley?"

Julia wondered how he could have learned such a thing but then remembered where he was lodging. "Yes. But I must tell you that she was having doubts about that relationship long ago."

"I see." Another paused lapsed, and then, "Do you think Vicar Phelps will ever change his mind and allow me to see her?"

"I believe anything is possible, Mr. Raleigh. You'll just have to continue being patient."

"I'm learning that patience is a hard schoolmaster, Mrs. Hollis."

She gave him a little smile. "But the prize is worth it, yes?"

His tone softening, he replied, "Very much worth it."

———

"You had Jonathan Raleigh over for *dinner?*" Andrew asked, incredulous, the next morning over their cups of tea, which the nip of the air had caused him and Julia to take in the *Larkspur*'s library with the door open a propriety-approving foot or so.

"He's my children's schoolmaster, Andrew," his fiancée reminded him, with no trace of repentance in her voice. "How long are you going to carry this grudge against him?"

The tea in Andrew's cup suddenly tasted bitter. He had gone through the latter part of the summer like a man who has inherited the world. Betrothed to the most beautiful, gracious woman in England, he had happily settled into village life and was living in harmony with his daughters in the vicarage. How long had he been allowed such bliss before Jonathan Raleigh decided to put an end to it. *Six weeks?*

"You don't understand. It's *my* daughter he treated so despicably."

"I do understand." She leaned forward to rest a soft hand upon the back of his. "But everyone is someone's daughter or son, Andrew. Should there be no forgiveness for anyone, then?"

"It's not a matter of forgiveness," he maintained adamantly. "It's a matter of not wanting to risk the same thing happening again."

"Life involves risk, dear. My late husband had an impeccable reputation, yet he betrayed his family."

As cynical as he sometimes was about human behavior, Andrew still could not understand how Doctor Philip Hollis, with such a wonderful family, could have given gambling first place in his heart. Andrew had to ask God's forgiveness more than once for having the guilty thought that he was glad the man had died. He was in danger of thinking it again if he did not return to the subject at hand, so he asked Julia, "What are you suggesting? That I should allow him to court her?"

"Not if you're not ready." She patted his hand as if he were a little child. In his present mood he should have minded, but he did not.

He wondered if she understood her power over him. She could render him silly with worry just by frowning.

"But I wish you would suspend judgment and allow Mr. Raleigh some more time to prove himself," Julia went on, her green eyes shining as he brought her hand up to his lips.

His heart told him that it was a reasonable request and that as a Christian he was expected to do no less. "Very well, Julia. We'll give him some time."

The strike of half-past eight signaled it was time to leave for the school, where he would see the subject of their discussion soon enough. He drained his tea, bitter or not, and, with a glance at the door, coaxed her into a kiss. He would have stayed long enough for another, but she reminded him that it was not a good example for the vicar to be late for Monday chapel.

At the schoolhouse door he paused to listen. A curious absence of pandemonium greeted his ears. He opened the door to find thirty-two faces trained upon their schoolmaster, who was in the process of reading aloud from something Andrew knew he should have easily recognized, but the calm of the classroom had befuddled his mind.

" 'I am glad, my brother, that thou didst withstand this villain so bravely; for of all, as thou sayest, I think he has the wrong name. . . .' "

Mr. Raleigh glanced up at him and stopped reading. "Good morning, sir."

"Good morning, Mr. Raleigh." Andrew nodded at the students. "Young men and young ladies."

"Good morning, Vicar Phelps," they returned politely. Even the Sanders boy, who had stuck his tongue out at him just a week ago as their wagon passed him on Market Lane, joined in the greeting.

"We were just enjoying a little of *The Pilgrim's Progress*," Mr. Raleigh said. "We read a chapter from it every day now."

In spite of his promise to Julia, it vexed Andrew slightly that the young man had known something that he himself—even temporarily—had forgotten. But he covered it with a smile and said, "What a splendid idea."

The smile seemed to take Mr. Raleigh completely by surprise, for a dazed look came over him. Andrew did not know how long it took him to recover, for having felt he had gone far beyond the extra mile, he turned to the students again and opened his Bible.

*M*ornings in the dormitories of the Josiah Smith Academy were becoming uncomfortably cold as the term advanced. Philip strongly suspected economic factors were behind this. Why warm up two whole floors in the mornings when the students were only allowed a half hour to make themselves presentable for their classes and would not return to those same rooms until afternoon? Perhaps he would have agreed with such a measure had he been an adult, but when his cold bare feet fumbled on the frigid floor for his slippers of mornings late, he found himself wishing he could send Mr. Houghton, the headmaster, for laps around the grounds.

After Westbrook had barked orders to "rise and shine" on Tuesday morning, Philip surrendered the warmth of his blankets and threw his feet over the side of his bed, mentally preparing himself for the meeting of warm feet and cold floor. But he was not prepared for the puddle of water. He was about to launch himself back into his bed and under his covers when another sense revealed to him that it was not plain water in which he stood. "Ugh!" he cried disgustingly, jumping out to the corridor between the rows of beds.

Other boys stopped grumbling about the cold, some coming over for a look and a snicker. "Watch out," Philip warned Milton Hayes in the next bed. Hayes sat up in bed and grimaced.

"You couldn't wait, Hollis?" jeered someone whom Philip saw fit to ignore.

"I thought I heard Whitby in here last night," Hayes said with an eye toward the lavatory door, behind which Westbrook had disappeared. "But I didn't know they'd done that. I'm sorry about your feet."

Philip rubbed his feet on the dry part of the floor while waiting for Westbrook to emerge so that he could show the monitor what happened and, more likely than not, be blamed for it. "Whitby has had it in for Patterson and me ever since—" Mention of his friend's name filled him with a sudden panic. "Gabriel!" he called, running down the corridor between

331

the beds. He was halfway to his friend's bed when there was an awful loud thumping sound and a much worse sharp groan. Westbrook burst from the lavatory at the other end, his face half lathered, and several boys ran to the scene.

As he had feared, Gabriel lay in a puddle in the space between two beds. "Are you all right?" Philip asked, bending to give him a hand. But Gabriel groaned again and shook his head.

"I can't move my arm, Philip."

"Don't tell me the whale got beached," Westbrook said sarcastically as he came closer, ordering the boys aside. Philip flung a scathing look at him.

"His arm's probably broken, Westbrook."

That wiped the sneer from the prefect's face. "Go get some help!" he yelled to no one in particular. Three boys scrambled for the door. In the turmoil that followed, Mr. Archer arrived with other housemasters, who carried Gabriel away on a stretcher. When Philip attempted to see his friend after classes were over, he was refused admission to the small infirmary by a stone-faced nurse. A broken arm was all the information she would give him.

The next day Gabriel Patterson was on his way back to Birmingham. *We didn't even exchange addresses,* Philip thought sadly as he passed the empty bed the next evening.

———

On the eighth of October, early morning thunderstorms assailed Gresham again. Jonathan rose from his bed, found his slippers, and padded, bleary eyed, to the window. Rivulets of water ran down the glass, making Y patterns as they joined other rivulets. *They'll be disappointed. Even if the rain stops soon, it likely won't dry up enough by recess to set up the target.*

It was only then that he remembered what day of the week it was. Saturday. And oddly enough, *he* felt a small stab of disappointment.

———

At least the butcher's cart won't be able to come, Seth thought, staring out at the rain from his open doorway. Nettle Lane would be too muddy for wagon wheels in such a deluge. Yet he had gone to the door three times during the past half hour, for what reason he was not sure. He was about to close the door again when he saw something looming above the drystone wall between his barnyard and the lane. It was moving toward his drive, and after staring at it through the rain for another second or two, he recognized it as an umbrella.

That can't be her! he told himself, yet he knew without a doubt that it was. How could he have imagined that the same bashful-looking woman who sang so sweetly before the church could possess such tenacity! With a sigh, he took up his own umbrella from an old churn crock near the door.

"I'll be back," Seth called to Thomas, who lay in front of the fire practicing his penmanship on his slate, his elbows propping him up in the front and his ankles crossed up in the air above his knees.

"Is it her?" he asked hopefully.

"It's her," Seth replied before stepping outside. She looked a sight with the umbrella over her shoulder, basket in one hand, and another bunching her skirts just above the ankles. There was no use attempting to talk in the downpour, and he certainly could not order her to turn around and go back, so he took the basket from her and accompanied her to the cottage.

Thomas, having temporarily abandoned his homework, held the door open and took their umbrellas as they entered.

"Hello, Miss Sanders!" the boy piped while their visitor took off a pair of oversized and surprisingly mudless men's boots and left them on the rag rug just inside the door. It appeared that she intended to go shoeless, with just the thick wool socks on her feet, until time to leave. In spite of her umbrella and bonnet, which she also removed to hang on the doorknob, several damp ringlets formed about her face.

"Good day to you, Thomas," she replied with an affectionate smile.

Seth found her kindness grossly unfair, because it would have warmed the heart of any boy on the receiving end. "I see that you've lessons to do today too?"

"Yes, ma'am." He ran to scoop up his slate and brought it back to show her the rows of *apple, bear,* and *candle* he had written as well as chalk would allow. "I'm learning script now."

"Why, that's fine work," she told him, eliciting a radiant grin from Thomas.

I told him the same thing not more than an hour ago! Seth thought. While the boy had smiled, he had not *glowed,* as he was doing now. "Miss Sanders, why didn't you stay home today?" he asked, barely able to keep the irritation from his voice. "The weather and all," he added lamely when she turned her hazel eyes to him.

She had the audacity to change the subject, explaining that she had walked on the grasses near the wall to keep her brother's boots from getting caked with mud. "I'm afraid it's just going to be vegetable soup today," she said, nodding toward the basket that sat on the floor now. "But I did bake some barley cakes this morning that will go nicely with it."

333

"Fine," Seth snapped, for he had no other choice. He returned to his chair and picked up the well-worn copy of *A Tale of Two Cities* on loan from the lending library. To add insult to injury, Thomas asked if he could take his slate in the kitchen and finish his homework at the table. "Fine," he snapped again.

He attempted to become absorbed again with the story, especially with reading time being so hard to come by. But his effort was thwarted by sounds of occasional clinks of dishes and conversation coming from the kitchen. It was not that they were too loud. On the contrary, they were too soft for him to tell what was going on without straining his ears. Finally he gave up and closed his book, making note of the page he had attempted about three times to read. He walked into the kitchen, pausing just inside to view the scene at the table with wonder. Thomas sat on his knees in one chair, his young face screwed up in concentration as he used his chalk. Miss Sanders, in the chair across from him, had in her lap what appeared to be a kitchen curtain and was pulling a needle and thread through it. She looked up at him and blushed a little.

"I noticed this tear last week," she said, raising the cloth a bit to show him. "I hope you don't mind my taking the liberty of mending it."

Bemused that she would concern herself about taking liberties when she already barged in on his life every Saturday, he replied softly, for the sake of the boy, "Would it matter if I did, Miss Sanders?"

"It would matter, Mr. Langford."

"But that wouldn't stop you, would it?" he could not resist asking.

"I suppose not," she answered frankly, then returned her attention to her mending.

Four more times, Seth consoled himself, purposely ignoring the savory aroma of the soup bubbling on the stove.

"It's so good to see you up and around!" Julia said to Miss Clark upon meeting her just outside the lending library early Tuesday afternoon.

"It's good to *be* up and around," Miss Clark smiled, switching a book into her left hand so that she could take Julia's hand with her right. "Doctor Rhodes advised that a daily walk would be good medicine."

Indeed, the advice seemed to be working, for there were bright spots of color in her cheeks. But then Julia wondered how much October's nippy wind had to do with it, for the schoolmistress still seemed much too frail. "Why don't you come back to the *Larkspur* with me and have some tea? You have to go home that way anyway."

"That sounds lovely, thank you." Ten minutes later, they sat in the hall and had ginger biscuits with their cups of tea. "Have your daughters not arrived from school yet?" Miss Clark asked.

"Mr. Raleigh has asked the children if they would be willing to stay another hour every school day for archery practice," Julia replied. "So many have to help on their parents' farms on Saturdays. And Grace asked to stay and watch Aleda practice."

"I see." Miss Clark raised her cup for another sip, but her forehead seemed knotted in thought.

Julia kicked herself mentally for bringing up the archery team, when it was obvious that Miss Clark was longing to assume the role of schoolmistress again. But what other answer could she have given but the truth? "Is something wrong?" she felt compelled to ask.

Miss Clark lowered her cup and smiled, softening the angular facial lines her illness had produced. "Are you wondering if I *mind* that the students are so enthusiastic about Mr. Raleigh?"

Julia would not have stated it that bluntly, but she had to reply in the affirmative.

"Not at all, Mrs. Hollis. In fact, I think it's wonderful. Yet of course I don't relish the idea of replacing someone who has sparked such a collective interest in them."

"They're going to love you, too, Miss Clark."

"I don't know," she admitted with a doubtful sigh. "I'm aware that Mr. Raleigh had some difficulty with some of the boys until he introduced the archery. Discipline was never an issue at Saint Margaret's. In spite of Doctor Rhodes' assurance that I'll be strong enough to teach in another three weeks, I have delayed notifying the board. I know nothing about archery, Mrs. Hollis, and wonder if I'll have the strength to maintain order in a class that size without such an incentive."

Recalling Andrew's description of the chaos he had witnessed on his previous Monday visits, Julia wondered as well. Perhaps if she were a man with the commanding presence Captain Powell had possessed, and not such a soft-spoken woman, her lack of knowledge regarding archery would not be a concern.

Presently her guest's voice pierced her thoughts. "You know, I do appreciate you having me over," she smiled gratefully. "It helps to discuss this with someone other than my parents. They're of the mind that I should take the whole year off."

"Are you considering it?" Julia had a feeling Mr. Raleigh would be happy for an excuse to stay longer and try to win Elizabeth's affection, but it was Miss Clark's wishes that had to be honored first. She was the one who had left Scotland because she was assured a position by the school board, while Mr. Raleigh's tenure was never supposed to last any longer than a month or so.

"Or at least waiting until after the tournament. That's in only a little less than six weeks. Teaching is the joy of my life, Mrs. Hollis, and I am eager to resume it, but there are the children to consider."

"Are you aware that Luke Smith has started attending the practices after school in the eventuality that Mr. Raleigh would have to give up the position before the tournament? So you wouldn't be taking that away from them."

Miss Clark gave her a sad smile. "The way I hear it, Mr. Raleigh inspires them. They've formed a team with their schoolmaster, and I cannot in good conscience destroy that now."

Shortly afterward Miss Clark left, with Julia accompanying her as far as the end of the courtyard. As they wished each other farewell, Julia did so almost distractedly, for the seed of an idea had been planted in her mind.

She spoke with Andrew about it two days later, in the library again, after giving the idea time to grow and bathing it in prayer.

"A secondary school?" he asked with raised eyebrows. "Here in Gresham?"

"Why not? Have you spoken with Ben Mayhew lately? He's dying to continue his education. His father would agree to it if it were free. No doubt there are others as well."

"My dear, it's a worthy idea," Andrew told her. He nodded thoughtfully. "A very worthy idea. But to hear the board tell it, finances are strained to the limit to maintain the grammar school. From whence would come the support? And what about a building?"

Julia smiled, thankful she had waited to consider all the possibilities before bringing it up. "The town hall sits empty most of the time. And even when it's in use, it is almost always on a Saturday or Sunday. There wouldn't be *that* many students, Andrew, because many graduates of the grammar school are content to work at their family farms or businesses."

He reached up to touch her cheek, his hazel eyes lit up with affection. "You've thought this out, haven't you?"

"I've thought of little else for two days," she admitted.

"And so have you thought up the funds as well?"

"No, but I've thought of the person who could easily afford to sponsor it. All that is really necessary would be books, which would be reused year after year. Some lamp oil and firewood will be needed during the cold weather. And the teacher's salary, of course."

"And who might this generous person be?" he asked, smiling. "One of your lodgers?"

Julia shook her head. "I can't ask them for money, even to support a school."

"Then who?"

336

She hesitated, preparing herself for the argument to come. "The squire."

"The squire?" Andrew raised his eyebrows again. "*Our* squire?"

"He donated those slates to the grammar school, remember?"

"Which doesn't exactly make him a philanthropist, Julia. A mere drop in the pail considering his fortune."

"Yes," Julia had to concede. "But I've found the way to his heart."

"You suggest we offer the squire *money*? But wouldn't that defeat the whole purpose of asking *him* for some?"

"No," she replied, smiling. "I'm referring to Mrs. Kingston."

"Ah . . . so he's that serious about her?"

"He has called on her here three times already this week, and once she even consented to take a carriage ride with him."

"I see." He became thoughtfully silent then, toying with the handle of his teacup.

Julia could see from his eyes that he was considering all the ramifications of the idea. Finally he looked at her and smiled.

"You know, it could work. It's a shame to have a sturdy building sitting idle most of the time, like the steward from the parable who doesn't use his talents. And the board would have several months with which to advertise for a teacher."

Now that she had sold him on the main part of her idea, it was time to sell him on the rest. But she knew it wouldn't be easy. "I'm talking about this year, Andrew. As soon as possible."

He blinked. "This year?"

"If the squire could be persuaded to sponsor it."

"But we're already well into the school year. Besides, there is no teacher."

"A mere matter of catching up, which would not be too difficult with a small class." She took a deep breath. "And we've already a teacher."

"Who?"

"Miss Clark."

"But she's already committed to the grammar school." His eyes narrowed suspiciously. "And without her, we've no *permanent* teacher to take her place."

In for a penny, in for a pound, Julia thought, urging herself on. "I believe Mr. Raleigh could be persuaded to stay the whole school year, giving the board all that time to advertise for someone to replace him next year."

He was shaking his head, his lips pressed together in a stubborn line, but she did not allow that to deter her. "In the first place, Andrew, I believe Miss Clark's health will still be too delicate to control that large of a class, even if she waits until after the tournament." She took a deep breath before advancing to her second point, the *coup de grace*. "And secondly, if you were Ben Mayhew, would you be willing to wait another whole year to pursue your dreams . . . just because the vicar doesn't like a certain young man?"

Her barb found its mark, for he peered back at her with a wounded expression, even raising a hand to his heart. "Julia . . ."

"I had to say it, Andrew," she said lovingly, but firmly.

*O*n the morning of October fifteenth, Andrew was waiting at the reins of the *Larkspur*'s landau as Elizabeth went inside Saint Julien's for Laurel when a familiar voice assailed his ears. "Hullo there, Vicar Phelps!"

He turned his head. Vicar Nippert had apparently sent his wife inside to fetch his daughter, for he sat alone at the reins of the carriage drawn next to his. "Good morning, Vicar Nippert," Andrew replied with a polite smile.

"Collecting your daughter, eh?"

"Yes," he replied, and then to his chagrin, he found himself responding to the obvious question with a rhetorical, "And you?"

"The same indeed! Say . . ." Vicar Nippert leaned a little closer, his eyes taking on a challenging glint above his toothy smile. "Looks like we'll be competing against each other next month, eh?"

"It would seem so."

"Well, you may wish to announce from your pulpit that our school board has commissioned a local metalsmith to fashion up a plaque. For the winning village to display on the wall of its school or town hall, you see?"

Andrew was truly impressed. "Why, that's a very generous gesture."

"Oh, not when you consider we'll more than likely be keeping it, eh?" Vicar Nippert slapped his knee, roaring with convulsive laughter at his own wit. This went on for several seconds, and when he finally chuckled down to a stop, he was panting as if he had run a mile. "Phew! Ever laugh so hard your sides ache?"

"Not lately," Andrew replied with the dignity befitting his avocation. "And have you ever considered that we might win that tournament?"

Vicar Nippert grinned and held up a silencing hand, the other digging into his ribcage. "Have a heart, eh? My sides!"

Stay calm, Andrew ordered himself. He reminded the vicar, "Your team isn't much older than Gresham's, you know."

"True, my worthy colleague . . . but all of Prescott is behind ours.

Makes a difference when you have the support of your village, eh?"

Andrew could feel the skin on the back of his neck burning by the time he spotted Elizabeth and Laurel strolling up the walk, absorbed in chatter with arms linked. He quelled the urge to hurry them on with an impatient beckoning of the hand. "Good day to you, Vicar," he aimed through his teeth toward the general direction of the neighboring carriage before hopping down sooner than necessary to assist his slowly ambling daughters.

"And to you as well, my good vicar!" Vicar Nippert chuckled to his back.

The ring of a hammer in the near distance told Mercy that Mr. Langford and Thomas were either repairing or building something behind their barnyard. She was relieved to hear it, for it meant she could get the meal underway—a Shropshire pie of rabbit and pork with a flaky crust—without having to undergo Mr. Langford's protests. Henry lent a courteous hand in getting the foodstuffs into the kitchen, and with a "see you next week?" left her to her own devices.

She had taken pity on her own family today, who grumbled every Saturday morning about the tinned meats and Fernie's propensity to either scorch them in the pot or serve them as gelled lukewarm clumps. On the back of the stove, she put a beef-and-turnip stew that would only have to be warmed. Her father seemed to have reconciled himself to her Saturday routine, for he had grunted "good bacon" over breakfast this morning—the first compliment she could recall ever receiving from his lips.

Her father was not the only person in her family to have acted in an uncharacteristic manner lately, she thought as she cut a lump of lard into some flour to make dough. Jack and Edgar, who still wrestled like fox cubs and were the scourge of the guineas, had returned from school an hour later the past few days actually declaring that Mr. Raleigh "weren't so bad a feller after all." Last night over supper they even begged their father to order a bow and some arrows so they could practice for the archery team at home, too, but thankfully her father had refused. "A waste o' good shillings," he had declared, while Mercy added silently, *A waste of good guineas would be more likely.*

Mr. Langford and Thomas appeared almost exactly at noon just as Mercy was considering going to look for them. Hearing them at the back door, she was struck by her usual nervousness at the boldness of her actions but covered it by taking up dry cloths to bring the pie to the table. Thomas brightened and hurried over. For just a second it appeared that he would embrace her, until his natural timidity asserted itself and he smiled up at her instead. "You're here, Miss Sanders?"

Mr. Langford, a few feet behind him, met her eyes and smiled at the boy's obvious question. She returned his smile—before her *own* natural timidity took over—and stared down again at the young face.

"Aye, that I am, young Thomas. Have you brought me an appetite today?"

He nodded enthusiastically. "We could smell it all the way to the pasture. Mr. Langford said it was likely—"

"Why don't we sit now?" the man behind him interrupted, pulling out a chair. His tone of voice matched the suddenly gray expression of his face. "We've still work to finish."

The boy's expression took on the same somber cast, but he climbed into the chair and lowered his eyes. Mr. Langford pulled out a chair for Mercy, sank into one himself, and without looking around to see if anyone else was ready, he bowed his head and mumbled, "Father, we thank Thee for the food we are about to receive. Bless the hands that prepared it. Amen."

The meal was eaten in silence except for a polite request now and then to pass a bowl or dish. Eyes were seldom raised, and when they did, it was to dart back down at their owner's plate. The years came rushing back to Mercy. She recalled the times she had pushed her hands against her ears in an effort to shut out the belligerent slurs her father would spew at her mother whenever he was in his cups. She felt as helpless now as she had back then and more than a little guilty. After all, if she had not come here uninvited, there would be no tension permeating the room.

And yet she could not stop herself from wondering. *Why did Thomas call him Mr. Langford?*

"Will you excuse us, Miss Sanders?" Mr. Langford asked afterward, pushing out his chair and putting a hand on the boy's shoulder. "I'll help you tidy up in a few minutes."

Mercy glanced at Thomas and bit her lip. Softly, she asked, "He's not to be punished, is he? I shouldn't have—"

"He's not going to be punished."

The tone of his reply did not invite query. The two walked back through the pantry to the outside, leaving Mercy with a knot gnawing in the pit of her stomach. Dully she cleared dishes from the table, storing the rest of the pie in the cupboard for their supper. After what seemed an hour but couldn't have been because she had just poured the kettle of hot dishwater into the dishpan, a set of heavy footsteps sounded through the pantry again. She turned to meet Mr. Langford's eyes across the room. Without the softening of a smile, his face had assumed its usual deep-set lines.

"Thomas is tending to his pony," he said in reply to the question that must have been on her face. He pulled out a chair. "Will you sit for a moment, Miss Sanders?"

Mercy nodded and complied. Mr. Langford sat in the chair next to her, stared at the fingers he held woven together on the table top, and looked at her again. "Thomas isn't my natural-born son. I adopted him from a London orphanage just before we settled here."

It was startling news, but relief eased through Mercy that it was nothing more serious than that. The nurturing he lavished upon the boy seemed no less strong than that of a natural father. *Perhaps even stronger*, she thought, considering her own family.

He spoke again before she could summon a response. "I wanted to keep that secret because it would surely lead to questions about his parentage. His father and mother perished in a fire, but they *were* married, Miss Sanders."

In spite of her nervousness, Mercy took umbrage at the distinct implicating tone of that last bit of information. "Mr. Langford," she said quietly, raising her chin a bit. "Do you think I would hold against any child the circumstances of his birth?"

"Why, no . . ." Now it was his turn to look uneasy. "I just wasn't expecting him to blurt out my name like that."

"Children forget, Mr. Langford."

"Yes." He passed a hand over his face, which now appeared weary. "But it's been 'sir' up until then. I just imagined after all this time . . ."

When he didn't finish, Mercy finished for him. "That he would call you 'father'?"

"I might as well be the postman or the baker."

"Now, it's not that way, Mr. Langford." Mercy did not know where her nervousness had fled, but she was glad to be shorn of it for the moment. "I've seen the affection shining in his eyes for you."

"You have?"

"Surely you have so yourself."

"Well . . ." he mused reflexively. "He *is* a winsome little fellow at that, isn't he?"

"A charmer, to be sure," Mercy smiled. "Perhaps it's shyness that makes the word so hard for him. Have you asked him again lately to address you so?"

"Again?"

"You *have* asked him, haven't you?" A hand raised from the table top briefly in what she could only assume to be a negative reply. Mercy peered up at him through widened eyes. "You expect a boy of such a tender age to take that on himself?"

"I wasn't quite sure how to ask him" was his sheepish admission.

"What if it's something he'd rather not do? He had a real father once, after all."

"He has a real one now as well, Mr. Langford," she replied softly.

As much as Seth prized self-sufficiency, he found it a relief to be able to talk about the thing that had troubled him for weeks. Indeed it was as if a weight had been lifted from his shoulders. *How could a Sanders be so wise?* he thought, then winced inwardly at his own arrogance. She had expressed that she would never hold a child's parentage against him, and all along *he* was guilty of doing so—even conveniently forgetting that his own family circumstances had been far from ideal. *At least her father stayed with his children.*

But as much as his esteem of her was increased, he would not be goaded into marrying her. And he felt no guilt over *that*, to be sure. If she wished to spend her Saturdays chasing rainbows, well, had he not insisted over and over again that she was wasting her time? She was a comely young woman, soft of voice and surely capable. But she deserved love, no matter how much she claimed it unnecessary to her contentment. If she would be patient, surely some young man would love her as much as he had loved Elaine. He had no intention of selfishly robbing her of some future happiness so he could have a cook and maidservant.

But he did intend to help her clean the kitchen, over her protestations. Twenty minutes later, after seeing about Thomas, who was happily brushing his pony's coat, he walked her home again. "I do want to thank you, Miss Sanders," he said as they moved along. "I'll talk to Thomas this evening."

"That's good to know, Mr. Langford." After a space of silence, she said, "May I ask you a question?"

As long as it's not pertaining to marriage, he thought wryly. "Are you wondering why I adopted Thomas?"

"Had you known him beforehand?"

He shook his head. "Just his mother. Years before."

"I see."

What exactly she did see, he couldn't know, but thankfully she didn't persist. When they reached the Sanders place he asked resignedly at the gate, "I suppose you're coming next week?"

She averted her eyes and said, "Yes, Mr. Langford."

Sympathy, for the boldness she obviously had to dredge up to carry out her ridiculous plan, found its way to his heart. He cleared his throat and before turning to leave, said, "The meal was delicious, Miss Sanders."

That evening, after a supper of warmed-over Shropshire pie, he sat by the fire with Thomas on the footstool at his knees, listening as the boy read aloud from a children's book from the lending library. *John Tucker's*

Path was rather a silly story, Seth thought, even though he enjoyed hearing Thomas read. John Tucker was a boy faced with the choice of associating himself with one group—ruffians who dipped snuff in secret, gambled with cards, and disobeyed their elders—and another consisting of children dedicated to industry and obedience. Etchings of the disagreeable crowd portrayed them with rumpled clothes, caps worn at cavalier angles, and frowning slashes for mouths. The good boys, on the other hand, wore respectful, serious expressions, neatly pressed clothing even at play, and lacked only wings. From the first page it was clear what John Tucker's choice would ultimately be, so why go to the trouble of printing out more pages?

But he had been assured by the librarian that such stories were good for developing children's moral fiber, and he certainly wanted Thomas to be influenced in the proper direction.

"Chair . . . actor . . ." Thomas frowned for several seconds at the word before looking up at Seth. "Chair-actor?"

Seth smiled. "This time the 'ch' sounds like a 'k' instead."

The boy stared at the word again, moving a finger across it until comprehension smoothed the drawn brow. "Is the word *character*, sir?"

"That it is," Seth affirmed, clapping the narrow shoulder. "That was a tough one."

A pleased smile lit up Thomas's face. "May I write it on my slate and show Mr. Raleigh?"

"Of course. Just remember to bring it back home for practice." He cleared his throat, almost wishing Miss Sanders were here again to lend him some of her support. "Thomas," he said directly.

The boy, who had been studying another word on the page, looked up at him again. "Yes, sir?"

Seth swallowed. "Do you think you would mind addressing me as 'father'?"

Thomas stared at Seth unblinkingly, while some intangible emotion seemed to be trying to surface in the young face. In an incredible awareness that brought a lump to his throat, Seth recognized it as love. He held out his arms, and the boy climbed up into them.

"I love you, Thomas," he said, awkwardly patting his back.

"I love you, Father," Thomas murmured into his shoulder.

Bless you, Miss Sanders, Seth thought hours later when the house was dark and still and his son lay sleeping in the next room.

———

When Jonathan arrived at the schoolhouse early Wednesday morning, he paused at the corner of the building to shout greetings to Luke Smith and the handful of older students who had coaxed him to allow them to come early and target practice. Several waves of hands were sent in return. Jonathan could not join them because of morning lesson preparations but trusted fully that Mr. Smith would not allow any careless behavior. The excitement for the archery team had gone beyond his most optimistic dreams, changing the whole character of the classroom from one of covert warfare to a team marching under one banner. Even the younger children frequently attended practice to watch, encouraging their older brothers and sisters with applause even for the lowest scores.

Seven more months, he thought, touching a desk on the way to his own up front. After requesting a few days to pray about it, he had given his answer to the members of the school board yesterday. That had been only the preliminary step, the men had explained to him, because now Miss Clark had to be asked if she would consider teaching the secondary school, and the squire if he would sponsor it. But Jonathan somehow knew that it would happen.

He smiled and brought out his planning ledger, in which he kept track of his responsibilities to the different levels of students. Seven more months in which to prove to Elizabeth that he loved her with all his heart. A gift from God, he had no doubt. And oddly enough, he was almost as happy about the seven more months he would be allowed to continue opening up the world to children, most of whom would never travel farther than Shrewsbury in their lifetimes.

A knock on the door snapped him out of his pleasant reverie just before Vicar Phelps stepped into the room with hat in hand.

"Vicar . . ." Jonathan said, taken by surprise.

"Mr. Raleigh," the man nodded tersely as he approached his desk.

Oh no. Jonathan had a feeling the minister had found out about his decision to stay and, of course, was livid about it. He stood but did not offer his hand for fear that the vicar might not return it in the same condition. "Good morning," he offered benignly.

Vicar Phelps planted his fists upon the desk and leaned forward slightly, propping himself up by his arms. "You've given the board your answer." Not a question, but a statement of fact.

"Yes, sir." *I don't want to fight a man twice my age.* Especially one who happened to be Elizabeth's father—and with shoulders as broad as a Viking's.

"How can we make sure we win that archery tournament next month?"

Jonathan blinked. "Sir?" he replied, not because he had not heard, but because he needed a moment to collect his wits.

"The tournament. What would it take to win the thing?"

Now that he could think, Jonathan had a ready answer. "Saturday practices, sir. If just for a month the children could be allowed a couple of hours away from chores—and still be given time to keep up with their schoolwork, of course."

"Hmmm." The vicar rubbed his bearded chin. "Would have to be on Saturday mornings, after the milk from the first milkings is delivered to the factory. If I call on the parents and can convince most of them, can you be ready this Saturday?"

"Of course."

Incredibly, Vicar Phelps stretched his hand over the desk. Even more incredibly, his face wore a grin. "Then let's give it all we've got."

*W*ith a parcel of peppermints lying on the nearby bench, Mrs. Kingston trimmed dead leaves from her prize *Rosa Allea* and waited for the Sanderses' wagon to appear on its return trip up Market Lane. She could only hope that neither of Mercy's older brothers had been commissioned to drive this Friday, for she was sure the candy would not serve as sufficient bribery for them. And being a strong temperance supporter, she could not in good conscience provide what would surely do the trick.

To her relief, the one named "Fernie" was at the reins and gladly agreed to wait. Actually he requested ten pence in addition to the peppermints, but after being subjected to Mrs. Kingston's shaming stare, he meekly held out his hand for the candy.

"I've been praying for you every day, dear," she told Mercy as they walked with linked arms in a remote part of the garden. "Can you see any weakening in Mr. Langford's refusal to marry?"

"None at all, ma'am," Mercy replied. In spite of the slight melancholy set of her hazel eyes, she looked rather endearing in a simple frock of dove gray crepeline that she must have sewn up this week.

Can't the man see what a jewel she is? Mrs. Kingston thought and briefly considered calling upon Mr. Langford to point out that fact. But it was a sad fact of life that some men could not be bullied, and if Mr. Langford happened to be of the same cast, she would be doing more harm than good.

"But we did have a good chat last week," the girl went on, as if fearing she was painting too dismal a picture.

"Well, that's *something*." Mrs. Kingston nodded. "And don't forget, you've three more times to go. I've ordered river trout this time. It's about time we tried some fish, don't you think?"

"I feel so beholden to you."

"Nonsense! I'm having the time of my life, so let's not dredge up that old issue," she added commandingly. She looked about for any lurking ears, then leaned her head closer. "Besides . . . there is a way you can repay the favor."

"There is? Anything!" the girl replied with fervor.

Lowering her voice, Mrs. Kingston replied, "You can sing at my wedding, dear."

The girl froze on the spot to gape at her in wide-eyed wonder. "The squire proposed!"

"Sh-h-h! No, he has not proposed . . . yet."

After a bemused silence, the straight line of Mercy's mouth curved into a smile. "No doubt it's only a matter of time, then?"

Mrs. Kingston smiled back. "Faith is a wonderful thing, child."

After lunch she changed from her gardening and walking clothes into the hunter green cashmere gown she wore when the squire met her train in Shrewsbury. She then settled a gray felt hat trimmed with black velvet ribbon above her chignon. She could have easily walked the distance to the manor house, but it seemed on the occasion of the formal request she was to make, a carriage would be more appropriate. Mr. Herrick, who was the most obliging man on earth, in her opinion, agreed to chauffeur her in the landau.

"Why, Octavia!" the squire said, rising from his chair and newspaper after she had been introduced at the sitting room door. It was tastefully furnished with walnut paneling and Brussels carpets, in spite of the rather dour portraits of Bartley forebears staring down from all four walls. Catching up her gloved hand to press it against his lips in a courtly fashion, he said, "What a pleasant surprise!"

"And no inconvenience, Thurmond, I trust?"

"None at all, madam! Would that I be so inconvenienced every day!"

If the hint of a future together was attached to this latter statement, Mrs. Kingston chose to treat it with a benign smile. She still harbored a suspicion that the squire uttered such vaguely promising things to see how she would react, thereby justifying himself in assuming she desired to marry him—and possibly losing interest in her.

"I'm afraid this is not a social call, Thurmond," she said from the leather high-backed chair he had offered near his after he had dispatched the maid for tea.

Uncertainty washed across his wrinkled face. "Is something wrong, Octavia?"

"Not at all," she reassured him but then amended that with a purse of the lips. "On second consideration, I would be forced to respond that there is."

"Pray tell . . . what is it?"

She gave a sigh and glanced up at the host of Bartleys captured in gilded frames. "Your ancestors founded this village, as you've told me."

"Yes, yes," he nodded. "Do go on, Octavia."

"I wonder what they would think if they could know how sadly Gresham neglects its older children."

"Neglects?" The squire's eyebrows raised, resembling two patches of white broom sedge sprung out of bare earth. "How so, Octavia?"

Now that she was confident he was in the correct frame of mind, she related the proposal for the secondary school as was put to her by Mrs. Hollis and Vicar Phelps. He listened, alternately pursing his lips and fingering the cuff of his velvet coat—sometimes both activities at the same time. The maid brought tea, and he sipped thoughtfully until he had drained his cup, then set it back on its saucer with a soft clink.

"And so the primary expenses would be the teacher's wages and some texts?"

"Yes," she replied. "Of course some lamp oil would be necessary and firewood during the cold months."

"That shouldn't be a liability," he mused aloud. "We've firewood in abundance in the woods, and the caretaker could see to delivering it."

Mrs. Kingston was not sure if that implied an affirmative answer, so when he became silent again, she waited. And then an idea suddenly struck her, one that would surely ensure his cooperation. *And if the board wants to complain, I'll tell them they shouldn't send an old woman to do their job!* She cleared her throat and gave him a prim smile.

"How silly of me, Thurmond! I've left out the most exciting part."

"You have?"

"The school would be named The Thurmond Bartley School of Advanced Learning," she replied, clasping her hands together rapturously. "With an elegant signboard, of course, attached to the one that says *Gresham Town Hall*." She reckoned she would end up feeling compelled to pay for that herself, but if the children would benefit from it, she would forever have the satisfaction of a wise investment.

It was clear to see from the slight shift forward in his chair that he was interested, but there was also a curious narrowing of his eyes—almost a cagey look directed at her. "I've a better idea."

An unsettling awareness of having lost control of the situation almost put her at a loss for words. "You have, Thurmond?"

"Yes." Slowly, a smile spread across his face. "I would prefer the sign read The Octavia Bartley School for Advanced Learning."

Mrs. Kingston had been expecting a proposal of marriage for weeks but still suffered a jolt when the time actually arrived. With her better instinct still demanding coyness, she affected an expression of incomprehension. "Thurmond . . . are you suggesting we become associates in sponsoring the school? Because I must tell you that while I have at my disposal considerable funds, this is a project that will need to continue indefinitely. I don't know if—"

He shook his bald head. "Octavia. Will you force me to get down on my aged knees?"

"Your knees, Thurmond?"

"I'm asking you to marry me!" When she did not reply at once, he sent her the cagey look again. "And it's the only way I'll support that school. Marry me, Octavia Kingston, and I'll even donate a new building next year!"

––––––––––

"Aleda is at archery practice," Julia explained to Philip after she and Grace had taken turns embracing him on the railway platform Saturday morning. "She says to come by the school and watch if they're still at it when we get home."

"My sister with a bow and arrow." The boy affected a shudder. "I suppose I'll have to stay on her good side from now on."

"She doesn't bring them home with her," Grace reassured him with a serious expression.

Julia laughed, more from the joy of seeing Philip than by their remarks. It was good to hear evidence of his same good humor, though she was disturbed by the presence of faint shadows lurking under his eyes whenever he held his head at a certain angle. Either her imagination was playing tricks upon her, or he had lost even more weight, for she had never noticed his Norfolk jacket hanging so loosely upon his frame.

Andrew hopped down from the driving seat of the landau upon first sight of them. Smiling, he shook Philip's hand. "I declare you've grown another foot."

"Why, no, sir, I still have just the two," Philip bantered, to which Andrew clapped him on the shoulder and laughed at the old joke.

However, as he assisted Julia into the carriage while Philip was storing his satchel in the boot, Andrew whispered, "Has he lost more weight?"

"I noticed the same thing," Julia whispered back.

They were halfway to Laurel's school when Julia realized what was the matter, for she had gone through something like this with Philip only a year ago. *He's pushing himself too hard again . . . just as he did when he wanted to win that trophy.* And no doubt at the Josiah Smith Preparatory Academy, competition was even more intense to be among the top students.

Relief seeped into her tensed nerves, for she had almost convinced herself he had contracted some mysterious disease. Surely this was something

350

that could be mended. She determined to speak with him alone sometime today and make him understand that while it was admirable to set lofty goals, few were worth ruining one's own health over. And if his appearance did not improve very soon, he would have to stay home and attend the new school, which was but a fortnight or so away from becoming a reality. If it broke his heart, so be it. Reconciling with disappointment was a lesson best learned earlier than later in life.

Her thoughts temporarily switched to another subject as the landau drew closer to Saint Julien's—Andrew's sudden strange behavior. For instead of reining Donny and Pete into the sweeping carriage drive, he had turned onto a side lane shaded by massive oaks. After the horses had come to a stop on the side of the lane, he twisted around in the driver's seat with a sheepish look across his face. "You went inside with your mother last month, didn't you?" he asked Philip above the noise of a passing chaise.

Philip sat up in his seat. "Yes, sir."

"Would you mind fetching Laurel this time? It's just a short walk across the grounds."

"I don't mind."

"May I go too?" Grace asked as her brother hopped from the carriage.

"That's up to Philip," Julia replied. All Grace had to do was turn her hopeful face toward him, and he grinned and held out his arms to help her alight. After watching them set out across the grounds hand in hand, Julia leaned forward to speak to Andrew.

"I never imagined you to be a coward," she teased, for the reason for his behavior had dawned upon her.

He winced, still twisted in his seat. "Those are words that pierce the heart, Julia."

"Surely he's not as obnoxious as you imply."

"And surely Henry the Eighth was just a little temperamental. You met him once. Did you not find him irritating?"

"Henry the Eighth?"

"No!" he replied after a little chuckle. "And I must tell you . . . if Gresham happens to lose that archery competition, I may start parking around back at the service entrance."

Julia smiled, then became serious again. "Is that why you've decided to forgive Mr. Raleigh?"

"No, Julia." Andrew shook his head to emphasis his point. "Although I'm aware the timing appears suspicious. It's actually because of what you said to me last time we spoke about him. About 'everyone being someone's son or daughter,' if you will recall. Mr. Raleigh has proven himself enough as far as I'm concerned."

"And if he asks permission to court Elizabeth again?"

He took in a deep breath. "That will be up to her, which means it will likely happen, for I believe she still has strong feelings for him. But if and when it does, it will be under my conditions, of course."

She recalled the "ten minutes alone after dark" rule he had enforced when Elizabeth was being courted by Mr. Treves and had a feeling the rules of conduct governing Mr. Raleigh would be even stricter. But she couldn't fault him for that. "I don't think you're making a mistake, Andrew," she smiled. "I like the young man."

"Well, even though I've forgiven him, I can't quite go *that* far yet." Returning her smile, he added, "But if he makes Vicar Nippert eat his words, I will likely be disposed much more favorably toward him."

The children returned with Laurel presently. "Why did you wait out here?" she queried her father.

"It's a long story," he replied. He urged the horses at a brisk trot most of the way home, then gave his apologies after the landau came to a stop in the *Larkspur*'s carriage drive. "I promised Mr. Raleigh I would help him with archery practice," he said, turning the horses over to Mr. Herrick. "Would any of you care to come and watch?"

Of course Grace wanted to go, and Laurel as well. They both turned pleading eyes upon Philip, who had just taken his satchel from the landau's boot. He grinned back at them. "Just let me change from this uniform and say hello to everyone in the house."

"I'll come along with Philip," Julia said. The short walk would not give them ample time to discuss his schooling, but she was painfully aware that the minutes were rapidly ticking away until it would be time for him to leave again. While her son was being greeted and embraced and teased by servants and lodgers, she sat next to Mrs. Dearing on the piano bench and listened to her halting efforts of a simplified version of "The Beautiful Blue Danube Waltz." The elderly woman paused from her music to proffer a cheek when Philip walked by, and he planted a hurried kiss upon it.

Ten minutes after her son had disappeared into his room, Julia was still seated with Mrs. Dearing, who now had begun to practice her scales. She didn't wish to hurry him, but mindful that he would regret missing the chance to see his sister shoot a bow and arrow, she walked down the corridor and tapped upon his door. He didn't answer, and she tapped again. "Philip?" she asked, turning the knob and slowly pushing open the door. He had not even changed his clothes but lay across his bed upon his side, with both arms wrapping his pillow so that only part of his face was visible.

Julia eased a couple of steps closer, but she could have stomped and not disturbed the deep slumber that produced soft snoring sounds from the space between his arm and pillow. She closed the door quietly on her way out, her earlier suspicions all but confirmed. Surely it was studying

352

long into the night that had put shadows under his eyes. Now she was more determined than ever to have that talk with him.

For the fifth time Mercy steeled herself and hopped into the back of the butcher's cart. Again Mr. Langford and Thomas were at chores somewhere outside, so she let herself into the house and set to work. She smiled to herself upon hearing them at the back door at noon. Apparently Mr. Langford was of the mind that since she was determined to show up at his cottage, he may as well be on time for meals.

After they had consumed a goodly portion of baked trout—seasoned with lemon slices and pepper—in relative quietness, Thomas told her proudly that he had made a perfect mark on his spelling examination yesterday.

"That's wonderful, Thomas," Mercy told the boy. "Would you spell a word for me now?"

He screwed up his face for only a second before replying, "Carriage. C-a-r-r-i-a-g-e."

"That's absolutely correct." She was so thankful for the boy's presence at these Saturday meals, first, because she had never realized children could be such delightful company, and second, because his joyful outlook almost always spilled over to his adoptive father. Mr. Langford sent her an appreciative look after she had listened to the spelling of three more words but then kindly told the boy that he should give her a chance to finish her meal.

"He's excited about the spelling bees Mr. Raleigh says they'll begin having after the Christmas holiday," Mr. Langford explained. "At first I was at a loss, because I never went to school. A spelling *bee*?"

Mercy, who had only yesterday had the same thing explained to her by Edgar, smiled. "They must be grand fun, all right."

"You never went to school either?" Thomas asked.

"I never even saw the inside of the schoolhouse until just recently."

"How did you learn to read?"

"Mrs. Brent taught me from her Bible. She would print out words for me to learn at home too."

"Didn't you have your own Bible? My father has one."

"Thomas." Mr. Langford's mildly stern tone did not quite match the shining of his eyes.

Thomas said "father," Mercy realized. "Oh, but I don't mind," she assured him, and in reply to the boy's question, she said, "Not until Mrs. Brent passed away and left me hers. But after I knew enough words to put sentences together, I began borrowing books from the lending library."

Thomas nodded, obviously fascinated that someone could learn to

353

read outside of a school setting. Of his father he inquired, "Who taught you to read?"

"Someone I once shared a . . . room with," Mr. Langford replied offhandedly while pushing out his chair. "We've still more work to get at, so let's put this kitchen to order while there is daylight left to burn. That was a fine meal, Miss Sanders."

Some half hour later, as he escorted her up the lane, he said, "I want to thank you for your advice regarding Thomas."

"I heard him call you father," Mercy replied with a smile.

Mr. Langford smiled too. "Your company has been good for him, Miss Sanders."

Such unexpected praise brought heat to her cheeks and caused her to lower her eyes to stare at the lane ahead. Apparently the delivering of it caused him the same shyness, for he became silent again. Mercy thought of Mrs. Kingston and how pleased she would be to hear next Friday that he had paid her a compliment. But then it seemed she could hear her friend fretting, *And you just sat there and allowed the moment to pass?*

Mercy swallowed. "The boy longs for a mother, Mr. Langford."

"We've discussed that, Miss Sanders," he said after an audible sigh that caused her cheeks to grow even warmer. Neither spoke until they had almost reached the gate in front of her father's cottage. Then he turned to her. "I'm not denying that you would make a fine wife and mother," he said in a regretful but firm tone. "And I'm flattered that you would want to make a future with Thomas and me. But I would be the worst kind of selfish monster if I married you solely for your housekeeping and mothering."

Don't back down, she told herself. "How can it be selfish of you to grant something I've requested? Something I've made a fool of myself these past five weeks to gain?"

A look of pain crossed his face. "Now, now. You've made no fool of yourself. In fact, I admire your determination, if the truth were told." He turned his head to send a brief glance toward the cottage, where thankfully, neither her father nor brothers loitered about with martyred expressions. Softening his voice, he went on. "You're still a young woman, Miss Sanders. I've noticed the way some of the young men in our congregation stare at you when you sing. If we married, you would grow to hate me for robbing you of the love that will surely come your way if you'll just be patient."

She had to will herself to reply to this. Still, her voice obliged her barely above the level of a whisper. "It has already come my way, Mr. Langford."

Mr. Langford gaped at her for a second before giving a violent shake of the head. "That's ridiculous! You know nothing of me!"

She opened her mouth to contradict him but found herself at a loss for any words that he would understand. And so for fear of angering him any further, she took her basket from his arm. "I will see you next week, Mr. Langford."

Again he sighed, before grumbling, "You *must* be the most stubborn woman in Shropshire, Miss Sanders."

It was a complaint this time, not a compliment, but Mercy could not help but smile wryly as she stared down at the packed earth of the lane. "The *second* most stubborn woman, Mr. Langford."

It was late evening before Julia could take Philip aside for a talk. Even then it took some doing, for in a moment of weakness she had allowed him to invite Ben and Jeremiah to spend the night, as in the old days. After tucking the girls into their beds, she had simply knocked at Philip's door and requested to see him alone. But it turned out that the library was occupied by Mr. Pitney, who appeared embarrassed to be caught thumbing through the row of the novelettes Miss Rawlins had contributed.

"He reads Miss Rawlins' books?" Philip whispered as they went back down the family corridor to Julia's room.

"Sh-h-h!" Julia scolded but could not blame him for his incredulous smile. It did seem quite odd, the thought of such a bashful, awkward, giant of a man reading love stories. "I think he's fond of her. But you must never tell anyone."

"I won't," he whispered back when they reached her door. Once inside her room, he said, still whispering, "Does she like him?"

"She seems to take very little notice of him. He's not like the aristocratic heroes of her stories." But it was time to talk over what had occupied her mind all day, and she motioned toward the dressing table bench. "We have to talk."

"Jeremiah and Ben. . . ?" he began.

Julia shook her head on her way to her chair and said, "They can amuse themselves for a little while longer."

Obediently he sat down on the bench. "We're not planning on walking the lanes tonight with anyone dressed as a ghost, if you're worried," he said in a half-teasing tone.

Julia smiled. "The thought never crossed my mind. But I'm reassured to hear that it hasn't crossed yours either. It's the state of your health that has me concerned, son."

"My health? But I'm fine."

"You're losing weight. And you look tired."

"You're worried because I fell asleep this morning," he shrugged. "I had to get up early to make the train. And the long ride—"

"Philip, one day shouldn't make such a difference in your appearance. You're losing weight, and you've shadows under your eyes."

"I have?" He twisted to study himself in the mirror. "I don't see any."

Julia couldn't either, she had to admit to herself when he turned back to face her again. "But I know I saw them this morning."

"It was probably soot from the train."

He had always been adept at convincing her that she didn't have to worry over him, but this time she refused to give ground. "You've lost weight, Philip. And I think I know why."

"You do?" For the fraction of a second, some uncertainty crept into his expression.

"You're studying too hard again. What good will it do you to win academic honors if your constitution is so feeble that you can't risk being near the sick when you finally become a doctor? There are people like that, you know."

"I know." He looked down at his shoes. "I'm sorry I've worried you, Mother. I'll do better."

"Just don't push yourself so hard, dear. That's all I ask."

"Yes, of course."

"And put a little more on your plate at mealtimes."

"I'll do that."

He was accepting her lecture with no argument, and it disturbed her a little. "Philip?"

His blue eyes raised to meet hers again. "Yes, Mother?"

"Is there anything else the matter? You're being treated well at school, aren't you?"

"Oh, famously," he reassured her with a smile.

"That's good to know," she said, letting out a relieved breath. As usual, she was looking for symptoms that were not there. But it certainly would not hurt to impress upon him that she was serious about his need to consider his health. It was easy enough for him to be reasonable while he was here, away from the pressures of academia. "I must warn you, Philip, that I still have some grave doubts about your being away at school. I allowed you and Doctor Rhodes to talk me into it, but—"

"I'll take better care of myself. I promise." He then rose, walked over to her, and got to his knees in front of her chair. "I do appreciate your providing me with such a good education, Mother. I know what a sacrifice it is."

Smiling, Julia rested her hand upon his shoulder. "It's no sacrifice if it helps you achieve your dreams, son."

He blinked and looked away for a second. "You're a good mother."

"And you have blessed my life in more ways than you can imagine." She could have sat like that exchanging endearments for hours, but she was mindful that a fourteen-year-old boy's capacity for them was infinitely smaller than a mother's. So to lighten the moment, she patted his shoulder. "I wonder what your friends are up to?"

"Oh, you know those two rogues," he replied, getting to his feet. "Probably no good. By the way, Ben is beside himself with excitement over the new school."

"Will Jeremiah enroll too?"

The boy smiled and shook his head. "Jeremiah has an aversion to books."

Casually, Julia broached the subject that had been upon her mind all day. "You know . . . with such a small class and a teacher as well educated as Miss Clark, a student willing to learn would likely do just as well as in the more prestigious schools."

"Yes? Perhaps I should come back here next year."

"You don't mind?"

"Why, no. It would save you money. And I would still study hard." Quickly he amended, "But not *too* hard for my health." While Julia was struck speechless at the ease of his decision, he leaned down to brush a quick kiss against her forehead. "I should see to Jeremiah and Ben now."

She stared with wonder at the door after it closed behind him. Seven more months at the Josiah Smith Preparatory Academy, and he would live at home until old enough to leave for university! With that hope waiting in the wings, she could endure seven more months.

You can take seven more months, Philip reassured himself on his way to his room. Even though the two months he had already spent at this wretched school had seemed to grind on forever, at least now he would not have to resign himself to three additional years.

It had taken all the restraint he could muster to keep from asking if he could stay home and begin the new school with Ben. Just the idea of not having to board the train to return to Worcester filled him with such longing that his eyes began to sting. He paused at his door to wipe his sleeve across his face. *Mother worked hard for that money,* he reminded himself. Running the *Larkspur* was easier now, but he could recall his mother scrubbing walls and floors during the days when Fiona was their only servant. He could not in good conscience ask her to throw that to the wind.

Ben and Jeremiah had begun a game of draughts in his absence. They used some of his chessmen as substitutes for the round game pieces. "You could have gotten the real game from the hall," he told them, dropping onto the side of his bed to watch.

"Mmm," Ben murmured, studying the board for his next move. "Too much trouble. What did your mother want?"

"To warn me not to pick up any bad habits from you two."

Jeremiah looked up from the game with a wounded expression. "What bad habits?"

"He's joshing, Jeremiah," Ben reassured him. He directed a smirking smile at Philip, but there was affection in his eyes. "No doubt he's become the class wit at the academy by now."

Philip smiled and wished he could tell them the truth. But it would serve no purpose and would make greater the chance of his mother finding out how miserable he was. He already regretted telling Vicar Phelps, but fortunately, the man had kept his word about keeping it secret.

However, he was drawn aside by Vicar Phelps after church the next day and asked if the situation was improving at all at school. Philip could not bring himself to lie to a vicar, especially while standing in front of a church, so he shook his head. "But I'll be coming home next year."

"Yes?" Vicar Phelps clapped him on the back. "Well, that's good news. A strong fellow like you can stand anything for a few more months, right?"

He carried that reassurance all the way back to Worcester. It fortified him enough to take without flinching the jeers and croaking noises sent his way by the upperclassmen he happened to pass. But it helped very little when he pulled back his covers that night and found two dead mice resting upon his pillow.

*Y*ou should see Cyril Towly shoot an arrow," Elizabeth's father said Monday over a supper of deviled kidneys and pease pudding. "He shot a bull's-eye three times at practice after school, Luke told me. And he's but twelve years old."

"Another William Tell?" she asked while sprinkling salt onto her potatoes.

"Well, we won't go so far as to test him with an apple, but I daresay Prescott will have no one to match him."

Elizabeth smiled indulgently. "And we very much want to win over Prescott, don't we?"

"It would be nice, yes, but winning isn't the most important thing, Beth." He buttered his bread lavishly as he spoke, inflecting a casual note into his voice.

"So you won't mind at all if it turns out that you have to congratulate that vicar?" she asked innocently, for she could see straight through him.

Her father paused to narrow his eyes at her. "You have a waggish sense of humor, daughter."

"I have? And from whom did I inherit it, I wonder?"

"Well, why couldn't you have inherited something like my singing talent instead?"

"I did, Papa," she reminded him.

"Oh . . . that's so." He affected a heavy sigh, for they were both just a hairsbreadth away from being completely tone deaf. "Sorry, Beth."

She sent him an affectionate smile across the table. "No matter, Papa. I would rather have the humor than the voice anyway."

"So would I," he replied with a wink. "Although you don't get requests to tell jokes at weddings, do you?"

They settled into a companionable silence for the remainder of the meal. It was only when her father had taken a second bite of his custard tart that Elizabeth broached the subject that had occupied the back of her mind for days. "I hear that Jonathan is proving himself quite competent in the classroom."

Her father's chewing slowed as he regarded her warily, but through closed lips he gave an affirmative reply. "Mm-hm."

Elizabeth took a deep breath. "May we invite him for supper, Papa?"

A stricken expression filled his hazel eyes, as if he had just been told the tart was laced with hemlock. *"Here?"*

"Of course, Papa. We could have him over on Saturday, when Laurel's home."

"Why, I don't know." He scratched his cheek beneath his beard, as was his habit when nervous or agitated "It's just too soon. He's going to be here for seven more months."

"Hasn't he proved himself enough?"

"To teach school, yes. But not to court my daughter. Don't forget what he did to you—"

"In Cambridge," she finished for him. "How could I, when you bring it up often enough?"

His expression darkened at the sharpness of her retort. "That was unnecessary, Beth. I've only wanted what's best for you."

For several seconds she stared back at him, fingernails digging into her palms. And then a picture came, unbidden, to her mind, of the tears that had clung to her father's lashes the morning he broke the news of Jonathan's unfaithfulness. *He was hurt by it almost as much as I was,* she realized for the first time. She uncurled her hands. "I'm sorry, Papa."

His chest rose and fell. "You care for him again."

Lowering her eyes, she replied, "I believe he's changed, Papa."

"If only I could be sure."

Now it was Elizabeth who sighed, but quietly. She had put such hope into her request. It was becoming more and more difficult to see Jonathan in church or in the village and be constrained to exchange only the most formal of pleasantries. "Then we'll wait a little longer."

"You think I'm unreasonable, don't you?" her father asked, pushing his unfinished tart away.

"No." She gave him a sad smile. "You're afraid I'll be hurt again."

"The thought of that frightens me more than I can tell you, Beth."

"But the only way to ensure my not getting hurt again would be to never allow me to leave the house." He opened his mouth to reply, but Elizabeth shook her head. "We'll wait, Papa."

———

It was with great reluctance that Andrew joined the students Mr. Raleigh assembled for after-school archery practice on Thursday so that Luke could attend a cousin's funeral in Nonely. After Monday evening's heart-to-heart talk with Elizabeth, he was unsure how he was supposed to feel in Jonathan Raleigh's presence. It was difficult to keep the old resentment bottled up now that he was positive his daughter loved the man.

Fortunately, there was enough to do to keep such thoughts at bay. While his main sports activity at college had been the rowing team, he had dabbled in archery and fencing enough to remember the basic form. From somewhere Mr. Raleigh had procured a cheval mirror mounted upon a frame for shadow drills. Andrew's responsibility, while Mr. Raleigh monitored activity at the target, was to stand one child at a time in front of it with a bow and have the student draw an imaginary arrow to practice proper stance.

It was not too long into practice that he noticed a face was missing. "Where is Cyril Towly?" he asked Aleda after reminding her to move her string elbow straight back at shoulder level.

She took her eyes off her reflection only long enough to reply with lowered voice, "He told Ruthie Derby she was stupid for missing most of her arithmetic answers. Mr. Raleigh made him apologize and stay away from practice today."

"He did?" Andrew looked over at Jonathan Raleigh, who was reminding one of the Sanders brothers to straddle the shooting line with his feet. The young man was likely as eager as Andrew was to win the competition, albeit for different reasons. To force his star marksman to sit out a practice must have taken some willpower. *And character*, Andrew realized.

When practice was over and the children dismissed to head for their homes, Andrew helped the schoolmaster gather equipment. "That was a good practice," Mr. Raleigh told him. "I believe they're developing some confidence."

"Yes." With a nod toward the cheval mirror, Andrew said, "Shall I deliver that somewhere?"

The young man grinned, raking his dark hair from his forehead with his fingers. "I'll have to slip it through the back door of the *Bow and Fiddle*. Mr. Pool lent it to me, but he's fearful of Mrs. Pool finding out."

"I can understand that." Andrew cleared his throat. "Would you care to join my family for supper this Saturday?"

"You mean me?" asked Mr. Raleigh after a short hesitation, as though uncertain his ears had functioned properly.

"Yes, of course."

"Why, I would be honored. Thank you, sir!"

Such happiness had filled the young man's expression that Andrew feared for a second he would bound over to him for an embrace, which would have been *too* much.

Brusquely he said, "We dine at seven."

————

Seth and Thomas sat down Saturday to a delicious meal of dumplings with thick beef gravy, smothered turnips, and almond pudding for dessert. As Seth watched the affection with which his son and Miss Sanders regarded each other, he felt like the most selfish scoundrel who ever lived. He had made feeble protests against her wasting her time by cooking for them, but had he really been serious he would have barred the door. Or even left the place with Thomas as soon as she insisted her way into his cottage. He could have packed sandwiches for them to picnic on somewhere—perhaps atop the Anwyl—until she became discouraged and left. It would have been cruel, yes, but not as cruel as allowing her to keep false hopes.

His conscience would not be assuaged by the reminder that he had told her flatly from the start that they could have no future together. Not while his plate was piled high with food from her hand. *God forgive me. Why can't I love her?* It would be wonderful having someone with her sweet nature to grace his cottage, and of course Thomas would benefit in many ways. But it was the years ahead that he had to consider, when bitterness would surely set in as she grew to realize his heart still belonged to a ghost.

It was too late to put an end to her visits when next week's would be the last. But for her own sake, he would have to treat her from now on with polite coolness. Then she would finally come to realize that her efforts had been wasted and would best be directed toward some other man.

————

"Careful. Don't burn your fingers," Elizabeth cautioned as her sister unwound a strand of her blond fringe from the curling iron. "And don't burn my hair either, please."

Laurel nodded absently. "Yes, the color becomes you."

"Did you hear a word I said?"

"Mmm. Something about your gown?"

"You're still dwelling on the new school, aren't you?"

With a shrug that belied her serious expression, her sister replied, "Well, I think the vicar's family ought to show support—don't you?"

"I didn't realized you disliked the academy so much. You never complained before."

"I don't *dislike* the academy." Again the shrug. "But I never had another option until now. I like it here much better. It's so much more serene."

"Serene?"

Laurel rolled her brown eyes. "Girls in large groups tend to become either hysterical, maudlin, or spiteful. Would you talk with Papa about it this week?"

"Well . . ."

"Mention the seven months' tuition he would be saving. And that there's a waiting list, so the academy wouldn't lose any money."

"Very well," Elizabeth sighed. "Are you finished?"

Tapping her cheek thoughtfully, Laurel added, "Well . . . you could tell him that the breakfast porridge is almost always lumpy."

"I mean, with my hair, scatterbrain!"

"Oh. See for yourself."

Elizabeth stood and turned to look in the wall mirror over her chest of drawers. Angling her face to study the mass of tendrils curling well above her eyebrows, she said, "You don't think it's too youthful?"

"It frames your face nicely," her sister assured her, reaching up to make sure the tortoise-shell comb was fastened securely upon the back of her crown. Laurel had talked her into wearing a style she had seen several times on the streets of Shrewsbury. The sides of her long blond hair were drawn up loosely into the comb, while the back, rolled smooth over a frizette, hung just below the ruffled collar of her navy calico gown.

"Yes?" Elizabeth slipped an arm across her sister's shoulders for a quick embrace. She was aware that the lavender poplin Laurel wore was her favorite dress-up gown. How heartening it was to know that she was not the only one looking forward to Jonathan's visit. "You look very nice yourself."

Laurel made a face at her reflection, for while she loved to be praised for her academic endeavors, any references to her beauty seemed to cause her embarrassment. "Thank you. But don't worry. I wouldn't dream of stealing your beau."

"He's not my beau, remember."

"But he would like to be." Laurel stepped up to the chest of drawers and picked up a brush. "How did you get Papa to invite him?"

"You know, I'm not sure. All I know is that he came home from archery practice Thursday and announced that Jonathan would be at supper on Saturday. He didn't seem open to interrogation, so I simply nodded and thanked him."

"Miss Phelps?" Both heads turned toward the doorway, where Dora stood in white apron and cap over a black gown.

"Yes, Dora?" Elizabeth said.

363

"That Mr. Raleigh is here."

"Did you invite him in?"

"He's in the parlor with the vicar."

Elizabeth thanked the maid and, after another glance at the mirror, left her room for the landing with Laurel on her heels. "Can't you move faster?" her sister whispered when they were halfway down the staircase.

"I don't want him to think I'm desperate for his attention," Elizabeth turned to whisper back. She had forgiven him for what happened in Cambridge, yes, and truly believed he had changed. But she would never allow him or any other man to assume he was her sole purpose in living. Mrs. Hollis had taught her only last year that it was nothing short of idol worship to put any other person up on a pedestal.

She paused just outside the parlor doorway to listen and was met with silence. "They're not even speaking," she whispered to Laurel.

"Well, go on in," her sister urged with a nudge. Sure enough, her father sat at the end of the sofa with his hands clasped upon his knees, and Jonathan sat in the same position in her father's favorite chair. It was not her father's generosity that had placed him there, Elizabeth knew at once, but his desire to avoid the possibility of her sitting next to Mr. Raleigh.

"Jonathan," Elizabeth said, smiling, as both men rose to their feet. She extended her hand, and he wisely shook it instead of pressing it to his lips. "How good of you to come."

"Good evening, Elizabeth," he replied with gray-green eyes shining. He then took Laurel's hand and kissed it quickly, causing her to flash Elizabeth a startled grin. "It was good of your father to invite me."

They seated themselves and settled into small talk devoted mainly to the weather—her father joining in only rarely—until Dora announced that supper was ready. Over Mrs. Paget's steak-and-kidney pie the polite chatter became strained, until Laurel asked Jonathan about the archery team. "Do you ever worry about someone losing an eye?"

He had just taken a sip of water and set his glass back down upon the cloth. "It's a perfectly safe sport as long as the safety rules are never compromised," he replied, smiling. "We keep the other children and spectators well behind the person shooting."

From the head of the table her father nodded agreement. "And once the shooter has drawn his arrow, if he turns his face away from the target for even a second, he must surrender his turn."

"That seems rather severe," Elizabeth commented. Actually, she understood the reason for that rule, but now that her father and Jonathan had found common ground, she wanted to encourage the conversation. It almost worked too well, for after each man took a turn explaining in his own words the wisdom of erring on the side of safety, conversation was dominated by talk of the archery team. They discussed the skills or need for improvement of every member, their relief that today's rain shower had come after this morning's practice, and the good news that the squire had donated a barn for use during the tournament in case the day should prove forbiddingly windy or frigid.

Judging by the amicableness of the conversation, Elizabeth was tempted to believe the past had been totally forgiven and forgotten. Only later, when Jonathan thanked them and took his leave, did she realize there was still some distance to go. She had assumed the ten minutes granted her to walk Paul to his horse would be allowed tonight as well, but the gentle though firm grip of her father's hand upon her elbow told her otherwise.

She nodded as she and Laurel passed Jonathan's church pew the next morning, and he smiled back warmly. At the end of the service, she walked out onto the green and was not surprised to see him standing at the fringe of those worshipers occupied with socializing. He was staring across at her, and even in the distance she could see that his expression was filled with as much adoration as any sonnet. Still, she ambled along, pausing to exchange pleasantries with Mrs. Hollis, who asked in a low voice, "Did the supper go well last night?"

"Very well. Papa and Jonathan discussed archery most of the time."

"But at least they're speaking, yes?"

"Oh, I'm most grateful for that."

Mrs. Hollis glanced over to where Jonathan was standing and arched an amused brow. "It appears he's waiting to speak with you."

"Yes," Elizabeth replied, smiling. "And I suppose I've kept him waiting long enough."

"Elizabeth," Jonathan said when she reached him, taking her proffered hand but wisely letting it go again after a gentle squeeze. "You don't know how overjoyed I was to receive your father's invitation Thursday. I barely slept the next two nights."

Elizabeth reckoned her own insomnia had been just as severe but merely gave him a serene smile. "It was good of you to come, Jonathan."

"Good of me to come?" Hurt was evident in his gray-green eyes. "Were you not at least a little happy to have me there?"

While she did not want to appear overeager, neither could she bring herself to be cruel to him. She was opening her mouth to assure him that his company had indeed been welcome, when a child's voice from nearby called, "Here he is!"

Within seconds he was surrounded by no less than eight schoolboys, each attempting at the same time to report that he had either finished his weekend homework last night, or been practicing his stance at home, or both.

He responded to them warmly, sending Elizabeth helpless looks while attempting to spread his attention out to each of them. She took a step back out of the way and smiled to herself. *I wonder if Jonathan will ever practice law?*

Laurel appeared then at her elbow, saying that their father was ready for them to return to the vicarage. Elizabeth lifted a hand in farewell to Jonathan, who appeared crestfallen as he responded with the same but was still in the clutches of his young captors. She shared his disappointment, for they had had scant opportunity to speak alone for any length of time since his move to Gresham. But one thing she had gleaned as a result of working for Mr. Ellis and Mr. Pitney was that Rome was not built in a day.

On Monday, November seventh, the new secondary school opened its doors. It was unnamed as yet, because while Mrs. Kingston had agreed to marry the squire, they both had their hearts set upon having the wedding in the manor garden when it was in full bloom, which would mean mid-May.

Both having had a hand in the reality of the school, Julia and Mrs. Kingston could not resist walking across the green early that morning to see how the village would respond. Miss Clark stood on the wide stoop, looking out across the green expectantly. As the distance closed between them, Julia noticed that she appeared somewhat healthier and infinitely happier than she had three weeks ago.

"Why, I daresay there is a glow to your cheeks," Mrs. Kingston said when the schoolmistress had hurried down the steps to greet them.

Miss Clark squeezed the elderly woman's hand, then Julia's. "I'm like a child on Christmas eve. I just hope we have students."

"Laurel Phelps will be here," Julia reassured her. Even as the words left her mouth, she could see Andrew and his daughter approaching from the direction of the vicarage. She lifted a hand to wave, and both returned the gesture. "And I spoke with Ben Mayhew's and Bessie Worthy's mothers at *Trumbles* just last week. Both are eager to study for university scholarships but hadn't the means to attend secondary school."

Mrs. Kingston nodded. "And Mrs. Casper—she's in my charity sewing group—mentioned a grandson who will be attending. Billy is his name. She claims that he's extremely bright, which may or may not be so." She shrugged. "We grandmothers are somewhat prejudiced toward our own grandchildren."

With a farewell and parting smile, Miss Clark turned and hurried over to greet Laurel at the bottom of the steps. Andrew joined Julia and Mrs. Kingston only for a moment before leaving for chapel at the grammar school. "We're a little early," he reassured them. "I'm sure more will come."

"But of *course* they will," Mrs. Kingston agreed as Julia nodded the same sentiment. Still, they sent hopeful glances here and there while attempting light conversation. As it turned out, five more children appeared in the following ten minutes—those Julia and Mrs. Kingston had already mentioned, as well as two factory workers' children from across the Bryce. It was a good beginning, considering most villagers still were of the opinion that grammar school was more than enough education for dairy farming and factory working. But as the idea of secondary education caught on, surely the school would grow.

And Aleda and Philip will be here next year too, Julia thought contentedly. It was as it should be. There would be time enough for the children to grow up and leave the nest. But at their tender ages, the wings they would need someday to carry them to their dreams could best be developed and strengthened within the confines of a loving family.

———

After seeing the new school off to a good start, Mrs. Kingston parted company with Mrs. Hollis to resume her walk. She strode west toward Worton Lane as a brisk northwestern breeze tugged insistently at her bonnet. *There is something I should do today*, she told herself—something which had nothing to do with the wedding plans that had preoccupied her thoughts lately.

And then it dawned upon her that Saturday past had been Mercy's last day to cook for Mr. Langford. They had not even discussed the significance of that on Friday, but then, their meeting had lasted only long enough for her to inform Mercy that the butcher would be sending mutton the next day. Dale Sanders had been the reason for the brevity of their meeting. His cross mood, Mercy had whispered, was because she had refused to give him some household money to spend on a bottle of gin at the *Bow and Fiddle*.

She would be speaking with Mercy again in four more days, but surely the child was wondering what to do next, and that was such a long time to wait. So when she returned to the *Larkspur*, she sought out Mr. Herrick. He was obliging, as usual, and agreed to deliver her in the landau to Nettle Lane.

Sanders men were visible in the barnyard, she saw with relief as the carriage slowed to a stop in the lane. She was still uneasy about subjecting Mr. Herrick to waiting in the drive, where he would be within shouting distance of Mercy's brothers and possibly ridiculed for his lack of height. "I shan't be long," she assured him, walking through the gate he held open.

She was startled when Mr. Sanders responded to her knock at the cottage door. The glare he slanted at her was anything but welcoming, but he jerked his head toward his shoulder to signify that his daughter was inside, then stalked out past her before she could bid him good morning. Mercy appeared a second later, apologizing and taking her by the arm. "I'm afraid he blames you for the Saturdays I was away," the girl explained. "But he holds back from scolding me too heavily for fear I'll take that position at the manor."

"He should be happy that they're over now," Mrs. Kingston said, settling at the table but raising a hand to decline Mercy's offer of tea. "I shouldn't detain Mr. Herrick from his duties for too long."

"Would he care to come inside?"

"He brought along a book to occupy himself. He orders them from a German bookseller in London. How was your visit with Mr. Langford Saturday?"

Mercy pulled out the opposite chair. The mixture of resignation and sadness in her expression leached all youthfulness from her face. "If it weren't for Thomas, there wouldn't have been two words exchanged between us."

Reaching across the table to pat her hand, Mrs. Kingston soothed, "There, there now. You mustn't give up hope."

"But the plan didn't work, and I've allowed you to waste all of that money."

"The plan has not run its course, dear child."

Now anxiety flooded her hazel eyes. "Please don't ask me to start all over again."

"Oh, I wouldn't dream of it," Mrs. Kingston replied with a shake of the head. "Now we must allow Mr. Langford the opportunity to *miss* you. And he will, my young friend. Of course if he's the stubborn sort, it may take some time. But patience is a virtue, is it not?"

"But how do you know—"

"That he will miss you? For the same reason that widowers tend to remarry much sooner than widows. No house seems emptier to a man than one in which a woman's presence has been felt but is no longer. All that is required of you now, Mercy Sanders, is to step back and allow that to happen. Don't catch his eye while you sing in front of your church. If he speaks to you, be polite, but then excuse yourself."

Some of the hopelessness left the girl's expression. "When you speak like that, Mrs. Kingston, I believe almost anything is possible."

368

"But of course it is, dear. All a woman with any sense needs is a plan. Just look at the squire and me. While your plan had to be altered to fit the circumstance, it is still a good one. By the way, you'll remember your promise to sing at my wedding, won't you?"

"I will be happy to," Mercy replied with a smile.

"Good enough!" Mrs. Kingston pushed out her chair and got to her feet before the girl could hurry around to assist her. "And now I mustn't keep Mr. Herrick waiting. Do let me know when Mr. Langford shows any sign of progress, dear."

"I will, thank you." At the door, Mercy gave her a quick embrace. "God is so good to give me a friend like you."

"Oh, come now," Mrs. Kingston said brusquely to hide her pleasure in the compliment. On her way to the gate, she prayed silently, *You heard her, Father. She's had so little hope in her life, and she's grateful to both of us for giving her some. We can't cause such a good-hearted girl to lose that hope, can we?*

*P*apa asked me to apologize for his not being here," Elizabeth told Julia after answering the vicarage door herself on the Friday morning of November eleventh. "He was called away on urgent business soon after Laurel left for school."

"Oh dear. I hope no one is gravely ill."

"I'm not sure. All he said was that he had to hurry and wouldn't be back until very late. But do come in."

"Why don't I come back some other time?" Julia asked. With the wedding less than a month away, Andrew had asked her to look over the two spare bedrooms that would belong to her children to determine if any furnishings would be needed from the *Larkspur.* "I shouldn't hinder your work."

"Oh, but I've been working hard all morning. A break would be nice. I'll even see about the rooms with you. Some of the furniture here was built around the time of the Stonehenge, so we may need to test it for sturdiness."

"I would appreciate your help," Julia said, smiling as they started for the staircase. "But you aren't suggesting we jump on beds, are you?"

"Haven't you always wanted to?" the girl returned with a glint of humor in her eyes.

"I purged myself of that desire long ago." She shrugged at Elizabeth's curious look. "I had an indulgent nanny."

"Really? I can't imagine any nanny allowing that."

"Well, it was gin she was indulgent with, so she wasn't aware of it at the time."

Elizabeth's laugh rang along the upstairs corridor as they reached the first spare bedroom and devoted their energies to taking inventory. It took less than twenty minutes to look over both rooms, so Julia felt relieved that she had not detained Elizabeth from her work for too long. But when it came time to leave, the girl pressed her into staying a little longer. "I'm afraid I'm in need of your counsel again," she admitted.

They settled into the parlor and chatted idly until Dora brought tea and shortbread. When the door closed after the maid, Elizabeth said, "I'm not sure if Papa has told you, but Jonathan has been allowed to call twice and has had supper with us once."

"It's so good to see that your father has changed his opinion of him," Julia told her, smiling. "I confess I wondered if I would ever see the day this would happen."

"As did I. But even so, Papa hasn't allowed us a minute alone together."

"You understand why, don't you?"

"I'm not sure that I do," Elizabeth replied frankly. "I don't think Papa realizes I'm not the infatuated girl I was in Cambridge. You've taught me how damaging it is to put someone on a pedestal, but I must confess it would be nice to have a conversation of some length without my father listening in. And surely Jonathan has proved himself trustworthy."

"I don't think it's a matter of doubting your maturity, Elizabeth. Or even Mr. Raleigh's trustworthiness."

With a searching look at Julia, the girl leaned forward in her chair and asked, "What has Papa told you? Please tell me."

"Actually, he has not confided in me regarding his reason. But I believe I understand it."

"What is it, Mrs. Hollis?"

It took Julia several seconds to arrange her thoughts so that they could be explained. She did not take young courtships lightly, for they became the foundations of either strong or disastrous marriages. "While your father has forgiven Mr. Raleigh, he wishes to prove a point to him."

Elizabeth shook her head uncomprehendingly. "I beg your pardon?"

After sending up a quick prayer for the right words, Julia went on. "Your father obviously now believes Jonathan's conversion to be real. But being in the ministry for so long, he's aware that even decent people have been known to stray. All of us value more highly the things that were obtained at a great price. Your father, I believe, is making this courtship difficult so that by the time Mr. Raleigh does win your hand, the thought of losing what he worked so hard to gain would be repugnant to him."

"In other words, he's forcing Jonathan to pay penance? While preaching grace from the pulpit?"

"Grace is a wonderful thing, Elizabeth. But sometimes penance is as well. It teaches us that there are consequences to our actions. I daresay Mr. Raleigh has grown even more in character from it."

They both took sips of tea in thoughtful silence, and then Elizabeth sighed. "I'll try to be more patient with Papa."

"You're a wise young woman," Julia said warmly.

371

"Wise? How can you say that? You see so deeply into things, while I'm still trying to understand the ripples on the surface."

"Because you are wise enough to know the limitations of your experience. A teachable spirit is a blessing, Elizabeth. Had I one at your age, perhaps I could have saved myself some heartache."

The girl's brow drew with concern. "Are you happy now, Mrs. Hollis?"

Julia smiled. "Very much so."

"I'm glad." Brown eyes shining, Elizabeth said, "I look forward to addressing you as 'mother,' Mrs. Hollis, but you've actually mothered me for over a year now. I appreciate your good advice more than you can know."

And I appreciate being allowed the opportunity to give it, Julia thought as she walked down Church Lane a quarter of an hour later, breathing in crisp air touched faintly with the scent of ripe apples from the squire's orchard. Above the roof of the *Larkspur* the brown and red Anwyl stood out in vast relief against a canvas of blue sky. *How sad it be would if no one ever asked.* By being allowed to point out some of the pitfalls she herself had stumbled into during the course of her three decades, she was able to redeem something of value from those mistakes.

At the crossroads she turned to the south and walked down to *Trumbles.* "Good morning, Mrs. Hollis!" Mr. Trumble paused from assembling an order for Mrs. Sykes, who turned to smile and echo the shopkeeper's greeting.

"Good morning," Julia greeted both. "Fine weather we're having, isn't it?"

"Fine indeed," the churchwarden's wife replied. "And the almanac says no snow until after Christmas, so your wedding day should be a lovely one."

Mr. Trumble chuckled. "In just a short while we'll have to get used to addressing her as Mrs. Phelps. I suppose you're terrible busy making plans for the coming nauticals?"

"There is quite a bit to do," Julia agreed. "But I'm blessed with some willing helpers." Indeed her women lodgers, even Mrs. Durwin so recently returned from her honeymoon, and Mrs. Kingston, busy with her own wedding plans, acted as if Julia's special day was the most important to them. The Worthy sisters had wanted to contribute as well. With their gnarled fingers they had spun nine yard lengths of silvery lace for trimming the ecru silk gown presently being assembled by Mrs. Ramsey.

"Well, what might I do for you today?" Mr. Trumble asked after Mrs. Sykes had bade them farewell and left the shop.

Julia produced the list drawn up by Mrs. Beemish. While there were certainly servants capable of shopping, she rather enjoyed taking care of it herself. For most of her life she had been unaware of the goods needed to keep a household properly supplied. Now she found it interesting to stay acquainted with the latest innovations in such things as tooth powder or silver polish.

"I'm afraid I'm out of vinegar until Monday," the shopkeeper murmured, perusing the list. "I'll have to send some over when it comes in. Shall I send the rest this afternoon?"

"Yes, thank you." Glancing to her left, she spotted a familiar canvas sack propped against the postal counter. "I don't suppose you've sorted any of tomorrow's mail, have you?"

His walrus mustache spread over a grin. "Enough to know that there are three letters so far aimed for the *Larkspur*. Would you care for them now?"

They both knew that since Philip had left for school, the question was unnecessary. But as it obviously amused Mr. Trumble to feign ignorance of what her answer would be, Julia repeated her line from the oft-rehearsed script. "If you're sure you wouldn't mind."

"Why, not at all, Mrs. Hollis," he said, stepping from behind the counter.

She looked over the letters after they were handed to her. One was addressed in childish block letters to Gertie, another, bearing a London publisher's return address, was for Miss Rawlins. She recognized Mr. Jensen's handwriting on the one addressed to her. Efficient as always, he was likely confirming that he would be arriving in a little over two weeks as planned.

There was nothing from Philip, but as Mr. Jones was out making rounds now with mail that had come in yesterday, there was always a chance one would appear in the letter box this afternoon. "Thank you, Mr. Trumble," she said and wished him good-day.

"And to yourself," he replied from behind his counter again. Julia was turning to leave when he said, "By the way, Mrs. Hollis, I hope nothing's wrong with any of the vicar's family."

"What do you mean?"

"He hasn't told you, then?"

"Told me what, Mr. Trumble?"

After a second or two of apparently wondering if he should speak any further, he replied, "Well, I'm not supposed to be disgusting what folks get in their mail, but I believe it would be all right to tell you, seeing as how you'll soon be married to the vicar. I was sortin' through this batch earlier, after Mr. Jones had already left, and found a letter addressed to 'Vicar of Gresham, Shropshire.' That's all it said except for the word *URGENT* underneath in big letters."

"That's odd. But if it were family, surely his name would have appeared on the envelope."

Mr. Trumble slapped the countertop. "You know, I didn't think about that. But being unsure if it could wait till tomorrow's delivery, I had Rupert run it over to him."

As Julia left the shop, she thought that Andrew's letter surely had to be the reason he had left the vicarage in such a rush this morning. Andrew still had a mother, as well as five brothers and their families. But again, any of these would have known to include his name—unless the sender was in a frantic hurry. In that case, though, why not send a telegram? And if it *did* involve family, why wouldn't Andrew have informed Elizabeth?

Whatever the problem—and obviously there was one—all she could do about it was pray on her way home, *Father, please be with Andrew and whoever is in need of his ministering.*

———

As the train pulled away from Droitwich Station, the last stop before Worcester, Andrew took Gabriel Patterson's letter from his waistcoat pocket and read it again.

> *Dear Sir,*
>
> *Please pardon me for not recalling your name, but I am sending this letter to you because Philip Hollis once told me that his mother was engaged to marry the vicar of Gresham. I do not think he would forgive me if I were to send this to his mother, because it was obvious to me that he is very protective of her.*
>
> *I was until recently a schoolmate of Philip's, until a prank caused me to fracture my arm. Now that I am no longer at the Josiah Smith Academy, I fear that Philip will bear the brunt of the cruelty that pervades the whole atmosphere of the school. At the time I left, he was most miserable and longed to go home.*

The letter went on to describe some incidents, such as a frog squashed into a textbook and even physical assaults. Behavior that one could expect when dozens of boys were housed under one roof, similar to things Andrew had experienced during his own boarding school years. While he had taken it upon himself to warn Philip to expect such treatment, he had also held the opinion held by most men—that bullies were an inevitable part of life and it built a boy's character to endure them. But it was the last paragraph of the letter that had prevented him from enjoying his breakfast, until he finally felt compelled to grab his hat and coat and hurry down to the Shrewsbury station.

> *Sir, I consider it my good fortune to have broken my arm, for it saved*

374

me from that wretched place. But I saw boys whose spirits were being broken every day. Is not a person's spirit more important than an arm? Will Philip have to wait until he is likewise physically injured before he can escape?

Overly dramatic it was, as if this Gabriel Patterson were an aspiring wordsmith at heart. But combined with Andrew's memory of Philip's declining weight and of the tears he had witnessed on the riverbank the day of the Durwins' wedding, he could not in good conscience ignore the letter. He was not sure what he hoped to accomplish today. Perhaps he would insist that Philip accompany him to meet with the school's headmaster. Or at least be able to reassure himself that he was doing right by keeping silent.

Whatever action he would decide to take, he was glad he had gone ahead and caught the morning train. He had promised to help with archery practice tomorrow, and Sunday was of course out of the question. And Monday seemed too far away, if Philip was as miserable as the letter stated. *Give me discernment, Father*, he prayed.

———

Philip could not tell who had tripped him as he lay with legs splayed across the staircase and his books were being trampled by dozens of pairs of feet hurrying to lectures. The worse part was not that his chin throbbed from violent contact with the edge of a step, but the knot of boys congregating on the landing below for the sole purpose of laughing at him. Glaring down at them, he roused himself to his knees and attempted to gather his textbooks. But no one would stop, until seconds later an authoritative voice demanded, "What's going on here?"

It was the Latin instructor, Mr. Blake, who spoke. "To classes—on with you!" he ordered the boys below while scooping up a chemistry text. When Philip was finally on his feet with textbooks gathered into his arms, Mr. Blake asked him what had happened.

Isn't it obvious? Philip thought, staring dully back at him. Surely any reasonable person could deduce what had happened from the intensity of the jeers launched up at him. *Are all the adults here blind?*

"I tripped, sir," he mumbled.

"Yes? Well, it was bound to happen, the way you boys rush down the stairs. Haste makes waste, you know."

"Yes, sir," Philip told him. "I'll be more careful."

When it happened again an hour later, this time as he was on his way down the busy corridor to another lecture, he forgot about his books and jumped to his feet in time to catch the self-congratulatory jeer Tupper was sending back in his direction. Elbowing his way through the boys between them, he jumped on the upperclassman's back and they both fell to the floor. He flailed into the older boy with his fists as a circle of shouting, laughing boys surrounded them. It was Westbrook who broke up the fight, grabbing Philip by the collar and jerking him to his feet.

"You know better than to touch an upperclassman, Hollis!" he growled. Meanwhile Tupper struggled to his knees, fishing for a handkerchief for his bleeding nose.

"He started it!" Philip answered, matching Westbrook's glare. "And I'll make him even more sorry if he trips me again!"

"I didn't touch you, Hollis!" Tupper exclaimed through the handkerchief held up to his face. "You're as daft as your fat friend!"

Westbrook shoved Philip in the direction of his strewn books. "Go to lecture, Hollis. And you can forget about lunch today—you'll be running laps."

Two hours later, as Philip was rounding the corner of the building to begin his fourth lap, he spotted a hackney cab drawn up the drive by two horses. He had no interest in learning who the passenger might be, so he resumed staring dully at the ground in front of him. Just as he made it to the far side of the building, a familiar voice hailed him.

"Philip?"

Incredulously, he halted and turned. Vicar Phelps stood next to the cab, waving an arm. Philip began running toward him, and forgetting how embarrassed he was at any public displays of affection, he threw himself into the vicar's arms. As he burst into tears against the man's broad shoulder, a hand clapped him gently on the back. "There, there now," the vicar soothed.

After a minute or two of this consolation, Philip became embarrassed and pulled away. "I'm sorry, sir. I just . . ."

Vicar Phelps would not let go of his arm. Narrowing his eyes, he said, "What happened to your chin?"

"I was tripped on the stairs." The memory of being laughed at again was far worse than the dull throbbing of his bruised chin, but he blinked his eyes and forbade any more tears. Then the question finally occurred to him. "Why are you here?"

The vicar's face wore a frown of concern. "To see about you, Philip. Why are you running out here by yourself? Isn't it close to lunchtime?"

Staring at the ground, he replied, "I fought with an upperclassman."

"Yes?"

Quickly Philip felt compelled to explain, lest the vicar think he was a troublemaker. "He tripped me twice, Vicar."

"You didn't have to tell me that, Philip. You're not the sort of boy who picks fights." Vicar Phelps glanced over at the building. "What do you think we should do? Talk with the headmaster?"

Hopelessness deflated Philip's shoulders. This was not Gresham. Beyond extending sympathy, there was nothing the vicar could do. "It won't do any good."

The man scratched at his bearded cheek. "Hmm. Then I suppose we've no other choice. Nip up to your room and collect your belongings while I inform whoever should be concerned that you're leaving."

"Sir?"

"Let's go home. Do hurry, will you? I didn't tell Elizabeth where I was going for fear she might let it slip to your mother. She'll fret herself sick if we miss that last train."

The mention of "home" brought intense longing. "But the money . . . Mother . . ." He swallowed a sob. "I don't want to waste Mother's money, and everybody will think I'm a quitter."

"Your mother will agree with my decision, Philip. No amount of money is as important to her as you are. There's no shame in leaving an intolerable situation. You gave it a try. *I* wouldn't stay in a place where I was repeatedly mistreated. I don't know why we force children to do so."

As Philip was opening his mouth to protest that he really thought he could tough it out for the rest of the school year, the vicar raised a finger to his lips. "If you don't want to spend another night in Worcester, you'll hurry!"

He thought his heart would burst. With a whoop of happiness, Philip caught the vicar into a ferocious embrace, then raced for the door. He was halfway up the stairs when he realized he had not told the vicar that the headmaster would be at lunch. But he thought it best to do as he was told. Fortunately, Westbrook was still at lunch with the rest of his dormitory mates, so he was able to collect his things unmolested.

Passing Westbrook's bed on his way to the door, Philip slowed his steps. Would he not enjoy the memory for years to come of having pitched the monitor's belongings and bedclothes out the window? The temptation lasted only a fraction of a second. God had answered his nightly prayer to take him out of this wretched place. He didn't think an act of pettiness was the proper way to show his gratitude.

"My name is Andrew Phelps, Mr. Houghton," Andrew said to the white-haired man at the head of the faculty table, where he had been directed by a student. "I'm withdrawing Philip Hollis as of this moment."

Headmaster Alfred Houghton swallowed the mouthful he had been chewing when Andrew approached and asked, "Under whose authority?"

"Under the authority that I'll be his father in another three weeks."

Glances were exchanged among the other men at the table. The man seated at the headmaster's right motioned him closer, and a whispered conference took place. Finally straightening, the elderly gentleman inquired, "Has the boy's mother granted permission for him to leave?"

"She will be glad of it, once she hears how your faculty denied your students protection from intense bullying."

Mr. Houghton's cheeks reddened. "It is not our policy to grant refunds, Mr. Phelps."

On impulse, Andrew took the envelope from his pocket. "I have a letter here written by a certain Gabriel Patterson, whom I'm sure you recall left this school with a fractured arm incurred under dubious circumstances. It would make compelling evidence in a court of law. Perhaps some newspapers would be interested as well."

There was another hurried whispered conference, and then the headmaster told him, "Mr. Courtland will draft a cheque. *Excluding* three full month's tuition and board, you understand."

That's better than what I expected, Andrew thought, nodding. Now that he had had a little time to think about it, he was a little stunned that he had taken it upon himself to withdraw Philip. But he knew Julia's heart. Even if she would have recovered nothing of the money, he was certain she would be of the mind that her son's welfare was more important.

They arrived in Shrewsbury at nine o'clock, and then Andrew had to retrieve Rusty and his trap from the livery stable near the station. It was almost ten by the time they reached Gresham. "I still can't believe this day is happening," Philip told him after knocking on the *Larkspur*'s courthouse door.

Andrew smiled back. "It's been a strange one, all right."

"Master Philip?" Mrs. Beemish said after answering the door with candle in hand. "Vicar? Is something wrong?"

For a second it appeared that the boy would wrap his arms around her. "I'm home to stay, Mrs. Beemish!"

"Indeed?" Still looking perplexed, the housekeeper smiled and stepped back out of their way. "Well, your mother turned in just a half hour ago. Perhaps you should wake her?"

Philip started off in that direction but then turned to Andrew. "I'm sure she'll want to speak with you too, sir. Will you come in?"

"My girls will be worried about me," Andrew replied. Dipping into his pocket for the cheque, he handed it out to the boy. "You can explain everything as well as I can. Be sure to give this to her, will you?"

"Is this a cheque?" the boy asked, studying the slip of paper.

"For the remainder of your tuition."

Again Andrew found himself caught up in an exuberant embrace. *I thought boys his age didn't like this sort of thing*, he thought but grinned his pleasure as his back was being pounded. Any misgivings he had entertained on the return train ride had completely vanished.

But by the following morning he realized Julia would be curious as to what had prompted him to leave for Worcester in such a hurry, so he left a little early for archery practice and stopped by the *Larkspur*. She greeted him in the hall, which was thankfully empty for a change, and pressed a quick kiss against his lips before saying a word.

"I take that to mean you're not angry at me?" he said, smiling as his arms circled her waist. He received another kiss in reply, but then she stepped back from his arms at the sound of approaching footsteps in the main corridor.

"Shall I bring some tea, missus?" Sarah asked from the doorway.

"I can stay but a minute," Andrew replied to Julia's questioning look.

Julia thanked the maid anyway, and when she was gone, said, "Philip told me how unhappy he was." Her emerald eyes filled. "I should have made him stay home after his last visit when I noticed his weight loss."

"It's not your fault, Julia. You gave him every chance to tell you what was wrong."

"I only wish he had. He could have spared himself so much misery."

Handing over his handkerchief, Andrew explained, "Well, in his eyes that was the same as running to his mother for protection. Not the sort of thing that a fourteen-year-old boy wants to be known for."

She sighed. "I suppose I'll never understand you men and your pride."

"Just take it as a compliment, dear. We're terrified that you women will find out how weak we really are and decide we're not worth the trouble."

"As if!" But then a smile lit her expression. "I'm terribly grateful to you, Andrew."

"It's no less than what you've done for Elizabeth." Reluctantly he had to add, "And as much as I'd rather stay here and hope to collect another kiss, I assured Mr. Raleigh I would help him set up for practice on the green today. You'll send Aleda on in a bit, won't you?"

"Yes. And no doubt Philip will want to watch." Her brow furrowed slightly. "But tell me . . . how did you know the extent of his unhappiness?"

"I received a letter from a former student who had struck up a friendship with him."

"You did? Philip mentioned no letter to me."

"No? Hmm—I gave it to him on the train." But then Andrew understood. Obviously Philip had only shared with his mother that he had been homesick and miserable, sparing her any details of his mistreatment. And wisely so, for the episode was over and done with now, and she had put herself through enough self-recrimination. "Then let's not mention it to him, shall we? A man likes to keep some things to himself."

As he walked out toward the green, Andrew thought of the waste it was that Julia's late husband had spent so little time with his children. If he had only understood the joy that a family could give a man, surely the gaming halls would have been less of an attraction. But he had seen it more than once during his ministry—men, and sometimes women, who trampled pure gold underfoot in their pursuit of garbage. *God, please strike me dead if I ever become that blind,* he prayed.

"Brush yourself off good now," Seth instructed Thomas on Saturday noon at the back door of their cottage. Sawdust from work on the new stables clung to their clothes and skin and had even managed somehow to creep up under their caps into their hair. He slapped at the front of his coat and raised a cloud, which made him sneeze three times in rapid succession. As he wiped his watering eyes, he heard Thomas laugh.

"Oh, that amused you, did it?" Seth asked. The boy's smile faded a little, uncertainty filling his large eyes. And then he shrieked as Seth lunged at him, caught him at the knees, and heaved him up over his shoulder upside-down like a sack. "This is a sure way to get the sawdust off a boy!" He held both feet tightly and trotted in a circle around the yard with the boy chuckling and bouncing against his back. "Do you find it so funny now?"

"Y-yes, sir!" Thomas replied in a spate of fresh giggles. Smiling, Seth swung him around and lowered him to his feet, then held him by the shoulders until his balance returned. The boy grinned and caught his breath, eyeing Seth as if torn between fear and the hope that he would be pounced upon again.

"I think we're both a mite cleaner now," Seth told him. He bent down to pick up the boy's cap. As he straightened, he heard a noise in the house.

"What was that?" Thomas asked with wide eyes.

"You heard it too?"

"Someone's in the kitchen." Hope suddenly filled his expression, and he started for the door. Seth beat him to it.

"It's not her," he said with his hand upon the knob. He could not allow the boy to rush in and have his hopes crushed. However, they had both heard *something.* And it was Saturday. Had she possibly lost count?

"Something must have fallen, that's all." But as he opened the door, there was a definite sound of movement—too far away to be the pantry, so it had to have come from the kitchen. He stepped into the pantry with Thomas close on his heels when another sound hit his ears.

Pot-rack?

Seth bounded into the kitchen. The guinea stood in the middle of the table, preening his gray speckled feathers as if he had every right to be there.

"I'll get the door, Father," Thomas said from behind. Seth nodded and eased around the table so that he could chase the bird toward the back. With a flutter of wings and an indignant squawk, it jumped from its perch and raced into the pantry. Seth heard the door slam a second later, and then the boy came into the kitchen.

"She's really not here," he said in a small voice.

"I told you she wouldn't be." Seth took a can of tinned beef from the cupboard and injected some cheer into his voice. "But we'll manage just fine. I bought some more ketchup yesterday, and we'll make some sandwiches."

"Perhaps we could invite her to have some with us? I could ride Lucy over and—"

"No, Thomas." Seth shook his head. "We can't do that."

Thankfully, the boy was not given to whining or sulking and helped him set the table. As they ate their sandwiches in silence, Seth thought that he could not blame the boy for missing her. He missed her visits a little himself, but of course how could anyone with a half-eaten tinned beef and ketchup sandwich in hand *not* miss the home-cooked meals? That was the only reason, he told himself, that his heart had jumped in his chest just a little when he had heard the sound earlier in the kitchen.

The following day, Miss Sanders' voice sounded especially pure, like a well-tuned instrument, as she sang "There Is a Fountain" at church. From the corner of his eye he could see how Thomas stared up at her with an enraptured little smile. He thought over the situation and decided that because the boy had grown so fond of her, it would be good to keep some casual contact. His conscience would be soothed as well by his showing her that even though there was no possibility of their having a future together, they could maintain a neighborly acquaintance. "Now remember," he instructed Thomas in a low voice as they waited at the side of the yard after church. "You mustn't ask her about cooking for us, or visiting or anything like that."

"Yes, Father," the boy replied obediently, in spite of the questioning look in his blue eyes.

Seth prompted himself as well. *If she even hints at marriage, I'll change the subject and we'll leave as soon as politely possible.*

Presently Miss Sanders emerged from the building. Thomas hurried over to greet her. "Good day, Miss Sanders!"

"Thomas! How good to see you!"

"It's good to see you too," he replied, basking under her affectionate smile.

Her smile did not waver at Seth's approach, but the expression in her hazel eyes became just a little more formal. "Mr. Langford. How are you?"

"Fine, thank you. And you?"

"Very well, thank you." She nodded toward the lane, where Seth could see one of the older brothers seated at the reins of the Sanders wagon. "I'd best be going now." With a parting smile for Seth and a touch of her hand upon Thomas's shoulder, she walked on toward the wagon.

That came off better than I expected, Seth thought as he hefted himself up in Soot's saddle with Thomas at his side astride Lucy. She had kept her promise about not pursuing him after the seventh Saturday and even seemed to have no bitter feelings about it.

Later, as he and Thomas cleaned the kitchen after a dinner of fried eggs and porridge, the boy looked up from a bowl he was drying and said, "That's the same song."

Seth blinked at him. "What?"

"That song you were humming. It's the same one Miss Sanders was singing this morning."

"Is it indeed?" *Means nothing*, he told himself.

*S*aturday, November nineteenth, dawned cold but windless and sunny, perfect for setting up two targets and marking shooting lines on the village green. Prescott's team, along with any spectators from that village, was due to arrive before ten o'clock. The time was very agreeable to Mr. Pool, for the tournament would likely take a couple of hours. Homemade signboards were propped in conspicuous places along the green, advertising that sandwiches and soup could be purchased at the *Bow and Fiddle*. Not to be outdone, Mr. Johnson planted his own signs next to Mr. Pool's, touting the Scotch eggs, meat pies, and sweets available at his bakery.

And to add their contribution to the event, the Women's Charity Society, of which Mrs. Kingston and Mrs. Durwin were members, had set up a hospitality table to provide free lemonade and samples of cheese donated from the squire's factory. While Mr. Raleigh, Luke Smith, and Vicar Phelps directed members of the archery team in stance drills, villagers exchanged pleasantries and gossip. Miss Clark enlisted the four secondary school boys to carry thirty-six chairs from the town hall for the comfort of any elderly or infirmed spectators.

"You know, we graduated a year too soon," Ben said to Philip while hooking the back of a chair from each elbow to bring outside. "First a merry-go-round and now archery!"

Philip caught up two more chairs in the same manner. "I'm so relieved to be back home, they could form a trapeze team and I wouldn't be jealous."

Sending a curious look at him, Ben asked, "It was that bad?"

"Awful." He gave a feeble shrug because of the weight of the chairs. "But now that it's over, I'm rather glad it happened. I had always dreamed of practicing medicine in a big hospital as my father did, but now I believe I'd like to move back here after university and work with Doctor Rhodes. He's already mentioned wanting me to take over his practice when he's no longer able to make calls."

"That's because you've already lived in the city, but I've never even seen it."

"You don't plan to settle here?"

Ben shook his head. "You can't build big buildings in a village, my friend."

A sadness rose up in Philip's chest at the thought of Gresham without Ben. In spite of his desire to grow up and become a doctor, he also wished he could freeze days like this and return to them whenever he wished. He had never fully appreciated how quickly time passed. But just as the waters of the Bryce, which appeared deceptively motionless most days, the years were constantly flowing and would not return.

"Philip, are you coming?" Ben's voice, from the doorway now, brought him out of his musings.

"Oh." He started for the door again with the chairs still attached to his rapidly fatiguing arms. But his friend did not step aside.

"I don't see how I can do this if you plan to stand there in the way all day," Philip complained.

Ben's expression became uncharacteristically sentimental. "No matter where we live, we'll always be friends. Won't we?"

"Friends to the end." Philip grinned, his mood lightening at once. "And I would shake on that if I had any feeling left in my arms."

———

At a quarter of ten the Prescott team arrived in three wagons, followed by several carriages and wagons of spectators. Andrew, having stepped away from the team just long enough to greet Julia and Grace, caught sight of a familiar carriage being reined to a stop with the others along the edge of the green.

"I take it your friend is here?" Julia said, her eyes bright with amusement as she held her daughter's hand.

Andrew rolled his eyes. "And I'd best leave you now, or I shall be forced to introduce you."

"Actually, I've met him—outside the academy when we fetched Laurel on the Durwins' wedding day. But we were not formally introduced."

"Count yourself blessed."

"Andrew, if he has introduced you to his family, you can't *not* introduce him to your fiancée. Surely he's aware that you're about to be married."

Of course she was right. Andrew sighed and from the corner of his eye spotted the vicar, flanked by his wife and daughter, advancing in their direction as if drawn by a magnet. "Very well, then, Julia. You've been warned. But are you sure you want to subject Grace to his company?"

"I'm not afraid," the girl said with her usual serious expression. She held up the forefinger of her left hand. "I didn't even cry when I caught my finger in the door."

Taking her small hand carefully in his, Andrew studied the bruised fingernail. "Poor Grace! Did it hurt?"

She nodded. "But I still didn't cry."

He kissed the injured spot. "Then you're certainly brave enough to endure this, all right."

"To endure what, eh?" asked Vicar Nippert, arriving at his elbow.

"Oh, just about anything." Andrew smiled and tipped his hat to the two Nippert females. "I would like you to meet my fiancée, Mrs. Hollis, and her youngest daughter, Grace."

"Welcome to Gresham," Julia said, extending her hand. After introductions were finished, Vicar Nippert's toothy smile faded into a concerned purse of the lips.

"Ernestine tells us that you've withdrawn your daughter from Saint Julien's. I say, I do wish she would have asked Ernestine to tutor her. Academic pressure too overwhelming, eh?"

"Not at all." Andrew had already expected on the day he withdrew Laurel that Vicar Nippert would have that impression, so he was able to reply with a smooth, "We founded our own secondary school here, and she wanted to be a part of it."

"Another school, eh?" For just the fraction of a second, something resembling envy passed over the vicar's features. "How interesting."

Mrs. Nippert waved a gloved hand toward Market Lane. "Quite a charming little village you have here."

"Thank you." It was Julia who spoke, and the glance she sent to Andrew seemed to say, *Now, aren't you ashamed for misjudging them?* "We're happy that so many of you could be here today."

"Oh, but I insisted upon it," said Vicar Nippert. "As I explained to my parishioners Sunday past, nothing makes a person appreciate the green of one's own pasture more than experiencing what else is out there, eh?"

Andrew was acutely aware that he and Julia and Gresham had just been insulted, however wide Vicar Nippert's smile now stretched around his prominent teeth. He had to choke back the impulse to point out that just because Saint Jude's windows could not aesthetically rival Saint Stephen's did not mean that Gresham was not as good a place to live as Prescott. Tipping his hat again, he said, "Forgive me, but I'm assisting with the tournament and must return to my duties." He took Julia's elbow. "And Mrs. Hollis and Grace should position themselves behind the Gresham team."

385

"May the best village win, eh?" was the parting shot Vicar Nippert directed to their backs.

"Don't say it, Andrew," Julia whispered as he tensed to turn. When out of earshot, she smiled and added in a low voice, "And thank you for not leaving me with them."

"May the best village win!" Andrew growled. "Is *best* now defined by how many points are scored on a target by school children?"

"It's just one person's opinion, Andrew," she said before leaving him to join the spectators well behind the shooting line of the Gresham target. "Don't allow it to ruin your day."

As if Vicar Nippert has the power to ruin my day! Andrew told himself. He only wished that he had thought to remind Vicar Nippert that archery was a sport designed to build self-discipline and confidence—not a means for one village to lord it over another. Reaching Mr. Raleigh, who was squatted on his heels to fasten a holster quiver to Nate Casper's waist, he leaned down to say, "We have to win this thing!"

"We'll give it all we've got, Vicar," the young man answered, raising his head to give him a bemused expression. "But you know as well as I that there are no guarantees."

The reminder tempered Andrew's ill humor a bit, and he returned his attention to queuing the Gresham children in the order in which they would compete. A third standard student from Prescott was the first to step up to the line, fifteen yards from the target on the right, with six arrows in his quiver. Because both village schools had differing numbers of students in each age group, it had been decided well in advance that the top score from each standard would be counted toward the grand totals at the tournament's end—deciding the winner.

There were hushed murmurings when the boy's first two arrows missed the target. Before pulling another arrow from his quiver he sent an embarrassed glance to a couple among the spectators, and Andrew felt sorry for him. It was not the lad's fault where he happened to live. Andrew's pity gave way to concern when the next shot landed within the innermost red zone to score nine points and raise a great cheer among the spectators assembled behind the Prescott team.

Mary Kerns from Gresham shot next, the sum of her scores amounting to sixteen; two less points than scored by the lad from Prescott. Mentally Andrew attempted to keep a tally of the top scores from each team but lost count between helping Luke fasten arm guards or quiver holsters and holding his breath every time an arrow was aimed at either target. Just as the first fifth standard student from Prescott had stepped up to take his turn, Mr. Raleigh touched Andrew's arm and whispered, "Vicar, perhaps you should sit down for a little while?"

"What do you mean?" Andrew asked, straining to look over the young man's shoulder at the target.

"Frankly, your face is flaming red. It's just a friendly competition, remember?"

That was the last straw. Andrew had looked forward to this day for weeks, and now the person who should get on his knees and thank him every day for granting him forgiveness dared to lecture him? "That's fresh talk coming from someone who wishes to court my daughter!" he seethed through clenched teeth.

He was stunned when Jonathan Raleigh spat back, "Well, her father dropping dead in front of me would put a damper on a courtship, now wouldn't it?"

Two seconds passed when all Andrew could do was gape at the face glaring back at him. Then the absurdity of his own behavior dawned upon him. He gave the young man a sheepish nod. "Sorry. I'll calm myself."

Andrew had to remember that promise when Cyril Towly scored thirty-eight points, the most accumulated by any one student, and stifled the impulse to run over to the boy and embrace him.

He was even more compelled to keep his word a half hour later when Mr. Sykes announced the final scores, declaring the Prescott team the victors by twenty-eight points, and the winner of the handsome plaque the village had commissioned. Handclaps and cheers went up among the people gathered behind the Prescott team. The Gresham spectators were much more subdued.

Get this over with now, Andrew ordered himself. With growing trepidation he hurried to Vicar Nippert's family and waited for a break in the congratulatory handshakes he was exchanging with parishioners. When the vicar noticed him, Andrew thrust out his hand. "Your team played admirably well."

"Why thank you!" Vicar Nippert said, pursing his lips sympathetically while pumping Andrew's hand. "Very big of you to say so!"

"Thank you." Andrew bade him and his family good day, but the other vicar did not release his grip upon his hand.

"Another tournament in the spring might be worth some thought, eh? It would be our turn to host, of course."

That was the last thing Andrew wanted to think about at the moment, but he responded with a polite, "That would be up to Mr. Raleigh and the school board. Why don't you write them?" Finally Andrew's hand was free, and with a tip of his hat, he turned and returned to where the team was still assembled. And what he saw shamed him.

While his first concern had been proving to Vicar Nippert that he could be a good sport, Mr. Raleigh's first thought had been for the children who had participated. Parents waited in the background as the schoolmaster patted shoulders and reminded the students that they were still new at this sport and had performed admirably. "We don't measure our worth to God by a few inches on a target, now do we?" Andrew heard him say.

It was wrong of me to subject them to this, Jonathan thought after the students scattered to their families. He had introduced archery as a tool to make his time in the classroom easier, not giving a thought to how losing a competition would affect the children. *They're too young. I should have waited until they've had more experience.*

"Should we gather up the equipment now?" Luke Smith's voice, whistling through his gaping teeth at the word *should*, interrupted his self-recrimination.

"Huh? Oh yes—thank you." Jonathan held a bow vertically against the ground, stepped his right foot through the space, and flexed it enough to remove the string. He felt a touch upon his back and turned to find Vicar Phelps staring at him. The words he had said during the heat of competition came rushing back to him, causing heat to rise in his face. "Vicar. What I said—"

"You did well, Mr. Raleigh."

Oddly, the vicar's hazel eyes were warm. Jonathan waved a hand toward the two targets. "All this was too soon. It only served to discourage them."

"Children are heartier than you think. Of course they wanted to win. We all wanted to. But this was only a sporting competition, not a life-or-death issue. Something that I forgot myself for a while. Thank you for calling me down when I was making a fool of myself."

Now Jonathan's cheeks burned like flatirons. "I had no right to do that, Vicar."

"You had every right." He actually grinned. "And it was funny too—that part about my dropping dead."

Not trusting himself to smile, just in case he was being set up for a tongue-lashing, Jonathan said, "I appreciate you saying that."

"I meant it." Vicar Phelps glanced past Jonathan for a second, then raised a hand to grip his shoulder lightly. "You know, while we've had our fun, Elizabeth has been hard at work with the charity ladies at the lemonade table. Why don't I help Luke here, and you go on over to see her? Perhaps a nice walk would be pleasant, don't you think? Then you join us at the vicarage for lunch."

"Why, yes. Thank you, sir."

The older man took the unstrung bow from his hands. "Good enough . . . Jonathan."

While Mercy's father had declared himself too busy to watch Jack and Edgar compete in the tournament, at least he had allowed Fernie and Oram to accompany her without too much grumbling. "You might as well get some o' them meat pies, since you ain't gonter be here to cook," he had even told Mercy, handing her some coins as she prepared to leave the cottage. "I don't fancy any more of thet tinned meat."

After the tournament was over, Mercy told her brothers to stay within sight of the wagon and hurried over to the bakery. Others had the same idea, for a queue of at least a dozen people from both villages had already formed, stretching until half waited outside the doors. She took her place at the end. The line moved quickly, for obviously Mr. Johnson had anticipated the rush of customers and prepared for them in advance. She was inside the shop and about fifth from the counter when she recognized the back of Mr. Langford's head as he gave his order. He turned a minute later, a parcel wrapped in brown paper under his arm. He had to pass by her in order to leave the shop. Still, Mercy was a little surprised when he stopped.

"Miss Sanders," he said with a smile that seemed almost bashful.

"Hello, Mr. Langford," she replied, returning his smile. "Where is Thomas?"

"He asked to sit in the wagon and watch the people still on the green. Did you enjoy the tournament?"

The woman in front of Mercy, who had been chatting with the woman in front of her, now held her head at a listening angle. This intimidated her, but even more intimidating was the prospect of having to tell Mrs. Kingston that she had failed to follow her advice. "Very much," Mercy replied before pretending to study the chalked signboard above the counter.

From the corner of her eye she watched him shift the parcel awkwardly to his other hand. After a second he said, "Good day, Miss Sanders."

She turned to smile at him again, as if she had momentarily forgotten he was standing there. "Good day, Mr. Langford. Please give my regards to Thomas."

"Yes, I will."

Did I overdo it? she wondered as a cold, miserable clamminess spread in her stomach. *Should I have looked away like that?* By the time she exited the bakery with her parcel, she had convinced herself that she had come just a fraction short of slapping the man's face.

"It was washing the cups so they could be used over and over that kept us busiest," Mrs. Kingston explained, her gloved hand resting in the crook of Squire Bartley's arm as they strolled along the west side of the green. "We had already made the crocks of lemonade yesterday."

Her fiancé's untamed eyebrows drew together sympathetically. "You poor dear. I could have had my servants helping you."

"Oh, but they would have missed the tournament. We were happy to do it."

Several feet away Mrs. Kingston caught sight of Mercy Sanders, handing a parcel to a lad in the back of their wagon. She wore a wool shawl over a brown calico dress, and the expression of someone deep in thought. "I'd like you to meet someone, Thurmond," she said, waving a beckoning hand. "Mercy, dear?"

The girl looked over at her and waved back. After saying something to the boy in the wagon, she walked over to join them. "Mrs. Kingston," she said, smiling.

"This is my fiancé, Squire Bartley," Mrs. Kingston said. "Mercy Sanders. She's the dear child who has agreed to sing at our wedding."

The girl blushed charmingly, dipping a timid curtsey to the squire. "I'm pleased to make your acquaintance, sir."

He touched the brim of his hat. "The pleasure is mine, Miss Sanders. Mrs. Kingston speaks highly of you."

"Mrs. Kingston is most kind, sir."

"Truthful, you mean," Mrs. Kingston corrected. "Tell me, has a certain young man spoken with you since we last met?"

"Ah . . . yes, ma'am."

Mercy sent an embarrassed glance toward the squire, who rolled his eyes. "I'll step over here and have a word with Mr. Sykes."

When he was out of earshot, the girl went on. "In the bakery just a little while ago. And at church last Sunday."

"Indeed? And how did you respond?"

She bit her lip. "I'm afraid I was rude."

"Nonsense."

"But you didn't hear how I—"

"I know you, Mercy, and you're incapable of rudeness. You're just digging up in doubt what was planted in faith."

"Am I?"

"Of course." Mrs. Kingston touched the girl's cheek. "Now stop tormenting yourself, dear child, and keep your mind on other things. This is a major commitment we're asking of Mr. Langford. We must give him time to think, mustn't we?"

The smile Mercy gave her appeared to require some effort, but at least some of the worry had eased from her expression. "I'll try to have more faith."

After they embraced, Mrs. Kingston watched the girl return to the wagon. The boy at the reins called to three other boys, who ran from the green to hop into the back.

The two horses were pulling the wagon onto Market Lane when the squire reappeared. His gray eyes followed the course of the wagon. "The Sanderses have had quite a notorious reputation for years. It was good of you to take that young woman under your wing, Octavia, and teach her the proper way to conduct herself."

She took his proffered arm, and they ambled toward the river. "She knew that long before I ever met her, Thurmond."

"Yes? I suppose there are nuggets of gold in every field."

"An appropriate description. I'm just hoping someone else recognizes the gold in her as well."

"Ah, so you're offering her advice on courtship?"

"Not exactly. You see, the reputation of her family has prevented her from being courted in the usual manner. So we've embarked upon a rather radical plan. Your willingness to hire her as a parlormaid was part of it, by the way."

"I didn't realize I was a co-conspirator."

"Oh, but you were, Thurmond—a very important part of the plan."

He chuckled. "Well, I hope it works. But I must say, I'm glad you and I have always enjoyed a straightforward courtship. I suppose maturity is the main factor. There has never been a need for intrigue between us."

Patting his arm, Mrs. Kingston coyly agreed. "It's the maturity, Thurmond."

———

"I can't believe my father suggested we walk together," Elizabeth told Jonathan as they strolled along the willows lining the Bryce. She kept her wool wrap drawn tightly about her so that she would be unable to take his arm. That would have been enough for the dozens of people still visiting on the green to link them together romantically. And after much thought, she had taken Julia's advice to heart about not making a reconciliation *too* easy. Her father had done his part. Now it was her turn.

"He practically insisted upon it," Jonathan said, wonder lighting his aristocratic face. "And he even addressed me as *Jonathan*!"

"No!"

"But he did. And I was afraid that after losing the tournament, he would despise me even more so."

They paused to exchange pleasantries with Mrs. Kingston and the squire, coming from the opposite direction. As they then moved on, Elizabeth told him, "My father didn't *despise* you, Jonathan."

"Never?" Her gave her a skeptical look.

"Well . . . perhaps for a little while."

"And what about his oldest daughter?"

She was unable to resist. "Perhaps for a little while longer."

"I deserved that," he winced.

They stopped walking at the bridge before turning back toward the vicarage. Even though Elizabeth was determined to allow their relationship to strengthen in small stages, she would draw the line at being unreasonable and cruel. "At one time, perhaps," she replied. "But no longer. You've asked my forgiveness, and you have it."

Jonathan's gray-green eyes acquired a sheen. "I have?"

"Yes, Jonathan. I'll not mention the past again."

"Dear Elizabeth! If only you could know how much I've prayed for this to happen!" For fear he would embrace her—and that she would allow it—she instinctively took a step backward and without her arms free to balance herself, lost her footing on the decline of the bank. Jonathan reached out both arms to steady her. He held her arms for only a second before dropping his hands back to his sides.

"Thank you, Jonathan," she said, more for the letting go than for his helping her regain her balance. They resumed their walk in the direction of the vicarage.

Still looking straight ahead, he cleared this throat. "You know, I came here assuming that because I had become a Christian, you would realize that I had changed and forgive me right away. Perhaps even come away with me to Cambridge." Now he looked at her. "After marrying me, of course."

It was the first time he had ever mentioned marriage to her. Aware of a blush stealing in her cheeks, Elizabeth did not trust herself to speak. Thankfully, he did not seem to resent her silence and went on after a spell.

"I was naïve and had no concept of restoration. I never thought I would feel this way, Elizabeth, but there were lessons here that I needed to learn."

"Lessons?"

He nodded. "Everything has been easy for me my whole life. School marks, sports—even joining my uncle's firm. He would have hired me had I been at the bottom of my class. By coming here and facing an uphill struggle with you—and with your father and with the school—I've grown to realize the joy that comes from little victories is preferable to the fun that comes from ease and the pursuit of pleasure."

"And what victories have you had, Jonathan?"

"Perhaps that's not the best word." He rubbed his chin thoughtfully. "I can't seem to think of a more appropriate one. But I'm referring to things I would not have known how to appreciate just a year ago. The children finally respecting me at school. Your father addressing me as Jonathan. Your walking with me like this." Turning to smile at her, he added, "And above all, your forgiveness."

She smiled back, thinking about the things she had learned as well. To distance herself from the emotions of her situation enough to see where a decision would affect her some ten, twenty years from now. Waiting could sometimes be a good thing, for had she thrown herself into Jonathan's arms the first time he appeared on the vicarage doorstep, she would not have allowed him to learn the lessons that were now obviously so important to him. She would share these things with him one day, she told herself. But for now, it seemed her heart was telling her that the waiting needed to go on just a little longer.

*T*he following day, Mrs. Jones had just begun the introductory notes of the closing hymn, "O Thou, in Whose Presence," when from his back row pew Seth heard the church door slam open. He twisted in his seat just in time to stare into the bloodshot eyes of one of the older Sanders boys. Swaying a little, the young man walked up the aisle. Reverend Seaton stopped singing to stare from his pulpit in disbelief, causing the voices of the few people up front who had not noticed the sound of the door to taper off. Mrs. Jones continued to play the piano, squinting with concentration at the hymnal propped open in front of her.

"Who is that, Father?" Thomas whispered from his side.

"Miss Sanders' brother," Seth whispered back. He considered getting up and escorting the young man outside but knew he could not do so without incurring some sort of scene. One look at Miss Sanders' face—white as whey as she rose to her feet from the front row—told him that it would be easier on her if she just left with her brother.

But it soon became apparent that fetching his sister was the last thing upon his sodden mind. Muttering to himself, the young man ambled over to a pew in the center of the church and dropped to his knees in the aisle.

"Why don't you love me, Mary?"

Over time Seth had learned most of the names of the small congregation. Even if he had not, it was obvious to whom the young man spoke. Mary Sloane, a serving girl at the *Bow and Fiddle*, sat at the end of the pew in crimson-faced humiliation.

Reverend Seaton reached the young man just as he was asking the question a second time. "You have to leave now, Mr. Sanders," he insisted calmly over the notes still coming from the piano.

The young man's back was to Seth, but from the thickness in his voice, it was apparent that tears had begun to flow. "But she don't ever speak to me when I come in the *Bow and Fiddle*!" He drew in a loud sniff, then wiped his coat sleeve across his nose. "She speaks to other people. I see her!"

"Why is he doing that?" Thomas whispered.

"He's drunk," Seth replied. *And stupid.*

Finally Mrs. Jones, in the pause between the first and second verse, looked out at the congregation and stopped playing abruptly. Miss Sanders walked down the aisle, chin lowered and shoulders set at an angle that suggested she was struggling to maintain control. The young man was content to sob until the pastor put his hand upon his shoulder and said with gentle firmness, "Why don't you wait outside in your wagon and I'll drive you home?"

With a roar of rage the man seized the hand and pulled himself to his feet. "I ain't leaving till Mary tells me she loves me!" He was drawing his arm back to launch his fist at the pastor when Seth jumped up, caught the man's arm, and twisted it behind his back.

"Outside!" he whispered fiercely into his ear.

"You're breakin' my—"

"Now!"

Still maintaining his grip, he forced the man to turn and head for the door. He let go only when they were outside and the door had closed behind them. The man spun around, crouched down as if to spring, and fixed him with a lethal glare. "I'm gonter kill you!"

Seth tensed for an attack just in case and hoped the situation would not escalate into a brawl right outside the church door. Raising a placating hand, he said, "You would do better to go home and sleep it off, don't you think?"

The door opened before the young man could make good on his threat and Miss Sanders walked out. She did not look at Seth, but he could see where crimson splotches replaced the earlier chalk white color of her face.

"Please go to the wagon, Dale," she said in a subdued tone. "It's time to go home now."

"But he broke my arm!" her brother protested with a spray of saliva.

"Your arm is fine. Please."

He motioned toward the door. "Mary . . ."

"You embarrassed her, Dale. Please go to the wagon."

At last her words seemed to pierce the haze of alcohol. Shoulders slumping with resignation, he turned and wove his way toward the lane where the horses and wagon waited. Miss Sanders finally looked at Seth. "Thank you, Mr. Langford."

With a skeptical glance at the wagon, Seth said, "Will he be able to get you home safely? Thomas and I could hitch our animals to the back and—"

"The horses know the way by now. But again, thank you."

It was the same politeness with which she had spoken to him yesterday. But this time he could see that the eyes were different. Tears gathered in the corners of her eyes, while their liquid depths revealed a painful mixture of humiliation and resignation. He had seen that expression innumerable times in the faces of his fellow convicts at Newgate.

"Miss Sanders?"

She had taken a couple of steps away from him but paused and turned to give him a questioning look. Unsure of why he had stopped her, Seth raised a hand helplessly while all he could think to say was, "I'm sorry."

Miss Sanders shook her head. "You've naught to be sorry for, Mr. Langford. But please explain to Thomas why . . ." She didn't finish but made a motion toward her brother, attempting to climb the spokes of a wagon wheel.

"I already have."

"Good."

You can't marry a woman out of pity! Seth told himself, watching the young man snap the reins as she sat beside him with her chin raised and her hands folded in her lap. There were things in the world beyond his control.

That afternoon as Thomas napped, Seth poured himself a cup of luke-warm tea and pulled out a chair at the kitchen table. He rested his elbows upon the table top and thought about the span of his life. Once he had loved with the whole essence of his being. When that was taken from him, he determined that the damage done to his heart now rendered it incapable of anything but pumping blood through his veins.

And then came Thomas. It was a different kind of love than what he had felt for Elaine, and yet it brought the same joy and contentment to his every waking moment. He had not purposed or expected to love Thomas in the beginning—only to provide him with a home. God had touched his heart while he was unaware of it even happening. Could He do the same again?

He took a sip of the tea, now tepid, and looked over at the curtain Mercy Sanders had mended. Even with nothing but a row of neat stitches of thread to prove she had ever been here, the kitchen seemed lacking something vital. Yet a room was not capable of feelings. Was it his heart that missed her? Only two hours ago he had reckoned himself feeling only pity for her, but would mere pity for a human being cause the ache he now felt in his soul as he remembered the sadness in her eyes?

Father, please . . . I need some clarity of thought, he prayed. *I don't want to do anything that would ultimately cause her more pain.*

The next morning he prepared a pot of porridge, then packed the lunch pail while Thomas ate breakfast. He was coming from the pantry with an apple in hand when the boy looked up at him, his laden spoon paused over his bowl. "May I have two today, Father?"

"Two? Certainly." The apple trees along the creek behind the pasture were as prolific as Miss Sanders had said, and he could have packed a dozen if he had wished. But for Thomas's small size, even two seemed unusual. Stepping back into the kitchen with another apple, he asked, "Am I not packing you enough food?"

Thomas's cheeks turned a faint shade of pink, and he glanced away before replying, "I want to give it to someone."

Mr. Raleigh, Seth realized. Of course. He had heard somewhere, or read in a story, that children sometimes brought apples to their teachers. He tossed the apple up in the air and caught it again. "You can bring Mr. Raleigh one every day if you like, Thomas. We've more than enough."

Oddly, the pink seemed to deepen. Glancing away again, the boy said, "It's not for Mr. Raleigh."

"Oh." And then Seth caught on. *At seven years old?* He had to walk over to the cupboard to hide a smile. "What's her name?" he asked casually when he could trust himself to speak again.

There was a hesitation and then a barely audible, "Grace Hollis."

"She's nice, huh?"

The boy nodded. "She showed me her smashed fingernail."

Seth's smile returned at odd hours of the morning, long after the boy had left on his pony's back for school. He found himself wishing he had someone with whom he could share the exchange that had occurred at breakfast. Mercy Sanders came immediately to his mind. Next to himself, she cared more about Thomas than did anyone, and it would certainly lighten the sadness in her eyes to hear that the boy's young heart had been captured by a little girl with a bruised fingernail. But of course, it was unthinkable to make any sort of social call next door.

Yet less than an hour later, he found himself walking the half mile down the lane. He had at least figured out a small way to help her. It was ludicrous of Mr. Sanders to refuse to allow his daughter to ride to and from chapel with him and Thomas when they passed right by their cottage every Sunday. Especially now, after he had allowed her to cook meals at his cottage for seven weeks in a row. And surely upon seeing the condition of his son yesterday, he would be more amenable to reason. *She wouldn't have to worry about being humiliated like that again.*

Over the hedgerow he caught sight of her on the west side of the cottage, hanging clothes upon a line stretched between two posts. A capricious wind whipped wet shirtsleeves and trouser legs into odd flapping movements, while from a kettle nearby, wisps of steam were sent up in all directions. She did not look his way, and he saw no other human outside. Voices drifted from the other side of the cottage door as he drew nearer. He was glad she was outside and knocked lightly so that she would not come to investigate. If he was to be throttled by a horde of Sanderses, he didn't want her to see it.

The door was opened by the younger looking of the two boys who had sold him the guineas. After gaping at Seth for a second, he stepped back and motioned to someone out of sight.

"Well, who is it?" demanded a recognizable voice.

"It's me, Mr. Sanders," Seth replied, taking the initiative and stepping across the threshold. What he saw irritated him immensely. While Mercy Sanders struggled outside with wet clothing, her father sat at the fireplace carving a short piece of wood, pipe in his mouth, and feet resting on a pile of shavings. The oldest three glared at him from the table, with playing cards fanned out in their hands. A pile of cards lying face down in front of an empty chair told Seth that he'd interrupted their game. On the stove behind them, a black pot made soft bubbling noises and sent up the same savory aroma that had permeated his kitchen on a rainy Saturday past.

Mr. Sanders took the pipe from his mouth. "What do you want?"

Forgetting the intention of his visit, he said, "I don't see how any of you can relax with your daughter out there working."

The man's green eyes narrowed. "What's it to you?"

"Yeah, what's it to him, huh, Papa?" said one of the younger boys at the table.

Returning Mr. Sanders' scowl, Seth replied, "It just pains me to see someone treated so unfairly."

"We done the mornin' milking already. She's got her chores, and we've got ours."

"Well, when do hers stop?"

"Want us to throw him out, Papa?" This came from Dale, who had made such a spectacle of himself at church yesterday. Two other brothers echoed the question.

The older man ignored them, but pointing the knife at Seth, he said, "You sure didn't mind her cookin' for you all those times, did you?"

That stung. "I had no idea she was so overworked . . . and under appreciated."

"If you're so concerned, why don't you go out there and help her?"

"Maybe I will." Seth swept a distasteful glance across all of them, turned on his heel, and left. Behind him the door slammed with such force that his already-pounding heart jumped in his chest. He stalked around to the west side of the cottage, where Miss Sanders now stood holding a wet shirt and stared in his direction. The wind had whipped color into her cheeks and pulled curls from her ribbon to dance about her face.

"Mr. Langford?"

"Miss Sanders." The shirt was an irritation because it belonged to one of the men loafing inside. He took it from her and tossed it into the basket at her feet, admiring his own restraint for not dropping it on the ground. Seth had no idea what he was about to say until the words started spilling out of his mouth. All he knew was that it felt good to say them. "I don't know that I will ever love you. But your presence in our home is a comfort to me . . . and to my son. If you still wish to marry me, I'll treat you kindly and sit with you in chapel as you asked."

She stared back at him, unspeaking, for so long that Seth began to worry that her recent cool politeness had been because she had changed her mind. He cleared his throat, which seemed to snap her out of some sort of reverie.

"Mr. Langford," she said, pushing curls from her face, while the rims of her eyes turned as red as her cheeks. "I would only want you to marry me because I would make you a good wife. Not because I cried yesterday."

"I want to marry you because you will make a good wife," he answered. *And because your tears touched something in my heart*, he thought but didn't know how to express it.

"Thank you, Mr. Langford." She put a hand up to cover her lips, which he suspected were trembling.

Seth felt suddenly lighthearted. Strange, in view of the fact that he was making a commitment of such monumental proportion. "A woman doesn't thank a man for asking her hand, Miss Sanders. You do me the honor of accepting my proposal. And speaking of which . . . I'm supposed to ask your father's permission. Not that it matters, because we can marry as soon as Thomas returns from school, if Reverend Seaton is willing."

"Today?" Mercy looked around her, grasping for her bearings. How could she have imagined as she carried the basket of wash out of doors less than an hour ago that *he* would appear and change the whole course of her life? But as disoriented as she felt, there was no confusion in her mind over the haste of his wedding plans. Her heart had taken up residence in the cottage next door a long time ago.

Her sense of duty then pushed itself to the forefront of her mind, and with great reluctance she asked, "May we wait until Saturday? I would like Mrs. Kingston to be there and to give my father some time to look for a cook."

"Saturday it is, then," he smiled.

Mercy could feel her pulse pounding at the base of her throat. In every novel she had ever read, engagements were sealed with a kiss. She did not expect that. Their marriage was to be based upon mutual benefit, not romance. But then Mr. Langford did the second-best thing. He reached down into the basket and picked up the shirt by the shoulder seams. With an expert snap that reminded her that he had been washing clothes at his own cottage for a while, he said, "We'll finish this little chore before speaking to your father so you won't have to return to it. And from the looks of things, your brothers' card playing days may become a little scarce."

Ten minutes later, as they walked toward the front of the cottage together, he stopped to face her, his expression suddenly grave. "I forgot to tell you something, Miss Sanders."

Mercy's heart sank. It had been too good to be true after all. "Y-yes?"

His chest rose and fell. "I was released from Newgate prison four months ago, after serving ten years."

"Ten years?"

"My sentence was for twenty, but my accusers came forth with proof of my innocence and I was set free."

She was torn between pity for him and her own relief that he was not calling off the wedding. "Mr. Langford, it was unnecessary to tell me that you were innocent. You're the most decent man I know besides Reverend Seaton."

He was clearly much relieved by this and reached for the doorknob. "Well, then . . . good. Let's get this over with."

Her father and brothers directed hostile stares at Mr. Langford as soon as they walked through the doorway, causing Mercy to appreciate just how difficult it must have been for him to come here. "We have something to ask you, Papa," she began in a shaky voice.

She felt a touch upon her sleeve. "I'll do it," the man beside her said in a voice as strong as hers was weak. Taking a step closer to her father's chair, he said, "Mr. Sanders, your daughter has consented to marry me, and we ask for your blessing."

As Mercy expected, her father jumped to his feet and accused her of being disloyal. Her brothers echoed that sentiment in the background. All the while Mercy stood with Mr. Langford, and out of respect, she allowed her father to have his say. But when he began to weep copious tears, telling her how much she reminded him of her dear departed mother, Mercy felt the scene had gone on long enough.

"The wedding will be today or Saturday, Papa," she said quietly. "You decide."

He dropped back down in his chair again and wiped his eyes. His pride would not allow him to answer, but the tight-lipped nod he gave Mercy was his way of choosing the latter.

Word of the wedding quickly spread among her tiny circle of friends, so when Saturday afternoon came, the first two rows at the Wesleyan Chapel were filled. On the front pew sat Thomas, Mrs. Seaton and her children, Mrs. Jones, Mrs. Kingston and Squire Bartley, and Mr. Trumble. Her father and brothers took up the second pew, managing to look at least cordial. With them sat Mrs. Winters, a fifty-year-old widow with broad shoulders and a stubborn set of the jaw. The reputation of Mercy's family had made finding a cook more difficult than imaginable, and so it was comical to see the males of her family taking it upon themselves to make life easier for their new house help.

She had seen Mr. Langford—she could not imagine addressing him as anything else—only once since Tuesday, when he had measured her finger with a piece of yarn for the gold band he would purchase in Shrewsbury. He had obviously made some purchases for himself and Thomas as well, for with their Sunday suits they wore new white silk cravats. Mercy, having not had time to sew, wore her newest gown of dove gray crepeline and over her chignon a length of lace purchased from the Worthy sisters. She did have three new nightgowns of lace-trimmed linen in her trousseau. Mrs. Kingston had made a special trip to Shrewsbury to purchase them, along with a silver fruit bowl. Mercy had been too embarrassed to tell her that the silver bowl would likely be more practical than the beautiful gowns, for this was not to be a marriage of the usual sort.

The ceremony was brief. Reverend Seaton read from the thirteenth chapter of Corinthians about "charity" and then had them repeat the vows. Mercy could hardly look at the man with whom she was pledging her troth, and indeed, he seemed to be struggling with shyness himself and directed his gaze in the vicinity of her eyebrows. Afterward there was cake and punch in the parsonage, for which Mr. Trumble could not stay because he had to reopen the shop. Her father and brothers stayed only long enough to consume their slices of cake and cups of punch, but at least they were polite, and Edgar even embraced Mercy before they left.

As soon as the door had closed behind her family, Mrs. Kingston called Mercy aside to say in a low voice, "The boy—Thomas. Would you like us to bring him back to the *Larkspur*? I'm sure Philip Hollis wouldn't mind sharing his bed for tonight."

Mercy was unable to look her friend in the eyes. Twisting the gold ring upon her finger, she murmured, "No, thank you, Mrs. Kingston."

"Are you quite sure?"

Impulsively she stood on tiptoes to kiss the softly wrinkled cheek. "But thank you for everything you've done for me. This is all because of you."

"Well, we must give God due credit," her friend reminded her while looking immensely pleased.

"Every day," Mercy agreed. *Every hour*, she corrected herself silently, for surely she had thanked Him that often since Tuesday.

It was half-past five when she walked across the threshold of Mr. Langford's cottage as the lady of the house. *I hope you can see this, Mrs. Brent*, she thought. While her husband and Thomas fed the horses and cattle—

seven, counting the six that Mrs. Brent had given her—she went upstairs to unpack the small tin trunk her brothers had delivered yesterday. It was in the spare bedroom, as she had supposed it would be.

Presently she heard the murmur of voices and went downstairs, where Mr. Langford and Thomas sat in front of the fireplace. They had saved the rocking chair for her. When she had sat down at their insistence, she noticed the boy was holding a parcel wrapped in brown paper. He approached her with flushed excitement, "We bought a gift for you in Shrewsbury, Miss Sanders."

Mercy did not correct him and appreciated that her husband did not either, though he sent her an apologetic look. This was new to all of them. "Why, you shouldn't have."

"But we wanted to," Thomas replied, grinning. He rose and placed the parcel in her lap, then shifted his weight from one foot to another while she carefully unwound the paper. It was a small hinged box of glossy jet paper-mache, about the size of her Bible, painted with colorful roses and birds.

"It's beautiful," Mercy breathed.

"You use the latch to raise the lid—see? You can keep things inside."

She did as instructed, opening it up to reveal a lining of royal blue velvet. And then music began to tinkle forth. "The shopkeeper said it's by a man named Mr. Mozart," Thomas explained.

Mercy shook her head in awe as the box blurred in her vision. "I've never owned anything so beautiful." She sat there listening to the music while Thomas got on his knees at the side of her chair and assigned himself the task of rewinding it when necessary. Mr. Langford presently went into the kitchen to make bacon sandwiches for supper. He apologized for his lack of cooking skills but was adamant that she should not have to cook her first night there. After supper the three of them played a game of dominos, also purchased in Shrewsbury, at the table.

Soon it was time for Thomas to go to bed. Mercy stood with head bowed at the foot of the bed while Mr. Langford led the boy in a prayer. When it was over and his father had tucked the quilt around his shoulders, Thomas's wide eyes studied Mercy. "Are you my mother now?"

Mercy glanced at Mr. Langford, who gave her a slight nod.

"Yes, Thomas."

"May I call you 'Mother'?"

"I would be honored, Thomas," she replied over a lump in her throat. She moved to the side of the bed as Mr. Langford stepped back out of her way and leaned down to press a kiss upon the boy's forehead.

"Are you all right?" Mr. Langford asked when they were outside the boy's door.

She nodded but had to dab at her eyes with her knuckles. "I wasn't expecting that."

They returned downstairs to their chairs at the fireplace. He began sharing with her his dreams of selling horses, and he answered her questions about prison. Kindly Seth also asked questions about her life, but there was little she could tell him. As far as she was concerned, her life had only begun two years ago. *That was when Mrs. Brent and you came into my life, Father,* she prayed during one of their comfortable silences.

Somewhere during that discourse, they began to address each other by their first names. And then when darkness pressed itself against the windowpanes, her husband got to his feet, took two steps over to her chair, and held out a hand. "Will you come upstairs with me, Mercy?"

Mercy stood, taking his hand, somehow aware that he was not referring to the extra room that housed her tin trunk. They walked upstairs in silence, while she berated herself for being too embarrassed to ask Mrs. Kingston or Mrs. Seaton for any information beyond her vague notion of what was to happen. It was only when they paused outside the door to his room that she regained control of her voice enough to confess, "I'm not exactly sure what I'm supposed to do, Mr. Langford."

"Seth," he gently reminded her.

"Seth."

To her surprise, he smiled and touched her cheek. "We'll have to teach each other, Mercy Langford."

———

One week later, Seth smiled at the memory of that night as he and Thomas sawed and hammered boards to construct new stables behind the hay barn. A wind from the west carried to them the aroma of bread baking in the kitchen. His cottage truly seemed like a home now.

He was not yet sure if what he held in his heart for his wife was love, but of one thing he was absolutely certain. There was not a man on earth with whom he would trade places—not even with a bushel of gold thrown in.

*P*lease remember to bring us each back a playbill," Mrs. Dearing reminded Julia in the dining room on the fifth of December as her lodgers made suggestions for the eight days she would be honeymooning in London. Their gaiety warded off any feelings of melancholy, just as the fire snapping in the grate warded off the chill of the evening.

It was not that Julia was not looking forward to her wedding the next morning. But she could not help but be mindful of the fact that this was her last supper as manager of the *Larkspur*, for she and her children would be moving into the vicarage as soon as she and Andrew returned.

"I'll be happy to," Julia replied, smiling. Tomorrow Mr. Jensen would move from his place between Mr. Pitney and the end of the table to take her position at the head. Professional to the core, he had learned his duties quickly during the past week so that she could concentrate on wedding plans. If it seemed strange to her that a man who had spent most of his sixty years in servitude now occupied a place at the main table, she could only imagine how odd he must feel. Still, her former butler was most pleasant, if just a bit reticent.

Miss Rawlins nodded her agreement to Mrs. Dearing's request. "And, Mrs. Hollis, if you could somehow persuade Mr. Clay to procure a poster, it would look quite nice in the hall."

"A poster would be lovely!" Mrs. Kingston declared, clasping her hands together. "Oh, but we should have it framed so the corners wouldn't curl. Do see that it's rolled up carefully, will you, Mrs. Hollis?"

"And perhaps you could ask all of the actors and actresses to sign their names," Mr. Ellis suggested.

Holding his fork, upon which a small potato was impaled, just above his plate, Mr. Durwin said, "That would certainly add to its worth. Although I can't imagine that you would ever desire to sell something with such sentimental value."

"But the autographs would still be interesting to look at." This came in a hopeful tone from Mrs. Durwin. "Do you agree, Mr. Pitney?"

Julia smiled to herself at how the rest of the lodgers had joined Mr. Ellis's mission of drawing Mr. Pitney into mealtime conversation.

"It's very interesting to see how people sign their names," the archeologist replied in his usual bashful manner.

"I wonder if Mr. Clay's picture is on the poster?" Aleda asked after receiving permission from Julia to join the discussion.

"Surely it is," Mrs. Kingston theorized. "After all, he has the lead role."

Mr. Jensen finally spoke. "I'm afraid it is not."

Eyes widening with interest, Mrs. Dearing looked across at him. "You have *seen* the poster, Mr. Jensen?"

"Actually, Mrs. Dearing, I have seen *The Barrister* as well. Mrs. Clay was kind enough to send me some tickets."

Julia had worried that Mr. Jensen would be too set in his ways to drop the deferential "sir" and "madam" from his vocabulary, but he had done so admirably. While he was there to provide for the comfort of the lodgers, it was important for the smooth operation of the house that his not be considered a servile position.

"Well, what *is* on the poster?" Mr. Durwin asked.

After a thoughtful pause, Mr. Jensen replied, "A wig, a gavel, and a toy tin trumpet strewn across the face of a legal brief, if my memory serves me correctly." He looked at Julia. "The colors are most vibrant and would indeed be quite becoming on display in the hall."

"A *toy trumpet*," Mr. Jensen?" Miss Rawlins shook her head. "But what has that to do with courts and such?"

"I'm afraid I am not at liberty to disclose that at this precise moment, Miss Rawlins. It would certainly impede some of Mrs. Hollis's enjoyment of the play."

"But you'll tell us after she and the vicar have left, won't you?" Mrs. Dearing asked with a conspiratorial glint in her eyes.

Mr. Jensen actually smiled. "As soon as their carriage wheels can no longer be heard, Mrs. Dearing, I shall be privileged to."

———

"I'm afraid I was very much the child about losing that tournament," Vicar Phelps confessed while carving the roast hen in the platter before him. "And congratulating the vicar from Prescott was one of the hardest things I've ever done. But would you care to know what Mrs. Hollis said to me afterward?"

"What was that, sir?" Jonathan asked, keeping his amusement hidden behind an attentive expression. It was obvious that the vicar was anxious about tomorrow, because he had told the same story when Jonathan suppered with them last week.

"She said with her usual frankness, 'Andrew, you just have to tell yourself that it's better to be beaten by someone like Vicar Nippert than to allow yourself to *become* someone like Vicar Nippert.' Wise advice—and to the point, wasn't it?"

"Very wise, Vicar." He winked across the table at Elizabeth, who sent him a grateful smile. *Please let me have some time alone with her tonight,* he prayed, knowing that a miracle of God would be the only way it would happen. Though the vicar now allowed them to take an occasional walk, he still did not allow them time alone after dark. Jonathan accepted his right to do so but was so bursting with the news he wanted to share with Elizabeth that he did not think he would sleep tonight if he had to hold it all in until tomorrow.

"Have you finished packing, Andrew?" Mrs. Phelps, the vicar's mother, asked from her place next to Laurel. Jonathan had met her previously in Cambridge. An energetic woman of about sixty-five, she wore her gray hair gathered back into intricate curls at the crown of her head, and gold earrings dangled like little pear-shaped sapphires whenever she spoke. She would be staying with Elizabeth and Laurel during their father's honeymoon in London.

Elizabeth had told him during their last walk that when her grandmother arrived three days ago, she was aghast to discover they had dropped the habit of changing their clothes for supper. "Aren't you carrying this 'when in Rome' notion a bit too far?" Mrs. Phelps had demanded, but the vicar had held his ground, telling her that it was a silly custom that would cause too much of a burden on Dora.

Now the vicar angled his head thoughtfully at the most recent question put to him by his mother. "I've almost finished. I can't pack my shaving kit and toothbrush until the morning. But you won't allow me to forget it, will you, Beth?"

"I'll remind you, Papa."

"And what about money?" Laurel asked. "Did you pack that?"

Absently the man patted the shirt over his stomach, where his breast-coat pocket would have been located, had he been wearing one. Meanwhile it appeared unlikely that the hen would be carved before dessert. "Oh yes. It's upstairs in my bureau. Laurel, please make sure I have that before I leave."

"What about Mrs. Hollis, Vicar?" Jonathan could not resist teasing. "Should someone remind you to bring her along tomorrow?"

Vicar Phelps chuckled appreciatively and pointed the carving fork at him. "That, Jonathan, can be your responsibility. But somehow I don't think you'll have to exercise it."

––––––––––

"What would you like us to bring you from London?" Julia asked her daughters after reading to them from the fairy tale book. Though she and Andrew planned to shop for Christmas presents while there, she wanted their children to have mementos they could enjoy as soon as they returned. The evening had a poignant quality about it, partly because this would be the last time she would tuck them into bed in the *Larkspur*. It was within these walls that she had fully come to understand what it meant to invest herself in the lives of her children.

"Would a heart-shaped locket be asking for too much?" Aleda asked.

Julia smoothed auburn hair from her daughter's forehead. "I think that's a lovely idea."

Grace had a to think for a minute. "Are there still toy stores there?"

"Certainly there are. What kind of toy would you like?"

"Something that winds up and moves? Like a bear who plays a drum?"

"A windup toy it is." The faces that stared back at her from their pillows were so sweet and trusting that Julia longed to stay for a little while and smooth their hair and tell them how loved they were. But tomorrow would be a busy day for all of them. "Now remember to obey Mrs. Beemish and Mr. Jensen while I'm gone. And wear your woollies to school every day."

"And clean our teeth and wash our faces?" Grace supplied helpfully.

Julia smiled. "That would be nice too."

Philip would have been mortified had she attempted to read to him, but he was willing for her to sit at his bedside for a chat instead of her usual good-night from the doorway. He asked for a set of draughts pieces so that he did not have to improvise with his chessmen whenever he had company. "And we'll have to leave the other draughts game in the hall anyway, or Mr. Durwin and Mr. Ellis won't be able to play."

"Will you miss living here?"

He glanced around the room, resting his head upon the arm propped upon his pillow. "I dreamt of this room a lot when I was away at school. And the hall, and even the kitchen. But I think it was the people I was missing most. You and the girls and everyone else. I don't think I'll mind living at the vicarage. And we can visit here anytime we like, right?"

"As long as we're considerate of the servants and Mr. Jensen," she replied, resisting the urge to smooth his hair as she had Aleda's. "The *Larkspur* still belongs to us, Philip."

"Good." He lapsed into silence for several seconds, then asked, "You

407

don't mind marrying Vicar Phelps, do you?"

"What do you mean?"

A line formed between his eyebrows. "You aren't marrying him just so we can have a father, are you? I mean, I know he'll be a good father, but you shouldn't let that be the only reason."

"I'm marrying him because I love him, Philip. But since you ask . . . I would never, never marry a man who couldn't be a good father to my children, no matter how I felt about him."

"Oh." He looked relieved. "Then it all works out just fine, doesn't it?"

She could no longer resist, but he only smiled long-sufferingly while she combed her fingers through his red hair. "Just fine indeed, Philip."

———

After supper, Elizabeth and Jonathan played whist with her father and sister at the parlor tea table while her grandmother sat on the sofa perusing a copy of *The Art Journal*. Her father did not rattle on as he had at supper. Either Mrs. Paget's cooking, Jonathan's joke, or simply having to devote himself to the strategy of the game had soothed his nerves. Or perhaps a combination of all three.

She and Laurel had discussed thoroughly how it would be to have their family more than double in size and had both concluded that the drawbacks—such as sharing their father's attention as well as time in the water closet—would be more than compensated for by having a mother and siblings around. Life certainly would not be boring!

And there was another reason Elizabeth was particularly glad—one that she had not felt ready to share with Laurel. She was certain that she would marry Jonathan Raleigh one day. Knowing that she was not drastically cutting down the size of her family would make leaving home easier on her conscience.

During the two weeks since the archery tournament she and Jonathan had taken other walks. Twice Jonathan had proposed, and twice Elizabeth had said she needed more time—not because she did not want to marry him—but because she wanted so much for everything to go right this time. She felt the need to be overly cautious. In the quiet of her room when she sought God's counsel, He seemed to be telling her that there was still something lacking. She had no idea what it was but had to trust that God would reveal it to her at the proper time.

It was only after her father won the match—a victory they had orchestrated by unspoken agreement as sort of a pre-wedding gift—that Jonathan looked at his watch and whistled softly through his teeth. "I'm sorry. I had no idea it was after ten."

"You couldn't very well leave the match, now, could you?" her father asked as he and Laurel gathered the cards. "By the way, I know that you all conspired to let me win." He grinned at their half-hearted protests and said, "I played as rotten a game as humanly possible to try to thwart your plans, but you were even worse. No wonder it took so long."

And then he did a curious thing. Looking up at Elizabeth, he said, "Be sure and take your wrap outside and be back in fifteen minutes."

"Fifteen minutes?" Jonathan whispered to her in the vestibule after bidding good evening to her family.

Elizabeth wound the shawl he handed her from the coatrack around her shoulders, whispering back, "Papa only allowed Paul Treves ten minutes."

"I wasn't complaining. I was just startled that—" His eyebrows rose. "Only ten? Really?"

"You let him win at whist, remember?"

They stepped out into a cold dark night bereft of stars. A low fog wrapped gauzy fingers in all directions, eerily shrouding the gravestones of the churchyard in the distance. But Elizabeth's mood was not somber. It had been a fine day, and tomorrow would be an even better one.

At the end of the porch, Jonathan turned to face her and took both hands. "I've longed for this moment all evening, Elizabeth."

She smiled. Even though she had delayed her answer to his proposal, she was not opposed to being kissed by him. Raising her chin just a little, she said, "You have?"

He made no move closer as he continued to talk with his eyes shining. "This afternoon I met with the school board at the *Bow and Fiddle*. They feel pressed to begin a search for a teacher for next year but wanted to see if I would possibly consider staying."

Elizabeth's breath caught in her throat. "You're considering it, Jonathan?"

"I'm more at peace here than I've ever been in my life, Elizabeth. I enjoy seeing a child's expression as he reads his first sentence, knowing that I helped to bring that about. Or having a student ask what causes thunder. Or watching a face glow simply because I praised a composition or sketch. It's so wonderful knowing that all of this was accomplished only by the grace of God and without any family connections."

"Then you have your answer, haven't you?" *And I have mine as well*, she realized, for it was as if some last remaining obstacle was fading away in her mind.

"Almost," he replied, now looking a little worried. "I wanted to find out how you felt about it first. After all, I initially moved here against your wishes."

She shook her head. "Things have changed since then. Of course I would like you to stay."

"Thank you, Elizabeth." He glanced toward the door and sent a breath between his teeth. "Ever wish you could freeze time?"

"Not until now," she replied, smiling. "But if you talk fast, you may be able to squeeze in another proposal."

"Another . . ." Utter surprise took over his face. "You would say yes?"

"That's not how it works, Jonathan. You have to propose before I give my answer."

His mouth curved into a smile. "Will you make me the happiest man alive, Elizabeth Phelps?"

"Gladly, Jonathan Raleigh."

"Oh, Elizabeth!" In spite of the passion in his voice, he gathered her gently into his arms as if she were a fragile doll. Automatically she raised her chin and closed her eyes. His lips were warm and sweet upon hers. When their lips parted and she opened her eyes again, his face was radiant, almost glowing. It took her a second, lightheaded as she was, to realize it was caused by rays of lamplight shining from the window.

"Oh," she said, releasing her arms from his shoulders. "I have to go."

He looked disappointed but nodded. "I'll see you at the wedding." With a glance at the door, he added, "I assume this isn't a good time to speak with your father."

"He's nervous enough as it is. Do you understand?"

"Of course. But when does he return?"

"In nine days."

"I'll speak with him then." Another kiss, this time hurried, and Jonathan bounded down the steps. He turned to grin and wave before the darkness swallowed him up completely. "We'll be sure to play whist first!"

"Will you, Andrew Royden Phelps, take this woman to be your lawfully wedded wife?" Bishop Edwards asked in the front of Saint Jude's the next morning. The filled-to-capacity church was decorated appropriately for the Christmas season with branches of holly and fir, red velvet bows, and rows of flickering candles.

Seated at the end of the first pew with Laurel, Grandmother, and the Hollis children, Elizabeth felt goose prickles as her father, looking quite handsome in a new black suit, answered, "I will." Two small words, spoken with such gravity as if he were verbally chiseling them in stone. And yet his expression was anything but grave. She could see even from the side that he stared at his wife-to-be with blatant adoration and joy across his face.

She had been happy from the first when her father and Mrs. Hollis announced their engagement. Even older people needed companionship, and the affection between the two was obvious. But she had never considered that the romance that made her pulse quicken whenever Jonathan smiled at her was just as strong in her father's heart. And from the way Mrs. Hollis, looking lovely in an ecru silk appliquéd with lace, smiled back at him, it was obvious that her heart was just as overwhelmed.

"Julia Mansfield Hollis, will you take this man to be your lawfully wedded husband?"

"I will."

Elizabeth squeezed her sister's hand as her father placed the ring upon Mrs. Hollis's finger. She heard sniffs coming from all directions behind her. Even her grandmother was wiping her eyes. Her father could have married years earlier, Grandmother had told her last night with not a little reproach in her voice, had he given any encouragement to the women who pursued him in Cambridge.

Yet he waited for the better thing, not even knowing when he would find it. He had trusted that God had a plan and knew that settling for second-best was not part of it. Because of his example, she had been able to restrain herself from rushing into another relationship with Jonathan before the appropriate time.

They that wait upon the Lord shall renew their strength; they shall mount up with wings as eagles. Elizabeth had heard her father read those words from the book of Isaiah countless times over the years without fully understanding their meaning. Now she understood and would one day teach them to her children as she had been taught.

She gave her full attention back to the ceremony before her.

"Now that Julia Mansfield Hollis and Andrew Royden Phelps have given themselves to each other in the sight of God and by solemn vows, and with the joining of hands and the giving and receiving of a ring, I pronounce that they are husband and wife, in the Name of the Father, and of the Son, and of the Holy Spirit. Those whom God has joined together let no one put asunder."

"Amen," Elizabeth said with the rest of the congregation.

"God the Father, God the Holy Spirit, bless, preserve, and keep you; the Lord mercifully with his favor look upon you, and fill you with all spiritual benediction and grace; that you may faithfully live together in this life, and in the age to come have life everlasting."

After the last congregational *Amen*, Bishop Edwards smiled. "You may kiss your bride." Now Elizabeth became aware that there were tears in her own eyes as she watched her father take his new wife's shoulders in his hands. She leaned forward just a bit to send a smile to her new brother and sisters. All three smiled back with their eyes shining as well. The kiss was appropriately brief for a vicar in front of his own congregation, but Elizabeth felt a strong certainty, watching his eyes as they drew apart, that there would be dozens more exchanged before sunset.

Don't Miss the First Book in This Charming Victorian Series

Julia Hollis's opulent life in Victorian London crashes to pieces when her husband passes away. Worse, she is told by his bankers that he gambled away their fortune. Now, the family's hope rests on The Larkspur, an old abandoned coaching inn in the quaint village of Gresham.

Driven by dread and her desire to provide for her children, Julia decides to turn the dilapidated inn into a lodging house. But can she—who was accustomed to servants attending to every need—do what needs to be done and cope when boarders begin arriving? And then an eligible new vicar moves into town....

The Widow of Larkspur Inn
by Lawana Blackwell
THE GRESHAM CHRONICLES #1

Looking for More Good Books to Read?

You can find out what is new and exciting with previews, descriptions, and reviews by signing up for Bethany House newsletters at

www.bethanynewsletters.com

We will send you updates for as many authors or categories as you desire so you get only the information you really want.

Sign up today!